Praise for
Eighty Days to Elsewhere

"For anyone who's ever longed to travel the world in search of adventure, love, security, danger, mystery—or themselves. A wild and wonderful journey in the company of the most engaging pilgrim since Phileas Fogg."

—Diana Gabaldon,
#1 *New York Times* bestselling author of the Outlander novels

"Dyer keeps readers engaged with scenic descriptions and a sweet, slow-burning love story. This is a delightful romp."

—*Publishers Weekly*

"This inspired series launch from Dyer (*Finding Fraser*) offers readers a journey around the world that is both entertaining and enlightening. Fans of new adult romance will enjoy watching Romy discover not only new landscapes but herself in the process."

—*Library Journal*

"Dyer takes readers on a journey of self-discovery that spans several continents, engages with various cultures, and touches on urgent sociopolitical issues. . . . A charming story detailing a woman's self-discovery through travel." —*Kirkus Reviews*

"I enjoyed *Eighty Days to Elsewhere* immensely and would highly recommend it to anyone looking for an entertaining adventure."

—The Bookish Libra

"A thought-provoking journey around the world." —Fresh Fiction

"A very entertaining and fun book while still being thought-provoking and smart. I highly recommend for anyone who is a fan of travel and romantic comedies." —Smitten by Books

"A book you'll devour in the weekend sunshine. . . . Dyer's examinations of race, culture, and the implications or consequences of travel were surprising and welcome. It is not enough for books to bury themselves in fluff anymore; we must accept that our lighthearted stories take place alongside the realities of the world we live in, and Dyer has started that trend here." —*Nuvo Magazine*

Praise for
Finding Fraser

"Jamie Fraser would be Deeply Gratified at having inspired such a charmingly funny, poignant story—and so am I."
—Diana Gabaldon,
#1 *New York Times* bestselling author of the Outlander series

"A must-read for *Outlander* fans eagerly awaiting their next Jamie fix."
—*Bustle*

"A humorous yet relatable self-discovery tale." —*Us Weekly*

An Accidental Odyssey

kc dyer

JOVE
NEW YORK

A JOVE BOOK
Published by Berkley
An imprint of Penguin Random House LLC
penguinrandomhouse.com

Copyright © 2021 by kc dyer

A JOVE BOOK, BERKLEY, and the BERKLEY & B colophon are registered trademarks
of Penguin Random House LLC.

Library of Congress Cataloging-in-Publication Data

Names: Dyer, K. C., author.
Title: An accidental odyssey / kc dyer.
Description: First edition. | New York: Jove, 2021. | Series: An ExLibris adventure
Identifiers: LCCN 2021031410 (print) | LCCN 2021031411 (ebook) |
ISBN 9780593102060 (trade paperback) | ISBN 9780593102077 (ebook)
Classification: LCC PR9199.4.D93 A63 2021 (print) |
LCC PR9199.4.D93 (ebook) | DDC 813/.6—dc23
LC record available at https://lccn.loc.gov/2021031410
LC ebook record available at https://lccn.loc.gov/2021031411

First Edition: December 2021

Printed in the United States of America
Scout Automated Print Code

Book design by Kristin del Rosario

1st Printing

For Finlay Mae
A most treasured artifact,
brilliantly unearthed by
my two favorite hot archeologists.

chapter one

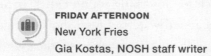

FRIDAY AFTERNOON
New York Fries
Gia Kostas, NOSH staff writer

I like my fries like I like my guys—a little greasy, a lot salty, and soft on the inside. This recipe tastes hot off the street cart . . . and if you're a purist, I've got a quick and dirty ketchup concoction waiting for you in the sidebar.

To feed four, all you need are six large potatoes—Yukon Gold, if you can get 'em—five cups of avocado oil, and a whole lot of finely ground sea salt.

To begin . . .

Reaching across my keyboard, I click the return button, and my piece shoots off with a tiny, audible zing into cyberspace. In reality, this means it only travels to the far end of the floor and behind a closed door before landing safely inside my editor's inbox. It's got the most smart-ass tone of any of the articles I've ever submitted— especially that opening line—which could *not* be further from the truth. But real journalists are always a little bit sassy, right?

Still, I can't suppress a sigh as I lean back in my chair. My final assignment submitted. I should be celebrating.

As if on cue, a head pops up, appearing through the smudgy

2 · kc dyer

plexiglass above the cubicle wall. The wall is one of those soft, grey fabric jobs; easily moveable and designed to absorb sound in an open-plan office. The grey color is soul-crushing on the best of days, and I'm not sure the things do much for absorbing sound either. In any case, mine is covered in recipes, mouthwatering food shots destined for Instagram, and a map of Manhattan with pushpins indicating all the places I've written pieces about. The plexiglass is left over from the company's social-distancing efforts. Even though the worst appears to be over, nobody seems willing to take these ugly things down just yet.

The head belongs to my cubicle neighbor, Janelle. She beams at me, her face poised above the shot of a beautifully plated selection of sushi that adorned an article I submitted last week.

"Drinks at five?" Janelle says and waggles her key chain at me. The key chain bears a little martini glass, complete with tiny olive. "Billy Rae's has two-for-one Fridays for the whole month of May."

In spite of my interior gloom, I can't help grinning back at her. Janelle's smile is infectious, her wide mouth bracketed with a pair of dimples on the left and a single on the right. The effect is just off-kilter enough to charm the hardest heart. She jingles the key chain again, plainly not convinced by my expression, and steps around the wall into my cubicle.

"I heard your story go through," she says, tapping my monitor with her pen. The pen, I can't help noticing, exactly matches the shade of lipstick she's wearing. Which, in turn, perfectly complements the blouse beneath her neatly tailored suit. "That means you're done, right?"

Janelle's ability to look uncreased at the end of her workday is a skill I've not managed to master in my time here. I sigh again and reflexively run my palms across my own crumpled skirt.

"Yeah, that was the last piece. Apart from edits, I guess I *am* done."

Janelle's grin widens. "And I've just finished the last of my three-parter on this year's local Michelin stars. So it's a celebration, then. Excellent." She perches on the corner of my desk, scrolling through her phone screen. "They do a classic Gibson too. Perfect for a rainy Friday."

My neck crackles as I push back my chair and stand up. "I'd love to, but I can't," I reply, averting my eyes. "I promised Anthony I'd meet him at Hudson Bakes. Cake tasting."

"*Hudson Bakes?* Cripes, Gia—that's the most expensive place in the city." Janelle, shocked out of her menu scrolling, drops her phone on the desk. "Forget drinks. I'll come with you. I'd give my right arm to taste their chocolate raspberry truffle cake again."

I contemplate Anthony's reaction to me showing up with a work colleague. Considering he's already vetoed me bringing Devi—my maid of honor—I don't think it'll go over very well.

"This is special, Gia," he'd told me on the phone that morning. "We're never going to have a day like this again. Who cares what everyone else thinks? Let's choose something we both love."

And so it was decided.

"I'd really like to," I tell her, entirely honestly. "But he's planned a special date night for us, with the tasting as the centerpiece. Sorry."

Janelle leans forward and puts a hand on my arm. "God, Gia— you're *so* lucky. When I got married, it was all I could do to get Mitch to show up for the ceremony. 'It's your day,' he'd say every time I asked for help making a decision. 'You just need to tell me where to stand, and I'll leave the rest up to you.'" She sighs. "I'd have done anything to have such a supportive partner."

There's a fine line between supportive and bossy, I think, and then clamp my lips shut on the thought, guiltily.

"You're right. I am lucky," I reply instead.

Reaching into a dark corner, I haul out an old box I've been hoarding from under my desk and start loading my things into it. In spite of the fact that the clock has just ticked past five, my boss's office door remains firmly closed. Charlotte Castle, my no-nonsense, incredibly organized editor, gave me a warm farewell when we passed in the hallway just after lunch and wished me luck. But she didn't offer me a contract.

"Last day and no job to come in for on Monday," I add gloomily. "I kinda wish I'd made a better impression on the powers that be."

Janelle folds her arms across her chest, and a careful look comes into her eyes. "Listen," she says. "It's not just you. It's a rough time for journalists everywhere. NOSH is a small company—one of the last independents. And we're only now getting back up to full speed after having to work from home for so long. Anyway, Charlotte has nothing but good things to say about you—you'll get a fantastic reference, for sure."

I step around her and begin pulling recipe cards off the wall. "I know. It's just . . ."

"Besides," she says, capturing my left hand as I reach for the last card, "you've got cake to look forward to, right?"

She turns my hand so the diamond catches one of the last rays of the setting sun gleaming in through the window.

I slip my hand out of hers and shoot her a wry grin. "The wedding's not until the summer. And I'd rather be thinking about my next story here, to tell you the truth. This whole 'big wedding' thing has me a bit freaked out."

"Girl! Anthony Hearst is one of the city's most eligible dudes. I wouldn't give working another thought if I were in your shoes. I'd be sitting back, drinking a Bellini, and leafing through *Billionaire Bridal*."

Rolling my eyes, I jam the last of my tear sheets into the box. "Janelle Olsen, you're the last person I thought would tell me to quit work because I'm getting married. What is this, the 1950s?"

As I say this, I collect the last item from my desk—a framed photo of Anthony and me from the day we got engaged. I drop it into the top of the box. With all personal traces removed, the cubicle looks like what it is. Empty desk space for a temporary intern.

Janelle's dimpled smile flashes as she plucks my coat from the hook and hands it to me. "Don't look so gloomy! All I'm saying is that you don't have to worry financially. You can take some time, plan the wedding, and keep an eye on the job market for when your schedule lightens up."

I'm just about to nail her again for her weirdly archaic attitude when my phone rings. It's slipped down inside the box, and I need to pull out my stapler and the framed photo to get to it. The photo is a little out of focus since it was taken from the Jumbotron at a Yankees game. It shows me standing on the infield looking stunned—and with one eye half closed—as Anthony beams straight into the camera from his position down on one knee.

Dropping the photo, I grab the phone, which is displaying a number I don't recognize, and answer it.

"Gia Kostas." I hold a finger up to Janelle to let her know she's not off the hook with me just yet. But every cogent thought vanishes in the next moment.

"It's Beth Israel ER, Ms. Kostas," a voice says through the line. "Your father has just been admitted with symptoms of stroke."

The NOSH offices are just off Union Square, so it's actually faster to run to the hospital than taking the L line. Janelle scoops up the box for me, offering to drop it at my place on her way home. I give her a quick squeeze before tossing my heels into the box and slamming my feet into Nikes. Charlotte's office door is still firmly closed, so I make an executive decision to call in my goodbyes and then bolt for the stairs. This building was renovated some time before the turn of the last century, and a person can age out before the elevator arrives.

As a native New Yorker, I am nothing if not an expert at typing on the fly, so by the time I hit Fourteenth Street, I've already left an e-mail for Anthony and a voice mail for my best friend. Anthony keeps himself on a strict communications schedule, so even though he doesn't reply, I know he'll be checking his e-mails on the hour. My friend Devi's residency is in the Emergency unit of the same hospital I'm running toward. So, while I don't expect her to pick up either, it's a relief to know she'll be nearby. It's not until I jog up to the front of the building that it occurs to me to call my mother, but the sight of an ambulance unloading pushes the thought out of my mind. I can call her when I have actual news. For now?

I just want to see my dad.

So. My dad.

Professionally, Dr. Aristotle Kostas is a well-regarded academic. He's got a string of initials behind his name and more degrees—earned and honorary—than I've ever actually counted. He's retired now, but since he's still technically professor emeritus at NYU in the Classics department, they let him keep an office there. Which mostly means he hangs out on weekdays, puttering around and giving the graduate students grief.

On the personal side, though, I can't really say things are as successful. My own relationship with him was totally rocky, at least while I was growing up. I almost never saw him, and my mom didn't have much to say that was positive. But lately—mostly since he's retired—things between us have been on the mend.

The biggest problem, if you ask me, is that my dad considers himself a lifelong romantic. He's told me many times—usually after too much ouzo—how helpless he is in the face of love. I know for a fact that others, out of his hearing, are less charitable. Having a reputation as a bit of a dog wasn't such a problem in the twentieth century, but it doesn't carry very far in the era of #MeToo. My dad's been married three times—his last wife being my mom, who is twenty-five years his junior, because they met when she was one of his students. By then, he was already a father to two boys. Both of my half brothers are much older than I am and married with families of their own. Alek lives in Los Angeles, and Tomas all the way over in London, England. With the uncomfortable situation between our respective mothers, we have never even exchanged Christmas cards. After my mom left a decade ago, my dad moved in with his girlfriend Kallie. They were still together until last year, when I'm pretty sure she threw him out. In fact, that might just be the longest time he'd been with one woman. So, yeah, like I said. He's a dog.

Once I started college and moved out on my own, though, things began to warm up a bit between my dad and me. Not having my mom in the room when we talk these days doesn't hurt, though I have to admit their relationship has improved, too, since she's remarried—and moved to Connecticut.

Now that he's retired, he makes more of an effort to spend time with me too. He's a lifelong season-ticket holder for the Yankees, and I'll tag along and take in a game with him now and then. During my whole internship at NOSH, he's treated me to lunch at least once a month. So now? The thought I might lose him just as I'm finally getting to know him is terrifying.

Hospitals feel like scarier places to me now than they did in the Before Times. There's nothing like a plague sweeping across the planet to give you a sense of your own mortality, I guess. And while everyday life has pretty much returned to my city, somehow it still doesn't really feel like it's back to normal. I'm not sure anymore what normal is, to tell you the truth. But as I pass through the front doors of Beth Israel, everyone around me just looks calm and efficient. Luckily, it's too early in the year for my hay fever to flare, so I can assure the nurse at the desk that I am symptom-free. She issues me a mask, and I skitter off along in the direction she points me, not quite running—but not quite not-running either.

The hospital is a maze, and by the time I find the correct floor and skid into the right room, I'm sweating and breathless. A nurse, standing just inside the door, raises her hand to stop me from going farther. Curtains encircle three beds, with a fourth partially drawn. I can see my dad inside, propped up in the bed, an IV tube taped to his arm. He's in conversation with a woman who appears to be holding his hand.

"Pops!" I gasp, and they both turn to look at me.

". . . entirely out of the question," the woman says, unclipping something from one of his fingers. She hands a tablet computer to the nurse, and I hurriedly sanitize my hands again at the station by the door before heading over to the bed.

"Ah! This is my daughter, Gianna," my dad says warmly as I scurry to his side. "Gia, meet Dr. McShane."

I nod at the doctor and reach for my dad's hand. "Are you okay? They said you had a . . ."

"I'm fine," he says, airily waving the arm attached to the IV. "A small anomaly, nothing more."

My dad is a Greek male, the sort who will lose a leg before admitting to a bit of a scratch, so I turn instead to Dr. McShane. "They said it was a stroke. Is there such a thing as a *small* stroke?"

The doctor nods, tucking her hands into the pockets of her lab coat. Like all the frontline professionals in the place, she is masked and gloved, but unlike several women I passed in the hallway, she's not wearing a face shield.

"Small, yes, but worrisome, nevertheless," the doctor replies, her voice only slightly muffled. "His vaccines are all up to date, and he's not showing any viral symptoms, which is good news. But we'll need to monitor your dad for the next forty-eight hours at least, just to rule out any further complications."

She turns back to him and gestures at a stack of books piled on the side table partially covered by my dad's overcoat. "That means bed rest, young man. Time to stay put and catch up on your reading." Raising an admonishing finger, she adds, "No exertion of any sort, you hear me?"

My phone jingles in my pocket, and I pull it out long enough to flick the sound off.

It's Anthony. I decide to call him later, and as I drop the phone back into my pocket, the doctor shoots my dad a thumbs-up and follows the nurse out past the curtain.

"Exertion?" I yank the lone chair closer to his bed. "What's she talking about?"

He glances away. "Overreaction. There's nothing much on my scan—I spoke with the radiologist, and that guy really knows his stuff. It's no big deal, trust me." He gestures at my mask. "Take that thing off so I can see your pretty face, eh?"

I slide my chair farther back before unlooping the mask from one ear. He grins at me. "That's better. Who's on the phone?"

"Just Anthony. I can talk to him later—this is more important. Start at the beginning. What happened?"

He sighs, and I hear a familiar note of exasperation enter his tone. "Nothing really. I was late this morning and missed my breakfast, so I had a little dizzy spell on the subway. When I got into the office, it returned, and . . ."

"They said it was a stroke, Pops. That's different from a little dizzy spell."

"Not a stroke—a TIA. You heard the doctor. Completely different kettle of fish, *koritsi*."

I glance around pointedly at all the equipment. "So, is 'TIA' medical shorthand for a stroke?"

"It stands for *transient ischemic attack*," he says, falling into his teacher voice. "It mimics the symptoms of a stroke but usually leaves no lasting damage."

"Usually?"

"Almost always," he says, cutting me off with another dismissive wave. "I'm fine. The dizziness is gone. They're giving me blood thinners and bad food." He sips ginger ale through a paper straw and grimaces. "All I need at the moment is some decent souvlaki. So, do you and Anthony have plans for the evening?"

I admit we were supposed to be tasting cakes. "But I'll cancel and bring you souvlaki, Pops."

He reaches across to pat my hand and shakes his head.

"Evan is already on his way over. He's bringing me some—ah— papers from the office, and he said he'd stop at Spiro's on the way. Don't worry about a thing, little girl. Papa will be fine. Go out and enjoy your Friday night. Eat cake. Have fun."

"Uh—don't you think I should stay and keep you company a while?"

"I'm fine, darling, I promise you." He gestures at the pile of books. "Reading to catch up on, remember?"

The adrenaline that carried me up here has drained away, replaced with a combination of annoyance and dismay at being so summarily dismissed. Then I feel guilty for this when he's stuck in bed with a tube in his arm.

"But, what about . . ." I begin, when his cell phone starts buzzing over on the table beside the books. I leap up and hurry around the bed to grab it, but he scoops it and answers before I can take more than a couple of steps.

"Evan!" he bellows cheerfully into the phone. "I'm fine—never better. Just hold a second, will you . . . ?" He pulls the receiver away from his ear. "This is going to take a few minutes, *Gianitsa*. Off you go. I'll speak to you in the morning, yes?"

"Are you sure, Pops?" I ask, the guilt surging again. "I can stay until Evan . . ."

"Go, go," he says. "That man of yours keeps a tight schedule. Is good for him to eat a bit of cake too, no?"

I step out of the room once it becomes clear my father won't be getting off his phone anytime soon. In the hall, I pause to hook my mask back around my ear and listen to the voice mail from Anthony. I click on the message with a little trepidation—my dad isn't wrong about Anthony and his schedules. But against all expectations, his voice is nothing but sympathetic: *Don't worry about a thing, babe. Stay with your dad as long as you need. Managed to reschedule the tasting for tomorrow, noon. Call if you need anything—turned the ringer on. Love you!*

As I begin dialing to return his call, a nurse gives me the evil eye, so I drop the phone back into my pocket and head toward the elevators. The doors slide open on Evan, my dad's most recent graduate student and resident gofer. His arms are piled with books and papers, and he's so intent on his phone call with my dad that he hurries past me without a second glance.

I sigh and step into the elevator. I can check with him again in the morning before the rescheduled cake tasting. It's only as the doors begin to close that I realize my dad never answered my question. Just what *had* the doctor been warning him against anyway?

chapter two

SATURDAY MORNING
Chocolate Raspberry Truffle Cake: Notes to self
Draft recipe by Gia Kostas, staff writer to no one at the moment

I haven't even tasted this cake yet, but the habit of food writing dies hard. Will make a note of all the varieties Anthony and I sample, and write a piece anyway. Someone's got to want a freelance story on wedding cakes . . .

As the train slows, I tuck my iPad away and stand up. It's not even ten yet, so I've got a full hour to check in with my dad—and try to get the whole story out of his doctor—before I meet Anthony at Hudson Bakes.

Stepping onto the platform at the First Avenue station, I think back to last night's conversation with my friend Devi. She'd buzzed me back right after I left my dad's room, so I got a chance for a quick check-in after all. Devi Patil has been my best friend since we shared a front-row desk in our third grade classroom. She'd chosen her seat because she was determined to be the smartest kid in the class. It says something about her that we still became friends even after she learned I was there because I was too easily distracted if I sat by the window. I got moved forward and she got straight A's, and we've been friends ever since.

Her brains—combined with a ridiculous work ethic—meant she

rocketed through high school, and I'm pretty sure she was the youngest person ever admitted to her medical school. These days, she's doing a stint in emergency medicine and is currently working pretty much day and night, between her courses and her clinical work. But even overcommitted med students are allowed a coffee break, so we met at the kiosk on the ground floor.

The good news, at least from my point of view, was that she didn't cry over my dad's situation. Devi might have the vocabulary of a trucker, but she has a heart as soft as the tummy fur on a new kitten. I'm secretly sure this is why she switched her focus from the neonatal unit to the less emotional—albeit more chaotic—emergency room. But far from crying, when I shared the news, she was quick to tell me that while a TIA isn't in any way desirable, as strokes go, it is less worrisome than many of the other varieties. She advised I go home, get some sleep, and leave my dad in the capable hands of the neurological unit.

This was reassuring advice. But since it was still only eight thirty, I made a detour by way of Billy Rae's just in case Janelle was still in residence. This proved a most excellent choice, as Janelle was not only holding court at a corner table, but my newly ex-boss Charlotte was sitting right beside her.

Charlotte Castle cut her teeth as a journalist in the golden age of New York newspapers. She interned at *The Post* as a young writer and was one of the first Black women in the country to edit a news desk on a daily. She even had a stint with the old grey lady herself—the *New York Times*—for a while. But as the digital age advanced, she saw the pixels on the wall and founded her own foodie publication way back in 2010. NOSH has had its struggles, but considering the dire state of many journalistic outlets these days, Charlotte and her company are doing pretty well.

Better still, by the time I pulled up a stool to the tall table in the bar, she'd spent enough time with Janelle and her Gibson to become a little garrulous. Charlotte not only bought me a drink but assured me that my skills were such that she would have hired me if she could justify it. All of which contributed to a far more cheerful night than I had anticipated.

Of course now, as I scamper up the subway steps, the rain, which had only spattered the shoulders of my coat earlier, begins in earnest. By the time I dash inside the hospital, my coat is drenched, and the sweater underneath feels like I've just stepped, fully clothed, out of the shower. I pause for a moment to wring the cuffs of my sleeves out over a conveniently positioned potted plant before rolling them up and heading for the elevator.

On the way, I decide to take the focus off my dad's health so he doesn't feel like I'm mother-henning him. Instead, I'll ask his advice about finding a position writing for his university's online newspaper. I've got three good questions lined up by the time I reach his floor, but when I step into his room, he's not there.

An orderly is stripping the bed, and the only sign he'd ever been there is a small yellow pill bottle on the metal side table. *Doctor Aristotle Kostas,* it reads. *One tablet 3x daily, with food. Important: Take as directed until finished.*

The next half hour is a tangled mix of confusion and recriminations. Dr. McShane is no longer on shift, and none of the ward nurses seem to know where my dad is. His regular practitioner's office is closed on Saturday, so there's no help to be found there. I spend a full ten minutes grilling a young man in scrubs only to learn he is a phlebotomist sent to draw blood from another of the residents of my dad's room. I finally corner the head nurse on the ward and blurt my dad's name, and when she rolls her eyes, I know I've found the right person.

"He's checked himself out," she says, shortly.

"Can you even do that?" I ask. "Don't you need a doctor's approval or something?"

"You do indeed. But your father, I'm afraid, took advantage of one of our student nurses."

"How—how do you mean?" I stammer. "Did he say something rude . . . ?"

The nurse reads the wariness in my eyes and shakes her head. "Nothing like that. He showed her his university identification, told her that as Dr. Kostas, he had a right to sign himself out on his own recognizance, and she bought it."

"He's a doctor of *philosophy*."

She nods wearily. "He's not the first to get away with it. These old guys can be wily. Of course, more of them try their luck the other way, I have to say."

"The other way?"

"Angling to keep their bed an extra day once they've been discharged. Most of 'em are lonely, and they like the extra attention. In any case, I'm sorry your dad escaped our clutches early, but if it's any consolation, he likely would have been discharged this afternoon. His preliminary tests all came back negative."

I can't help releasing a shaky sigh of relief. "At least there's that. But he left his meds. I found them on the bedside table."

I hold up the bottle, and she peers at the label. "Well, that's not good," she says. "These are blood thinners. He needs to take them for a couple of weeks, or at least until he's been cleared by his own physician." She shoots me a harried look.

"I'll find him," I say, dropping the bottle into my shoulder bag. "I'm pretty sure I know where he's headed."

After thanking her—and apologizing again—I toss my mask into a bin and hurry back out onto the street. My clothes are still unpleasantly damp, and the cold breeze swirling old leaves on the pavement outside the hospital makes it feel more like February than the middle of April. The grey clouds are so low, the tops of most of the buildings on the street have vanished. Competing odors of exhaust fumes and old cooking oil linger in the air. I pause to leave a voice mail for Anthony, suggesting he head over to the cake tasting without me and promising to join him as soon as I can.

Anthony's reply, uncharacteristically, pings into my e-mail almost instantly. He is *not* happy.

Please come, he writes. *They won't postpone again, and if his tests are negative, he can wait until tonight for the meds, can't he?*

I stare at my screen for a long moment before taking the easy way out, stepping into one of the many MTA cellphone dead zones, and heading for the Classics department at NYU.

W hen I arrive at the university offices, the door to my dad's floor is open, which is a good sign. As I hurry along the corridor, the familiar musty scent of the place envelops me. The department is usually deserted and locked up tight on a Saturday, so the fact the door is not only ajar but propped open with a copy of *Ovid* bodes well. Unfortunately, when I poke my head into his office, there's no sign of my father.

Instead, I find his grad student, Evan, seated behind a pile of papers at my dad's desk. He jumps to his feet as I come charging into the room. A bit of a pip-squeak at the best of times, Evan takes one look at my face and caves almost immediately.

"He's gone," he says, his tone somewhat defensive. "He told me he has a doctor's permission."

"Gone? Gone where? He signed *himself* out of the hospital, Evan.

And the last time I checked, the Classics department was not issuing medical degrees."

Evan steps sideways, effectively putting the desk between us. His voice takes on a pleading note. "I've—I've got a special tutorial scheduled in five minutes."

I yank my dad's abandoned pill bottle out of my bag and rattle it in his face. "He left his *meds*, Evan."

Pointing up at the clock on the wall, I add, "He's already overdue for one dose, which is putting him at risk of another stroke. I'm sure you wouldn't want to be party to that—would you?"

He swallows hard and visibly blanches when I rattle the pill bottle again.

"I—I didn't know," he whispers, his voice catching in his throat. "He didn't say anything about medication. Only that he was feeling better and that he had a flight to catch."

"A—a *flight*?" I sink onto a chair at the magnitude of this. As I do, my phone pings in my pocket, but I ignore it. "Dude," I say, ratcheting my tone down from demanding to merely pleading. "I'm supposed to be somewhere else too. But I'm really worried about my dad."

Evan glances at his watch, takes a deep breath, and then yanks out a file folder from the top drawer of the desk. "If he finds out I told you, he'll kill me," he says faintly.

I glance into the folder and then meet his eyes one last time. "You'd better get to your session," I say firmly. "I can take it from here."

Evan doesn't wait to be told twice. He's out the door in an instant, a trail of papers literally swirling in his wake.

As for me? I glance back down at the folder.

And this is how, less than a day after waving my magazine internship goodbye and without tasting even a single morsel of wedding cake, I find myself on a plane bound for Athens, Greece.

chapter three

SATURDAY, SOMETIME LATER
Budget Airline Bits and Bites
Gia Kostas, former staff writer, currently airborne, possibly insane

You know things are bad when you steal the foil pack of pretzels off a stranger's tray when they're sleeping. In my defense . . .

Okay, so there's really nothing I can say in my own defense apart from the fact that remembering to feed myself was the last thing on an already too-long agenda in what is turning out to be a too-short day.

Here's the thing. I don't think the reality that my dad's gone a little crazy can be called into question. What it comes down to is whether I'm willing to accept this new truth and go eat cake—or not.

The fact I'm sitting in the back row of this airplane trying to justify the stealing of pretzels says it all. Any eating of cake, at least by me, did not happen today. Worse, the e-mail conversation I've just had with my fiancé might actually mean that whatever's going on with my dad is either catching or familial. Or both.

Deep breath. Which is hard to take, considering I'm wearing a mask.

This is my first time leaving the city since—well, since Life Changed—and it's eye-opening. At home in New York, after that crazy first year of the pandemic, I feel like we all sort of settled into a new reality. Whatever that means.

For me, I guess it means I've gotten used to seeing more people wearing masks and even gloves than in the Before Times. Where it was unnerving at first, it's not so much anymore. And of course, on an airplane, it just makes sense. Who knows where all these people have been? On the streets of Manhattan, even after that killer third wave, mask-wearing is nowhere near a hundred percent compliance, at least lately. But on this plane? Everyone.

Including the guy sleeping across the aisle from me, who has added an intricately hand-stitched eye cover to the mix. So while the mask over his nose and mouth ripples a little on every snore, the one above it stares out at the world with unblinking embroidered blue eyes fringed in long lashes under faux-fur eyebrows.

Aaannnd we're back to unnerving, again. Is it any wonder I stole the guy's pretzels?

I lean across the aisle to stuff the empty pretzel package into his seat pocket and then yank Evan's file folder out of my bag. It's too late to know if I've done the right thing. What I need to figure out now—having made this series of questionable-at-best decisions—is what do I do next?

The contents of the file folder are, in some ways, a revelation. In others? They are a total freaking mystery. A mystery that, on first glance back in my dad's office, I was sure I could solve with a quick trip to New Jersey. And maybe even be finished in time to meet up with Anthony for a little apology sex and a lot of groveling.

This did not happen.

I take another deep breath and stare again at the contents of the folder. The first three pages are essentially a printed version of what looks like a long text thread between my dad and Evan. The conversation is mostly confusing, with elliptical references to both a theory and a journey that don't make a lot of sense. Things get a little clearer on the following pages, which are printouts of an airline ticket—dated today—with my dad's name on it and what looks like a reservation at a hotel in a town whose name I don't recognize.

Mostly because it is literally all Greek to me.

And so here I am. On a plane, taking a flight I not only cannot afford but have put on a credit card with an impossibly high rate of interest. I don't even have a real suitcase with me. Instead, when I realized what my dad had done, I grabbed my gym bag, dumped out the sweaty remnants of my last workout, and tossed in a few things from the clean-but-not-yet-folded basket in my bedroom. Then I headed to the airport to see if anyone would let me on a plane.

As expected, this decision does not sit well with Anthony.

Not because he's upset with me—not really. If I read between the lines of his e-mail, it's clear he just wants to help. Of course, for Anthony, helping often means throwing money at the problem.

If I'm being honest, I have to admit this usually works. Speaking as a person who has never in her life been able to solve a problem in that particular way. I mean, I know how lucky I am to have had a paying internship, but all the same, I barely have enough money to cover my rent and groceries these days.

Still, right now I'm so sick with worry about my dad, I can't imagine that even hiring someone to ensure he takes his meds would result in any actual, measurable change in his behavior. So when Anthony's e-mail arrives, outlining the name of a company I can hire to chase down my dad in Greece, I turn off my "read receipts" and don't reply.

I know he won't agree with my choice to follow my dad. And from my spot here in this legroomless plane seat, I'm not so sure he's wrong. The fact that he is so often right about things—and so relentlessly optimistic of his own success—is one of the things that attracted me to him in the first place.

We met last year, when I was taking my final semester of classes in journalism school at NYU. He's three years older, which I did not discover until after our first date. Later, he told me that he'd read a story I'd published in the *Washington Square News* and wanted to meet the person who'd written it. It took him until just before Halloween to track me down, which meant that at our first meeting, I was dressed as a Ghostbuster.

Accessorized with a proton backpack, of course.

Since literally every other female was wearing a skimpier costume at the party, I was pretty surprised when the good-looking young reporter sporting a porkpie hat and suspenders sauntered up toward me, a beer in each hand.

"Two-fisting Jimmy Olsen?" I guessed when he grinned at me.

"Close," he said and, handing off one of the cans, pulled a pair of heavy black horn-rimmed glasses out of his pocket.

"Nearsighted Jimmy Olsen?"

He rolled his eyes at me, handed over the other beer, and pulled open his shirt at the neck to reveal a Superman t-shirt underneath.

I beamed at him. "My second-favorite reporter!"

"Why only *second* favorite?" he asked, taking one of the beers back and cracking the top. "Everyone loves Clark Kent."

I shrugged. "I've always been on Team Jimmy."

"There's no accounting for taste," he said and clinked his beer can against the one I was still holding.

I'm not a beer drinker, but I cracked my own can to be polite. After he introduced himself as Anthony Hearst, I swallowed the rest of the can out of sheer nerves.

I'd heard his name bandied about the department before, of course. I mean, the faculty—in that "it's no big deal, but how great are we?" way—made a lot of hay of the fact that a Hearst was in attendance at our J-school here in New York and not at Yale or somewhere more high-profile.

I remember him telling me he liked my costume and not much else, to tell you the truth. After the beer, I switched to some kind of hideous pumpkin-spiced rum concoction. I don't actually remember much more of the party, though I'm pretty sure I had fun. In any case, when he later offered to drive me back to the tiny apartment I share with Devi, the make-out session in the front seat of his car was somewhat—ah—more heated than I might usually engage in upon first meeting. Nevertheless, when I did eventually lurch up the stairs to the apartment, it was alone.

Of course, the fact I was strapped into a Ghostbuster costume may have had some bearing. Also? I had a boyfriend. On-again, off-again, mind you. But technically, even though he was out of town, at that moment we were still on-again. His name was Ryan.

The next morning, my hangover and I staggered down to answer the front door only to have a huge bouquet of red roses stuffed into my arms by a grinning delivery girl.

There were three dozen of them in all. Three dozen. I mean, I've had a few boyfriends, but none of them had ever ponied up for even a single dozen roses for me before that moment. Devi stopped counting blooms long enough to proffer tea and aspirin for my headache, and the two of us spent the morning Googling my newfound Superman.

Right after, that is, I texted Ryan a firm—but admittedly chicken-livered—goodbye, relegating him back to off-again status, much to Devi's disapproval. Not that she was on Team Ryan or anything. It's just, she's always been a big believer in the face-to-face breakup.

Mostly because she is much braver than I will ever be.

In any case, we learned online that while Anthony Hearst might be only a distant relative of the famous family, he had big plans of his own. His father's e-publishing firm was on the cusp of going public, and Anthony himself was apparently leading the charge.

It was heady stuff, and when he asked me out again the following weekend, I accepted. I didn't know then—and I still don't really know now—what he sees in me. He was finishing his master's, and I was still a lowly undergrad.

Also? Our backgrounds can't be more different. I mean, I grew up as the only daughter of a single mother and an often absentee father, so when I finally got to meet Anthony's family in their Fifth Avenue pied-à-terre, I felt more than a little out of place. But I promise you, I have never known a more romantic man. Just when I thought that three dozen couldn't be topped, he filled—literally filled—my apartment with more roses on my birthday. Roses in every color of the rainbow.

And somehow, with little more than five months having passed since that first meeting of Ghostbuster and reporter, I find myself engaged to this man. It's every girl's dream come true.

Isn't it?

chapter four

SUDDENLY SUNDAY
Ellinikos Kafe: Jet-Lag Jolter
Gia Kostas, former journalist, currently pursuing wild (Greek)
goose

For a drink with only three ingredients, Greek coffee is surprisingly difficult to get right. You need to find a briki *to start, and of course the grind of the beans is everything . . .*

I stagger off the plane in Greece, exhausted and with a stiff neck from sleeping sitting up. This was my second flight after a huge layover in Frankfurt since, apparently, no one wants to fly straight to Athens from New York. Even though the plane was only half full, the ramp is already crowded with people milling around together much closer than I've become used to in postviral New York City. Still, the ceilings are high, and I peel off my own travel mask with relief. It's good to feel like I can take a full, unfiltered breath again.

As I walk through the airport, the last rays of the setting sun beat through the large windows. The scents of hot cooking oil and roasting meats in the air are overlaid with airline diesel and something that smells like wood smoke. The concourse is even more jammed than the exit ramp, and I am swept along in a zombie haze through to Greek customs.

"Is this all your luggage?" demands the officer, pointing a blue-gloved hand at my hastily stuffed gym bag.

"Yes. I'm not staying long," I begin, but he cuts me off with a wave of the hand.

"You're in Greece now, *glykoúla*. You don't need more than a bikini, eh?"

I nod, because it seems the expedient thing to do, and refrain from informing him that I haven't worn a bikini since I joined my first swim team at twelve years old.

The crowd thins noticeably once the customs guard waves me through, which is lucky, because as soon as I exit the gates, I realize I have no idea what to do next. Around me in the Arrivals hall, a version of the opening scene from *Love, Actually* is unfolding, except bigger and Greeker. As each new person emerges through the doors, a cheer goes up, and they are swept into a scrum of screaming and sometimes sobbing relatives. Cheeks are pinched and slapped until they are apple red, flowers are proffered, and the arriving passengers, looking dazed, are ushered away in a surging cacophony of loving family.

Apart from myself and a pair of quite clearly newlywed tourists, every arriving passenger is met with some form of this chaotic greeting at the gate.

Feeling like a bit of an outcast, I look around to orient myself. The stark blue-and-white Greek signage is completely baffling to me, so it's a great relief to see most of the things I need are also spelled out in English. Homing in on a sign I recognize beside a coffee shop cash register, I immediately log on to the airport Wi-Fi and fire off messages to Anthony and Devi in quick succession.

Then I order a coffee.

Greek coffee is thick and black, and served very, very hot. When the girl passes it to me in a demitasse china cup, I decide not to pro-test. I don't really have a free hand for carrying a to-go cup anyway, so I steel myself and drain it in one.

The kick to my head is immediate and so satisfying, I almost don't notice that I've scalded my entire mouth.

For some reason, the message to Anthony doesn't want to go through, but seconds after I hit "Send" on the text to Devi, the phone rings in my hand. Worse, she's calling from a hospital line.

"Why are you calling me?" I hiss into the phone. "I'm in Athens. Are you allowed to call long-distance from work?"

"*I'm in Athens?*" she repeats, her voice squawking through the phone. "What do you mean you're in Athens? Why the hell have you gone to Georgia? Are you on location for NOSH?"

I shoulder my gym bag and try to sidle sideways around a noisy group of people who have encircled a young woman whose Knicks jersey I recognize from the plane.

"*Agápi mou,*" cries one man, placing both his giant palms on her freshly reddened cheeks. "You are home with us, at last! Come— your *yiayia* cannot wait a moment longer."

From the single, desperation-filled glance she shoots at me, I can't tell if she's upset about the fragile state of her grandmother or just mortally embarrassed by the volume of the welcome. As she is finally swept away toward the airport entrance, I can hear Devi again.

". . . texting and calling all day," she's saying.

"I know," I yell into the phone, as yet another noisy family swoops past. "All your notifications just came through. Listen, I'm sorry. I didn't have time to call before I left. And—I'm not in Georgia. I've never even been to Georgia."

"Yeah, I know that," she says, and I can hear the relief in her voice. "I've never been there either. Are you at some bakery, or . . ."

"I'm in Greece," I confess, before she can go off in the wrong direction again. "I'm chasing down my father."

I listen to the sound of silence on the other end for a full ten seconds before I cave. "Dev? You still there?"

"Your dad has run away to ATHENS, GREECE?" she shrieks. "What the fuck, Gia?"

"My words exactly. Or at least, slightly less blasphemous."

"*Fuck* is not blasphemous. It's profane. And don't change the subject. What's going on?"

I honestly do not know and tell her so. "But I've got the name of his hotel. I'm going to hunt him down, hand over his meds, and then come home." I pause, not sure if I should risk it, and then blurt it out. "I missed both scheduled cake tastings."

"Oooo. Bet Tony's pissed."

"*Anthony,*" I say, enunciating carefully, "has been an angel. He only wants to help."

"By organizing your whole life for you."

I can't help sighing. This is familiar ground with Devi. Somehow, she and Anthony got off on the wrong foot, and I haven't been able to make her see how great he really is. And of course, he senses it and is crusty with her too. It's frustrating. But I don't have time for this right now.

"Anyway. I just wanted to let you know I'm safe."

"Well, thank you for that," she says, the sarcasm not entirely gone from her voice. "But as soon as you find your dad, text me, okay? I mean—do you even speak the language?"

"*Ochi. Den miláo elliniká,*" I reply, automatically.

"I take it that means no?" she says.

I can't help grinning as I glance around again. "Right. But most of the signs are in English too. I'll be okay—I'm not going to be here long."

A bell begins to ring through the phone. "Yikes—that's a code blue. I gotta go," she says. "But stay in touch, okay? I'll be checking for your texts."

"I promise. Love you, Dev."

"Love you too, crazy person. Be safe."

And without another word, she's gone, off to put out whatever the emergency room fire of the moment is. She's very good at what she does.

I check my phone to see if a message has come through from Anthony, but when there's no joy, I tuck it into my pocket and head for the nearest exit. Time to find the *real* crazy person in this scenario.

Luck is with me, in that my cab driver speaks excellent—if heavily accented—English, and we are soon hurtling away from the palm tree–lined streets around the airport and heading toward the city. My eyes are burning from lack of sleep, but I can't tear them away from the view outside the window. The airport itself is—apart from the Greek signage—almost identical to every airport I've ever been to at home. Buses line up outside, surrounded by yellow cabs zipping across the lines of traffic. But as soon as we pull away from the airport, it's clear I'm not in Kansas anymore.

There's not a single cloud in the sky, which has darkened to a deep indigo blue. To one side of the perfectly ordinary freeway, rolling hills in the distance are backlit with a single line of gold where they rise up to form low, rounded mountains. Seconds later, the palms disappear, and the trees lining the freeway become short and scrubby. The air swirling in through the window has a tang to it that I can't quite place. It smells of the sea, yes, but is different from the funky, industrial odor that lingers around the docks at home. Saltier.

Can air smell like olives?

I lean back in my seat and close my eyes at last, breathing in the fragrance that is Greece and wishing my best friend and my fiancé liked each other a little more.

If I try to pinpoint it, I think I first noticed her active animosity toward him after the proposal. In the beginning, she'd been as dazzled as I was with the flowers and the expensive restaurant dates. In a way, she benefited too, at least in the form of the foil packets twisted into swans that I brought home to share after elegant dinners with Anthony. But Devi is a Yankees girl, born and bred, and the day Anthony proposed, she watched the whole thing on television while she was supposed to be studying for her last exam.

When I finally made it home that night feeling—I have to say—thrilled and stunned in equal measure, she started in on me as soon as I walked through the door.

"Three months," she said, pointing to the calendar we have hung on the only open wall space in our tiny kitchen. "Two months and twenty-nine days, if you want to get technical. That's less than a hundred days you've known this guy, Gia. And you said *yes*?"

I remember feeling immediately deflated. "Don't you want to see the ring?" I pleaded, forcing my left hand into hers. But she barely gave it a glance.

"It's huge," she said flatly. "No surprise there."

"It's gorgeous," I said, still feeling shocked at the weight of it on my finger. "Rose gold and platinum, Devi. And the diamond is . . ."

"I don't care how fucking big the diamond is," she snapped. "It's too soon. You're being railroaded, Gia. Did you know what was coming when you went to the game tonight?"

I admitted that I hadn't. And by the end of our conversation, I was forced to concede that the public nature of the proposal *had* thrown me. It had been one of the first games that a large crowd had been allowed back into the stands, and the mood of the place was boisterous.

"How could I say no? The entire stadium was watching."

Devi scoffed. "The entire country, more like. It was the game of the week, Gia. People watching in Omaha saw him drop to one knee. People in Kentucky."

I plopped down beside her on our old sofa and put my newly heavy left hand on her knee. "Exactly. Like, I'm going to say no under *those* circumstances?"

She clutched my hand in both of hers. "Did you want to say no? Because if you even thought about it—that's intimidation, Gia. He's using his wealth and his power to intimidate you into saying yes."

"I wanted to say yes," I insisted. "I did. I do, I mean. It's just—unexpected, is all."

She snorted. "I'll say. You hardly know this guy."

"Come on, Dev! I know him—I do. Anyway, he's a public figure. Everyone knows he's a great guy."

Devi rolled her eyes at me. "Oh my god, girl. Will you *listen* to yourself? Look—I'm happy for you. I mean—I *will be* happy for you if this is what you want. It just feels too early. Too rushed somehow. Less than three months together, and you're ready to commit for the rest of your life?"

"I love him," I said, fighting back weepiness. "I do. Life has been so awful for so long, and getting married is supposed to be a celebration, Devi. You're my best friend. You'll be my only bridesmaid. I want you—of *all* people—to be happy for me."

She flattened my palm against her pajama-clad thigh and stared down at my new ring for a long moment before letting out a tremendous sigh.

"Okay. I will be happy for you. But just promise me you won't have a whirlwind engagement. Give it some time, okay? It'll be a big society wedding, of course. Those things take at least a year to plan, don't they?"

I duly promised and was freed at last to take my spinning head to bed.

Of course, within a couple of weeks I found myself explaining to Devi how lucky Anthony had been to secure a venue—the venue of our dreams—with only two months' notice. And worse—how Anthony's three younger cousins had counted on standing up for him at his wedding their whole lives. Besides, no one ever just has one bridesmaid, do they?

But even as I assured Devi of her inalienable position as maid of honor, I could see she was digging in her heels. And when that girl makes up her mind?

It's not easy to change, is all I'm saying.

chapter five

SUNDAY LATE
Pink Lemon Ouzo
Gia Kostas, once aspiring-journalist, now parental overseer

A unique, Greek take on spiked pink lemonade. This sweet, licoricey concoction goes down like candy floss, but it's got a kick like a bronco if you're not careful. Begin with a handful of mint, crushed into a tall, slender glass . . .

My phone rings for a second time just as I collect my credit card back from the cab driver. He's pulled over at the side of a cobbled lane that runs in front of the hotel address I culled from Evan's file folder. I climb out, slam the car door before the taxi pulls away, and manage to answer the phone on the third ring.

"What. The. Actual. Fuck. Gia?" Anthony's voice comes exploding out at me in a tone I've never heard before.

"I—uh—hi, Anthony." I can't help glancing up at the hotel entrance, where a young woman dressed in a yellow bikini top and black sparkly miniskirt is staring at me with undisguised interest. "I guess you got my voice mail?"

He has indeed and is not at all happy about it, he tells me, in no uncertain terms. He is not happy, the cake baker is not happy, and—worst of all—his mother is not happy. She has, he tells me, called half a dozen times since I've gone AWOL, her list of concerns growing with each call. I listen in jet-lagged silence until the tirade finally slows enough that I can get a word in.

"Of course, I want a lovely wedding—I want that as much as you do. But it's months away, Anthony. This situation with my dad is an emergency that I need to deal with right now."

At the mention of my dad, Anthony's tone softens a little.

"Look, honey," he says. "I know you're worried. But flying to Athens? I just hope it's worth losing the best baker in the city."

The lights of a small bar next door to the hotel twinkle gaily in the darkness, in direct contrast to the feelings inside me. I can hear the quiet strains of a piano through the open door.

"I—don't even know how to answer that, Anthony. This is my dad's life. Yes, it's worth missing out on some stupid cake—*god*!"

Tears of fury and exhaustion spring to my eyes, and I slump back against a car parked at the curb. This is the first real argument I've ever had with Anthony, and on top of the fear for my dad and the jet lag, I don't have any resources left to deal.

Clearly, I'm not the only one. All traces of Anthony's earlier conciliatory tone disappear in an instant. I yank the phone away from my ear and punch the volume button down.

"Seriously? Seriously? Gia, if you'd been paying attention, you'd know that tomorrow is my company's initial public offering. And the entire thing has fallen on my shoulders because my father is less than useless. As a result, I have had an incredibly shitty day, *everything* is going wrong, and now I've got my mother all over my ass about wedding plans. I'm just fucking ready to call this whole thing off, do you hear me?"

"Call what off?" I say, slowly. "The public offering?"

His voice explodes out of my phone. "Jesus CHRIST, are you a complete idiot? This IPO is my *entire* future. I thought you knew how important this was to me, Gia. I—I don't even know what to say to you. We're done, man. Done."

I suddenly feel entirely awake. A cool wind swirls around me, raising goose bumps on my arms. Propping the phone to my ear with my shoulder, I tug down the sleeves of my cardigan. I have never heard him sound so angry.

"You don't mean that," I whisper, but he's not listening.

The dark, such as it is on a city street, has folded in on me now, which at least gives me a little cover. I wipe my nose with the cuff of my cardigan and take a shaky breath.

"I just need to find my dad, okay? I'll hand over the medication he left behind and make him promise to take it. I can be back in a couple of days, and I'll—"

"What is it about the word *done* you don't understand?" he says coldly. "Call me when you get home, and we can sort things out then."

And he's gone.

I pocket my phone and turn to find the girl in the bikini top proffering a somewhat tattered-looking tissue at me. I can feel myself blushing as I reach to accept it and swipe quickly at my eyes.

"No need to be embarrass." The girl offers a sympathetic smile. "My boyfriend asshole too. We fight all the time."

She swings open the doorway to the hotel and gestures me inside with a sweep of the hand.

"Oh, we weren't—that is—he's not . . ." I begin, and then give up entirely and step through the doorway. As I hurry toward the front desk, her voice follows me, a clarion call from the dark entranceway.

"I keep him around because he has nice motor and is excellent lover. Does your man have nice motor?"

I affect the time-honored tradition of pretending not to hear her and cross the floor at a swift trot. The hair on my arms stands up as I hurry through the startlingly cool interior. A scent of onions cooking permeates the air, coupled with the slightly unsettling undertones of mildew and Pine-Sol. As I reach the front desk, an elderly man wearing a stiff, black polyester suit and an enormous mustache nods at me formally. A shiny gold bar pinned to his lapel identifies him as *Konstantin*.

"Good evening, madam. You have reservation?"

"Vroom, vroom!" calls the girl from the door, and the elderly man leans to one side.

"Sikka," he warns. *"Figue!"*

She gives a last giggle before slamming the door behind her.

"My apologies, madam," Konstantin murmurs. He runs a finger over one unruly eyebrow, which is only marginally less bushy than his mustache. "My niece, Sikka. Just returned from her semester at English university, and she is quite impossible. These young people, so filled with high spirits, eh?"

I join him in shaking my head at the state of young people these days and then confess that while I don't have a reservation, my father should be in residence. When I give him my dad's name, Konstantin's face breaks into a wide smile.

"Ah—you are daughter of Dr. Kostas? Lovely man, your father. Lovely man. Is not so busy right now. I find you a room."

I feel a flash of fury at my father, the lovely man. Chasing him down has just cost me the most romantic relationship of my life, and I could just as easily strangle him at the moment. But before I can say another word, Konstantin pulls out a registration card for me to sign.

"No need to fill details—I get from your papa in the morning." He slides a key across the desk and points me toward a darkened corridor. "Room sixteen. Sleep well!"

"Oh, but I was hoping to meet up with my father tonight." I pick up the key. "Can you tell me which room he's in?"

Konstantin points to the stairs. "Room thirty-six. Top floor. Only the best for your papa. But he is sleep early—much jet lag."

I stare up the steps for a long moment, trying to decide what to do.

"You need assistance with your bags?" Konstantin asks, at last.

"No—no thank you," I say, unable to keep the defeat from my voice. "This is all I have. Good night."

I shoulder my bag and aim myself toward my room.

I'm just about to turn the key in the lock of room sixteen when fury overtakes me. I've come all this way—at a huge cost to my life and my own relationship—and I'm supposed to respect *his* beauty sleep?

Not *this* Kostas.

Trembling a little from the combination of anger and exhaustion, it takes me a couple of minutes of fishing around in my bag before my fingers close around the pill bottle. I yank the bottle out, toss the bag inside my room, and stomp up the stairs.

It turns out that room thirty-six is three winding and super rickety sets of stairs up. By the time I get to the top, I have to pause and gasp a few times to catch my breath, which takes the edge off my fury, a little.

There's only the one numbered door on this floor, so I feel very little guilt about pounding on it. No answer.

"Pops?" I not-quite yell and then knock again, so hard that the number six spins on its nail to become a nine.

Still nothing.

I'm just balling up my fist to go again when the door to the tiniest elevator I've ever seen clanks open behind me, and Sikka steps out. She's carrying a teetering stack of folded towels.

"Heavy sleeper, your papa?" she says, as I resume pounding. "I can hear you all the way up in lift."

"I just need to get him to take his medication," I say, pausing long enough to rub my knuckles, which are getting seriously sore. "I don't know why I'm bothering. He drives me crazy."

Sikka shoots a glance down the stairwell I've just climbed up and thrusts the towels into my arms. "All Greek men are like that. Is a curse on us women."

Reaching into her pocket, she grins at me. As the key clicks in the lock, her eyes meet mine.

"Don't tell Konstantin, okay?"

"I won't," I promise, and she gives me a final grin before scooping up the towels and heading off down the hall.

Inside, the room is shrouded in darkness, but a thin line of light shines from what turns out to be the bathroom door. My father is an indistinct, snoring lump under the bedclothes.

I march into the bathroom, fill a glass with water, and leaving the door wide open, return to my dad's still sleeping form. He's always been a heavy sleeper, but I'm not going to let that stop me now.

"Pops," I say into his face. "Wake up."

I have to actually shake his shoulder before he sits up and stares at me blurrily. "Marta? What are you doing here?"

I thrust the glass of water into his hand, and when some of it slops over the edge and onto the covers, I feel grimly delighted. "It's me, Pops—Gia. You forgot to bring your pills, and you need to take one now."

He blinks slowly, twice. Then without another word he pops the proffered pill into his mouth and takes a swallow of water before rolling back under the covers. "Thank you, *koritsi*," he mumbles. "You always take such good care of me."

I stare down at him. "For crying out loud, Pops. You are seriously not even going to speak to me after I've come all this way?"

A gentle snore is the only reply.

The light from the bathroom illuminates the shock of grey curly hair that is now the only part of him visible above the bedclothes, and I briefly consider murdering him in his sleep.

But in the end, I give it up as a lost cause and stomp back down the stairs to my own room.

The room is very small, but like my dad's, it's got a tiny en suite bathroom and a bed, and at the moment, that's all I care about. A night-light glows in one corner, and I can't be bothered to even flick on the light switch. It's not until I throw myself down on the bed that I realize his pill bottle is still clutched in my hand.

I gaze at it blankly and, for a moment, contemplate heading back up to shake the stupid things in his face, but the thought of those three flights of rickety stairs is too daunting.

And there's no way I'm setting foot in that tiny, creaking elevator.

Rolling over, I stare at the ceiling feeling exhausted and strung out and helplessly angry. At my dad, for creating this situation.

But also at Anthony.

I replay the argument in my head, and the more I think about it, the less reasonable his whole diatribe seems. His life is crazy at the moment, I know. All the same, my actions—however ill-advised—definitely did not deserve that kind of response. I'm just worried about my father. Who doesn't worry about their parents?

Snatching up my phone, I try dialing him twice before I realize my plan likely doesn't work outside of the US. I grab the receiver of the phone beside my bed and try again. This takes several attempts, as I need to get an outside line *and* find the country code for the US. Which is apparently 01. But even after all this, when the call finally goes through, it clicks immediately into Anthony's voice mail.

At the sound of his voice on the recording, I burst into tears.

Not wanting to leave a sniveling message, I slam the phone down, accidentally catching the little plastic information card holder beside the phone with the receiver. It shatters, sending shards skittering across the floorboards.

Dropping my head into my hands, I force myself to get a grip. I'm so angry, heartbroken, and strung out by exhaustion that I know I'll never be able to sleep.

I get up, splash my face with water in the tiny bathroom, and then commence a hunt for the minibar.

It turns out that Greek guesthouses do not have minibars.

And in retrospect? This sad fact is entirely to blame for everything that happens next.

At least—that's what I tell myself.

If this hadn't been a wild goose chase from the start, I likely would have just turned on the television and tried to late-night bore myself to sleep. I've done it before. But along with no minibar, this little room also doesn't have a television. Glancing at the clock, I see it's just past midnight.

I suddenly remember the lights and music coming from the building next door to the guesthouse. Then I recall just how loudly Anthony was yelling at me in that moment. And then? I get angry all over again.

A drink will help. I can get a drink in the little nightclub. Maybe just a glass of wine to help me sleep.

I sling my purse over my shoulder, grab my room key, and step into the corridor.

Standing in the street, I discover the place next door turns out to be more of a pub than a bar. Through the door, I hear the strains of quiet music being piped over the speakers. This is perfect. I can drink my wine, head back to my room, go to sleep, and deal with my dad in the morning. Then I can call and sort things out with Anthony.

I reach out to open the door when I feel a hand on my arm.

Jerking my arm away, I whirl around to find Sikka grinning at me. Her hair, the lower half of which is platinum blond, is now pulled up with a jeweled clip, and she has exchanged her yellow bikini top for what I can only describe as a silver flapper dress. It looks to be entirely made of Christmas tinsel.

"Good girl," she says. "Going out will cheer you up, and you will forget your problems." She looks around. "But this place is a dump. I take you better place—lots of Greek boys. Greek boys, they good at helping you forget."

I can't suppress a sigh. "I don't want a Greek boy. I want Anthony."

"Okay, fine—tomorrow. But tonight? You come with me. Just one block, there is perfect place. You dance. You drink. You forget."

I point down to my travel-stained dress. "Look—I can't go out to some nice place in this. I just want to get a glass of wine and go to bed."

Sikka links her arm through mine. "You come with me. Two minutes. I get you sorted."

She leads me around the corner and through a side door back into the guesthouse.

"You know I'm Sikka, yes?" she says, resting her bright yellow manicure on her own chest. "And you? You are Gianna?"

At my surprised look, she grins. "I check registration card. I like to drive Konstantin a little mad sometimes. Is good fun."

"Just Gia," I reply absently, looking around the room.

There are two industrial-size machines, washer and dryer, but the rest of the room is strewn in everything from heavy overcoats to piles of high-heeled shoes.

"I do laundry here," she says, wiggling her eyebrows at me. "You would *not* believe what people leave behind."

In less than two minutes, I'm out of my own clothes and wearing a little black strapless number that's about a half size too tight. I throw my teal cardigan over it.

Sikka shakes her head. "You don't need. Too warm for dancing. Greek boys like bare shoulders."

I put it on anyway. My cleavage is spilling over the top of the dress.

She points to my left hand. "Take that off," she orders. "He no spoil your fun tonight."

I stare at her, suddenly overcome with the memory of Anthony's voice. *We'll sort out the details when you get home.*

"Should I give it back?" I ask her, suddenly.

She looks scandalized. "Never! He dump you—you keep ring! But wear on your chain now, for be safe."

Other than the ring, the only piece of jewelry I happened to be wearing when I jumped on the plane was a necklace my dad gave me when I was thirteen. It's a little silver Coptic cross on a matching chain that belonged to his mother, I think. My dad grew up Catholic, of course, but nonpracticing, and my own mother's family belonged to one of the Dutch reformed churches. Organized religion has never appealed to me, although—optimist that I am—I like to think that there is something to aspire to after we're done here on earth. Nevertheless, this necklace, with its perfectly square little cross, has always been one of my favorites.

I slide the ring onto my necklace, where it nestles into my slightly-more-voluminous-than-usual cleavage. And then I try—and fail—to not touch the indentation on the bare third finger of my left hand.

Sikka takes my mind off the ring by handing me a pair of shoes with at least five-inch heels.

"Are you crazy?" I stare down at the shoes. "I can't walk in those."

She shrugs. "You can. They have big platform, see? So only three-inch heel. Like magic!"

Her own dress is so short I catch a glimpse of her butt cheek when she squats to buckle my shoe.

"I don't know . . ." I begin, but she rolls her eyes at me and plunges her own feet into a pair of thigh-high leather boots.

"Is only for dance." She takes me by the hand, which is a good thing since I can't walk in these crazy shoes without support, and we totter back out onto the street.

Luckily, the nightclub is indeed only a block away. And compared to the pub next door—well, there's really no comparing them. This place is bigger, noisier, and totally jammed with unmasked, mostly inebriated, writhing bodies.

An extremely sweaty man dances over to us as we walk in the door. He's wearing a pink dress shirt, unbuttoned almost to the waist, and stands about two inches shorter than Sikka in her high-heeled boots. He does a little shimmy in front of her, and she laughs uproariously and throws herself into his arms, latching her lips onto his.

"Gia, this is my Ivo," she says as they break apart. "Ivo, Gia's heart is broke. We need drinks, okay?"

Ivo gives me a broad, gap-toothed smile and shimmies off into the crowd.

"Only one drink," I shout at Sikka, who is already pulling me onto the dance floor.

"Sure, sure."

The music shifts, and it's Daft Punk, and suddenly? I'm dancing. I mean, only a monster doesn't dance to Daft Punk.

When Ivo brings me a pink drink, I down it in two swallows and immediately start to feel better. After all, between the jet lag and the crying I'm probably a little dehydrated, so this lemonadey concoction is likely just what I need. Ivo grabs Sikka by the hips, and since she's still holding my hands, the three of us dance together, which seems to make him extremely happy. Then Sikka straddles her legs around one of his knees and starts grinding on him, which is my cue to back away. In under a second, they are swallowed by the crowd.

I find myself standing beside the bar with one of Sikka's ridiculous, not-quite-stolen shoes in my hand, which has come off in all the dancing. And as it turns out, I am just fuzzy enough to not be able to sort out the buckle.

Defeated, I drop the shoe on the floor, balance on the other one, and order a drink for the road. Sikka was right. I do feel better.

I also feel someone slide in beside me at the bar.

"I think you've possibly lost your shoe," he says and holds it up.

This is no Greek boy.

He's got a British accent for one. Tall with dark eyes and darker hair, a little curly. Persian origin, maybe, or possibly South Asian. In any case, he has soft, olive skin, which is also tanned—in fact, I can see where his nose is peeling, just a little.

"Yours?" he repeats. He's got a half-finished glass of beer in his other hand.

"Sort of." I take the shoe back from him. "I mean, it's—ah—mostly borrowed, to tell you the truth. I was just having a little trouble getting it back on."

The bartender slides my drink over at this moment. It's a refill of whatever Ivo brought me before, consisting, I now realize, of pink lemonade mixed with something akin to jet fuel. I knock it back in one.

My tall, hot, shoe-returning friend raises his eyebrows and smiles. "Thirsty?"

Um. Yes. Very, *very* thirsty.

But of course, I don't say this. Instead, I lift one shoulder casually. "Just a bit dehydrated actually. Jet lag."

"Ah. That explains the shoe." He smiles and is about to turn away when I grab his arm.

I hear myself say, "Can I buy you a drink?" and then—worse—I actually do.

Things might get just a little—ah—crazy after that.

chapter six

MONDAY, WEE HOURS
Tzatziki and Pita Triangles
Gia Kostas, once aspiring-journalist, now washed-up hack

Bar food in Athens has its own unique flair and is never quite what you expect. Everything from pork skewers to Greek salad is available in nightclubs, and the fuel is needed because the Greeks know how to dance. This favorite begins with . . .

Here's the thing.

I've been to nightclubs. They're not really my scene, but I grew up in New York. Of course I've been. I've had wild nights out. I mean, I'm a twenty-five-year-old human. Devi and I barely survived eleventh grade, which is why neither of us can touch tequila to this day.

But to tell you the truth, I mostly got it out of my system way back then. After we were legal, a lot of the fun dropped away. Of course, I go out to bars now and then, but . . . you know. I was the one dressed as a Ghostbuster at that Halloween party, after all.

And then, of course, there was the virus. I mean, it was a world-changing event, and I'm not sure we're in the clear, even now. During the worst of it, my name might as well have been Caution, not Kostas, since I was such a careful hand-washer. I followed the science, listened to the recommendations, and still have at least a dozen face masks tucked into my underwear drawer.

I guess if I had to put my finger on the actual trigger that kicked off events tonight—it was being dumped. Over the phone. I mean, before this happened, my biggest argument with Anthony was when I left a towel on the floor in the bathroom.

For the record, I *did* hang it up. I'm pretty sure I did, anyway.

All this to say what just happened is . . . out of character.

The first thing I do after pushing Sikka out of my room—she in-sisted on seeing me home safely—is to check the phone. It's three in the morning here in Athens, which means it's only just after eight at night in New York. My head is spinning from exhaustion and jet lag and guilt and exhilaration, and it's all too much.

Too much to cope with alone.

I haven't been to church since my confirmation when I was eleven, but—dammit. I lead such a disgustingly boring life. The need to confess my sins—my delicious, *delicious* sins—and to bare my soul to Anthony is almost too much to handle.

Almost.

Instead, I dial Devi and tell her everything.

"You did WHAT?" she squawks when I blurt the whole thing out. "Who are you, and what have you done with my friend Gianna?"

"I know—I know it sounds crazy."

"Crazy? You've never done anything like this in your whole life."

"I know I haven't. Devi, I don't know what happened. It was all so fast. I only meant to have a glass of wine to help me sleep, and then . . ."

"What time is it there now?"

I peer at the clock. "Like—three fifteen."

"Gianna Marie Kostas, I have less than ten minutes before I go on shift. And I hope I don't have to remind you I haven't had sex in four months since I broke up with Jordan. I need details and I need them *now*."

"I—I really can't explain it. I'd been dancing, and one of my shoes fell off, and he helped me put it back on, and . . ."

"Holy crap. You're a fuckin' Cinderella." And then she loses it, repeating "*literally* fucking" in between guffaws.

"Dev. Get a grip."

"That's what *she* said . . ." she shrieks, and this sends her off again, giggling like a teenager. "Okay—sorry, Gia, sorry. I'm just a little overtired. Keep going."

"*You're* overtired? I think I last slept on Friday night, and it's now Monday morning."

"Geez, no wonder you're getting jiggy with strange guys. You must be exhausted . . ."

"I am," I say, just as she adds, "and also drunk."

"I only had two drinks, or maybe three. But then, he offered to help me with my shoe, and . . ."

I suddenly remember the brush of his fingers against my ankle, and the zing that shoots through me—even now—is enough to make my knees buckle.

"Did he kiss you?"

I flash back to the moment, me literally throwing myself into his arms, him backed against the door in the corner.

"I—uh—yeah, I guess you could say that," I admit. "It's possible I sorta kissed him."

"And then what happened? I've got two minutes, Gia, and I swear . . ."

"I'm telling you as fast as I can, Dev. I don't know how it happened. We were kissing, and then this door opened behind him, and we kind of fell inside, and one thing led to another . . ."

"Hosanna on a bagel," Devi's voice explodes through the phone. "Don't give me this 'one thing led to another' garbage. Are you telling me you had sex with this man in the toilets?"

"Not—not technically in the toilet. I think maybe it was a janitorial closet? There was a sink. I—I don't really remember."

I remember it vividly.

The closet door had been an accident, for sure, but we'd been making out so hard against it that when it fell open, there was no other option. It was even darker in there than on the dance floor, and it definitely smelled of bleach and old mop. I slammed the door behind us, but there was a tiny gleam of light coming through the crack around the door. Just for an instant, the mirror over the sink reflected the heat in his eyes. So yeah. It was me who hopped up on the sink and pulled him closer. All me.

Devi's voice crashes through these memories. "Okay, okay. But please, *please* tell me you had fun, at least."

I have a sudden vision of just exactly what happened the moment he slid his fingers under my thighs and I felt the warmth of his skin against mine, and I have to swallow, hard, before I can speak. Even so, my voice comes out with a croak.

"Yes, okay, it was a little fun."

It was the best sex I have ever had in my life.

"So—you're going to see him again?"

"Devi," I hiss into the phone. "What is it about 'one night' that you don't understand?"

I stop immediately, appalled at how I have just—even accidentally—echoed Anthony. But Devi doesn't notice.

"Nothing," she says, still sounding delighted. "I couldn't be happier for you." Her voice drops into a warning tone. "As long as there was a condom involved."

I sigh heavily. "There was. I carry a couple around in my purse for Anthony."

She chuckles. "You naughty minx."

I don't mention we've never had occasion to use them.

"Look," I say firmly. "After I talk to my dad in the morning, I'm going to hop a flight home as soon as possible. I need to try to patch things up with Anthony. This thing tonight was a one-off. A mistake."

I can hear her sigh through the phone. "*Anthony* is the mistake, Gia. He puts his own needs over everyone around him. It's *good* you had this fight. You need to take time to think of . . . *shit*."

A distorted voice echoes through the phone, drowning out her words. "Dev? What is it?"

"Gotta go. They're paging me. Text you later!"

And she's gone.

I peel off Sikka's dress, unhook my bra, and realize, to my horror, that I am missing my underwear.

Shame floods through me. I am *that* girl. *That* girl who bangs some stranger in a toilet. Okay, so it wasn't a toilet, but it may as well have been. A janitorial closet is not exactly a step up.

I drop into bed, wrap my shame around me like a cloak, and fall into the deepest, most contented sleep I've had in months.

chapter seven

MONDAY MORNING
Orange Mango Juice
Gia Kostas, ex-journalist wannabe, now parental drug runner

This lively day starter is an excellent counterpart to the rich, dark Greek coffee that is offered with breakfast everywhere. Particularly refreshing after a late evening's revels or perhaps a few drinks too many the night before . . .

His voice is contrite and very, very confusing. "Oh, babe, were you asleep?"

After I realize I'm somehow already holding the phone to my ear, I struggle to sit up. My head gives a little spin, but not too bad.

"No—no," I mutter groggily. The red LED lights on the little clock by the bed read 8:15. "I have to get up. I need to talk to my dad."

I try desperately to concentrate as Anthony's voice floats through the phone. He sounds almost—pleading.

"Gia, babe, listen," he says. "You just caught me at a bad time earlier, okay? I feel lousy about how we ended the call."

"I do too." Swinging my legs over the side of the bed, I see with a pang of something close to horror that I am topless and still wearing Sikka's sparkly black dress, which is pushed down around my waist. I hastily pull the sheet up, as if that will change anything, and drag my attention back to Anthony's voice. "Sorry—what did you say?"

"Babe. It's after one and I'm super tired, but I couldn't go to sleep with things so bad between us. So listen—I need you to know it's all good now, okay?"

"It's all good?" I repeat stupidly.

"Yeah. The markets are still a mess, and it means we can delay the fucking IPO for a week. It'll give me time to get all my ducks in a row."

"Your ducks?" I get an absurd image of Sikka making duck lips in one of the selfies she was taking last night, and my stomach knots in a way that has nothing to do with my hangover.

"Right. And listen, I talked to my mom, and we've got it all worked out. I know you're worried about your dad, and seriously, it's okay with me. Stay as long as you need to."

"I'm—I just have to see him this morning, and then I'm coming home. Anthony, are you saying . . ."

"I'm saying I love you, babe. It was all a misunderstanding—our first fight can't be our last, can it? I need you, Gia."

"You still—you still want to marry me?"

"Of course I do. I never said anything otherwise . . ."

I think back to him saying, *We are* done, *man. Done.*

"But . . ."

He cuts me off. "No buts. Listen, I even managed to keep the cake people happy, and they accepted the booking over the phone. It's all taken care of, babes. Deal with your dad, and I'll see you soon, okay?"

"All taken care of . . . ?" I can't seem to knock my brain out of repeat mode. And stupidly, all I can take from this is that I'm not going to get a taste of that chocolate raspberry truffle cake, after all.

"Right," he says, and his tone softens again. "Honey, listen. I'm sorry if you misunderstood my intentions. I only want what's best for us—for both of us—right? Now, I've got to go before I fall asleep on my feet. Love you!"

"Love you too . . ." I begin, but he is gone.

My phone falls from my numb fingers, and I clutch my hands to my only slightly aching head.

What—in the name of all that is holy—have I done?

Clean yellow light slants through the shutters over my windows and illuminates my face in the mirror on the wall beside my bed. My hair is sticking straight up on one side, both eyes are raccooned with mascara and eyeliner, and every inch of my exposed skin is apparently covered in glitter.

Apart from the glitter, I am the spitting image of the horrified face in Edvard Munch's famous painting.

I leap to my feet and flee to the bathroom before I live up to the title and scream.

It turns out that curling up in a ball on the floor of a tiny en suite bathroom can't really solve any problems. And worse, when I pillow my head on the cardigan I find discarded behind the door, I get the faintest scent of the hot guy's aftershave.

The visceral pang this shoots through me sends me leaping into the shower. I can't think about how, even when we were both slicked in sweat, he still smelled fantastic. I have to erase everything that happened last night from my memory.

Ten minutes later, I step out of the shower and wrap my hair in a towel. I have a little headache behind one eye, but nothing that an aspirin and a cup of coffee won't fix. It's the giant headache I'm worried about, and that one has nothing to do with alcohol.

A headache that comes from the tiny, niggling thought that Devi might be right.

No. No. I'm engaged to be married. I love Anthony and he loves me. What happened last night was—well, we were on a break. An admittedly very short break, but . . .

Suddenly, I have a thought. Undoing the clasp of my necklace, I replace the ring firmly back on my left hand. There. Physical evidence that Anthony and I are together. All my mistakes are behind me now.

I'm just drying myself off when there's a rapid knock on the door. Quickly looking around, I see there's only a single hand towel remaining in the bathroom.

The knock comes again, and this time, a voice hisses through the door. "Gia, is me. Open up!"

"Just a minute," I yelp, and yanking the towel out of my hair, wrap it around myself.

I grab the handle just as the third set of knocks rattles the door in its frame.

"What the hell?" I say as the door flings open and Sikka pushes herself inside.

"Oh, good." She looks relieved. "I thought I have to run back for key."

"What? You can't just . . ."

"I need dress. Woman came back for it—can you believe?" She strides across the room and plucks the sparkly strapless dress from its spot on the floor where I kicked it off earlier.

She shakes it out and—to my embarrassment—sniffs it. "Is good," she concedes, and folds the dress neatly. "Good enough, at least. I take now."

"Fine, fine," I say. "Happy to be rid of it."

She looks into my face suddenly and waggles her eyebrows. "You have good time with that gorgeous man last night, eh?"

I nod before I can stop myself and then shake my head hard.

"No. No. It was a mistake. I should have just gone to bed."

She looks puzzled. "You did go bed. I put you there—early early—myself."

I sigh. "I know. I just—I should never have gone out. My—my fiancé just called."

She chuckles. "Your ex? I thought he dump you last night?"

I swallow hard. "Apparently not."

This makes her laugh out loud. "Oh—ho! So he was home feeling bad, and you were out having sexy times with *elkystika Ellines agoria.*"

My face immediately flushes at the memory. I *so* was.

"No—nothing happened, okay? It was a little harmless flirtation, nothing more."

Sikka shakes her head and sets the dress firmly on the table beside my bed. "Gia. I saw you come out of that room. I saw his face—*and* his neck! You don't need to be ashame. I would have gone for him if I didn't have Ivo. He was—how you Americans say?—so much a hunk!"

I clutch her arm. "I know, but you have Ivo. Just like I have Anthony. I'm not a cheater, Sikka. I've never had anything like this happen before."

Her face clouds. "You no cheat. He dump you—your man dump you. I saw you cry!"

"I know, but it was a mistake. He was just—there's too much going on right now, and me coming all the way here to Athens to find my dad—he was upset."

She shrugs and picks up the dress. "You no cheat. He dump. If he wants you back now, fine. No problemo." She grins at me. "Or maybe you stay apart? I bet I could find your hot man for you, and you give him another chance before you choose?"

I'm shaking my head furiously, but she's not paying attention.

"No way he from here." She taps one temple. "Must be guest. I do laundry in many hotels. You want me find him? What's his name?"

"No—no. It was a mistake, I told you. I—"

Sikka shakes the dress at me. "Unless you don't know his name?"

Opening the door, she roars with laughter at the look on my face. "Okay, I go. And you? Have happy memory, nothing more."

She steps out the door, then pauses, and sticks her head back inside. "Every girl need happy memory sometimes, eh?"

Then she winks at me and vanishes down the hall.

B y the time I'm dressed, I've got the worst of the anxiety under control. Right now, my focus has to be my dad. He must have missed a couple of doses of his meds, but at least I got the pill into him last night. I'd planned to be up at six, ready to plant myself outside his door, but—well, there's nothing I can do about this now.

I drape my cardigan over the back of a chair so it has a chance to air out and leave to find my father.

I n the corridor, I run into Konstantin, who is in the middle of yawning widely.

"I beg your pardon, Meez Kostas," he says apologetically. "My shift is end now. Time for me to go to bed."

"No worries," I say. "I'm still a bit jet-lagged myself. Can you point me to the breakfast room? I'm trying to find my dad."

"Point you?" Konstantin says, looking horrified. "I take you there this minute!"

He sweeps an arm out to indicate our direction, and then bustles ahead of me down a long, dark corridor.

"Is just this way," he says, making a sharp left and then, before I can quite negotiate it, a second.

I crash full out into his back as he stops abruptly to throw open a door. The light from outside pours into the dark entranceway, effectively blinding me for a moment. Eyes narrowed to slits, I am in the midst of apologizing for the collision when a voice drifts in from outside that I recognize.

Before I can react, Konstantin strides out, sweeping an arm back toward me like he's announcing the arrival of royalty. "Dr. Ari— your beautiful daughter. She is here!"

Embarrassed, I scuttle behind him into a tiny, sunlit courtyard. The flagstone surface is large enough to hold only three slightly rusty wrought iron tables. The whitewashed brick walls are overgrown in lush greenery dotted with nodding pink flowers. A large tree dominates the space, providing shade for the diners at the only occupied table.

As I step out onto the patio, the conversation falls silent, and I find myself looking at a statuesque blond woman sitting beside my father. Her tremendous height is clear from the impossibly lengthy legs crossed beside the table, and she smiles up at me. Most of her face is obscured by sunglasses, but I can't miss the lift of a single eyebrow as she glances from my face to my dad's. Beside her, my father looks up in surprise.

"*Gianitsa!* You *are* here after all. I thought I only dreamed of you last night!"

He leaps to his feet and wraps his arms around me.

"Not a dream, Pops." I thrust my hand in my bag for his pill bottle. "The real question of the moment is—why are *you* here?"

In the silence that follows my words, the attractive woman turns to my father and clears her throat. "Perhaps we should continue our discussion another time, Dr. Kostas," she says quietly.

Her voice is deeper than I expect, and clearly American, and the sight of my dad's abashed expression suddenly infuriates me. Finally, my hand closes around the familiar shape of the pill bottle inside my bag.

"No. No—don't let me interrupt. I'm only here as an errand girl."

I toss the bottle of pills at my father, who snags them out of the air and slips them into his pocket in a single smooth move.

Evidently pleased with this feat of hand-eye coordination, he smiles and gestures at an open chair. "Darling—sit down. Let me introduce you to my friend, and then all will become clear, hmm?"

As much as I want to vent my exasperation into his face, I'm genetically unable to create a scene in front of a stranger. And with the warmth of the sunlight on this little alfresco patio, relief surges ahead of my anger. I've done my job. My dad has his medication. The rest is up to him.

I slump onto the chair and watch Ari pour me a drink from a frosted pitcher sitting on the table.

The blonde slides her glass forward with one perfectly manicured red nail, and my dad hurries to fill it as well. The liquid is the palest orange and cold enough to immediately frost over the outside of both glasses.

"Thank you, Dr. Kostas," she says in a throaty baritone.

This is confusing on several levels. My dad's conquests often run to the squeaky-voiced, ingenue variety, but this woman definitely does not tick any of his usual boxes. She's wearing a light linen dress, which fits her toned body like it was made for her, and four-inch turquoise stilettos, the quality of which I've only gazed at longingly in Fifth Avenue window displays. Her hands and feet are both larger than my father's, but she moves with a grace that I can only aspire to. And while entirely glamorous, she is no ingenue. Her makeup is immaculate, but in this clear, Greek sunlight, the fine lines around her eyes are unmistakable. Whether she's midthirties or midfifties, I cannot hazard a guess, but at least she is not—praise the gods—younger than me.

My dad's hand closes around one of mine and gives it a quick squeeze before I yank it away. "Darling, I know you are upset, but hear me out. This is my friend Teresa Cipher. Ms. Cipher is the proprietor of a company called ExLibris Expeditions, and I have been working with her for the past six months."

"Delighted to meet you," Teresa Cipher says with a nod. "*Gianitsa*, is it?"

"Just Gia," I reply shortly, and sip my drink to avoid further explanations.

My mind reels. So at least my dad hasn't run off with another conquest, then. In any case—not one of his usuals. But six months? Before any of the questions squelching around my brain can take a useful form, my dad is speaking again.

"Between Ms. Cipher here and an archeology colleague I've just connected with, I plan to retrace the steps of Odysseus on his way home from the Trojan War."

chapter eight

MONDAY AFTERNOON
Bougatsa
A recipe by Gia Kostas, aspiring journalist, poor social skills

Generally considered an after-dinner sweet, or perhaps an addition to afternoon tea if one is feeling decadent, this flaky custard pie is an Athenian favorite. It's served in tiny, rich slices garnished with . . .

I narrow my eyes at my father, who is beaming across the table at me like he's just announced a cure for cancer. "Who?"

"His name is Dr. Rajnish Malik. I'm sorry you missed him—he was here last night before you arrived. He's made some amazing new discoveries at old sites using a new technology known as photogrammetry."

I sigh impatiently. "No—I meant *Odysseus*. You're following in the footsteps of Odysseus? Why on earth would you do that?"

Just as my dad takes a deep breath, ready to launch into whatever weird justification he has for traveling halfway around the world, Teresa Cipher leans forward.

"I'm afraid I'm going to have to step away from this fascinating discussion," she says. "Your completed file is here as we discussed, Dr. Kostas, with paper tickets clipped inside to the itinerary"—she shoots me the ghost of a smile—"since you weren't comfortable using the e-tickets. If you have any questions, I won't be far away. You have my contact details."

"Not heading straight back to New York, then?" My dad jumps to his feet as she rises, and beams up at her. She is a full head taller than he is, and my stomach clenches just a little. He always goes for the tall ones.

She settles her sunglasses firmly into place. "No, not back to New York, at least for the moment. I'm in London at present, setting up a new satellite office there."

My dad chuckles. "Glad to hear business is good, Teresa. So I'm not the only one following an ExLibris flight of fancy these days?"

She gives a little sigh. "Well, like everything, it was touch and go there for a while. I'm not completely confident the travel industry is out of the woods just yet. But ExLibris serves a certain clientele, and of course no one offers the level of service that we do, so I hold out hope. Thank you again for your custom, Dr. Kostas. It's been a real pleasure revisiting Homer again, I must say. My card is inside the package, and should you need anything on your journey, I am always at your disposal. Lovely to meet you, Ms. Kostas."

Scooping up the manila envelope, my dad starts to reach a hand across the table but hesitates and then hastily withdraws his arm.

"Old habits die hard—I know," Teresa Cipher says, smiling again. "However, the whole elbow-touch alternative to the handshake appalls me, I must say, so I prefer to default to literary precedent."

She steps away from her chair, bends gently at the waist, and gives my father an unmistakable, formal bow.

After bestowing a final, smaller nod to me, she strides off. The distinctive click of those turquoise Manolos fades quickly away into the darkened interior of the hotel. My dad settles into his seat with a sigh and leans forward to pour the last of the carafe's contents into his glass. Returning the empty container to the table, he glances across to my glass.

"Oh, you need a refill, darling. Let me order another pitcher."

I stare at him in exasperation. "I don't need a drink, Pops. I need an explanation. A *proper* explanation."

He chuckles uneasily. "Well, in that case, *I'm* the one who needs a drink."

I lean back in my chair and cross my arms, waiting. He drains his glass and then rattles the ice cubes inside. If I didn't know better, I'd think he was nervous.

"Papa," I begin, in the most menacing tone I can muster, but he waves me to silence.

"I'd planned to tell you everything," he says quietly. "Before the—the *incident* at work."

"The *stroke*, you mean?" I say brutally. "It was a stroke, Pops. And you took off without your meds. To *Greece*, for crying out loud. What was I supposed to do?"

He nods, his eyes almost closed in the glare of the morning sun. "Look, I'm telling you now, okay?"

I wait until he actually meets my gaze before nodding. He sips unthinkingly at his empty glass, returns it to the tabletop, and in a voice so low I have to lean forward to hear him, he begins.

Apparently, things kicked off almost a year ago when—in the course of doing research for a book he has been supposedly writing since his retirement—he spotted a video online. The star of the video was an archeologist who'd been documenting a number of projects on a bunch of obscure digs in and around the Mediterranean.

"His program—it was called a vlog," he says, "which means video log, understand?" He smiles at my expression. "You see? Your old man can learn something new, eh?"

I roll my eyes at this, mostly just to keep myself awake. I can feel one of the famous Ari Kostas lectures coming on, and I'm not sure my sleep-deprived brain can take it.

He goes on to say that, with the help of his assistant, Evan, he reached out to the YouTuber, who turned out to be less of a social media influencer and more of a nerdy scholar. The guy was doing postdoctorate work in a region of the Mediterranean that he—my dad—has always felt held clues relating to the true journey of Odysseus returning home from the Trojan War. Clues that the latest translation of Homer's classic made even clearer.

"I'd set it all up before the—the TIA," he admits grudgingly. "I'd already delayed my plans more than a year because of the virus. And damned if I'm going to let some tiny burst blood vessel stand in my way. This trip means everything to me, Gianna."

Around the same time, he heard of a company called ExLibris Expeditions, which specializes in recreating adventures drawn from the pages of famous literary works. When he reached out to the CEO of ExLibris, Teresa Cipher was so delighted with his idea, that she personally planned and organized the entire trip. Once this was underway, he'd connected with the archeologist to tell him of the decision to retrace Odysseus's famous journey, and they agreed to meet here to arrange site visits.

"Pops, how is any of this even possible?" I say when he stops at last for breath. "I mean, the story is, like, an allegory, isn't it? Half of the places Odysseus traveled don't even exist, right? And was Homer even a real person?"

Maddeningly, my dad shrugs. "This is true. But there are sites in the region that speak to the storytelling history that gave rise to all of the Homeric works. I want to visit the places that are significant to the story, and Gia? If I can find the evidence, I promise you it will be worth all the trouble."

I narrow my eyes at him. "And just how much is all this going to cost?"

My dad's grin broadens. "That's the best part," he says. "Evan pulled off a miracle and arranged a research grant funded through an American-Grecian think tank." He reaches into the inside pocket of his sport coat, pulls out a crumpled envelope, and thrusts it at me.

I slide the letter back to him with one finger. "Truthfully? I don't care at all about the financing, Pops. What bothers me is that you've taken off on some sketchy project *without your meds*."

It takes a full minute of me staring pointedly—and silently—at his pocket before he pulls out the pill bottle.

"I'm sorry, Gianna," he says, finally. "The last thing I wanted to do was worry you. It's just . . ." He pauses before the words gush out of him in a sudden torrent. "If I'm going to die—if this thing is going to take me—I need to leave something behind for you. The boys, they have their own lives. But you? You've always been different."

He reaches across the table and clutches my hands in his. "I want to show you that your papa's work means something. If my theory pans out, I'll cement my place in history beside Homer—add my voice to his to show the significance of this ancient culture to our modern day. If I can prove with hard evidence that the early transcription I've been researching exists, it'll mean something. It'll be a legacy that I can—that *you* can—be proud of. That's why I came here so suddenly, my darling girl. I don't know how much time I have left. And I am so, so close."

As he finishes, his eyes are damp, and suddenly mine are too.

"You don't have to prove anything to me, Pops." I can't find a tissue in my bag, so I use the cuff of my sleeve to swipe at my eyes. "I don't care if you're the world's foremost expert on Homer, for goodness' sake. I just want you to take your health seriously. I need you to care whether you live or die—or at least try to do what the doctors tell you, okay?"

He reaches across to squeeze my hand. "Fine. I will take the pills they give. I will not overdo the stress, I promise you. But one way or another, I need to make this journey, darling. It may seem like nothing to you now, but if I'm proved right, it will mean everything, I promise you."

I slump back in my chair with a sigh. "Okay, Pops. And you've got your meds with you, at least, so I've done my part. Now it's your turn."

A small, round woman suddenly materializes behind my left elbow, making me jump.

"Your pardon, sir, madam," she says and slides a platter heavily loaded with something that smells of roasted meat and calories onto our table.

In spite of my exhaustion, my mouth immediately begins to water.

"Madame Konstantin," my dad cries, "you have outdone yourself!"

The lady, clearly pleased, nods her head and smiles. "I like hear your thoughts, Doctor," she says. "And of course, your beautiful daughter. She must be hungry after her travels."

She positions the platter on the table and then lays a fresh, white plate in front of each of us.

"Thank you so much, Mrs. Konstantin," my father says. "I cannot wait to taste your marvelous offering today. Your moussaka last night was simply sublime."

"I shouldn't," I say as the lady quickly pockets the bills my father slips to her. This speedy disappearance of his euros goes a long way toward explaining her husband's earlier effusiveness. "I need to sort out my flight home as soon as possible."

"Darling, darling, you have to eat. You must at least try a sample. Madame Konstantin is the most marvelous cook, I promise you."

Mrs. Konstantin looks like she might burst with pride at this pronouncement and immediately starts spooning hummus into a ramekin beside my plate.

"Is very special *bougatsa*," she says. "A savory rather than sweet, yes? Like my *yiayia*, I make with lamb." She shoots me a pointed gaze. "My *bougatsa* melt in mouth, I promise."

As she spoons hummus onto my father's plate, the rich aroma of the roasted meat fills all my senses. And I do need to eat, after all. Both of them watch as I stab one of the fine slices of pastry with my fork, dip it, and deliver it to my mouth. At my expression, Mrs. Konstantin's anxious face melts into a smile.

"You like?" she says, happily pushing the platter nearer my plate.

"I guess a few bites won't hurt," I say hastily, sputtering crumbs.

My dad sweeps half the platter onto his own plate, and between us, we devour the entire thing.

Awash in the delicious food and the somnolent atmosphere of the alfresco courtyard, I find the worst of my fears quieting. The frozen, frantic pace of life in New York feels an eternity away from this relaxed, idyllic place. My father's face has color, and his eyes are animated as he outlines his plans. The fact that he shakes the bottle at me and pops in a pill when Mrs. Konstantin returns with a platter of baklava goes a long way to lulling my fears. My stomach isn't clenched with anxiety for the first time in days and is instead pleasantly full of Greek delicacies.

Propping my head on my hand, I angle my face into the light as the lowering rays of the afternoon sun shine down on us. Half my blood might be Greek, but my skin tone is pure, pallid Dutch, and returning home with sun-kissed cheeks will not be the worst thing that comes out of this crazy little jaunt. I'm thoroughly sick of our icy New York winter, and no matter how short, this visit has been a welcome respite. My dad is explaining the significance of ancient pottery to storytelling, and suddenly, without any effort on my part—I'm asleep.

It's not like this hasn't happened before. But generally, when I nod off over one of his long stories, it's usually after a heavy restaurant meal, and I'm sitting in some comfy banquette where, with my dad on his third ouzo, he doesn't really notice if I tilt a little into a darkened corner.

This time, all I know is that one minute I'm back on the dance floor with the guy from the nightclub who is looking super hot even though he's wearing Sikka's silver icicle dress, and the next, my dad is wiping yogurt out of my hair with one corner of the tablecloth.

"I—ah—sorry, Pops—you were saying?" I push aside the plate with a clear imprint of my nose still outlined in yogurt.

He shakes his head and makes the little tut-tutting noise that he usually only brings out when he's mother-henning me. "I was saying—I *am* saying—why it is so important that I complete my research now. But you're too sleepy to think clearly, *Gianitsa*. Tomorrow is soon enough to sort out your plane home, yes?"

I grab a glass that I'm pretty sure only contains melted ice cubes and drain it. This ends up giving me a piercing brain freeze for a moment, which serves to stab me back into my right mind. I've done what I came for. I need to focus on planning my wedding to Anthony, not dreaming about some smoking hot guy in a sparkly dress.

"*Our* plane, Dad. Why don't you come home with me? You can return this summer, right after the wedding."

My dad rolls up the yogurt-stained edge of the tablecloth with a sigh.

"I've worked my whole life to prove this theory. I need to see it through."

"You won't, Pops, if you get sick again. At the very least, you need to get your plans signed off by your doctor. You left before most of your test results were even in!"

He squeezes my hand. "If you are so worried, my girl, maybe you should stay and keep me company." He shoots me a sly grin. "Give me a chance to show you where your papa hails from, *Gianitsa*," he says, sweeping out a hand to take in the charming garden-bedecked courtyard. "Your roots are here too, remember."

I raise one hand. "Uh, my roots are half Dutch, Pops. Half of my genetic code is cycling through Amsterdam."

"How could I forget?" My dad snorts dismissively. "But darling, you know your mother's family don't give two figs about their heritage. When they moved to America, they never looked back. This is where I was born—let me show it to you."

His smile broadens. "Hear me out. You could sell NOSH a story about all the Mediterranean foods you'll be eating on your journey. On *our* journey. We can make an adventure of it, Gianna. One last adventure with your papa before you run off to marry your millionaire."

Above us, a bird trills softly from the bougainvillea that lines the tiny courtyard. Everything that's happened in the last forty-eight hours jostles around in my brain.

"Enough talk," he says before I can muster a reply. Pushing his chair away from the table with a clatter, he offers me his hand. "Sleep on it, darling. We can talk it through later, when your head is not nodding into the dessert course, hmm?"

I can't find the strength of character to argue any longer, and I'm tired enough to curl up on the flagstones underneath the table. The truth is, any real fight I had in me was gone before my face hit the yogurt. Still, before I close the door to my room, I manage to extract a promise from my dad that he'll take his medication. He taps the side of his nose and rattles the bottle at me.

I'm asleep before I have time to pull back the floral duvet.

chapter nine

TUESDAY, BEFORE DAWN
Greek Breakfast: Fetoydia
Gia Kostas, former journalist, still jet-lagged

The key to this luscious take on French toast is tsoureki, a delicious braided sweet bread often spotted around Easter time, but a staple in most Greek kitchens year-round. Instead of tossing away the stale leftovers, the best cooks . . .

I awaken in pitch darkness, startled out of restless, uneasy dreams by a sound I can't identify. I lie there, staring up at the ceiling and wondering why my room is so dark. It never really gets dark if you live in New York City, which is why we all have blackout curtains. Then the sound comes again. I recognize it this time—the trill of the bird in the bougainvillea. I'm not in New York. I'm in Athens, facing another ten-hour plane ride, complete with an impatient fiancé at the other end. The little clock on my bedside table tells me it's 4:30 a.m., and I'm suddenly wide awake.

I have somehow managed to sleep my way through almost twelve full hours.

My dream floods back to me. Ridiculously, it was about the guy in the nightclub again. This time, he wasn't wearing Sikka's sparkly dress. He wasn't wearing anything at all, really. Just his skin, dusky and hot against my . . .

I jump out of bed, bolt for the tiny sink, and splash my face with cold water. I need to wash the dream—and the memories of that night—down the drain, where they belong.

Face freshly washed, I flick on the bedside light and grab the tablet out of my bag. The bed has a creaky, wrought iron frame, so I prop a large, mango-colored cushion behind my back, pull my knees up to act as a desk, and start composing an e-mail to Anthony. I need to tell him how much he means to me. That I came here because my dad is important to me, but how he, Anthony, is so important to me too.

This turns out to be harder than it should be.

As I type, delete, and retype, the rosy fingers of dawn begin to slant through the slats of the window blinds. Details of the room around me slowly rise into focus, starting with the shutters themselves, which are cornflower blue and a little dusty. The room's furniture is old and mostly sturdy, with mismatched wooden end tables and a wrought iron corner table rusted in all the places where the once-white paint has chipped away. There is a faint scent of lemon furniture polish.

By six thirty, I've written and erased the e-mail exactly nineteen times. In any case, I can't stand the feeling of my teeth against my tongue for a single moment longer. I snatch my toothbrush out of my bag and head for the bathroom.

Ten minutes later, teeth clean and wearing my favorite cotton sundress from last summer, I emerge to the warm scents of coffee and baked goods wafting from somewhere down the hall. I turn to follow them without a second thought.

Breakfast is set up in a tiny room that abuts the open courtyard. Outside, a gentle rain is falling on the bougainvillea. Inside, there are three small tables, one of which holds the remains of a recently deserted breakfast. I choose a seat at one of the others and head over to investigate the covered dishes on the sideboard.

"Help yourself, help yourself," comes a voice from behind me, and

I turn to see Konstantin dressed in the same shiny black suit as before. He gestures at the sideboard, which holds a basket filled with croissants and a loaf of braided bread that is still steaming gently. Next to the bread, a platter of sliced cheeses nestles beside a bowl of hard-boiled eggs, and several smaller bowls hold hummus, dill-sprinkled yogurt, and a couple of other sauces I don't recognize immediately.

As I begin filling a plate, he beams at me and lifts the carafe he carries in one hand. "Coffee, miss? Or you prefer tea?"

"Coffee's fine," I say gratefully.

"Of course. Though, your father likes his tea, yes?"

I can't help grinning back at him as he fills my cup with what smells like black magic. "I guess so. No accounting for tastes."

"A good breakfast is just the ticket," Konstantin replies diplomatically. "I bring you *fetoydia*. My wife just make a new batch, fresh, with eggs from Sikka's chickens, yes?"

He vanishes without waiting for an answer. I sit back and think what a Renaissance woman Sikka is. Laundry and chickens and all the Greek boys. A woman bustles over to clear the table next to mine as I take my first steaming sip of the Greek coffee. It's hot and rich and sears right through to my brain stem.

Perfect.

I've just arranged a sliver of cheese onto a slice of the oven-warm bread when the woman clearing the table beside me speaks.

"Oi, Konstantin," she says to his retreating back. When he doesn't turn, she holds something up and rattles it to get his attention.

The familiar sound cuts right through my morning fog, and I spin in my seat to look at her. She's holding a small plastic bottle in one hand.

"Is that my dad's medication?" I blurt.

The woman smiles over her shoulder at me. "No Engleesh," she says, handing the bottle to Konstantin. "Sorry, sorry."

Konstantin glances at the bottle before slipping it into a pocket. "Finish your breakfast, *louloudi mou*," he says soothingly. "I will pass these to your father when he returns."

"Returns? What do you mean, *returns*? From where?"

This comes out perhaps a shade louder than I intend, and Konstantin takes a hurried step backward. "I—I not sure, miss. Your papa leave not so long ago, but . . ."

I take a deep breath in an effort to keep my voice even. "It's fine— I'll give the pills back to him. I just—I can't believe he's left them behind again."

I hold out my hand, and as Konstantin drops the bottle into my palm, the rattle of the pills inside is like the ring of truth finally hitting home. After another fortifying sip of coffee, I pull out my phone and log into the hotel Wi-Fi.

By the time I'm finished, I realize what I've written is really too long for a text, but I fire it off to my boss at NOSH anyway before I can change my mind.

Then I take a picture of my laden breakfast plate and send that too.

At that very moment, my dad comes striding into the room. Eyes twinkling, he scoops up a piece of sticky baklava from a plate beside the coffee carafe and pops it in. Then he licks his fingers flamboyantly, like a man who's performed more of a magic trick than just disappearing a piece of sticky Greek pastry.

"That's disgusting, Pops." I stuff a linen napkin into his hand.

My dad looks unrepentant and kisses his still-damp fingers toward the door. "Your wife's talent with baklava—perfection!" he says to Konstantin. "The flavor of the honey—it tastes just like my mother's."

Konstantin beams. "I tell her. Honey is raw, from one of Greek islands. Which one? I can't remember. It don't matter—best in world, yes? More tea, sir?"

He places a fresh teacup and saucer across the table from my breakfast. As my dad sits down, I pour one of the tablets from his bottle into my palm and place it beside the saucer.

He rolls his eyes at me, but swallows the pill without comment.

I spoon sliced melon into my mouth and chew it up more vigorously than is perhaps strictly necessary before speaking. "You left the bottle on the table again."

He spreads his hands wide. "I left only to take a phone call, *koritsi*," he says. "I promise you I will not forget them again."

Draining the last, delicious drop of my coffee, I sigh. "I'm not going to give you the chance. I'm coming with you."

My father's face travels the gamut of expressions from stunned to delighted in an instant. "*Gianitsa!* You have seen the light!"

This makes me snort. "Seen you in action, more like. The only way I'll know for sure that you're looking after yourself is if I'm with you."

He raises an eyebrow. "Your papa is fine," he says, slapping his stomach with such a ringing blow I'm sure it's got to hurt. "I don't need looking after."

"Too late," I snap and push back from the table. "I've just pitched Charlotte a Mediterranean travel food blog. But I'm coming even if she says no."

My dad leaps up to join me, his face wreathed in delight. "I can't believe you take your papa's advice, for once!"

Before I can reply, his face falls. "But what about Anthony—the wedding plans? Is it not best for you to return to New York?"

"I can handle Anthony," I say recklessly. "His family's company is just about to go public, and he's working all the time. I can probably manage most of what I need to do online, and the wedding's not until July, anyway. He'll understand."

My stomach clenches on this last sentence. I make a sudden decision to e-mail him first, before I call. Just to be on the safe side.

Once he realizes I'm serious, my dad grabs my head in both his hands and plants a loud kiss just above my eyebrows. Then, while he hurries out front to meet his driver, I return to my room to collect my things. Flipping open the cover of my iPad, I pull up the latest draft of the morning's apology e-mail. I replace it with a short note explaining to Anthony that my dad needs me to stay with him for a couple of weeks and that I will call and explain as soon as I can.

Pressing "Send," I try to ignore the tiny but pervasive sense of delight I feel at the thought of being away from the wedding-planning frenzy.

It's just relief about Pops, I tell myself as I gather the last of my things. Pure relief, stemming strictly from how well he's doing.

Scooping up my bag, I hurry through the dark corridors to the front door of the hotel. Outside, my dad climbs into the back seat of a tiny blue car waiting at the curb. The sun is already dazzling, gleaming off the windshields and bumpers of other vehicles whizzing off into the balmy Athens morning.

Konstantin makes a show of sweeping the door open for me and gives me a little bow as I lift my hand in farewell. Sliding into the car, I slam the door closed, and feeling strangely light in spirit, I grin across the back seat at my father.

"Ready?" he says, beaming back at me.

I take a deep breath. "Almost. But before we go anywhere, I'm going to need a big hat."

chapter ten

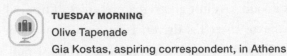

TUESDAY MORNING
Olive Tapenade
Gia Kostas, aspiring correspondent, in Athens

I used to believe olives were for adults only—to be avoided in antipasto and even scraped off the occasional pizza. Perhaps this speaks to my own experience, but their tart, salty flavor was too much for me when I was growing up. Here on the shores of the lush, sun-dappled Mediterranean, however, spotting an olive means it's time to embrace adventure . . .

As I slam the car door closed, the driver immediately pulls out into traffic, and I'm flung back against the seat. Luckily, I've been well trained by New York City cab drivers, so I just feel around for my seat belt, and try to readjust my dad's suitcase, which is inexplicably between us on the back seat. As the buckle clicks into place, I'm startled to suddenly come face-to-face with a bird, which I think might be a parrot. The bird hops onto the seat in front of me and clings on to a well-lacerated section of fabric beside the passenger headrest.

It turns one, bright yellow eye at me and dips its head as the driver performs a series of rapid lane changes. *"Kalimera,"* it croaks, and winks.

I manage to stifle my gasp of surprise, but the driver locks eyes with me in the rearview mirror and laughs.

"You catch Herman's attention," he says, and reaches a finger up to scratch under the bird's chin. "He like you already—I can tell."

The bird preens himself on the driver's finger for a moment and then repeats his greeting.

I look over at my dad, but his eyes are locked on the passing city. No way to tell if he has even noticed the creature.

The bird bobs its head twice, whether to compensate for the weaving vehicle or in greeting, I can't tell. *"Kalimera,"* it barks again. *"Kalimera!"*

"Kalimera," I repeat hurriedly. This seems to be the correct response, because the bird winks its eye at me again and then hops out of sight down onto the front seat.

I lean forward toward the driver. "Is your bird—uh—Herman— is he a parrot?"

"Cockatoo," replies the driver, and then he executes the kind of screeching U-turn that I've only seen employed by getaway drivers in heist movies. "He is my copilot, yes?"

I swallow hard and clutch the door handle, suddenly thrust back into the memory of the only Uber drive I've ever taken. It was a couple of years ago in New York, making my way across town for a university event. The car was nice enough, but the driver had a lizard curled around his neck that stared at me, unblinking, all the way to Javits Center. I've never taken another Uber, but I guess that trip was good preparation for the presence of a random bird in a Greek cab. The cockatoo almost seems less weird, somehow.

The driver turns out to be Konstantin's cousin Panagiotakis—"call me Taki"—who is a barrel of a man with a shiny bald head and an enormous black mustache. I soon learn that while Taki might well drive like a maniac, at least he knows where he's going. Within five minutes of diving into Athens traffic, he's screeched to a stop outside a little market. Shortly thereafter, I am not only safely behatted but have also snapped up six pairs of underwear, a pair of slightly-too-large aviators, and a phone charger that will work all over Europe.

Clutching the world's largest floppy hat in my lap, I buckle myself into the back seat of the car, a crazy feeling of lightness flowing through me. I think it's the hat that does it—soft straw with a brim large enough to shade most of my shoulders. With a hat like this, I'm committed now.

Sliding myself as far as my seat belt will allow from the curious bird, I turn to watch as the cheerful chaos of Athens unfolds outside the window. In some ways, it reminds me of every large city I've ever seen. This district is filled with three-story walk-ups, the city blocks interrupted by the occasional tree-filled public square. Still, tiny details keep leaping out to slap me with colorful Grecian reality. Flowers climbing walls, and here and there a brilliant blue or yellow door gleams out from beneath a shadowy overhang. Still, as we drive through the city, most of the buildings are a little on the dusty side, with back alleys as loaded with graffiti and tags as any block in the Bronx.

"The garbage in the streets is much worse than I remember," my dad says quietly. He leans forward and asks Taki a question in Greek.

As he listens carefully to the driver's reply, I marvel at my dad's comfort with the language. I've heard him speak Greek perhaps a handful of times in my life, usually only a word or two thrown into the sentence for emphasis. But maybe it's like riding a bike?

I have to admit it's pretty cool.

When he leans back in his seat, I can't help grinning at him. His expression, however, is more serious.

"Taki says the money has fled—first taxes and then corrupt government officials. When the plague took the tourists away, all hope left with them," he explains. He turns and looks out the window, and my good humor drains away.

The car isn't air-conditioned, or if it is, none of it reaches the back where I am sitting. I push the button on the armrest only to see the lock click into place. After a moment of staring blankly at the door, clicking the lock up and down, I realize the window is hand-cranked. I grasp what's left of the plastic handle and roll the window open. The thing jams halfway down, and sounds of honking horns and squealing brakes fill the car, the inevitable accompaniment to city driving anywhere. But we are moving fast enough that the whoosh of air cuts through the plastic and fake pine-scented heat in the back of the car, and I lean toward the open window in relief.

We soon leave the sketchier parts of the city behind, and here the streets are wide open and broad. A boulevard dividing the lanes is dotted with intermittent palm trees, and large signs periodically appear, some of them even in English. But just as I'm getting comfortable—or as comfortable as I can get with the handle of my dad's suitcase jammed into my side—a motorcycle overtakes our car, and then another, and suddenly we find ourselves amid a swarm of motorbikes buzzing like bees and changing lanes as though the whole idea of signaling is merely optional. It's impetuous and chaotic and very Greek.

Even after being here only a day, I'm beginning to get a bit of insight into why my dad is the way he is.

The bird squawks, and suddenly I see the ancient stone lines of the Parthenon rising above us like a venerable, crumbling fortress atop the Acropolis. Large sections of the monument are girded in scaffolding, and only a handful of tourists are scattered across the entire hillside.

The car takes a sharp corner, and the Parthenon vanishes as we whiz through an open market flagged in tidy-looking square bricks. Taki expertly steers us past vendors under umbrellas who sell everything from flip-flops to bicycles. There are more people down here, but there's not a single camera—or baseball cap—in sight. Mostly round, dark-haired women carrying net shopping bags and baskets.

Spying a section of fenced-off ruins behind the last row of market stalls, I turn to my dad and jam my thumb out the window. "Is this a part of the Parthenon too?"

He leans forward to look. "An element of the Acropolis, yes," he says, and reaches across me to point a finger as the crumbling walls hurtle past. "This was Hadrian's Library," he says. "He was a tremendous scholar. You can still walk through and see the remains of his reading rooms and the places where they shelved books."

I stare back over my shoulder as the last of the marble pillars disappear from view. "Isn't he the guy who built the wall in England?"

There's a bark of laughter from the front. "He was trying to keep the damned Scots in the north, where they belonged," Taki calls over his shoulder. "Not sure how it worked out for them in Britain, but there's not many of the redheaded buggers here, anyway."

I clutch the back of the passenger headrest as we take another corner on two wheels. "I guess Hadrian got around," I remark to my dad.

He nods approvingly. "A fellow traveler and a true man of vision. Not a bad guy, for an Italian."

As the car gains altitude, I can see other hilltops rising out of the bustling streets. Beneath our feet, the city unfurls like an earth-toned carpet as far as I can see in every direction. The terra-cotta roofs intermingle with tiny dots of color—blossoming vines and the odd splash of green. From this height, I can see that while modern buildings abound, none are really more than ten or twelve stories high, and I can't spot a single skyscraper.

Also? I'm pretty sure I've never seen quite so many cats in one place. The streets are teeming with them, virtually every one sporting the same bored, vaguely annoyed expression as they saunter nonchalantly away from certain death under the wheels of Taki's car. After lurching around yet another feline obstacle, the car crests a rise, and for the first time, in the distance I spot the twinkling blue of the Aegean.

This, it turns out, is our destination for the day. According to my dad, Odysseus decided to pause on his way home from the Trojan War and raid a small community called Ismaros. And so our trip today is taking us to the place he thinks is the closest present-day settlement to that stop: Alexandroupoli in Thrace, along the south coast of mainland Greece.

As the sea stretches out—impossibly blue—before us, Herman flaps his wings once and hops onto the back of the front seat. His skill at moving through an erratically speeding vehicle is remarkable. With a gait similar to a swaying sailor, he makes his way behind Taki's head, sidles along the narrow verge of the back door, and to my father's clear delight, onto his outstretched arm.

I take advantage of his enchanted conversation with Herman to reach for a familiar-looking file folder poking out of the open flap of his briefcase. The last time I saw this folder, Teresa Cipher had been sliding it across the table toward my dad. Since I still haven't looked at the itinerary in any detail, I flip open the folder and begin to read.

Turns out the back seat of a lurching vehicle driven by a mad, bird-owning Greek is not really the best place to do any sustained reading. I can only manage a moment or two of focusing on the page before nausea is clutching at my throat. All the same, as the car settles onto a smoother section of tarmac, I manage to take in a bit of the big picture.

This itinerary is far more detailed than the one I got from Evan. I count eleven separate destinations, spread out across the entire region. This seems to encompass far more ground than we can possibly hope to cover in a mere three weeks. Still, a quick scan of the details tells me that Odysseus would likely have benefited from having Ex-Libris plan his route. There would have been fewer useless dashes across the Mediterranean, at least. Teresa Cipher's careful notes spell out the timing of each leg of the journey in specific terms.

My phone buzzes against my thigh, but by the time I yank it out of my pocket, I've got no bars again. I've missed a call, but I can't tell who it's from. Guilt washes over me, this time tinged with regret. I should be heading back to New York, not sitting with my guts churning in the back of this rattling little car, heading out on some wild goose chase.

I glance up from the folder to find my dad looking at me. He opens his mouth to say something and then closes it again.

I choke back all the recriminations that I want to hurl at him. He told me to go home. This is all on me. And I need to at least pretend to take an interest.

Taking a deep breath, I drop the folder onto the seat between us.

"Why Thrace?" I ask. "If we're retracing Odysseus's route home from the war, shouldn't we start in Troy?" I glance back down at the map of the Mediterranean stapled into the front of the folder. "Where *is* Troy, anyway?"

My dad's expression clears, and he chuckles. "You won't find it on that map, *Gianitsa*. Troy once existed far from here, deep in Anatolia in a region of present-day Turkey. Regardless, the great man's journey across Asia Minor is of little interest to me. The real magic doesn't begin until he and his crew try to raid Ismaros, only to be swept away by a storm." He pulls down his sunglasses and wiggles his eyebrows at me before opening the top of his briefcase.

With some alarm, I see that he is retrieving his very dog-eared copy of *The Odyssey*, bristling with a rainbow of Post-it notes. Before I can object, my dad settles back into his seat and begins to recount the saga of the failed raid on Ismaros.

I think I last five minutes.

Sometime later, the slam of the car door awakens me, and I open my eyes to find I'm lying stiff-necked with my head against one of the backseat windows. Outside, Taki is leaning against the front of the car, which is currently parked on a dusty hilltop. The rest of the car is empty. Even the bird is gone.

I circle my neck to shake out the stiffness and haul myself out of the back seat into the warmth of the afternoon.

Taki, eyes slitted against the smoke drifting up from the cigarette in his mouth, reaches into the front seat, pulls a bottle of water from a cooler, and hands it to me.

"You good sleeper, eh?" he says, wrinkling his eyes at me approvingly as I twist off the cap. "You been out two hours, at least."

There's a flutter of wings, and Herman alights on his shoulder.

"I think I'm still a little jet-lagged," I manage after swallowing a sip of the water. "Where are we?"

Taki takes a last drag of his cigarette before grinding it out under one heel on the dusty ground. He points back down the gravel road behind us.

"Is little village called Makri. Your papa decide he want make a stop here since you out cold, eh?"

For the first time, I notice we have pulled up beside a small, black motorcycle. It's an old Yamaha, seat worn and wheels dusty, with a black helmet dangling from one of the handlebars.

Taki reaches into his pocket and jams a fresh cigarette into the corner of his mouth. He gestures with his lighter toward a rough path carved through scrubby brush and dry, sunbaked earth.

"Is along there, just a few hundred yards. Watch for the wire fence, eh?"

"Uh, my dad, you mean? My dad's down there?"

He lights the cigarette one-handed and squints at me through the smoke. "The dig. Your papa, he visit the site where the team work. Just that way. You can't miss. I collect you both later, eh?"

Before I can even open my mouth to reply, he slides back into the car and throws it into gear. I catch a glimpse of Herman clinging onto his perch for dear life, and then the car disappears in a cloud of dust that leaves me coughing.

As the roar of Taki's motor recedes into the distance, I turn to look out over the view. Below me, the sea gently undulates a few hundred yards down, reflecting the clean denim blue of the sky. The silence feels profound, but when I stop to really listen, I realize it's just human-generated noise that's vanished. A small breeze whispers through the bracken on the hillside below me, and above, a single puff of cotton cloud floats across the sky. A dozen snow white birds soar past, calling to each other in voices that pierce the air like silver.

As the fresh breeze tugs at my ponytail and lifts the hem of my sundress, I think I hear voices coming from the direction Taki pointed, so I drag my attention away from the bird ballet above my head and step cautiously onto the path. Almost immediately it takes a precipitous angle downward, and my feet slip a little in the dust as I hurry along. The sound of voices fades away under a sudden gust of wind, and on both sides of the path, the grasses flatten as the air swirls around me, suddenly chill, tasting of salt from the water below. I clutch at my hat, catching it before it can blow off to join the birds in their midair dance.

Suddenly feeling exposed on this rocky cliffside, I pause and glance up to see the fluffy white cloud isn't so tiny anymore, and a lot greyer than it had looked when it was bobbing in the distance over the ocean. The next swirl of wind pulls the scarf I had knotted around my ponytail right out of my hair, and it flutters high out of reach, a flash of red and yellow against the suddenly tumultuous grey bank of clouds.

In the distance, the sky is still blue, but I can see flecks of white breaking up the formerly undulating surface of the now wine-dark sea. Above me, the sun vanishes.

I spin in a circle, torn by whether to go back up to the top or continue down the cliff path. It's steep enough to make me feel a little teetery. A flash of lightning makes everything oddly pink for a moment, but it's the almost instant boom of thunder that makes the decision for me. I scuttle, crablike, down the cliff path, which soon weaves through a low collection of thorny bushes, offering a bit of shelter at least. I have no interest in drawing the attention of the next bolt of that lightning.

Through all of this, not a drop of rain falls, though the air is thick with an odd, muddy combination of humidity and dust. Around me, a tiny maelstrom is swirling, and as I duck into the somewhat questionable shelter of the bushes, the dust coalesces above me into an intense mass of whirling debris. Dead leaves, pine needles, and salty particles form a tightly spinning vortex less than fifteen feet away.

I've seen footage of dust devils on YouTube, careening crazily through the deserts of Arizona and elsewhere, but I can tell you, nothing like this ever shows up on the streets of New York. It looks less like a funnel cloud and instead has an unnervingly human shape—narrow at the bottom and the top, but also in the middle—like the visual you get when watching an ice skater do a tight spin. The dust it throws off is thick enough to make me close my eyes, and I instinctively crouch down and wedge myself between two of the scrubby bushes lining the path. I can't even take a full breath without my mouth filling with grit.

Clutching the brim of my hat in one hand and a thorny branch in the other, I make myself as small as possible and wait for the wind to pluck me from my inadequate hiding place and hurl me off the edge of the cliff.

chapter eleven

This, the most famous of Greek exports, is a salad best constructed from freshly sown summer ripe tomatoes, coarsely chopped cucumber, and tangy red . . .

nstead?

Nothing happens.

By *nothing*, I mean literally a single moment passes—not even long enough for me to risk taking another breath of the gritty debris passing itself off as air—and the storm is gone.

I stand up again and take a cautious step away from the shelter of the shrubbery in time to spot the surface of the sea directly below me rise up in a tiny whorl, looking kind of like the reverse of the water going down the sink. For an instant, it holds the same vaguely human form as the dust had taken as it spun beside me, then shatters with a near audible *poof!* and settles like mist into the waves. The surface of the ocean calms almost immediately, the waves tucking their white caps away and returning to a deceptively gentle swell.

I'm still staring openmouthed when below me I hear a shout. Farther down the path, my father's face suddenly appears, shortly followed by the rest of him.

"Koritsi!" He waves enthusiastically and hurries up the hillside toward me. "I was just coming up to get you. I'm glad you came down—there's so much to see!"

My dad's hair always looks like a curly grey mop, so it's hard to tell at this distance if he was caught up in the wind or not, but his expression doesn't look at all worried.

"Holy mackerel, Pops." I try to take a step toward him and realize my legs are trembling. *"That* was the weirdest thing ever."

Strangely enough, his grin broadens. "Did you get caught in that little squall? I *thought* I heard a clap of thunder! The weather—it wants to stay warm now that spring is here. These little storms, they pass through so quickly, yes?"

As he nears, I see that his face has begun to tan a little, the unhealthy pallor of his skin tone in the hospital already reduced to little more than a bad memory.

I clutch his arm, grateful to have something—someone—to hold on to, and he folds me into a welcome hug.

"What is this?" he asks into my ear. "You are shaking, *Gianitsa.* Are you cold?"

"No," I say, my voice muffled by his sleeve.

I have a sudden memory from when I was small, my head buried in his shoulder, my legs clinging on to him for dear life after I'd fallen off my bike. I push the memory away and step back, suddenly feeling ridiculous.

"I'm—I'm fine." My voice sounds stiff even in my own ears. "It was nothing, really. Just a weird little storm, but the wind swirled up so suddenly, I was worried I'd get blown off the cliff."

"Tsk, we can't have that." My father playfully tucks his arm through mine. "I've only just got you here, and you haven't seen the dig yet. This way, this way!"

I allow myself to be led back onto the path, which crests a little rise, then begins to wind downward through the low, thorny bushes. As we walk, I can see that if I'd been on this part of the path well below the cliff-top, I would have missed the little maelstrom entirely, which has clearly been my dad's experience.

"That's what I get for cowering up there like a big chicken," I mutter.

"What's that?" he asks but then interrupts me before I can reply. "Watch your step here, eh? This gravel is tricky."

I skitter downward, bone-dry pebbles rolling under my feet like marbles. This makes me grateful I donned my Converse today instead of the strappy sandals I usually wear with this dress.

The path takes a sharp hairpin turn and then levels out. My dad releases my arm and strides confidently downward. I hurry along behind him, keeping one eye on the footing of the rocky path. Below us, the water is now once again glinting a benign, impossible blue. There are a couple of long docks, or perhaps just breakwaters, jutting out into the surf, but beyond them, nothing but calm, serene sea all the way to the horizon. In the distance, my little black cloud has wafted toward what might be an island. Above us, the sun shines down, suddenly hot.

If someone told me there had been a flash storm here, I wouldn't have believed them either.

My dad turns and beams at me, interrupting my thoughts. "This Neolithic site has been known for more than a century." He pauses beside a sagging barbed-wire fence, unlatches a rickety wooden gate, and holds it open so I can step through. "It's a rich site, and even today, they are finding new evidence of settlement."

I jam my hat more firmly on my head and try to put the storm out of my mind. "Okay, but the *Neolithic*? Isn't that a little before when Odysseus set off on his adventures?"

He laughs and latches the gate behind us. "No question. Some of the artifacts they've uncovered here have been dated to three thousand years BCE. The fact that people have been here so long—that plays into the stories they tell, yes? Into the histories. But darling," he says, pausing to reach back and clutch my arm, "what I came to see is *not* what I found. What I found is so much better! You must come meet him."

He winds his way around a large pile of stones, and I hurry along behind only to career into his back when he stops suddenly.

In front of us, two men, both stripped to the waist and speckled in dust, grapple with an enormous boulder.

"Need a hand there, boys?" cries my dad, and before I can react, he hops into the hole beside the men.

"Pops," I begin, but as I do, he throws his shoulder against the rock and heaves. There is a moment of doubt, and then the boulder shudders slightly. "That's got it, boys," my dad yells encouragingly.

Sure enough, the huge stone rolls off to one side. As it settles, the men straighten up, cheering. The larger of the two men steps out from behind the boulder with one hand in the air, and my dad gleefully slaps it. The man is so tall, my dad literally has to hop to reach his hand. The skin of his bare chest is the color of an old saddle, deeply tanned. His trousers are covered in dust, and he's wearing a seventies-style headband over his long grey hair, which is pulled back into a ponytail with a leather lace. He is the most enormous human being I have ever seen.

"Look at that, *koritsi*," my dad crows from below my feet. "Your papa still has some life in him yet!"

The huge man steps away from the boulder, and I see that what I thought was a headband is, in reality, an eye patch. It's a wide strip of black leather angled across his face so as to cover the place his left eye should be. Beneath it, a white scar snakes, livid across his brown face, from under the leather all the way down to the corner of his mouth. In one hand, he's clutching an enormous, rusty iron rod. The rod, which he's been using as a crowbar, is itself at least a foot longer than my dad is tall—and tops out just under the man's shoulder.

"Holy mackerel," I blurt, "that's *huge*! The—that rock, I mean."

Either my dad doesn't notice my near gaffe or chooses to ignore it.

"Not so huge when you have enough manpower, eh, Paulo?" he says, beaming up at the man. "Let me introduce you to my daughter, Gianna. Gia, Paulo is the man I wanted you to meet. He grew up here, so he knows everything about this region. And he is also the one responsible for feeding everyone on-site."

"Feeding *and moving boulders*, hey?" Paulo replies and flexes a bicep the size of a bowling ball. He swivels his gaze up to me. "Nice to meet you, Gianna."

I manage a nod and smile.

"Nothing moved until I got here," counters my dad, his grin broadening.

"Which is a hundred percent what you are not supposed to be doing," I remind him. "The doctor said you're not to exert . . ."

At this moment, the second man strides out from behind the boulder.

"Nonsense," my dad interrupts, cutting me off. "Just lending a hand to my young friend here. Gia, this is my colleague, Dr. Rajnish Malik. Rajnish? My daughter, Gia."

Anything I was about to say dries up on my tongue.

It's Hot Nightclub Guy.

Frozen to the spot, I catch a glimpse of a brown, muscled chest before he bends to collect a very dusty t-shirt from where it's been lying on the ground. Yanking it over his head, the fabric falls over his long, chiseled torso, catching a little on the small of his back. As he reaches around to free it, I stare helplessly down at his khakis, which are buckled so low on his hips that I get a clear look at the dusky yet slightly sun-reddened skin above the green-and-pink floral waistband of his boxers.

I've seen that skin before. I've touched it.

I've *tasted* it.

"Nice to meet you," he says, squinting up into the sunshine and smiling.

On his neck, just below the line of his jaw, is a small, almost perfectly round bruise.

At the sight of that bruise, a wave of sensation jolts me with an intensity that is equal parts desire and mortification. In an instant, I'm swept back to the moment when it happened. To the moment when I bit his neck to keep from screaming. To the moment when I may have screamed—just a little, anyway. And how we both laughed afterward, the way two young, single people who have just really enjoyed something spontaneous and unexpected—and *perfect*—together laugh.

Single people.

The skin of my face and neck is suddenly on fire. Panic lurches through me like a punch to the stomach. I consider turning to flee, but there is nowhere to run. Taki has driven away, so I can't even go hide in the car.

Hysteria bubbles in my throat, and I only just manage to cover it with a cough. "Nice to meet you too," I choke out, at last.

"Very dry out here." A look of concern crosses his face at the sound of my croaky voice. He points a trowel across the dusty ground toward a portable table piled with gear. "Help yourself to some of our water. There are a few bottles in the cooler, just over there."

"I'm okay. I mean—that is—I've got some already." I hold up the bottle Taki gave me.

"Excellent." His smile gleams up at me for a moment until my dad suddenly grips him by the arm.

"Look at this layer, Rajnish!" My dad's voice is quivering with excitement. As he squats in the trench, I can hear his knees crackle from where I'm standing.

After shooting me a last apologetic grin, Hot Nightclub Guy drops to one knee beside my dad.

With everyone safely peering at whatever they've found in the wall of the trench, I edge slowly away and struggle to get a grip on myself. Too much is happening at once, and I don't know where to start. Making sense of the weird little windstorm earlier or the fact that my dad is working with a one-eyed giant pales in comparison with this current problem.

Even under the cover of my enormous hat, the afternoon sun beating down on this bare section of the hillside is making it hard for me to think clearly. The only shelter on the site is a battered blue tarp that has been strung between the branches of a pair of gnarled bushes. Under its dust-crusted surface rests a collection of assorted excavation gear—shovels and sieves and a single old work boot. I make a beeline away from the animated discussion still going on in the trench, position myself in the tiny square of shade thrown down by the tarp, and try to collect my thoughts.

Front and center, of course, is Hot Nightclub Guy. Rajnish Malik. Now no longer a delicious nameless memory, but a colleague of my father.

Also? Possibly the best kisser I've ever met.

To push this thought away, I take a glug from the tepid water in my bottle, and then splash the last of it on my wrists for good measure. But instead of clarity, this only brings mud—dampening the dust on my hands and arms just enough to glue it in a thick, grey layer to my skin. Lovely.

Giving up, I jam the bottle into my bag and try to look for positives.

Could it be possible he hasn't recognized me? It *could* be. I mean, I'm wearing my big hat. And my sunglasses. Our meeting just now was little more than a brief encounter—a polite hello between two people who, if I have anything to say about it, will never meet again.

I risk a quick glance over at where the three men are still on their knees, talking in the trench. Just Paulo is fully visible, with his head and shoulders above the ground. The hot archeologist has his back to me, and I can only see my dad from the nose up. Behind the tarp, the dusty hillside rises above us. Nothing is stopping me from bolting back up the cliff path and waiting for Taki's return on the hilltop, right?

Just as I decide to make a run for it, Paulo straightens up. "Now your daughter is here, Aristotle, I go see to the food, eh?"

My dad creaks back to his feet and glances up at me. "Paulo has a treat in store for us, *koritsi*—just you wait!"

So much for my escape plan.

As Paulo raises one leg to step out of the trench as easily as I would step over—I don't know, a Manhattan curb?—my dad puts his hand on the shoulder of the man beside him.

"Dr. Malik here specializes in repatriation of archeological finds, *koritsi*. His expertise to my project is invaluable."

The hot archeologist gives a little shrug. "It's always exciting to find something new, but there's nothing like the satisfaction of returning lost objects to their original owners."

My dad nods sagely. "And you never know what you'll find either. Not just pottery."

Rajnish Malik grins, his teeth a flash of white in the dusty landscape. "It's amazing what turns up, really. I've found tools, jewelry, shoes . . ." His voice trailing off on this final word, he looks straight up at me and lifts his eyebrows, just once.

My heart lurches and then drops like a rock.

Shoes? He knows. He's recognized me.

And worse—he knows I know too.

Paulo's voice interrupts my frantic thoughts, calling from across the site. "Ten minutes and then eat, yes?"

"Yes," agrees my father and slaps his hands together enthusiastically. The dust rises off them like a cloud, and he laughs, looking up at me. "Come down here, girlie, come down. Paulo has given us ten minutes. Let us see together what our young friend has uncovered."

And with a polite smile at my father, as if the whole eyebrow thing hadn't just happened, "our young friend" replies, "Delighted, Ms. Kostas," and offers his hand to help me step down.

chapter twelve

TUESDAY EVENING
Ovelias
Gia Kostas, special correspondent to no one, near
Makri, Greece

*This spit-roasted lamb is not a spontaneous meal but worth every
minute of preparation. Hot and delicious, for this delectable feast
to taste as good as it deserves, thinking ahead is essential. You
begin the day before . . .*

I swallow hard at the touch of his hand. "It's just Gia," I manage, at
last.

"Just Raj, then," he says, still grinning that wide, white smile
at me.

As the enormous man retreats toward a wisp of smoke in the
distance, I step into the trench, and Raj Malik releases me at last.

My dad reaches out and puts a hand on each of our shoulders.
"There," he says, beaming. "You finally meet. My two favorite young
people. I have the feeling you will hit it off, yes?"

"Do you?" Raj turns to look at my dad. "I think you might be right."

My stomach muscles cramp at the effort it takes to retain a bray
of hysterical laughter.

Instead, I take a deep breath. There's no use trying to sort out
what I'm feeling right now. I need all my resources to just play it cool.

"So—Paulo," I say, as casually as I can manage. "He works for you?"

"When it suits him," Raj Malik replies. "He really wanted to meet Dr. Kostas today."

My dad nods in agreement. "I've spent the last hour listening to his stories," he says. "The man is a positive *font* of information."

"The man," I whisper, "is a *giant*."

"Yes. Yes, he is." Raj, still grinning, pats his stomach. "And an excellent cook, besides."

He squats down near the spot where the boulder had been seated, and my father drops gingerly to one knee beside him. With their attention on the wall of the trench, I can finally unclench my shoulders.

The ground is baked dry here—deeply dry, as if even the idea of falling rain is merely a memory. I glance up to look for my storm cloud, but the sky is a clear, endless blue above us. It's like the windstorm never even happened.

And, staring at the sky, I'm hit with inspiration. I just have to send the whole nightclub experience off with that vanishing storm. If this guy has recognized me, surely he won't say anything to my dad. I mean—why would he? I decide to just ride out the rest of the afternoon by pretending nothing happened in that nightclub and staying out of the way as much as possible.

I take another shaky breath and step back as Raj Malik pulls what looks like a paintbrush out of the pocket of his khakis and gestures at the wall of the trench. The place where the giant boulder was seated is now open to the air. The exposed earth, while still quite dry, is a darker color than farther along the trench and is marked with several obvious layers.

"It's exactly as I thought," he says quietly. "Look at this line here, Dr. Kostas, and this one. The stratification is very similar to the Ithacan site we were discussing earlier. This is going to make dating any finds a piece of cake."

The two of them beam at each other like the lines of rock in the dirt are made of solid gold.

"It looks just like a layer of ordinary rock to me." This comes out a little more snappily than I intend, but neither one of them appears to have even heard me.

In any case, I realize the last thing I want to do is engage at all. Attempting to remove myself from the discussion entirely, I sidle away from the trench. And as I do, my shock begins to morph into annoyance at myself for being such a coward.

It was just one night. This is embarrassing, there's no doubt about it, but I've got no one to blame but myself. I just need to make it through today, and I never have to see this guy again. I'm engaged to be married, and that's all that matters.

In any case, this guy is *so* not my type. When I was single, I generally went for blond boys closer to my own height. Tall and gangly is definitely not my jam, and Raj Malik has got to be at least five eleven. My first boyfriend was six feet tall, and I endured a three-month kink in my neck before we finally broke up. Admittedly, the kink came mostly because when we weren't kissing, he talked about himself incessantly, but still. Anthony is five nine, which makes him a perfect three-inch heel taller than I am.

". . . evidence that this side has been truly untouched," continues Raj, the excitement in his voice almost palpable.

I force myself to tune back in.

"Which means locating the piece is a possibility?" My dad leans forward, running a finger along the line of stone in the sand.

Raj's smile falters. "Now, Dr. Kostas—I have to remind you of what I've been saying all along."

"I know, I know," my dad says, impatiently. "Context is every-thing. But . . ."

Raj jams his hands into the pockets of his khakis. "I'm still con-vinced the other site is more likely," he insists quietly. "The stratification looks right here, but until we open this section up, we won't know for sure. Still, the layering is very evident—which makes it measurable. Most important is that this area is quite clearly undisturbed until now. Whatever was left behind then is likely here still. This is going to be huge news for the society."

My dad's reply is interrupted, this time by a distant shout.

It's Paulo.

"Lunch," says my father, rubbing his hands together again. "Let's make a plan while we eat, yes?"

I hurriedly reach for his hand, and he helps me out of the trench, still talking over one shoulder to Raj.

As I follow them—at a safe distance—across to the far side of the dig, I spot the site's cooking facilities for the first time. Paulo is kneel-ing beside a kind of open brazier, filled at the moment with grey and white-hot coals. He turns and I see he is bearing what looks like an enormous blade with a huge chunk of meat skewered on it, charred and steaming. The aroma of barbecued lamb envelops us, enlivened with hints of rosemary and oregano.

"It smells delicious," I whisper to my dad, and I realize suddenly that I actually feel hungry.

This is a good sign. I can put the whole nightclub incident behind me. I can focus on other things. I *can*.

My dad grins broadly. "Paulo had the fire lit long before we ar-rived, and we have been subject to the torture of these aromas since we got here. Four—almost five hours the lamb has been on this spit, eh? But you know it will be worth the wait."

As we watch, Paulo slides the contents of the skewer onto a huge metal platter, and I realize that the carcass of an entire lamb, complete with head, is now lying in front of us.

The table, which is the collapsible, plastic variety with metal legs I remember seeing by the hundreds in every exam room at college, is sporting a red gingham cover. Atop the brightly checked cloth, a few small containers have been opened and lined up beside a stack of plates and cutlery. The first is a shallow clay bowl piled with charred, foil-wrapped bundles. Beside this mountain of potatoes are smaller bowls containing condiments and sauces, of which I recognize only hummus and tzatziki.

As Paulo sets the platter down, I see great chunks of meat are already falling away from the bone. He reaches across to a small square cellar beside the potatoes, dips his enormous fingers into roughly ground sea salt, and sprinkles it across the meat before deftly serving portions onto a stack of mismatched ceramic crockery. He quickly adds fragrant servings of Greek salad and, after carefully wiping the grease from his fingers, offers each of us a plate.

The mingling aromas of lamb and spices combine to ensure even my anxiety over meeting Raj Malik again isn't enough to stop me from picking up my fork.

It's only just in time that I remember to grab my phone and document the contents of my plate as he's laid it out. Of course, there's been no word from Charlotte, but there are also exactly zero bars on my phone. Harboring the faintest hope she might still agree to my pitch, I start snapping pictures.

On the large, white plate, glistening pieces of roasted lamb dusted in sea salt nestle up to the fluffy, white potatoes flecked in bits of their own skin charred from the fire. The lustrous, fragrant salad adds a brilliant pop of color to complete the presentation.

The lamb is crisply seared on the outside but melts away as soon as I close my mouth around it. Warm flavors of rosemary, oregano, and perhaps even some kind of chili permeate the meat, and I can't swallow it fast enough. I don't think I've ever tasted anything better in my life.

No one speaks for at least five minutes as the people who have been doing manual labor all morning dig in. And I, who have not heaved a single boulder, participate no less eagerly.

I do manage to keep myself to only one serving, however, so when Raj and Paulo go back for seconds, I slide over to sit beside my dad.

"I still don't get it," I say to him quietly. "Just what is it you are looking for? Surely a few lines in the dirt aren't going to prove your thesis? I mean, don't you need Indiana Jones's holy grail or something?"

My dad shakes his head and says, "Yes," at the same time as Raj, sitting down beside him, says, "No!"

They both laugh.

"Rajnish is right," my dad says through a mouthful of food. "That is—he doesn't believe we'll find the actual evidence I am looking for."

"If we find a few sherds of pottery in the right context, that should still prove your point, sir," Raj says before digging in to his own second helping.

My dad shrugs. "I still hold out hope for an actual intact piece," he says, a trifle wistfully. "This trip—it is a special one. I'm counting on my girl to bring me a little magic, eh?"

"A little magic?" Raj repeats, and I make the mistake of looking at him. His eyes are twinkling, and I feel my face growing hot again as I hurriedly look away. "Greece is a magical place, no question. You never know what you're going to find from one day to the next. Or who."

"Correct!" roars my dad and lifts his water bottle in a toast. "Anything can happen in this magical place."

Desperate to change the subject, I pull the notebook out of my bag and busy myself jotting down the ingredients and presentation of the meal.

Paulo, who has accumulated a sizeable stack of well-cleaned bones on his plate, looks up.

"Can you tell me the spices you used on the lamb?" I ask him, pen poised.

He pauses, a half-gnawed lamb's rib in one hand. "Just the usual—rosemary, thyme, a little sage. Why?"

I explain that I am hoping to sell an article about the food I eat while I'm here. "It's for an American food magazine I interned with. I'd like to know a little about your process—you know—how you came to discover this recipe."

There is a sound like a roll of thunder deep in his chest, and I realize he is laughing.

"My *process* is to walk through my flock and select a fat, slow lamb. I take away from the rest and crack his neck, quick-fast, eh? Then I bring here, gut and spear on the *souvla* over low, hot fire. Then we eat."

His smile broadens as I take notes. "Why you write? Your father not teach you this? Every good Greek knows how to roast a lamb."

I look over at my dad, but he's grinning, and he pauses from re-filling his plate yet again to tap the side of his head. "I give her my brains, Paulo. I leave the cooking to her mama."

I bite back the remark that leaps to my lips at this and turn my face to Paulo. "What's the most important part of the process? Selecting the fattest lamb? What about the seasoning?"

Paulo shrugs. "The fire's most important," he says and leans over to stir the embers with a rusted iron fork. "You need a good, hard wood that hold heat a long time."

My father nods sagely. "The spits they use in New York?" he says wistfully. "Not the same. Nothing tastes like this does, with the flavor of these gnarly old trees cooked right into the meat."

Paulo turns and points his fork at me. "Trees bent because of the winds here. Your papa say the wind blow you nearly off cliff on your way down. Is true?"

"Nearly," I admit. "It was a scary little squall, for sure."

His large brown eye locks onto mine. "You see a goddess in the wind? The earth spin in the sky?"

I swallow and wipe my chin with a paper napkin, which comes away with a smear of tzatziki.

Of course it does.

"Well, I don't know about any goddess, but for sure the wind swirled up a bunch of leaves and maybe sand? I couldn't tell if it came from the ground where I was standing, or if it got blown up from the beach below."

"Oh, she is blown up from below without a doubt," he says. "Depending on which of the Furies visits, she will have hair of snakes or perhaps wings of bats." He drops the bone noisily onto his plate. "Did you see any wings? Bird wings or maybe bats?"

"I—I can't say that I did." I am seriously beginning to regret the direction this conversation is taking.

My dad tries to say something but is hampered by a mouthful of lamb from interjecting. Paulo surges to his feet and unearths an unlabeled bottle from under the table. My dad's eyes light up, and he hurriedly tosses the water out of his plastic bottle onto the dusty earth at his feet.

"They come from the earth—from *below* the earth—the Erinyes," Paulo continues, running the blade of his knife around the cork. "The Furies, some call them, they blow up into the sky to take vengeance on those who would swear a false oath or who commit murder."

"Aha! Well, this is unlikely," splutters my dad, who has managed to swallow his mouthful. "Unless you have been recently committing murder, *Gianitsa*?" He holds up his empty bottle to Paulo.

Before I can say a word, Paulo upends his bottle, splashing wine onto the ground behind my chair. "It needn't be murder," he says, his voice dropping to a low rumble. "Alecto, she punishes those who commit moral crimes, and Megaera, those who break oaths or commit infidelity and theft. Have you done anyone wrong, *néa gynaíka*? Broken any promises?"

I give a little involuntary jump and stare at him, speechless, as he strides with the bottle toward my father. But instead of aiming for his glass, Paulo once again splashes the wine on the ground behind his chair.

"An offering. Appeasement to the Furies," he rumbles and then puts my dad out of his misery by directing a stream into his upraised water bottle.

"To the Furies!" my dad echoes triumphantly and drains his bottle, while Paulo does the same with the wine bottle.

They both roar with laughter.

Raj shoots me a look across the table and then leans toward the two other men.

"Paulo," he says suddenly. "Death—that's Thánatos, right? Or is it Dolofonía?"

"It depends," Paulo replies, and for the first time, he breaks into a smile. "On whether the death is natural or the result of murder!"

I sit back, relieved of Paulo's strange attentions for the moment as the two older men get safely sidetracked by Raj. The little windstorm was so unnerving at the time, and now the word *infidelity* has seriously shaken me. Paulo's take on it does nothing to make me feel better. I remind myself that I've never given a minute of credibility to all my dad's Greek mythology stories over the years. I refuse to get freaked out by brief spring weather anomalies that may or may not be related to my own questionable behavior.

Giving myself a shake, I take up my notebook again as the conversation rages on around me. I need to use this time to get as many details of the meal down as I can. Jumping up, I snap a few pictures of Paulo's fire. For the first time, I see that the spit is attached to a motor. Of course it is. This is twenty-first-century Greece. It's not like my lunch was just made by a giant who hand-turned his slaughtered lamb over a dragon-spawned fire. Get a grip, Gia.

I close my notebook and return to the table. As an outsider, it sounds like a yelling match, but really? Every conversation my dad has in Greek ends up the same—waving hands, jumping up, slamming the table. Only the fact they are all smiling, my dad often slapping Raj on the back when he pronounces a word correctly, betrays the benign nature of the conversation.

I feel strangely grateful to Raj for his ability to read the room, if nothing else. Of course, I can't afford to think of anything else. Not now.

As I help myself to a second serving of salad, I watch him continue this halting conversation with Paulo in Greek, my dad interjecting periodically—and loudly—with the correct word. Raj's hair is sticking straight up from his forehead, cemented skyward by a combination of sweat and dust. I can't help thinking of Anthony, who would never be caught dead with a hair out of place. Even after his regular noontime game of handball—twice weekly—he emerges from the court with his hair unruffled and little more than a healthy glow along his cheekbones. But I get the feeling that even when Raj

Malik isn't too busy concentrating on his conversational skills, his hair isn't really a priority. It's long—not pandemic long, but still—and more windblown than it looked the other night.

The other night, when our sweat-slicked bodies were glued together. When things got so hot, I bit his neck in pure lust.

I tear my eyes away from the blue bruise above his shirt collar, my face flushing at the memory, and when the three men burst into laughter, it's a welcome distraction.

My dad slides his plate away. "Excuse me a moment. I'm just going . . ." He makes a vague gesture with one hand.

"Good idea." Paulo jumps up, and the two of them quickly disappear along a path leading into the scrubby underbrush.

The panic I felt earlier surges like a wave through me again. My fingers suddenly go so numb, I drop my pen.

Scooping it up, Raj Malik hands it back to me. "I—ah—like your hat," he says, his voice low.

I realize I am staring at him with my mouth open. "Thanks," I reply, at last.

"I almost didn't recognize you earlier," he adds, giving me a sideways glance. He touches the bruise on his throat, almost involuntarily.

"I'm really sorry about that," I begin. "I didn't mean . . ." but before I can finish, Paulo suddenly reappears with my father. Both of them are sporting that look of relief common to men of a certain age everywhere.

I set down my own plate and edge closer to my dad. "Is the latrine nearby?"

He points in the direction he just returned from, and sure enough, now that I'm standing, I can see the roofline in an unmistakable color of green.

"It's a composting toilet," whispers my dad. "Not too bad."

The three men are all standing now, so I take the opportunity to flee. The facilities, indeed, are not the worst I've ever been in, but not exactly the kind of place a person wants to linger. Finally, after fifteen full minutes of stalling, I squirt my hands with liquid sanitizer from the bottle attached to the outside wall and head up the path.

Still smoothing the cool alcohol rub onto my hands, I pause to stare out over the vast, blue, perfect Mediterranean. From the site, I hear a distant roar of laughter—Paulo still telling stories no doubt. But I need to face reality. The writing—my writing for NOSH, at least—is on the wall. There's no way Charlotte will agree to my pitch. And in any case, my dad is being responsible. He even winked at me earlier as he swallowed a pill with his meal. He's an adult, he doesn't need me, and I've more than done my part. My fiancé wants me with him, and that's where I should be. The last thing I need is to be reminded of the mistakes I made that night in the club when I should be focusing on my wedding.

I need to go home.

Mentally practicing the wording to let my dad down easy, I trudge back along the path. I'm still shaking the cool alcohol rub off my hands as I walk onto the site only to discover my dad has, once again, disappeared. And standing alone by the remains of the feast is Raj Malik.

Maybe Paulo is right.

Maybe I am cursed.

chapter thirteen

These potatoes—hot, creamy, and incredibly flavorful—are a standard with many Greek meals, but when served with a fully spitted roasted lamb, there is no comparison. The secret, of course, is . . .

I return to find Raj standing beside the table, neatly scraping plates into a paper bag. "Everything goes into the compost," he says as I walk up.

Not knowing what else to do, I pick up a plate and begin to scrape it off.

"I can do that," Raj says shortly.

I glance at him, but he doesn't meet my eyes. He seems suddenly—almost formal.

"My dad is—ah—very good at getting other people to clean up after him." I finish scraping the first plate and pick up a second. "Also at disappearing."

Raj pauses and then gently sets his scraped plate down inside one of the storage tubs. "Paulo took him for a tour of the cave." His voice sounds carefully neutral as he points at a path through the scrubby bushes. "It's just down the hill a bit. I'm sure they'll be back in a minute, but I can take you down there, if you like."

What I really want to do is flee down the cliff path after them, but I suppress the urge.

"No, I can give you a hand here first." Using a stray spoon, I scoop the last few tomato seeds into his compost bag. Stacking my freshly scraped plate on top of Raj's in the bin, I grab the nearly empty tzatziki bowl.

"Sorry to be so snappy about my dad. But honestly, it's like looking after a toddler. He gets interested in something and wanders off, and the next thing I know, he's on the other side of the world. He not only refuses to look after himself; he neglects to inform those of us who care about him."

"I can see where that might be a problem," Raj says and then reaches over and takes the bowl out of my hand.

"I—uh—I think we should just clear the air a little, while we have a minute," he adds quietly. For the first time, he meets my eyes, and it's plain that all the earlier lightness in his expression has vanished.

I shoot a quick glance at the path down the hill, but it remains deserted. "Right. Okay. Good. Fine," I blurt before I am finally able to shut myself up. "Let's do that."

He's silent again, and around us, the only noise is the rustle of the wind in the grass and the distant cry of a bird.

"The other night was a mistake," I blurt right at the same moment he says, "I think we just need to forget about . . ."

We both stop suddenly, and the silence stretches out again, uncomfortably long.

"I'll go first," I manage, at last. I have to take a deep breath in order to continue. "What happened the other night—well, I was in sort of a bad place, and . . ."

"I should let you know"—he cuts me off—"that while you were gone, your father filled me in on your whole background. He's very proud of you."

"He is?"

"Indeed. The job with the newspaper, your recent engagement—everything."

I stare up at him, suddenly speechless. "My—ah—engagement was . . ."

He lifts a hand. "We don't need to talk about it," he says stiffly. "Honestly, let's just treat the thing in the club like it didn't happen."

"Okay," I manage. But any sense of relief I have is laced heavily with something else, leaving my stomach feeling sick and sour.

"Good. Good. We're in agreement, then," he says, still not looking at me.

He wipes his hands on a piece of burlap and glances at his watch. "I have an appointment this evening, so I'm afraid I'm going to have to head out shortly. Perhaps we should go find your father."

"Contrary to my dad's opinion, I don't actually require any looking after." I can feel my shoulders stiffen. "I'm okay to wait here for him. When he gets back, I'll tell him you've been called away."

"It's just, I suspect you've likely had a bit too much sun today," he says quietly. "I don't feel comfortable leaving you on your own out here. I'm sure your dad has just lost track of time prowling around in the cave with Paulo. It's not far, and it'll provide a little relief from the sun."

I had the sense to throw a light linen top over my dress this morning, so between that and my big hat, my shoulders and back have been safely covered all afternoon. But there is no denying that my forearms, in spite of liberally applied sunscreen, have taken on a shade of pink that might well come back to haunt me later. I nod stiffly and follow Raj down a winding, dusty path along the hillside.

The path is too narrow to walk side by side and almost immediately becomes fairly steep—a thin, grey line separated from the precipice by only the occasional prickly bush clinging to the scanty soil. But as we progress downward, it's less dry underfoot, and more greenery appears on either side of the path. Thick, wiry grasses that smell of sage are studded with tiny white and yellow wildflowers. As the path continues, we pass a patch of wild, white daffodils bobbing their heads in the late afternoon sun.

Raj walks with an easy, loping stride, but it takes all my concentration to keep up and not to skid on the slippery gravel surface. After a couple of quick turns along the cliff face, the path is little more than a narrow indentation in the dusty rock below our feet.

I've forgotten to refill my water bottle from the big plastic container up at the dig, and I'm suddenly deeply thirsty. Also? I'm regretting my earlier inability to articulate my actual thoughts regarding our—ah—first contact.

Yes, I feel guilty about what happened. I should never have gone out that night, let alone followed Sikka into a situation where I could get into such a mess. But I should be able to stand up for myself—at least enough to tell him what was really going on. That I don't make a practice of being a cheating, one-night-stand-having sleazebag.

Not as a rule, anyway.

Just as I reach this conclusion, we come to another switchback in the path. I take an unwisely large step, and my foot skids right off the edge of the cliff face.

There's time for a shot of raw adrenaline to rocket through me before I feel Raj's hands on my arms, and suddenly, both my feet are securely back on the path.

"Careful," he says mildly and turns to head back down. I try to follow, to pretend my heart isn't doing a full-out drum solo, but it's no use.

Raj only carries on a step or two farther before turning back. The path is steep enough here that he is looking up at me, shading his eyes against the lowering sun.

"You didn't turn an ankle, did you?" he asks and lifts his sunglasses to squint up at me.

"Ah—I—no." I scramble for something—anything—I can use as an excuse for my unwillingness to move any further. "It's just—look, I need you to know I had a huge fight with my fiancé the other night and that he dumped me."

Glancing pointedly at my left hand, he says, "So—you're not together anymore?"

He's shading his eyes from the sun, so I can't read his expression.

"No—I mean—yes. Yes, we're together. We patched things up."

"Ah."

"But not until—later. After. After everything that happened. Between us—you and I—that is."

My voice trails off, and neither one of us says a word for a long moment.

When he speaks again, his voice is quiet. "Look. We're both adults. I'm not sure we could have designed a more awkward situation if we tried, obviously, since I work with your dad. But I actually really admire what he's trying to do here. And your life is your own. You're getting married. It was one night—it didn't mean anything. Let's—let's just get through this, okay?"

"It's only . . ." I begin but am interrupted by a roar of laughter rising up from directly below us.

"Okay," I say, at last.

Raj reaches up to guide me down the final, steep section. I clutch his waiting hand, and it feels so good, I don't want to let go. But as soon as the ground flattens out a bit, he releases his hold on me immediately.

And then we are standing outside a cave, and my father is sitting on the ground, leaning against a large smooth rock. Paulo is perched on a flat boulder beside him, and they are passing another green bottle back and forth. Beyond Paulo, two more bottles lie empty on their sides in the dust.

"Gia—darling!" calls my dad when he spots us. "Come join us! Paulo has been sharing family stories."

My dad's face is red, and his hair is sticking out from his head like tufts of grey steel wool.

"Not only stories." I gaze pointedly down at the dead bottles. "Pops, how much have you had to drink?"

With a grunt, Paulo lurches to his feet. He collects the empties and waves one of them at me. "Local grapes. We share bounty with gods."

Without another word, he turns and disappears inside the cave. My dad, still clutching his own bottle, smiles absently out at the sea.

Raj flicks a glance at me and then, pulling a flashlight from his pocket, starts into the cave after Paulo.

Embarrassed, I offer a hand to my dad, who takes it, and I haul him to his feet.

"Raj—I mean, Dr. Malik needs to go," I hiss under my breath.

He gives me a goofy grin. "Now that I'm on my feet, I *also* need to go."

I roll my eyes. "That's not what I mean, obviously. He has an appointment, and he's likely going to be late because we've had to come down here to rescue you."

My dad burps gently. "Darling, I'm doing research. I don't need rescuing."

He takes a couple of wobbly steps before sinking down onto the boulder that Paulo had been sitting on. "See? No problem at all."

"Right." I give him another glare and then step around him to peer into the cave. The sky is taking on the deep gold of late afternoon, and the jagged mouth of the cave is dark against its brilliance. My eyes don't easily adjust to the blackness, but the cool shade is intoxicating when I walk inside. I turn back to look at my dad, who is tilting dangerously atop his stone perch. "Is Paulo coming back out?"

He shrugs. "The man does what he wants." My dad's accent always thickens when he drinks, and the slur in his voice stokes my annoyance.

"He has been telling me stories of Cyclops's cave." His voice drops to a stage whisper. "It never really belonged to the Cyclopes. It's called that for the tourists only."

"Okay, whatever. We need to go, and you're sitting down here getting sloshed. You *know* you shouldn't be drinking when you're on medication. It's so frustrating, Pops—it's like you go out of your way to ignore everything the doctor said."

He shakes his head at me. "Ah, *koritsi*, I'm sorry. I just got caught up in his stories. And a man could sit in the sun and look at this view all day, yes?" He hauls himself to his feet.

"I get that. I just wish you would listen to me—or at least to what your doctor told you."

"I do, my darling. I will. It's just—to be back here . . ."

He pauses and caresses the boulder by the doorway gently with one hand. To my horror, I see his eyes have welled with tears.

"It means so much to me, *Gianitsa*. To be here, at last, and to be able to show it all to my beautiful girl . . ."

A sort of scuffling sound comes from behind us, and I whirl to see the glow of a flashlight bobbing toward the cave entrance. I'm suddenly awash in embarrassment that the men inside will see my dad maudlin from day-drinking.

"We've got to get going." Scooping up my dad's sunglasses from a patch of grass near the cave entrance, I hand them over, and he slips them on. "Dr. Malik needs to leave, and I've somehow got to get you up that hill to meet Taki."

"It's not a problem," says Raj, emerging from the darkness of the cave behind us. He flicks off the flashlight and shoots his broad, white smile at my dad. "Ready to head back?"

Ari grins blearily and swings his arm to clap Raj on the shoulder but misses and takes a few wobbling steps forward in a way that makes my earlier stumbles look sure-footed. Raj places a steadying hand on my dad's arm, and I catch sight of him peeking at his watch.

"Maybe we can call Taki from here," I suggest hurriedly. "He can come down and give us a hand."

"No need," Raj begins, but then Paulo shambles out of the cave and presses a fresh bottle into my dad's hands.

"A gift," he bellows, clapping him on the back. My dad stumbles, and the only reason he doesn't fall is that Raj is still holding his arm.

Instead, he reaches out to wring Paulo's giant hand. "No one can tell a story like you, Paulo," he says, fervently. "Your generosity will not be forgotten."

Raj grins up at Paulo and, without a word, swings his head under one of my dad's arms and sets off up the hill. The path is barely wide enough for one, so I follow along, awash in embarrassment. At the first bend, I look back to see Paulo pulling the cork out of a fresh bottle. He holds it up to me in salute and hollers, "To Nobody!" before tilting it back.

I turn and follow them at what almost qualifies as a run.

While this speed doesn't last long, I find going up is a piece of cake compared to the journey down. I never do catch up to Raj and my dad, but I arrive at the top a scant moment or two behind them, only slightly out of breath. And miracle of miracles, Taki is already waiting for us with Herman on one shoulder and the car doors open to catch the breeze.

I hurry over just in time to see Raj carefully arranging my dad into the back of Taki's car.

Feeling mortified, I whisper, "He's never like this. He probably shouldn't have had wine with the medication he's on."

Raj stands up and shrugs it off. "It's fine. Don't worry about a thing."

As I climb in through my own door, Raj leans down beside my dad's window.

"I've got to head off now, but I'll meet you at the next site, Dr. Kostas," he says.

Raj steps back from the car, but in the end, he can't get away without a round of handshakes with the men present. Herman does them all one better by jumping onto Raj's shoulder and rubbing a cheek against his ear.

When at last Taki and Herman take their seats, I slam my door closed and watch Raj swing a leg over his bike. He catches me looking and shoots me a grin before pulling on his helmet and gunning his bike to life.

I think he is as happy as I am that this day is almost over.

The drive to the guesthouse is as noisy and bumpy as this morning's had been, but my dad just leans back, eyes closed and a gentle smile on his face. Herman sidles along the back seat and begins crooning into my dad's ear.

I sigh and lean my own head back. "What were you even thinking, Pops?"

His smile broadens. "I was trying to get Paulo to tell me the story of how he lost his eye."

I turn and stare out the window until I can't stand it any longer. "How did he?" I ask in spite of myself.

But my dad only shrugs as Taki bumps the car up against the curb. "When I ask him, all he will say is 'Nobody knows.'"

As I open the door, a wave of exhaustion wafts over me. My dad, perversely, seems to have recovered and climbs out of the back seat by himself with only a small groan at the effort.

I've always felt in pretty good shape for a city girl, but it turns out my ability to walk sixty blocks in Manhattan at the drop of a hat doesn't translate all that well to having to mountain-goat my way around these Mediterranean highlands. I don't know what I would have done if Raj hadn't been there to help get my dad back to the top of the path. I feel torn between being grateful to him and being mortified by the entire afternoon.

I trail in the front door of the guesthouse behind my dad, determined to put this day behind me. I'm going to send Anthony a little love note and then spend the rest of the evening finding a flight home. Drunken father be damned—I can't stand the idea of having my own mistakes thrown into my face every time I look at Raj Malik.

My own searing hot mistakes.

Grabbing a handful of grapes from the huge bowl on the front desk, I turn and head up to my room.

The cool of the guesthouse is so welcome after the long, hot afternoon in the sun. In the bathroom, as I'm washing my hands and splashing my face, I notice my engagement ring is covered in dust. This rapidly turns to mud as the water hits it, clogging all the fittings. I snatch the ring off in horror.

It's a gorgeous ring, a ten-karat diamond surrounded by twenty smaller but perfectly identical stones, though it's always felt a little too big for my hand. There's no doubt this is the most expensive thing I have ever owned, and for that alone, I feel duty bound to look after it. I think of all the times Anthony has held my hand up to the light so we can admire the sparkling radiance dancing off all the stones.

It's not sparkling now. I close the drain carefully to prevent disaster and spend half an hour gently scrubbing away the ancient dust and grime from the site. When the ring is sparkling again the way it should be, I unfasten the chain around my neck and return the ring onto it, where it clinks against my small cross. Just for now, and only for safety's sake.

Throwing open the window of my bedroom, I take a deep breath of the cool night air. The heat of the day has abruptly fallen away, and I can smell the salty tang of the sea on the cool breeze. It smells so different from the sea at home, notes of fish mingling with the fresh scent coming from the grove of trees planted below the guesthouse. Leaving the windows wide open, I sink down onto my bed, log on to the internet, and type the airline into the search bar.

As the Wi-Fi connects, my tablet pings with notifications of new mail. Scrolling through, I see most of it is wedding-related spam, but a note from Charlotte Castle catches my eye. The subject line reads: *Your crazy idea.*

My heart sinks. Charlotte has been a great boss, but one thing I have learned over the past few months is that she has no time for banter. She's also almost militant in her ability to maintain an empty inbox.

I lean against the wrought iron of my headboard and steel myself for the worst. So it is with total shock that I click open the e-mail to find that she is not only open to my idea of a modern Mediterranean odyssey but already has a plan for publishing a series of installments in NOSH over the coming weeks.

I'm visualizing a new post from each of your destinations. Simple, local food, deliciously described and with accompanying recipes. We'll need good, clear photographs to highlight the stories and will promote the series through social media and on the blog. Travel stories are so rare these days, people are clamoring for them. Think you can manage it?

I'm so delighted with this news that I've leapt right out of bed before I notice a second e-mail has arrived while I was reading Charlotte's.

This one is from Anthony. My heart sinks when I see the subject line, which, strangely enough, echoes Charlotte's: *This crazy idea of yours.*

Why would he bother sending an e-mail when he could just message me back? Or call? I quickly scan the contents.

If this is more important to you than planning your own wedding, so be it. I've spoken with my mother, who is quite frankly delighted by this turn of events. Luckily, she is known for her exquisite taste, and I will oversee any major decisions until you can get home.

It begins to make more sense when I get to the bottom and see the message was sent by Anthony's executive assistant. Melanie's worked for him for less than two months—a month shorter than our engagement, in fact—and though I haven't met her in person, I've got a pretty clear impression. I picture her as a woman in her midfifties, her hair in a French twist, her look efficient and severe. And the truth is that while she's a perfectly capable business correspondent, and is apparently so organized that Anthony's office has never functioned more smoothly, her notes lack any kind of personal touch.

Regardless, Anthony has a right to feel disappointed, and I am determined to serve my penance. After a snack featuring perhaps the best olive tapenade I've ever tasted, I use the inn's Wi-Fi to file my first proper story with NOSH. Then I leave my dad drinking ouzo in the lounge with Taki and spend the evening scanning celebrity wedding websites on the veranda under the reflected glow of a Mediterranean moon.

chapter fourteen

WEDNESDAY MORNING
Rizogalo
Gia Kostas, special correspondent to NOSH, in
   Alexandroupoli, Greece

This simple, delightful rice pudding is a Grecian favorite, harkening back to childhood. It can be served at any time of the day but is a welcome comfort for breakfast on a spring morning. Start with your preferred rice—I always go for jasmati—and . . .

I knew last night that my dad's plans involved an early morning visit to another site, so before I drifted off, I set the alarm on my phone. Not that I plan to accompany him. Now that Charlotte has accepted my story idea, I have work of my own to do. Also? The last thing I need is to have to face Raj Malik again.

Now that I am proudly writing as a special correspondent to NOSH, my goals for the morning are to make a list of article possibilities and to check in with Anthony. I found a cache of Idris Elba's wedding photos last night, and I want him to have a look at the tux.

I mean, Idris in a tux . . .

I fully don't expect Anthony to have the same reaction I do, but it *is* a nice tux. The fit is *perfect*.

So when the ting of an e-mail coming through awakens me, it takes a moment before I realize I must have slept right through the alarm. My first scrambled thought is that the e-mail must be from Anthony. But when I blearily stare at the screen, the NOSH icon jumps out at me. At the same time, the sounds of voices and traffic noise drifting in my window remind me that morning is well under-way in Alexandroupoli. Dropping my phone onto the end table, I make a dash for the tiny bathroom.

After throwing on a pair of yoga pants and cleaning my teeth, I stumble out of my room and head for the stairs. Just as I round the last bend in the stairwell, I spot my dad climbing into Taki's little blue car outside the front door. I lift my hand to wave, but he doesn't see me before the door slams and the car hurtles away. I'm left stand-ing in the doorway, mouth open, one hand in the air.

"Meez Kostas?" says a voice behind me.

I turn to see a young man, maybe fifteen or sixteen. He's wearing casual shorts topped with a carefully pressed white shirt and what is obviously a clip-on black tie. He holds out a plastic tray, yellowed, with a cigarette ad laminated to the top. On the tray is a slip of paper with my name on it.

My Gia,

Dr. Malik has found something he wants to show me in situ. Context is everything. Back before lunch. See you soon!

Papa xxx
PS: Took pills with breakfast. You see? I remember.

By the time I finish reading, the boy in the clip-on tie has van-ished with his tray. With at least one obligation safely out of the way, I turn around and head back inside in search of breakfast.

Just past the tiny front desk, I spy an open door and peek through it. Inside, a half dozen small tables are scattered about. There are people seated at only two of them, and behind the nearest couple, a buffet board stretches across the room, crowded with serving platters.

As I step inside, Clip-On Tie reappears, his white shirt now safely wrapped up in an apron. "Welcome, welcome," he says, his voice squeaking a little on the second word. A blush rises up from his collar as he directs me to an empty table.

As I sit down, I remember to pull out my phone and open Charlotte's e-mail to find a disappointingly tepid review of my first submission.

> Workmanlike. But it lacks magic. Needs punching up with sensory detail. I want to *taste* this food. Rewrite and submit again *ASAP!*

Italicized commands from Charlotte are too much before I've had coffee. I've never been a big breakfast person, usually content to grab a banana or, at most, a bagel with my coffee before heading into work in the morning. But I no sooner lift my head from my phone before Clip-On Tie and a young girl, who looks so much like him she could be his twin, leap into action. My small tabletop is swiftly adorned with cutlery, a basket with a selection of different bread rolls and rusks, and a tiny cup filled with muesli-sprinkled yogurt that smells like fresh raspberries.

The girl, who I only just notice now is also wearing a clip-on tie—though hers is a bow tie, and thus more forgivable than her colleague's Windsor knot version—ushers me over to the buffet. It is, as far as my foggy brain can recall, definitely a weekday, but the food before me has more of a ring of Sunday brunch to it. She gestures me toward a huge platter of sliced cold meats—a selection of which I'm almost positive includes jellied tongue—and slips a plate into my hand. The rest of the table is laden with bowls of fruit, platters of sliced tomatoes, and several varieties of cheese, including a chunk of Roquefort that I can smell from across the room. There's also a small mountain of baklava awash in slivered almonds and oozing with golden honey, and what looks like a spinach quiche.

My stomach is still in knots from Charlotte's e-mail, so in the end, I settle on a bowl of fresh fruit with a piece of the baklava perched precariously on one side. This selection is clearly not up to the house standard, however, because when I return to my table, I not only find a cup of coffee waiting for me but a bowl of what I'm almost positive is rice pudding, sprinkled in cinnamon and steaming.

I slide the dishes aside, pull up the article on my iPad, and stare at it glumly. Around me, couples at the other tables engage in lively discussion while they eat, but I tune them out. If only Charlotte had been more specific—I mean, she wants to *taste* the food? How the hell is that possible?

Defeated for the moment, I remember to take a few shots of my breakfast before I start to eat. This draws the attention of the two elegantly clad servers. They are visibly delighted when I pull out my phone to document the feast, and their enthusiasm cheers me up a little. In no time, we are all fast Insta-friends. I learn that they are indeed twins, and while Ilias has a great deal to say, his sister, Iliana, seems quite shy. She shares his leonine head of thick hair but sports a worry line between her brows that is unmatched in his open expression. Their parents own the guesthouse, and since it is a school break, they are both helping out. Their Instagram accounts, which I dutifully follow, are filled with typically teenage shots; lots of sand and sea and parties, and at least half of Ilias's recent posts involve some variety of bare-chested flexing.

Which he does pretty well, to tell you the truth.

The twins' phones vanish in a twinkling when a shout rings out from the kitchen, and I return to the last of my breakfast.

"You America?" Iliana asks quietly as she returns to refill my coffee cup.

"American," corrects Ilias, discreetly whisking crumbs off my tabletop into his palm. His sister looks mortified, the worry line between her brows deepening.

I nod and smile at Iliana, though my mouth is too full at the moment to actually reply. Her expression clears a little, and she gives me an embarrassed smile back before hurrying off into the kitchen.

"She does accounting books with our mother," says Ilias by way of explanation. "Very good at numbers, not so good at English."

"Well, your English is excellent," I reply. "Much better than my Greek."

He puffs up his chest. "When I finish exams this year, I plan to head to America."

"For college?" I ask between bites of baklava.

He shakes his head impatiently and then leans across the table.

"Hollywood," he says in a stage whisper, "is calling."

This makes me laugh out loud. "Oh, so you want to be in the movies?"

He shoots me a startlingly white smile in lieu of a reply and disappears into the kitchen after his sister. I can't help grinning back as the kitchen door swings on its hinges. A smile like his—coupled with that beefcake Instagram—is not going to hurt his chances in Hollywood.

Ten minutes later, my stomach distended but happy, I manage to make my escape from the food-pushing twins. I head back to my room to give the article another shot.

Someone has made my bed while I've been out for breakfast, and suddenly, I feel pathetically grateful that one element of my life is in order. But when I perch on the freshly made bed, the reality of what I'm doing sinks in. I'm here in Greece to keep an eye on my dad, yes, but also—I need to remember the importance of this golden ticket I've somehow been granted. Charlotte has given me a shot at actually being able to call myself a journalist. I do *not* want to blow this opportunity.

I don my sundress—still a trifle dusty from yesterday, but the only one I have with me—and whip on a little eyeliner. Tying my hair into a high ponytail, I briefly mourn the loss of my scarf to the winds and head out to find something in Alexandroupoli that will make my piece *sing*.

At the front door of the inn, after a single glance into the crystalline blue sky, I shoulder my bag and set out.

Because of our late arrival last night, I didn't get much of a sense of the city apart from spotting a lighthouse standing sentinel near the sea. Maybe in the daylight, I can garner inspiration to help improve my piece for Charlotte. Armed with a paper map I collected from the front desk, I aim myself toward the sun-dappled waterfront.

This port city, which was a fishing village until the last century, is today the largest in Thrace. As I stroll along the promenade, I'm struck by the fact that Alexandroupoli has all the earmarks of any American resort city. I mean, there's no Starbucks in view, but the waterfront is peppered with expensive resort-style hotels and restaurants. The biggest difference seems to be the size of the buildings. I remember walking along the Atlantic City boardwalk almost a year ago, celebrating Devi's twenty-fifth birthday. We strolled from one hotel bar to the next, each one more floodlit and elaborate than the one before.

Here, much like the neighborhood in Athens and very unlike Atlantic City, there's not a bunch of high-rise hotels. Instead, streets are lined with multiuse three-story walk-ups. At street level, these buildings are filled with storefronts and cafés. Everything seems pretty quiet, with hardly a camera-toting tourist to be seen. People don't feel comfortable yet traveling around the way they used to, and in any case, it's shoulder season, which means fewer visitors on the streets than in the busier summer and winter months.

This suits me fine, because it means I've got my choice of un-crowded vistas for optimum photography. I spend a happy morning wandering the streets, taking pictures of all the food I can find in windows and on street carts, and—determined to punch up the story Charlotte deemed "workmanlike"—whispering descriptive phrases into the recorder app on my phone.

I've just added "the delicate beauty of lotus petals scattered across the plate . . ." when I spy a cute coffee shop overlooking the beach. The thought strikes me that a little refreshment after the morning's exten-sive perambulations might be a good idea. I've just settled into a chair on the deserted patio when my phone pings. It's a reply from Anthony.

Gia baby,

Counting the hours until you return. I miss you more every day. Keeping myself busy by thinking up surprises for you so you know how much you are loved. I have worked out three—yes, THREE— so far, each better than the one before. I'd promise more, but I fear that my talent with gift-giving might encourage you to stay away longer, and we can't have that, can we? Ha ha.

For now, I will content myself with giving you a hint as to the first of the surprises. Take a look at this, my darling almost-wife, and picture yourself inside something just like it. Soon!

Anthony xxoo

I lean back in my chair to read his note and find myself beaming at the server when she arrives with my coffee. I feel suddenly grateful that Anthony and I managed to get past the rough patch. I mean, apart from that single bad argument, his patience with my weird dad has been amazing. As I take my first searing sip, I mentally enumerate all the ways I'm going to show him my gratitude when I get home. This backfires a little, as I get lost just for a moment remembering the feel of Raj's hands on my bare thighs, but I manage to dismiss the thought quickly enough.

No more thinking about Raj. Instead, I vow to devote all this new bad-girl energy to making Anthony happy to see me when I get home.

It's not until I'm paying my bill that I remember he embedded a link, so I pause beside my table and click through before the Wi-Fi can drop off.

The window on my screen opens to a page on the British *Vogue* bridal site, and one look at the image makes me sink back down into my seat. It's a shot of a famously tall supermodel, swathed in a columnar confection of ruched satin. The white sheath has delicate, lacy straps and an elegant train sweeping the floor. But beginning at the bodice, the dress sports an almost egg-shaped explosion of layered ruffles—dozens of them—cascading almost to the knee. The model, of course, looks beautiful, with her long neck and even longer legs balancing out the ludicrous explosion of tulle across her torso. How could Anthony's mother think this dress would suit me? It's designed to hide every curve.

And the price?

The price is fifteen thousand. *Pounds*, not dollars. It's British *Vogue*, after all.

The server leans across in front of me and wipes the table. Taking the hint, I get to my feet again and walk toward the little gate separating the tables from the street, but not before I scroll down to load the full page.

Anthony and I have often discussed the disparity in our financial backgrounds. I'm not sure he really gets it, to tell you the truth. He's never had to save for anything in his life. But he knows my mom has offered to buy my dress for me—we've talked about that, for sure. And there is absolutely an extra zero in the price tag of this dress that she will definitely not be counting on.

Now, my mother is nothing if not practical, and I'm sure she wants me to be happy. If this designer dress was the one I wanted, she'd find a way. But it's not—and the dress is her wedding gift to me. She's making a special trip up to the city next month so we can pick it out together.

All thoughts of sending a sexy little reply back to Anthony fly out of my head. The only thing worse than the price tag is the silhouette. What this willowy model pulls off with ease would leave me looking like the Stay-Puft Marshmallow Man.

Don't get me wrong—I love my body. I do. I'm strong and reasonably fit, mostly because I spend my life walking everywhere. I even do Zumba with Devi, at least when she's off on Thursday evenings. I kept up with my swimming all the way through university, so my shoulders are *strong*. I also like to eat, which—you know—kind of comes with the territory in my line of work.

I think back to the few times I've shared a meal with Anthony's parents and try to remember if I've ever seen his mother actually eat anything. I mean, she sips her tea, but . . .

Suddenly, the memory of her raised eyebrow as I scraped out every last, luscious crumb of my tiramisu that time after dinner at La Bernadine takes on a whole new meaning. Could those ruffles be intentional?

Quickly scrolling through the remainder of the dresses on the page, I see they are, if anything, even uglier than the one Cara is wearing. I take a deep breath and try to use logic to calm the sudden emotional maelstrom swirling in my gut. Maybe his mother isn't being passive aggressive about my figure. Maybe we just have wildly different tastes.

In any case, this is all wrong. The plan was to pick out a pretty dress with my mom. I'm not willing to bury my body under an explosion of tulle designed to hide every curve.

Let alone spend more than twenty grand on.

My good feelings evaporating, I step onto the sidewalk. It's my own fault. This is what I get for sending Anthony that picture of Idris Elba in a tux.

As I drop my phone into the pocket of my sundress, a car screeches to a halt beside me on the street.

My dad rolls down the side window as I try to get a grip on my heart rate. He's waving his phone at me wildly.

"There you are! I just got off the line with Teresa. She's managed to move up the flight. Get in—we need to pick up your things from the guesthouse."

He reaches back awkwardly and unlatches the rear door.

"I thought we were spending the day here in Alexandroupoli." I slide inside. "I need to punch up my . . ."

"Sorry, *koritsi*, but there is no time. I'll explain on the way, yes?"

He pulls his medication bottle from the breast pocket of his pink shirt and rattles it at me. "I have so much energy today! These things must be working. I think maybe you're right, eh?"

This is likely the closest thing I'll ever get to an apology, but before I can work myself into any kind of a decent gloat, we pull up to the guesthouse. Ari leaps in through the door ahead of me, and as I head to my room, he's over beside the front desk pressing cash into the clerk's hand.

My dad never *has* gotten the hang of the contactless purchase.

I have so little stuff, it takes me only a moment or two to collect everything. By the time I get back to the front desk, my dad is gone.

Instead of the desk clerk, a round little woman wearing chef's whites—and who looks exactly like an older version of Iliana—greets me.

"Your papa waits in the car," she says with a shy smile before pressing a foil-wrapped packet into my hands.

"Ilias tell me you like my baklava. For your trip, yes?"

She vanishes back into the kitchen so quickly I have to call out my thanks through the swinging door as it closes behind her.

A woman after my own heart. Bet *she* didn't wear a puffball dress to her wedding either.

Seconds later, I'm hopping into the back door of Taki's car, while my father taps his watch impatiently from the front seat.

Herman is clearly delighted to see my dad again. "Dr. ARI!" he croaks as I slam the door closed. His tone is so note-perfect that at first I'm sure it's Taki's voice, and it's not until I slide across the back seat that I see the excited cockatoo bouncing on his perch.

As the car rockets away from the curb, Herman flutters suddenly past me into the back window—which is startling—and then sidles sideways along the back of the bench seat, stopping only when he reaches a spot next to my dad's ear. Raising his crest, he leans forward to peer into my dad's face.

"Hello, Hermy." My dad runs a finger along the bird's beak.

I swear that bird begins to purr.

Taki takes a tight corner, and I grab for the door handle and glance over at my dad. "Pops, I'm supposed to submit my rewrites today. I thought the next flight wasn't scheduled until tomorrow?"

He shrugs. "That dig is no good—not for what I want. That Malik kid cares so much for the layers in the earth, but . . ." He gives a dismissive flick of his fingers, and his voice trails off as Taki pulls out onto a highway and accelerates to light speed. We are both forced back in our seats, and even Herman staggers a little on his perch beside my dad's ear.

After a moment, Ari somehow manages, against all laws of gravity and momentum, to lean forward and pluck his worn copy of *The Odyssey* out of his bag. He riffles through the pages until he finds what he is looking for.

"It was Paulo's stories that gave me the idea," he begins and pulls his reading glasses down from their usual place on his forehead. "Here!" he shouts over the roar of the wind pouring through the front windows. "This is it, exactly!"

I feel a rising sense of dread creep into my gut, which must show on my face, because my dad pauses in his explanation and laughs. "You needn't look so worried, *koritsi*. In fact, this should please you. Going a day early is a shortcut, yes?"

This is not what I'm worried about.

Holding the book up, he takes a deep theatrical breath as I make my move. I dive forward, pluck the book from his fingers, and toss it onto the empty seat beside me. I've had that book read to me so often I can recite whole swaths of it from memory. And *not* by choice.

"Why don't you just tell me in your own words?"

His eyes narrow. "Well," he snorts, clearly insulted, "I wouldn't want to bore you with the details. The object I'm looking for was not in Makri. I didn't think it would be but needed to confirm to be sure. This means I can head south early and make my way directly to the next site."

He turns away huffily and stares out the window as the scenery hurtles by.

I consider reminding him how his reading always puts me to

sleep and instead decide to try pacifying him by asking for more detail. "South? Where in the south? One of the islands?"

My father arches an eyebrow. "Perhaps if you *read* a little more widely, it would be obvious." Then he snaps his mouth shut and returns to the view out his window.

I sigh and watch the sea go by as Taki hurtles down the highway to the airport. It's astonishing how sitting beside my father makes me feel like a teenager again. On the rare occasion we'd hang out together when I was growing up, it was just like this. In retrospect, my guess is he was so used to everyone at the university acceding to his every whim that having to actually communicate with his own daughter, someone who wasn't contractually obligated to listen to him or obey his orders, threw him off his stride. Also? Once he takes offense, it can be hours before he forgets why he's mad and starts talking again.

Before now, I've always had my own life to return to until he recovers from his huff. But stuck here in this moment, all I can do is stare at the sea and regret every choice I've made in the past three days.

I should be home tasting cakes and trying on dresses with my fiancé. Or at worst, I should be sitting on a shady Grecian portico gently rubbing aloe vera into my singed forearms and refining the text of my submission for Charlotte. But instead, I'm sitting in the back of a car driven by a bird-loving maniac beside a sulking man-baby.

I take a deep breath and vow to spend less energy on catering to my dad and more on editing. At the moment, I'm more concerned about impressing Charlotte than I am over the wedding dress, and that's saying something.

Since my dad is still refusing to speak with me, it's not until we get into the airport that I learn that our flight is bound for Crete. I take advantage of his snit to sit by myself in the departure lounge and have another look at the original itinerary. Digging around in my bag, I pull out the file folder I snatched away from Evan that day in my dad's office.

It feels like an eternity ago.

In any case, looking at the itinerary does cheer me up a little. We'll be flying into Heraklion Airport on the north coast of Crete, where we're scheduled to spend only a single day. If my dad can get whatever he needs to see wrapped up in a day, I for one am not going to argue about moving things along.

Nevertheless, while distances in Europe don't really compare with those in the US, this part of the journey is no short hop. The flight to Athens is just over an hour, and then we have to wait for a second flight to get to Crete.

I jam Evan's file back into my bag with a sigh and pull out my tablet, but just at that moment, they call us to board. Stepping into line behind my still-distant father I look for the bright side. I can always work on the plane.

Which means, of course, that I get exactly zero work done.

In the first place, the plane is the smallest I've ever flown in—seating maybe forty people?—and to my surprise, Taki is coming along for the ride. I spend the entire time jammed ignominiously into a seat between my dad and Taki, who is holding Herman's cage on his lap as carry-on luggage. Our route crosses the Aegean Sea all the way down to Athens, and there's no real option to get any work done onboard. The plane is so buffeted by gusting spring winds that the flight attendants have to remain buckled in for the duration of both flights. I don't get a chance to lower my tray table even once.

Instead, I spend my time fretting. While we wait for our second flight, I use the airport Wi-Fi in Athens for a quick text exchange with a very sleep-deprived Devi. This doesn't really help, as it turns out she's pulling an all-nighter in the hospital's ER and sounds almost as out of sorts as my dad. I should note that his mood did improve eventually, especially after he spent the layover in Athens in the airport bar with Taki.

"Only a small gin and tonic, darling," he calls from his seat. "Practically medicinal!"

While Taki and my dad live it up in the bar, I sit out in the departure lounge and finally manage to put together a reply to Anthony. Lots of emphasis on our shortcut and the time saved, and a promise to discuss the dress in more detail when I get home. But between his refusal to text and his disciplined approach to his inbox, I know it's likely I won't hear back from him until later tonight, at the soonest. There hasn't really been time for a full accounting, but I send him a list of all the wedding-related sites I've been perusing, with my favorites underlined. And even after that, I spend the second flight alternating between nausea from airsickness and worry that I am letting my fiancé down.

Nearly five hours of teeth-rattling, legroomless travel later, we finally begin to spiral down toward the airport. As the plane circles, I watch a large ferry steam past an enormous breakwater protecting the port city. The waters lapping the shore as we land are a brilliant, impossible shade of blue, even compared with those off mainland Greece. We touch down with a gently vertiginous bounce in Heraklion, Crete. The relief I feel at having my feet on the ground is clearly shared by Herman, who squawks loudly as we shudder to a halt and then carols "Olé, Olé" all the way out through security.

However, even our arrival in Crete doesn't offer my anxiety a reprieve. A quick check of my e-mail while we wait for my dad's bag shows no reply from Anthony. Worse, there *is* an e-mail from Charlotte. The subject line is just a series of question marks, and there is no text in the body of the e-mail. The sense of panic in my gut ratchets up a notch. My fiancé is incommunicado, and the woman I want most in the world to impress decidedly . . . is not.

Lost in my own thoughts, I trail along after my dad, who is at least looking a bit more cheerful now that we're on the ground. But Taki, who was born here, is glowing. As we walk out of the airport, he pauses and then raises his hands in the air like he's just scored a goal. Suddenly there is a roar and a rushing sound, and the three of us find ourselves in the middle of a cheering, bouncing mob. With a sense of self-preservation far superior to my own, Herman flies into the sky above us as the mob surges around in joyous rapture.

A short, barrel-chested man, the spitting image of Taki but with the addition of a mop of grey curls and a possibly even lusher mustache, throws his arms around both my father and me.

"Kalos IRTHATE!" he bellows. "Welcome! Welcome to Crete!"

And as the crowd takes up this chant, from in the air above us, I hear Herman squawk, *"Olé!"*

chapter fifteen

WEDNESDAY AFTERNOON
Tsakiris Chips
Gia Kostas, special correspondent to NOSH, in
Heraklion, Crete

*Snacking is universal in any culture, and what greater delight than
when something you assume you know well surprises you. Just
when you think the staid potato has seen and done it all, these
salty, spicy specimens come along to offer a new take on an old
theme . . .*

The chaos outside the arrivals level at the airport takes a while to
settle down. By the time it does, I have learned that (a) Taki has a
very large family, and (b) they are extremely happy to have him home.

As all the yelling and kissing and pinching of cheeks and crying
swirls around me, I am suddenly reminded of my own jet-lagged
introduction to Greece in the Athens airport. The large, joyous family greetings then seemed so much a part of an alien culture to which
I had no connection at all. Can that really have only been last Monday? Less than a week ago—way less. Five days.

Amazing what a difference five days can make. I am with my
own father, for starters, and am now surrounded by one of those
surging, loving families that I so desperately tried to avoid that day
back in Athens.

Yet somehow, here in Crete, the fact that I am not *of* this family

does not seem to matter at all. I remember that Taki is only a nick-
name, and his actual given name being Stavros Panagiotakis means
this whole crazy family are Panagiotakises. My hands are shaken and
squeezed, my cheeks are pinched and patted, and the rest of me is
thoroughly hugged in both group and singular iterations, without
the least regard for any attempt at social distancing. Almost everyone
is crying tears of joy, and I am surrounded by a surging sea of human
emotion. As the only child of a single mother, I've never been greeted
even remotely like this before. It's overwhelming and shocking
and . . . quite, quite lovely.

As there is very little English being spoken; in the moment, I am
able only to grasp a couple of the introductions. Taki's brother, whose
name is Spiro; and Giagiá—pronounced Ya-ya—his grandmother.
She is a round little woman, dressed entirely in black. Her white hair
is pulled back under a grey scarf, and even in this heat, she is firmly
buttoned into a well-worn cardigan. As Taki introduces her to me,
there is a sudden flurry of feathers, and Herman alights on her shoulder. I steel myself, expecting a shriek to rival the one she let out when
she caught sight of her grandson, but no.

Instead, Herman steps gingerly along her shoulder and settles in
right beside her ear. He places his cheek against hers, and the two of
them coo at each other so quietly I can barely hear it under the cacophony of family greetings.

"Ermie!" she whispers. *"Ermie-mou!"*

The tiny pink patch on Herman's cheekbones darkens, and he
drops his crest as she caresses him with one thick, wrinkled finger.

After a few moments, the noise level drops enough that Taki's
brother Spiro is able to shepherd everyone, still all talking at once,
into the airport parking lot. After several false starts, since each Panagiotakis seems to have a distinct—and opposed—memory of where

the family car is parked in this remarkably small lot, we finally stop in front of what has to be the strangest vehicle I have ever seen.

The main body—which may have once been a shade of blue or perhaps grey—appears to be the chassis of an old truck with parts of several other vehicles soldered, Frankenstein-like, onto it. Oxidation along every seam gives the impression that rust itself might be holding the whole thing together. The back of the vehicle is an open-bed truck framed in wood and edged in what looks like the remains of a repurposed picket fence. There is no roof, and in fact, no windscreen. The seats, of which there are three, are all long, bench-style, with the first tucked well under the giant steering wheel, and the subsequent seats sort of layered upward behind, like a mobile stadium section. It is a car chimera or—perhaps more accurately—a hybrid truck in the truest sense of the word.

The family all piles inside, with Giagiá being given the seat of honor next to Spiro, who is driving. My dad and Taki end up crammed together behind Giagiá on the seat, which appears to be engineered so she can most easily cling to Taki's hand. As one of the youngs, I am shuffled along with a half dozen others into the open back of the truck, which gives me an unobstructed view.

I gather from the tiny bits of shouted conversation I can actually understand that we are being driven to our accommodation, which may or may not belong to a family member called Tira. When everyone is finally seated up front, we begin the slow process of backing out of the space. Of course there are no seat belts in the bed of the truck, so those of us in the back each grab hold of whatever the most solid-seeming section of picket fence nearby is and hold on. Around me, Taki's younger family members are alternatively chatting to each other or beaming at me and repeating "Hello, how are you?" at odd intervals in heavily accented English.

None of them wait to hear a reply.

There are several false starts at reversing, until one of my companions in the back, a boy of fifteen or so, vaults over the fence and, standing to the side, offers directions that help Spiro make his way out of the parking spot. Once this is achieved, a cheer goes up and Spiro starts forward with a lurch. The direction-giving boy, whose name I determine from the cheer to be Nico, trots up behind us and easily scrambles back into the moving truck.

As the truck bumps along over the gravel surface, it seems we are taking a fairly circuitous route through airport parking. This may well be because everyone is still talking at once, with most of the family shouting directions at Spiro. Herman, whom I have come to think of as Taki's navigator, has abandoned his place on Giagiá's shoulder and fluttered up to roost behind the top row of seats out of the wind.

We haven't gathered too much speed, which seems appropriate for a vehicle with no windscreen, and are cruising toward what might be a cashier's booth. I've made myself fairly comfortable, sitting on my gym bag, and have just begun contemplating how this truck can be allowed to drive on any road legally when disaster strikes.

The volume of what I believe must be a combination of opinions, direction-giving, and just general cheerful chatter has not abated at all since we entered the lot, so when Spiro turns out of a row of parked cars toward the booth and there is a loud chorused shout, he slams on the brakes. Later, I will discover that he was about to turn the wrong way into a one-way lane. But in the moment, I join the rest of the untethered humans as we are flung forward into what is suddenly a giant pile of assorted body parts. This precipitous stop is followed by an equally sudden bang, as a car traveling behind us—a small red Mini Cooper station wagon—slams into our tailgate.

The collision serves to counteract our collective forward motion, and the group of Taki's assorted younger family members, myself irretrievably tangled among them, soar backward, ending piled in a new heap against the wooden tailgate.

I should probably stress that none of this has been terribly painful, but as I haven't known any of these people for more than ten minutes, it does feel a trifle intimate.

Not surprisingly, there is a great deal of fairly shrill verbiage springing from the forward section of our vehicle, but as I can't understand most of it anyway, I concentrate on trying to get myself as upright as possible. Doing so requires unwrapping my legs from various other people's limbs, with much awkward maneuvering involved. I'm just trying to apologize to the young man whose name I'm pretty sure is Nico for stepping on the palm of his hand when the doors to the Mini Cooper fly open.

While the loud voices from the front of the truck continue, sounding more acrimonious by the second, all conversation in the back fades away at the sight of the people pouring out of the Mini. I'm fairly certain that even with the sudden stop and the collision, I did not hit my head, but I can't help doubting myself at the number of young men emerging from the vehicle behind us. The front end of their car has crumpled, and the bumper is wedged under the bed of the truck, so the windshield of the Mini is a mere foot or two from where I am peering over the tailgate. For a moment, all I can see through the windshield is a sea of faces staring upward, the whites of everyone's eyes rounded in shock. And when the exodus begins, there are fully three or four people outside the car before I see they are all in uniform.

Basketball uniforms. We have been rear-ended by a basketball team. As I stare, openmouthed, more members of the team spill out of the Mini like clowns from a circus car. I'm fairly certain a Mini

Cooper—even the station-wagon variety—has seating for a maximum of five or maybe six regular-sized people, but I count at least ten young men, all in their blue-and-white sleeveless jerseys and knee-length shorts, milling around outside the crushed remains of their car.

Like the members of my own vehicle, they are all shouting—at us and at each other. After a moment, with a bit of help from his teammates, the driver manages to unfold himself from behind the wheel and step out of the car. His shouting, by contrast, is entirely directed at us. Clearly incensed, he kicks the front tire and slams his door closed in such a fury that, somehow, the hatchback of the vehicle springs open, and dozens of basketballs, as though released from the barrel of a cannon, come surging out, bouncing off across the parking lot like they are making a getaway.

With a cheer, the younger contingent of Taki's family leap over the tailgate as one and dash off to corral the escaping basketballs.

In the meantime, the driver storms past to confront Spiro, looming over the smaller man like an avenging giant. I have a brief moment of fear that he is going to take Spiro's head right off, but at that moment, Giagiá leans out of the door and shakes her finger right in the younger driver's face.

The power of Taki's Giagiá is such that the driver immediately takes a step back. Holding his hands palm forward in an "I surrender" gesture, he listens wordlessly as she makes her opinion of just who was at fault perfectly clear.

After Giagiá's intervention, things settle down quickly, and soon the airport police service arrives. Both the officers are women, which I find strangely comforting. And while things remain pretty confused for the next hour or so, there is exactly zero I can do to affect the outcome of any of this. I resume my comfy seat atop my gym bag in the back of the truck, share a package of something called Tsakiris Crisps—oregano-flavored potato chips—with Nico, and watch it all play out.

The airport policewomen handle things with utmost efficiency. The only injury turns out to be where Spiro bashed his forehead on the steering wheel when the Mini didn't stop in time, but Giagiá has not only a clean linen handkerchief in her mammoth handbag, but a Band-Aid large enough to cover the wound entirely.

All the same, with two such passenger-heavy vehicles, there is a lot of milling about while the police take statements. The basketball team, who are here to pick up a member flying in from Olympic tryouts in Athens, are generally in good spirits. The car belongs to the team owner, luckily fully insured, though the driver is cautioned for carrying too many passengers.

Whether a similar admonition is offered to Spiro for his Panagiotakis-mobile, I never do discover.

Once the police wrap up their investigation, things begin to move quickly. The fact that both our truck and the Mini were heading the wrong direction on a one-way road goes a long way to calming the Mini driver. In the end, all the members of the basketball team each wrap their giant hands around the sheet of metal passing for a back bumper on the truck and lift it bodily off the Mini. The Mini proves to be too damaged to drive, but watching the team members tuck themselves into the back of the tow truck, I'm convinced they actually might have a bit more space for their onward journey.

More legroom, anyway.

chapter sixteen

 STILL WEDNESDAY
Tea Bags and Sugar Packets: Notes to self
Gia Kostas, former food writer, now emaciated starvation
   victim, near Matala, Crete

*Legend tells us that the saddest thing for an eager chef is an
empty pantry. Foraging is indeed an art, but the sorry truth is,
there is almost nothing more pathetic than a grown woman . . .*

Once we leave the airport behind, a certain level of calm returns.
My dad plans to scoot off to whatever dig Raj is working on,
and my goal, of course, is to stay as far away from both of them as
possible.

Also to rewrite my story and send it off to Charlotte.

It's my last chance to get it right, and I need to find some way to
add the magic she's looking for.

Heraklion is the largest city on Crete, but we're not staying here.
After all the to-do at the airport, we're soon bumping along a two-
lane road that heads in the direction of the south coast, the sun lowering to one side. The road is lined with white walls overhung by
gnarly trees with shiny green leaves. The terrain around us seems as
dry as the mainland, and a fairly steep cliff below the highway leads
down to the brilliant, crystalline waters of the Mediterranean Sea. A
steady, cool breeze is blowing from off the water, and combined with

the wind stirred up just from sitting in the open bed of the truck, I'm convinced I will never untangle my hair again.

More than an hour later, and shortly after ambling through a bustling, waterfront village, we pull up in front of the guesthouse in our giant, weird ride. It is a charming little villa, perched by itself at the end of a dusty gravel lane.

Unfortunately, standing by the front door is Raj Malik. I've been watching people's faces on the journey from the airport, and to tell you the truth, nobody really bats an eye as we drive past. But as we pull up, I have time to watch Raj replace his initial look of shock with a carefully neutral expression.

He may think he's got it covered, but I can read the amusement flowing off him in waves. For the first time, I feel a little defensive of my dad and his journey. If he has to surround himself with weirdos in order to achieve his lifetime goal—well, why shouldn't he?

The truck gives a final shudder as it rolls to a stop, and Nico—the boy who shared his potato chips with me—gallantly vaults over the side, opens the tailgate, and offers me a hand down. In the meantime, my dad is slowly working his way through all of Taki's family, each of them wringing his hand, or in the case of Giagiá, literally grabbing his head by the ears and firmly kissing each cheek twice.

Beside the front door, I spot Raj surreptitiously checking his watch. The accident in the parking lot has delayed our arrival by at least an hour, and this current goodbye ritual is also taking forever, so I lean in and link my arm with my dad's, physically prying him away from the loving embrace of Spiro.

Yet as the truck finally lurches away, with Taki gazing slightly imploringly at us over one shoulder, Raj doesn't look at all put out. Instead, he can't seem to hold back a grin. "That vehicle is really— something."

"Apologies for keeping you waiting, my friend," my dad says, smiling wryly. "Taki hasn't been back to Crete for two years, and his family are—you understand—clearly happy to see him."

"Are they giving you all the credit for bringing him home?"

My dad shrugs and looks at his watch. "Perhaps. Listen, young man, we have maybe two hours of daylight left. What say we go look at your site?"

Raj nods and then glances politely over at me, but I wave him off. "I've got work to do," I say quickly. "I'll sign us into the guesthouse, Pops. You go on ahead."

"Thank you, darling. See you for dinner, eh?"

He trots ahead with his suitcase and deposits it on the front step. I follow him up to the door and pause to wave before stepping inside. With some alarm, I see my dad is strapping on a motorcycle helmet. Raj is already wearing his, but instead of a motor bike, I notice he's climbing onto a Vespa scooter. My dad hops on behind him and lifts his hand to me as Raj putt-putts away.

I can't help grinning at the sight. Definitely not as cool as the black bike Raj was driving on the mainland, but still a huge step up from the Frankentruck that got us here. And likely safer too.

The guesthouse is a small whitewashed cottage clinging to the cliffside, with a sweeping vista of crystal clear sea as a backdrop. In the distance to the west, I can see the white sail of a yacht soaring across the waters of the Mediterranean.

The proprietress of this cottage, Tira, is waiting for me inside. She has ridden her own scooter from her home in the nearby village of Matala.

"Is used to be a fishing village, but now mostly tourists," she explains while walking me through the cottage. "Though maybe we go back to fish if the tourists keep away, yes?"

The guesthouse is painted entirely white, inside and out, with the characteristic Hellenic blue as an accent. It is tiny and perfect, with two small bedrooms and a living area that opens onto a stone balcony above the ocean. Below us, the water takes on a dozen shades of blue as the waves crash into the base of the cliff, topped with a spray of snow white foam.

The one downside to this little piece of paradise is that the Wi-Fi is down, a fact I don't discover until after my father is long gone.

"You come into the village tonight," Tira says soothingly. "Matala has everything you need. Good food, perfect beach, nice taverna. You sit under stars and surf internet to your heart content, eh? And by tomorrow, the nice internet people promise is all fix." She smiles apologetically and shrugs. "Life on Crete."

I start to tell her that I need to be online to check in with my boss and then stop myself. "Life on Crete," I echo instead, and even manage a smile in return.

After leaving me a key to the front door and pointing out a safe path down to a tiny beach, Tira heads back into town, and I am alone for the first time in so long memory fails me. I savor the silence for a few minutes. This is perfect—no distractions. And in spite of the fact that I feel a little cut off without Wi-Fi, it still means I should be able to focus on my edits undisturbed.

Instead of getting straight to work, I indulge in the luxury of my first shower of the day, washing all the travel dust—most of which was acquired while sitting in the back of the Taki family Frankentruck—down the drain. Refreshed, I pause only to slather myself in sunscreen before bringing my tablet and a bottle of water onto the flagstone balcony. The wall surrounding the small open space is whitewashed limestone, and one whole corner is covered in grapevine, which grows up to form a green canopy beside the cottage.

I crank open a faded blue umbrella furled in the center of a slightly rust-dappled metal table and set up a workstation beneath it: tablet, notebook, pen, and phone. The water bottle has beads of condensation coating the outside already. I pull up a metal garden chair, open my most recent file, and fingers poised above the keyboard, I take a deep breath, ready to write.

Nothing comes.

I read over my existing draft; the one I sent through to Charlotte.

Still nothing.

Over the course of the next two hours, I pace, drink the whole bottle of water, check out the inside of every cupboard for possible snacks, find nothing but a box of tea bags and three sugar packets, drink another whole bottle of water, consider eating one of the sugar packets, unpack my bag in case I've stashed a granola bar somewhere, find nothing except unwashed laundry, return to the balcony, stare at the first draft, add the word *the* twice, erasing it both times, and finally swallow the contents of all three sugar packets in despair.

I'm just hiding the evidence of my shame by jamming the torn little packets to the bottom of the trash pail I find under the sink when I hear a distant *putt-putt-putt* sound followed by a not-so-distant spray of gravel.

I hurriedly brush away the few remaining sugar grains adhering to the sunscreen on my face and plant myself back in my chair. When my dad walks in, I look up and then throw in a big stretch to add authenticity.

"Wow—hi! Has it been two hours already? I've been grinding away here the whole time," I say, hastily exiting the barely touched document on my screen.

"Had a good afternoon, darling?" My dad swoops out onto the deck to give me a kiss on the top of my head, then strides over to the balcony rail and flings his arms wide.

"Look at this view, *koritsi*! Raj, come here and just look at this view! Isn't it something?"

I turn to see Raj Malik has followed him out onto the deck. He smiles a little shyly and joins my dad by the balcony rail.

"This *is* a magical place," he says softly.

His hair is sticking up in the back from the helmet he's still carrying, but he closes his eyes for a minute, smiling into the evening breeze.

I don't realize that I, too, am smiling until my dad turns back to face me, rubbing his hands together.

"What's for dinner, darling? We've been walking around Rajnish's site all afternoon, and I'm starving!"

My short-lived cheeriness evaporates and I stare at him pointedly without replying. This clearly does not get through his thick skull, as his benign, slightly inquiring expression doesn't change.

"Uh—Pops?" I fling open one of the empty cupboards. "There's nothing to eat in this place. Like nothing. Not a cracker. In any case, as you can clearly see, I've been working all afternoon, myself." I somehow manage this last with a straight face, mostly because I'm so irritated at his presumption.

"Oh, of course, of course," he crows, oblivious. "Self-catering, and we didn't bring anything with us. I forgot completely. But not to worry, darling. Taki promised to drop by later to bring a few essentials. You can whip up breakfast tomorrow to make it up to me, eh?"

He turns and winks at Raj, who has taken an unconscious step back. Only the irritation I feel at myself for wasting the whole afternoon prevents me from taking my dad's head right off.

Instead, I smile sweetly and pick up my cardigan. "I didn't realize you brought me along as domestic help, Pops. But since there's nothing I can *whip up* for you at the moment, should we go in search of some food in the village?"

Raj winces at this, but my dad, curse him, still misses my sarcastic tone entirely. Instead, he claps his hands delightedly.

"Of course, of course! But darling, you'll have to stay here. I'm quite sure that our friend doesn't want to double us both on his scooter."

I narrow my eyes at him and snatch up my bag.

"Quite unnecessary, I promise you." I stomp out of the house ahead of both of them. "As I plan to *walk*."

chapter seventeen

STILL, ASTONISHINGLY, WEDNESDAY
Scampi
Gia Kostas, special correspondent to NOSH, outside
Matala, Crete

A dive into the cuisine of Greece is like slipping beneath the crystal clear waters of the Mediterranean; filled with adventure and with new knowledge at every turn. You may well have gone all your long life believing scampi to be shrimp, but I am here to tell you . . .

In the end, we all walk down to the village together. The two men follow behind me, Ari telling Raj about the accident with the basketball players.

"Damnedest thing you ever saw, all those enormous boys pouring out of that tiny car," he says.

I'm still cranky, so I snort a little at this, coming from a man who had been safely ensconced in the front of the vehicle and who couldn't possibly have seen any of what he's describing.

My dad crinkles his eyes at me. "Of course, Gia had a bird's-eye view, didn't you, *koritsi?*"

I think back to the accident, to being at the bottom of a pile of bodies when Spiro hit the brakes and then suddenly being at the top of the pile after the Mini bumped us.

"It was more like being in a rugby scrum." The ocean breeze has loosened my ponytail, so I tuck a stray curl behind my ear. "I had to disentangle myself from all those Panagiotakises in the back, first. But yeah—I have no idea how they crammed so many giant guys into one tiny car."

Raj laughs out loud. "I am so sorry I missed it," he says. The wind has finally blown the helmet-head out of his hair, and he's rolled up the sleeves of his white shirt.

I grin back at him. "You have to understand, these guys were huge—like, almost the size of Paulo, every one of them. Watching them tumble out of that little car . . . It was pretty amazing."

My dad waggles his eyebrows. "I think we got away lucky. When Odysseus met *his* giants, the Laestrygonians, they wrecked all his ships and ate his men."

As he speaks, he catches the toe of one of his shoes in a section of crumbled sidewalk and stumbles. Quick as a flash, Raj reaches over and steadies my dad back onto his feet.

"Whoa—thank you," gasps Ari. "It's been a long day. I'm ready for a bite to eat and a nice cold G&T."

Raj smiles. "Almost there. I've had enough of this sun too."

As we carry on walking, I notice he positions himself just a little closer to my dad's side, one tanned, muscular forearm held cautiously at the ready.

My heart gives a thump that I am so not ready for, it actually stops me in my tracks for a minute.

As my dad describes the experience of driving in Spiro's amazing vehicle, I try to shake it off and hurry to catch up with them again. I spend the rest of the walk into the village silently castigating myself. This is Greece, filled with the buffest of man bods, and here I am, fixated on an unexpected kindness and a glimpse of forearm.

I've been away from home—and from Anthony—too long.

As we walk up to a likely looking taverna on the waterfront, I decide to throw expense to the winds and call Anthony as soon as I can get service on my phone.

There are a handful of tables scattered on a deck hewn from the smooth wood of olive trees. We are seated right away at a table beside the water. The deck is bleached almost white from the sun and forms a part of the dock. There is a quiet splash of waves against the hulls of a dozen or more fishing boats that are moored nearby, and the air is alive with the gentle tinkling of wind through the riggings. The taverna deck is festive, draped in wisteria and fairy lights, though only two of the tables have diners. A family of four, plus a round, happy baby, enjoy a meal consisting of a dozen communal dishes crammed into the center of a large table. I resist the urge to lean over and photograph the whole thing.

Barely.

Once I know where we are to be seated, I mumble something about needing the washroom and then head off to find a quiet spot to make my call.

The time difference is seven hours, so I feel like I have a good chance to catch him, especially if he's on his lunch hour. I check my phone and see I've got three out of four bars—that should be plenty.

It takes a moment for the call to click through, but it only rings once before it's picked up.

"Anthony Hearst's office," says a light, young, decidedly *not-* Anthony voice.

"Uh—his office?" I ask, feeling stupid. "Isn't this his cell phone?"

"Yes—yes it *is!*" the voice chirps animatedly. "But Mr. Hearst is in a meeting and can't be disturbed. Who's calling, please?"

I am so thrown off I forget my own name for a moment. Anthony never hands off his cell phone. He turns it off all the time—*most* irritatingly—but will never relinquish it to anyone.

"I—it's Gia. His fiancée," I stammer before I manage to get a grip on myself.

"Gianna!" The woman's voice warms immediately. "I *thought* I spotted your name on the screen. How *are* you? Are you still in Athens?"

This warm, lovely voice throws me right off. In the first place, it does not sound *at all* like it belongs to a fifty-year-old spinster. "Is this Melanie?" I ask cautiously.

There is a squeal on the other end of the phone that makes me pull it away from my ear for a moment. By the time I put it back, I've missed half of what she's said. ". . . told you about me? I've heard so much about you! It's great to finally meet you, even if it's only over the phone. Are you so excited to see all the plans falling into place for the wedding? And when will you be back? Sometime this week?"

This barrage of questions is too much, when all I have in my head is an exchange of a bit of anticipatory sexual banter with my fiancé. "I—uh—no, probably not this week," I say, grasping onto the easiest question to answer. "Is there any way I can speak to Anthony for a moment?"

"Not right now—oh, hold on, Gianna, just a sec—"

Melanie's giggle is almost as shrill as her shriek, and even though she's no longer talking to me, her voice is still so loud I have to yank the phone away from my ear a second time.

"Suze!" she crows. "You are *such* a babe! I love cupcakes! This *totally* slaps!"

Suddenly Melanie's voice is back and thankfully closer to a regular volume. "Oh, hey, Gianna, sorry 'bout that. The people who work in this place are *so* sweet, honestly. Listen, let me make a note, and I'll have him call you back this afternoon."

"Uh—thanks," I mumble. At that moment she gets interrupted again, and I'm finally able to end the call.

I take a minute to go stare at myself in the ladies' room mirror, but it's cracked across and makes me look even more discombobulated than I feel. This is my own doing—I'm the one who took off on this trip, leaving Anthony to deal with all the wedding stuff right in the week before his company goes public. It's no wonder he doesn't have time to talk with me.

I use a tissue to clean up the sweat-smudged eyeliner under my eyes and decide that when he does call back, I'm definitely going to make it worth his while. Then I make the mistake of Googling "best phone sex techniques," and after a moment or two of scrolling, I wonder if I'm going to need to bleach my phone—and maybe my eyes—before I go out to meet my dad again.

When I finally do make it back to the table, I find that my dad and Raj have been joined by Taki, who has managed to escape his family and order a round of appetizers, in the time I was frantically trying to erase the search history on my phone. Luckily, the food is so good, it's all anyone can talk about. I get a ton of pictures of a brilliantly yellow salad of squash blossoms known as *kolokoythoanthoi*, some deliciously fragrant lamb *apáki*, and the most warm and garlicky pita bread I've ever tasted.

But before we can order the main course, my dad pushes back his chair. I roll my eyes, fully expecting the usual garrulous Aristotle Kostas toast. Instead, he gives me a gentle smile.

"I've had a bite, *koritsi*, and I've taken my medication, and believe it or not, right now your papa is done for the day. Can you drop me at the villa, Taki? I think a good sleep is in order for this old man."

Raj and I both jump to our feet. "I can come with you, Pops," I begin just as Raj says, "Let me see you home, Ari."

But my dad waves his hand at both of us and points at the bottle of wine the server has left in an ice bucket by the table. "Nonsense.

You two sit down. Finish your dinner. Drink the wine—it's the specialty of the house, yes? Infused with lotus flower."

In the flickering candlelight from the tables, he does look tired.

"Are you sure, Papa? I'm happy to . . ."

"Stay, darling. And don't forget our walk down on the beach in the morning," he says. For the first time, his eyes twinkle a little. "After you make my breakfast."

With a chuckle, he takes Taki by the arm, and the two of them head out the door.

The air is warm, slightly sweetened by the flowering wisteria, and heavy with humidity. I should follow my dad's lead and head home, but when Raj holds up the wine bottle, I slide over my glass.

The wine is rich, and its fruity sweetness masks a solid kick that doesn't arrive until a moment or two after swallowing. However, without my dad and Taki present, the atmosphere becomes instantly awkward.

"Listen," I manage, at last. "We can just head off after this drink."

"If that's what you'd prefer. But seriously, I think we've already established that we can have an adult conversation without me being—ah—indiscreet."

"Indiscreet?" This makes me laugh out loud, and he actually blushes a little.

I take a big swallow of the wine. "Considering it was *me* ripping your clothes off that night, I don't think your indiscretion was ever the issue."

"That's—not the way I remember it." He leans back in his chair. "In any case—we've already decided to put the whole thing behind us. And since we both love your dad, I think we'd best just agree to be friends, all right?"

He holds out his wineglass, and I clink the edge with my own. "Friends."

Raj smiles, and we are both saved from saying anything else by the arrival of the server, who recommends the scampi. As she leaves, I narrow my eyes across the table.

"What do you mean 'we both love your dad'?"

He smiles without a trace of embarrassment. "Just what I said. He's a world-renowned scholar and a lovely gent. I feel honored to work with him. Who wouldn't want to?"

I shrug. "Lots of people."

His eyes meet mine again, questioning.

"He's just—such a handful." I glance down at the wine in my glass. "He's used to being the boss, and he's—well, obviously he's an aging Greek male. He's got some pretty old-fashioned views."

Raj's expression softens. "He knows how to push one's buttons, no question," he says, and I can't argue with that.

The scampi arrives, and rather than objecting to me taking a picture of his plate, Raj offers to assist and gets several great shots. Then, as we dig into the luscious dish, between bites he asks me about the writing gig. Less than halfway into the bottle of wine, and I'm suddenly as garrulous as a teenager. When he asks how I spent the afternoon, I actually tell him, and before I know it, all my anxieties about keeping the job and finding my way as a journalist spill out.

"I don't know what you're worried about," he says. "I mean—I know you're following your dad as he chases down Odysseus, but this is your adventure too. That story you told me about the basketball players? Hysterical. You obviously come by your storytelling genes honestly. Work an anecdote like that one in, and you'll win your editor's heart."

"What do you mean, come by it honestly? My dad's an academic, not a journalist."

He takes a long sip of wine and leans back in his chair. "You have to understand, I grew up in London. Every year we had school trips to the British Museum, which is filled with items from India. Watching your dad's show—seeing his interest in repatriating Greek treasures like the Elgin Marbles—inspired me to become an archeologist in the first place. To make new finds, yes, but also to help return objects to the cultures they came from."

Raj traces a finger along the stem of his wineglass. "Your dad? He's a storyteller, first. And when he reached out to me last year, I was totally thrilled, to tell you the truth. A chance to work with someone the caliber of Aristotle Kostas? I'm in."

He drains his wine and then recklessly splits the rest of the bottle between our glasses. "The truth is, I'm supposed to be spending this summer swotting over postdoc grant applications in London. But I'm here because his ideas—well, they captivate me. I want to help him succeed, if I can."

I shake my head. "He talks a good game, my dad."

"Agreed, he does. But so do you."

Enlivened by the warmth and beauty of the night, we end up talking until way too late. The incredible seafood and rich red wine go straight to my head, and soon I am babbling not only about my fears about my father's health but about my relationship with Anthony and all the balls I am dropping for the wedding by being here.

Raj leans forward in his chair and looks at me with an expression I cannot read. "Did you say Anthony Hearst?"

He pronounces it the British way, "Antony," but I nod. "That's him. Why—do you know him?"

He shakes his head. "I—I went to school with someone by that name years ago. But it's such a common name. I'm sure it's not the same person."

"He's from New York, not London, so you're probably right."

Raj leans back in his chair, staring out into the darkened marina, and then with a start, glances at his watch. "Is that the time? I need to get you back. You have an early day with your dad tomorrow."

He gives our server a little wave, and she starts over to our table.

He taps his card on the server's machine and then gives me a tight smile. "Ready?"

I tuck my arms through the sleeves of my cardigan and stand up.

His voice takes on an effusively cheerful note. "Now, about that basketball team," he says as we make our way to the door. "Can you find a way to tie them in to an article about food?"

And, having effectively taken a swift left turn away from all personal subjects, he finds me a cab and waves me off.

chapter eighteen

THURSDAY
Lotus-Infused Wine
Gia Kostas, special correspondent to NOSH, on the south
coast of Crete

*Lotus blossom is native to more southern climes than those of
Crete but somehow still works its beautiful way into the local
cuisine. According to legend, the lotus-eaters were an indolent
crew, all hedonists to the core. Rightly so, for who could resist . . .*

I sleep through my alarm the next morning and instead awaken to
the smell of frying onions and coffee. This provokes a feeling of
nausea so great that I pull the covers back over my head. Why did I
drink all that wine?

The evening comes back to me in snippets that leave me awash in
regret for more than the alcohol. I remember telling Raj my worries
about work and about the wedding—a massive overshare brought on
by wine and the kind of naturally flowing conversation that has been
so absent in all my exchanges with Anthony lately. What I do not
remember is him talking about *his* life.

At all.

So. Once again, slightly sloshed girl acts the fool. At least this
time, I didn't jump his bones. Of course, babbling on about the man
he thinks I cheated on, is exactly *no* better.

I jam the pillow over my face. What. An. Idiot.

The good news is that he's heading back to his dig very early today, so I won't have to face him. He is my dad's colleague. It shouldn't matter if he can't stand me.

The bad news is that somehow—it does matter.

I sit up in bed, suddenly struck by another memory. I'm almost positive I took Raj's advice and wove the story of Paulo into the piece on the lamb souvlaki and drunk-submitted it before I fell into bed. It's always been a hard-and-fast rule of mine to never submit anything—anything—after I've been drinking.

This thought pushes all worries about Raj's feelings toward me aside and nauseates me for real. I throw back the covers, intent on heading straight to the bathroom.

Unfortunately, standing up proves more of a challenge than I expect, and it takes me a full five minutes to navigate the space between my bed and the tiny en suite bathroom. By the time I get there, the nausea has dropped back a little, tamped down behind the giant bass drum that is pounding just beneath the surface of my forehead.

I wash two Tylenol down with water from the shower head and then think, *What the hell?* and climb in, pj's and all. Fifteen minutes later, by the time I emerge from my room, I'm freshly showered and feeling well enough to face the smell of food, at least.

My dad is standing at the stove, humming a little and stirring something in a frying pan.

"Just in time for breakfast, darling!" he cries, waving a pink floral oven mitt at me. "Can I interest you in some eggs? I have a hankering for an omelet."

Catching a glimpse of my expression, he points at an actual *briki*—a Greek coffee pot—steaming on the table and laughs. "Oh, it's like that, is it? Luckily, your coffee is ready."

The coffee is brewed and is so hot and lovely, I'm almost prepared to forgive him for his sexist remarks of the night before.

"This place is nice." I sip the fragrant coffee gingerly. "More work when you have your own kitchen, though."

My dad shrugs and then cracks two eggs with one hand into a mixing bowl. This is a trick I haven't seen him perform since I was very small, and it makes me suddenly nostalgic.

"It's the only accommodation Teresa Cipher could find near the caves. Matala is such a small village. And I like to cook breakfast. We'll go out for a nice dinner with Taki tonight, yes?"

"Where *is* Taki?" I look around. No wonder the place seems so quiet—no morning chatter from Herman.

"He's visiting his family for the day. You and me, we walk down to the caves this morning. Taki will pick us up later, okay?"

"Okay." Flipping open my iPad, I discover that the local internet company has come through, as Tira predicted, and the Wi-Fi is working. I take another sip of coffee to steel me for the horrifying task of checking my e-mail, but there's nothing new waiting in my inbox. Hope surges through me. Maybe the Wi-Fi is still down and last night's ill-advised e-mail didn't send?

I click through to "Sent Mail," and sadly my e-mail to Charlotte is at the top, complete with the drunkenly penned subject line "GIANT Edits." This so discourages me, I toss my phone over onto the couch and swallow the rest of my still-warm cup of coffee. Between the coffee and the Tylenol, my headache is starting to recede, but the sick feeling in my stomach settles over me like a shroud.

"All ready!" My dad flips his spatula in a display of showmanship that backfires when he misses catching it. As the spatula clatters into the sink, he says, "Ha! Meant to do that!"

Scooping up a plate in each hand, he waltzes across to the table and slides one of them in front of me. It contains a perfectly formed omelet, two golden-brown pieces of toast, glistening with butter, and a pair of cherry tomatoes that have been fashioned to resemble rosettes.

"What on earth is this?" I'm shocked out of my gloom by the sheer prettiness of the presentation.

My dad sets his own plate down, discards his floral oven mitts, and gives me a shy grin.

"I want to make up for giving you a hard time last night," he says, spoiling the effect by shaking pepper all over his plate.

"Okay, that's nice and all, but when did you learn to make a perfect omelet like this? And what about these?" I hold up one of the intricately sliced tomato rosettes.

He shrugs and scoops a section of omelet onto his toast before devouring an enormous bite. "I take a cooking class with Kallie—uh—maybe two years ago?" he says, gently spraying toast crumbs.

"So—before she threw you out?" This comes out perhaps a teeny bit more cuttingly than I intend.

His face takes on the resigned look I know so well. "Before she threw me out." He points at my plate with his fork. "You should eat this. You need strength for our hike today, yes?"

I pour a second cup of coffee. I notice someone has freshly replenished the store of sugar packets on the table, so I grab a couple.

"Maybe I'll save mine for later," I say, ripping open the packets. "I'm not feeling that great at the moment."

My dad shovels another forkful of food into his mouth and chuckles. "No? But I hear from Rajnish that you had a lovely meal last night." He points at his phone. "Scampi was it? I'm sorry I missed it."

I manage to answer without blushing.

"It *was* really good. The wine was too. I only had a couple of glasses, but it was clearly too much."

My dad waves his fork dismissively. "Greek wine takes getting used to, *koritsi*. You just need more practice." He points again at my plate. "This sort of breakfast is very good for hangover."

Before I can say anything, he adds, "And yes, I learned *that* after Kallie threw me out too."

I sip my coffee, vowing silently that I will never drink again.

My dad mops the last of the egg off his plate with a crust of toast, pops it in, and then reaches for his backpack.

"I've already packed treats for later, darling. Taki brought a whole selection of *kalitsounia*, perfect for our hike down to the beach. We go explore the caves, yes?"

I groan inwardly and possibly aloud too. "Uh—Pops, I need to do some . . ."

"Gianna Marie Kostas," he interrupts. "Don't forget your promises to your papa, eh? This is our last full day in Crete, and these caves? They have art from the Minoans. The Minoans, *koritsi*. Old when even Odysseus made his way past. You will not regret it. And I promise, I have you back to your precious computer by three. That is only eight a.m. in New York, yes?"

"Okay, fine. Let me . . ."

But just as I reach for my phone on the couch, it pings.

A text from Charlotte. Shit. I haven't even had a chance for a sober look through the file I sent her last night. And it's—I check the time—got to be after one in the morning where she is. This can't be good.

I swallow hard and click on her text.

Now THAT'S what I'm talking about, baby!

Baby? I hastily check the source. It *is* Charlotte's number. As I'm checking, another text comes through.

LOVE Paulo. More like this, Gianna. I'm going to run this
one on Friday. Need another piece for Sunday's newsletter.
Same length. More pix, tho. Give me lots to choose from.
Way to go!

"Holy shit," I blurt, feeling stunned.

"What kind of language is that, coming from the mouth of my baby girl?"

I look up at him and grin. "Sorry, Pops. But—listen to this! Charlotte loved my edits. She's running the piece in the Friday edition and wants another one to run on Sunday!"

"Woo HOO!" He throws his arms wide and dances a quick Greek *sirtaki* across the tiny kitchen, crossing his legs and bobbing a few times for good measure. "That's my little Barbara Walters!"

"Geez, Pops—can you come up with a more contemporary role model for me, please?"

He laughs. "Okay, she's too old, but she is a go-getter, and so are you."

I'm so stoked by this good news, my headache vanishes. A strange feeling of lightness floods through me. I have, quite literally, zero obligations at the moment. The wedding plans are under control. Anthony's mother may come across as a little—ah—opinionated, but she seems very happy to tackle jobs on the wedding list. We can decide on the details—and the dress—when I get back. And my piece for NOSH has been submitted and accepted. A day of wandering in and out of a few caves down by the beach might be just what I need.

To celebrate, I pull up the camera app on my phone, take a picture of my breakfast, and then sit down and eat it. The omelet is nearly cold, but it's loaded with mushrooms and onions and is actually quite tasty.

Since Taki is spending the day with his family and Raj is over at his own worksite on the other side of the island, there's no one else I can pawn the care of my dad off onto, so as I finish the last of my toast, I concede defeat. Tucking my phone into my pocket, I join him at the door.

"That was a most excellent breakfast, Pops," I admit and scoop the key into the pocket of my sundress.

He beams. "A man who lives alone has to learn to look after himself," he says. "Besides, Taki brought almost all the ingredients."

I grin and swing the door open. "Well, you added your own magic, anyway. It's a memorable meal just because you cooked it."

He smiles skeptically at this, but as I will soon discover, truer words were never spoken.

"Maybe you write a story about it?" he says, shouldering his backpack.

"Maybe," I agree, and we head out down the path to the beach.

chapter nineteen

FREAKY FRIDAY
Mushroom Omelet
Gia Kostas, special correspondent to NOSH, along the
southern shore of Crete

Who can deny the pleasures of a warm, cheesy omelet to start the day? Strewn through with mushrooms, which bring their own special something, this omelet is an adventure in eating. You might not be surprised to learn this fine meal is standard the world over, but is never more Greek than when served with . . .

After breakfast, it's an easy fifteen-minute stroll to the beach from our villa. I'm feeling uncomfortably full, so a walk is just what I need. I left my bag behind, tucking my phone and wallet into my pocket with the key. No use risking sand getting into my tablet. In any case, after that weird and joyful text from Charlotte, I'm ready to take a few hours off, for real.

My dad, on the other hand, is wearing his little canvas rucksack, a water bottle for each of us tucked into the outside pockets, and god knows what else inside. In his hands, he carries some kind of elaborately folded paper map, which keeps catching the breeze off the ocean and snapping into his face.

"It's a surveyor's map of the caves," he replies when I ask. "They are usually filled with tourists, but maybe not so much lately. Best to have a map to be safe."

"Can't you just use Google Earth?" I point out the app on his phone. "Easier to read it off your screen, don't you think?"

The delight I get from the look of horror on his face lasts the rest of the way down to the beach.

The sky is a clear, perfect blue; paler over the land than the sea. Where the water and sky meet, the competition between the shades of blue is breathtaking. It is a simply gorgeous day.

I don't really know how the tides work here, but as we step off the path onto the rocky shore, the water seems very close. There's no sandy or pebbled beach, just a shelf of carved volcanic rock against which the waves slap and splash. This section of the cliff face has been eroded by wind and water, and as we turn our backs on the ocean to face the rocky cliff, a cave entrance looms up only a few feet away.

"Okay, well, this is way scarier than I pictured it." I step closer to peek inside. "I thought it was just going to be a few little holes in the rocks by the beach."

"Darling, it looks worse than it is. And see?" He rustles around inside his pack. "I've brought us both headlamps. It'll be as bright as daylight in there, I promise you."

It takes a few minutes to strap on the headlamps, and when we do, the little beams of light jump all over the inside of the cave walls, bringing back my earlier feelings of nausea.

"How deep does this one go, anyway?" I ask as I follow him inside. My head *is* actually starting to spin a little.

"Not far." My dad trains the beam of his headlamp onto his map. "Perhaps a few hundred yards to the next section."

"The *next* section? Just how many caves are there down here?"

"We don't have to go all the way through them, darling, if you are nervous."

"I'm not freaking nervous," I snap.

I totally am.

"It's just your damn headlamp is making me feel sick."

This is the truth—I really am starting to feel quite weird. In the harsh halogen light from the lamps, the wet, rocky walls of the cave begin to undulate at the edge of my vision.

Suddenly, though I could have sworn he was at least twenty feet away, I can feel my dad's hand on my arm.

"Why don't you just sit down for a minute, *koritsi*? Look—here's a nice flat rock. If you're sitting still, you'll get used to the light in no time. I'll just have a peek ahead to the end of this section and be right back."

And then his hand is gone, and his light is gone, and I am sitting alone in a dank cave that smells of seaweed and salt and maybe something dead.

I drop my head into my hands and rub my eyes. When I look up again, the cave walls ripple out and in, out and in, like they're made of tidal water and not of rock.

"Pops?" I'm yelling, but instead of carrying, my voice falls like a clump of tangled seaweed from my mouth. Aren't caves supposed to be echoey?

Not this one.

"Papa?" I try again.

He doesn't reply.

I stare down at the sand between my feet and watch the clump of tangled seaweed that had been my voice begin to writhe and twist. Like it might really be snakes and not seaweed.

My stomach clenches again, and I scramble away from the seaweed snakes, just in case. My head thrums. The walls shimmy.

"This isn't the freaking headlamp." I feel my forehead with both hands. "Maybe I really am sick? What if those eggs were bad?"

My head throbs under the strap of the headlamp, and when I rub the sore spot, one of my fingers trips the switch. I'm suddenly plunged into absolute darkness. There's a moment where the weird head-spinning is superseded by raw fear pulsing through me like a silver lightning bolt—bright and vicious and murderous.

Then I find the switch and flip it on, and the sharp, almost blue halogen beam shoots across the cave again. Just the sight of the light helps slow my heart rate, but when I turn my head in the direction I think my dad went, the stupid walls are still dancing. Worse, as the light from my headlamp bounces around, the wet cave walls begin to light up with some kind of phosphorescence, flashing green and blue and red and gold. It's like being at a seventies party with a glitter ball. Except without the party. Or the glitter ball.

I'm suddenly sure the flashing lights are going to drive me into some kind of aneurysm—it's in the family, after all—so I hurriedly look down again, aiming the light at the sandy floor of the cave. And suddenly, my phone begins to ring.

This makes me jump, triggering the walls again, which means it takes me something like five rings before I finally get the thing out of my pocket.

As I yank it out, I realize I've been carrying the solution to my little headlamp problem with me all this time.

"Idiot." I slide my thumb across the screen. "You've got a flash-light on your freaking phone."

Using the other hand, I snatch the stupid headlamp off and put the phone to my ear.

"Darling," my mother's voice trills, a little tinny through the phone. "The headlamp is not the problem."

"Well, *something* is making me sick," I complain.

The beam of my headlamp catches a sudden movement across the sand near one of my feet. I'm pretty sure it's only a tiny crab, but when I jump, I land almost all the way back at my sitting rock out of sheer nerves.

My mother's voice continues. "It was your father who made *me* sick, darling, but you know that. Biggest mistake I ever made in my life, that man. So delighted to not have him to look after anymore. He's *your* problem now."

I shine the light from my phone back at the rock I was just sitting on. My mother appears there now, reclining a little on one elbow. She's wearing her cropped jean jacket with the cuffs rolled up, yoga pants, and Uggs. She's got her big coffee mug that reads "One Cranky Bitch" and takes a swig from the side without the chip in it.

I look back down at my phone. The flashlight is still shining, but the screen reads zero bars.

So. Many. Questions.

"*My* problem?" is what comes out when I finally manage to form words. It's not really what I want to ask first, but she's laughing now, and her voice is still coming out of the phone.

"Yessiree, all yours. I mean, the man can't even buy groceries without screwing up, right?"

I look down at the phone. The screen actually fades out, but the flashlight is still shining on my mother, who is sitting in front of me clear as day.

"Just a minute, here . . ." I begin, but she cuts me off. And as she speaks, the screen of the phone lights up again.

"Oh, don't get me wrong. You are the best thing that ever happened to me. But I was nineteen, for Chrissakes. My whole life was rainbows and unicorns. *Literal* unicorns, Gia. I mean, I still had a unicorn on my backpack that year at university when I first met Aristotle."

I can't help wincing, and she raises an eyebrow as she sips her coffee.

"Oh, he was no pedophile," she says chummily. "I was nearly twenty-one the first time we had sex, and he was cruising in on fifty. But he likes 'em young. How old is that Kallie?"

I lift one shoulder. "Thirty-one, I think. But she's dumped him now too."

My mom barks a laugh and pours the dregs of her coffee cup onto the sand. I laugh too—I can't help it—but I edge a little closer. In the light from my phone, I can see the lines around her eyes. She does love to laugh, my mom.

"I guess he's on the hunt again, then?" She brushes a fleck of sand from one sleeve.

I shrug and sidle still closer. "He's looking for something else right now. I'm not really sure what. It's to do with Odysseus—with his work."

For the first time, my mom's smile falters. "Always the work. What is it with men and their work?"

"Everybody has to work, Mom. I mean, isn't Harold still a mailman?"

The smile returns to her eyes and she gives a throaty chuckle. "Yeah, but unlike your father, he leaves his work at the office. And anyway, the sex with him is *so* much better."

I suddenly remember why I don't like talking to my mother about relationships.

Her relationships, anyway.

"Darling, can you tilt that light away a little? You're shining it right into my eyes," she complains.

"Sorry," I say automatically and point my phone at a spot on the sand about halfway between us.

"Thank you, darling. And in any case, don't forget what I told you," she says.

The screen on my phone winks out in my hand.

"Mom?" I look from the phone back up to where she's sitting, but the rock is empty.

Snatching my headlamp up from the ground, I jam it back onto my head. The light bounces off the wet rock inside the cave, and as I look down, a swirl of water washes over my feet.

I shake my phone to get the screen to light up, but it no longer has a screen. Instead, it's a small stone tablet, just like the ancient Greeks used to write on.

Just like the one my dad is looking for.

That does it. Clutching the no-longer-a-phone, I hurry toward the rocky opening that my dad vanished through, calling his name into the darkness. Around me, the walls sparkle and wobble like an unstable galaxy.

Rushing blindly forward, I hit the stalecti—stalegmi—the stupid pointy rock hanging from the ceiling. It's just a glancing blow, but enough to knock me to my knees; the sound of my cry still strangely muted.

Luckily, the water isn't deep, but it's definitely covering the floor. The place I've landed is sandy, not rocky, so my knees are fine. I've only grazed my skull, but it was enough to knock my headlamp out. After feeling my forehead and determining the damage is minimal, I manage to get the light back on. The rocky ceiling appears to have broken at least one of the tiny halogen bulbs, because the light is much dimmer when I finally get it working again. I try flipping my phone light on, but it's still a stone tablet.

"There's no service in here," says a voice, and I look up to see Devi leaning against the cave wall. She's wearing her scrubs, which I think are green, though it's hard to tell in the dark, and her stethoscope is looped around her neck. "And that phone of yours is looking pretty odd at the moment, to tell you the truth."

"For crying out loud, Devi—not you too!" I peer at her in the reflected light from my headlamp. "I was just talking to my mom."

"I love your mom," says Devi warmly. "Everything important I needed to know in life, I learned from your mom when I was a teenager."

I sigh, remembering this all too well. Case in point: her very Hindu mom side-eyeing mine at school pickup after Devi came home full of a joyful description of gay marriage.

"Trust me, she's just the same. Oversharing about her sex life. Ugh."

Devi stuffs her stethoscope into a pocket. "You're too sensitive. She's just got a happy life. You should celebrate that."

"Look, I'm too busy trying to keep track of my dad, okay? He's somewhere in here, but as usual, I've lost him."

"He's fine," she says reassuringly. "Small doses of psilocybin have been shown to really assist people, particularly seniors. Opens their minds."

"What do you mean, psilocybin? Is that in his blood thinners?"

"Ha! No fear. Why don't you ask Ryan?"

And there, just around the corner of a particularly shiny rock, I spot Ryan, smoke curling up from behind his back.

Ryan Taylor. Ex-boyfriend, part-time comic book store clerk, and closet smoker. I am now officially surprised by nothing.

"I can see you," I say drily. "You might as well come out."

He doesn't really, just sidles a little closer to the now fairly dim circle of light generated by my headlamp. He's wearing the exact clothes he was wearing when I last saw him. Jeans, plaid shirt rolled to the elbows, displaying a full right sleeve of tattoos—every image referencing a separate Bukowski poem—and Blundstones. It will shock no one to note that his hair is shaved to a perfect number two on the sides, his man bun is neatly knotted on top, and his beard smells of cedar and sage.

He blows a puff of chocolate-scented smoke out of the corner of his mouth. "Dev," he says, not even speaking to me. "You know I haven't done shrooms since second year. Edibles only these days."

"You're still smoking." I cough a little. I really have no interest in talking to Ryan ever again, either in actual human form or as some kind of apparition, but I can't help feeling hurt that the conversation between these two beings manifested by my own brain doesn't include me.

"I never smoked in your room, Gia," he says, meeting my eyes at last. "I feel like that was more than generous. All your harping was the second strike toward our breakup, you know. And anyway, I'm not smoking anymore. Vaping isn't the same."

There is a lot I want to say on this subject, but I'm distracted.

"The *second* strike? What was the first?"

His gaze shifts away from me in the darkness, and he fidgets with his e-cigarette.

"Ryan. You told me you broke up with me the first time because I didn't like slam poetry. You never even mentioned the smoking. Or—like—my aversion to the smoking."

"Yeah, well, your lack of any literary interest at all was also a problem, right? But really, it was the third strike. We would never have worked, Gia."

I do not disagree with this final statement.

But.

"What do you mean the third strike? What was the *first* strike? And why are you using a baseball analogy when you abhor organized sporting events?"

I hear him mumble something under his breath.

"What? What did you say?"

"I said—I knew you were faking it."

"I wasn't . . ." I begin, but don't quite find a way to finish the sentence.

"You were," comes Devi's voice out of the darkness.

I whip my headlamp around but can't see her anywhere. She must have slipped through the opening to the next cave.

"Well, not *all* the time," I admit.

"Honesty," says Ryan virtuously, "is important in a relationship. And what about Anthony?"

"What *about* Anthony?" I'm feeling fully exasperated now. "We're not talking about Anthony here."

Ryan exhales a mouthful of chocolate vapor. "You need to be more honest with yourself," he says. "If you ever get out of here. Which, you know, you might not."

For the first time in this conversation with the ghost of boyfriends past, I feel a chill. "Can you help me?" I whisper.

He shrugs and gives me his most charming smile. "Not really. Besides, you're not the one who needs help at the moment."

And he literally vanishes in a puff of chocolate-scented smoke.

Vapor. Whatever.

After Ryan leaves, the walls lose most of their sparkle. Or maybe the one remaining functional bulb in my headlamp is slowly beginning to fade. A metaphor for my situation?

I call out for help—from my dad, from Devi and my mom, even from Ryan—so long and so loud that my voice begins to hurt.

I don't mind admitting that I quite nearly lose it here. Abandoned—and not for the first time—by my father, lost in some cavern near the shore of the Mediterranean Sea, which at the moment is lapping gently around my ankles, and plainly no longer in my right mind. Anyone would cry.

I'm not sure how long I wander after that, one hand out in front of my face to ward off further stalactite encounters, and the other tracing my route by following the damp, rocky wall of the cave.

A long time.

As the sparkling walls dull, the water rises, and soon I am trudging, zombielike, through knee-deep water. I step through the entrance to yet another cavern, when, from above me, a spray of water douses me in the face. It's a freezing splash, and like any cold shower, it brings me a moment of clarity.

I am in *real* trouble here.

And right then, with a tiny, audible click, my headlamp dies for good.

chapter twenty

POSSIBLY STILL FRIDAY
Sardi's Manhattan
Gia Kostas, special correspondent to NOSH, in an ancient
  Minoan labyrinth, Crete

The treasured memory of a past experience can often be inspiration in itself. And who can forget the first sips of a drink served by a master . . .

Okay, I just have to pause here to say that it's taken me a while, but I think I've finally figured it out. And in retrospect, I can say with some certainty that as much as I want to blame my dad for all of this, it *was* likely an honest mistake.

An honest mistake that finds me sitting here in this sweet, indigo hour after the sun has vanished but the stars have not yet emerged. Sitting here on the sand holding the hand of an old man who has his eyes closed and is singing quietly to himself in Greek. Perhaps he is singing about the stars? After our last conversation, I am unwilling to ask.

We are both leaning back on a still-warm log, waiting for Taki to arrive. My earlier plan to return to the guesthouse and be working by three has long vanished by the wayside. Instead, we are here on the sand waiting for Taki to collect us at seven and take us for dinner. An early dinner and then an early night.

It will not be an early night.

Because what *is* seven, even? What *is* dinner? What is—that is—*who* is Taki?

These words, you may guess, are from our last conversation. The conversation with my dad, one Dr. Aristotle Evangelos Alexandros Kostas, seventy-two-year-old stoner extraordinaire.

You know, I think there's gotta be more stars in the sky over the Mediterranean than over New York. Even accounting for light pollution, I've seen more stars in my short stay in this country than I have in a lifetime in my own city. But right now, thinking of what we've just been through and staring up into the endless, limitless depths of the Milky Way, I am sure of only one thing.

There are no stars in hell.

W ell now. Where was I? Ah, yes—lost in a labyrinth, deep under the earth, never to be seen again. That's where. So, yeah, no flames, maybe, but still hell.

I have no idea how much time has passed when I finally, finally have a bit of luck. My phone not functional, my headlamp totally dead, my voice no longer able to yell, I stumble through yet another gap in this stony, endless hellscape. But something has changed. This time, I feel a definite gust of air—cool air—in my face. Enough to blow my hair back.

"Pops!" My voice hisses into the darkness.

No answer.

"Pops?"

And then—because it's really, *really* dark—"Papa?"

The air swirls around my face again, and I hear a faint dripping noise; distant, like a neighbor's leaky tap, followed by what can only be described as a tiny giggle.

And then—maybe fifteen feet away—the screen of an iPhone lights up, and I can see his glasses reflecting the glare. He's perched on a rocky outcropping on the far side of this cavern.

I'm beside him in a second, which turns out to be lucky, as his phone turns itself off almost immediately.

Stupid low-power mode.

"Pops, it's me. I'm right here."

"Oh!" His voice comes through the velvet darkness. "My beautiful Gianna! I am *so* proud of you, my girl." Somehow he finds my hand and squeezes it gently.

"Okay, Pops, that's really nice, but—listen, I'm trying to tell you something important. We have to get out of here—I think I need to see a doctor."

"First place, ahead of everyone. The red ribbon. My girl."

I take a deep breath and give up feeling around for the phone. Instead, I squeeze his hand back, hard.

"Pops, listen to me. That red ribbon came from a spelling bee which took place at least fifteen years ago. I need you to focus. We have a problem here—this is serious."

"Of course, my darling. My ears are open to you. My soul is open to you."

The total weirdness of this shuts me up, and I take an inadvertent step back and drop his hand for a moment. This turns out to be a mistake. I hear the giggle again and then a rustle, and he's gone.

"Pops!" I'm yelling now and stumble a little. "This is *so* not funny."

For the first time, I realize I can see the shape of the rock walls around me. Two or three more tentative steps and the smooth, damp surface of a huge boulder is under my fingers. I sidle around it to find I'm at the mouth of the cave. Lurching out of the entrance, I literally fall over my father, who is sitting just outside on the sand.

I am, at the same time, both completely freaked out by this whole experience and entirely grateful to be breathing the fresh sea air. The spot where my dad is sitting looks nothing like the location where we entered the caves what seems like an eternity ago. Here, instead of sea-polished stone, there is sand; mostly white but flecked with red and tan and black sparkles.

Across the water, the sun has dropped below the horizon, so the beach isn't blazing with color but rather glowing in a rich, golden light. Which means I have been trapped in that underground hell for the entire day. The blue of the sea is now a plummy, wine red, and as I sink down beside my father, it is lapping at his legs, rising a little higher as each new breaker swooshes in.

Kneeling beside him in the water, I can see that behind his little, round John Lennon sunglasses, his eyes are open. He smiles gently.

I clutch his arm. "Pops, do you feel sick? Are you—are you seeing things?"

His smile broadens, but I have to admit there's not really a person I recognize behind those eyes.

"I am filled with love," he intones, almost like a chant. "I *am* love made manifest. I so love you, my sweet Penny—my *lucky* Penny. There's never been anyone but you."

I take a deep breath of the warm, salty air and try again. I can't remember him ever referring to me as his lucky penny before, but nothing is really making sense at the moment.

I take his face in my hands and force him to look at me. "Pops, it's me—Gia. Are you good to stand up?"

The lids of his eyes close behind his glasses again, and I can feel panic returning to my gut. Eyes tightly closed, he says, "I am *so* good. I am love. I am the universe."

Okay then.

"Papa," I say again. "I—I think I've been drugged. I'm—ah—I've been seeing some really weird stuff that I'm almost positive isn't actually there."

The next wave slaps me firmly in the chest, and I'm now wet to the shoulders. As it has before on this endlessly long day, the cool water brings clarity. But this time?

It also brings understanding.

My dad is not hearing what I'm spelling out. And there is no universe in which Ari Kostas would not be entirely horrified to hear his daughter has ingested an illegal substance. Which leaves open only two possibilities.

One: That Ari Kostas has well and truly lost his mind. Or two . . .

Another wave splashes up, soaking us both. I have questions that need answers, but first? I have to get us out of the sea.

Grabbing my father under one arm, I struggle a minute to ensure my own feet are solidly underneath me before I stand up. Below the waves, the sand shifts under the soles of my shoes. The water, which is starting to chill in the cooling air, tugs gently at the hem of my sundress.

Or two: We both ingested said substance together.

"For crying out loud, Pops." I haul on his arm, trying to pull him to his feet. "Where did you get those mushrooms?"

He blinks at me owlishly but actually puts some effort into standing. By the time we're both vertical, the water is swirling above our knees. The tide is rising very fast.

"Mushrooms?" he repeats. "You mean—from breakfast?"

I stagger forward, one arm around his waist. The angle of the sand beneath the water is steeper than I expect, so we actually have to lift our feet quite high to make forward progress toward the beach. It takes my dad a few tries to get the hang of this. We're finally making headway when he catches his foot and drops to one knee.

"Yes. From breakfast." I'm puffing with exertion but manage to haul him back up. The water is only ankle-deep here, and my raw panic is receding. Into its place steps something else. Something like fury.

"The mushrooms in the omelet, Pops. Did Taki bring them home with the rest of the groceries?"

"I'm really quite wet," my dad says, looking down at his legs as we stagger up onto dry land for the first time. "Goodness. I should have worn my swim trunks instead of these trousers."

I give his arm a little, exasperated shake. "Never mind your trousers. Did Taki give you those mushrooms, Pops?"

For the first time, his eyes clear a little, and he chuckles. "No, I bought them myself. From a girl—a sweet little thing wearing a tie-dye shirt like I haven't seen since I was a boy. Pink and purple and indigo blue."

Okay. My fury at Taki eases a little. By this time, I've hauled my dad up the beach past the tide line, which is marked with a thick layer of dry, black kelp. We shuffle onto a section of almost pure white sand, still warm from the sun. The beaches here don't seem to have as many stray logs strewn about as the Jersey Shore has at home, but I spot one at last and half push, half guide my dad toward it.

"You sit here." I point at the end of the log where wind and water have worn the wood smooth as glass. "Tell me about this girl."

Instead of perching where I direct him, he sinks down into the sand beside the log and leans back against it. As he does, the breast pocket of his shirt lights up briefly, and I realize his phone is not lost in the Mediterranean after all. But when I reach for it, he captures my hand and clasps it flat against his chest and closes his eyes.

For a moment, I think I can feel his heart beating against my fingertips, but exasperation is starting to push back my own fuzziness, and I snatch my hand away.

"The girl?"

He sighs, eyes still tightly closed. "On the way home from dinner last night, Taki and I go in the *magazi*. We buy eggs and milk and bread inside, but they have no mushrooms."

His glasses slide down to the very tip of his nose, and behind them, his eyes flutter open again. "I'm not worried. We have feta. But then Taki forgets his grappa and goes back inside, and I see this girl. She is standing just around the corner, and she's holding two little plastic bags with fresh mushrooms. I buy only one small bag because they were expensive. But delicious, don't you think?"

I'm not even sure where to begin. I slump down into the sand and lean on the log beside him.

I mean, yes, my dad was a child of the sixties, but if you could have heard his antidrug diatribes aimed at teenaged Gia? OMG. Drugs were the Antichrist. Drugs of any stripe—including weed— were the root of everything that was wrong with the world. They were the scourge of society. The bathroom stalls of corporate America were awash in the white powder of their own destruction, and there's no way a daughter of his was . . .

Well, you get the picture. Of course, double standards abounded, and in fact, my dad took me to Sardi's for my "first drink"—his words—when I turned twenty-one. I got to order whatever I wanted, so I ordered a double Manhattan. Manhattans happened to be the specialty of the house at the Rusty Nail, the little corner pub which was a favorite with my journalism class. Unbeknownst to my father, of course. The Nail was conveniently located just around the corner from Cooper Square, home to the Arthur L. Carter Journalism Institute, and from second year onward, my friends and I were regulars. Gillian, the bartender, specialized in sixties-era drinks and schooled us well.

Still, that Sardi's Manhattan was pretty special.

In any case, my dad's institutional blindness toward the evils of alcohol aside, he didn't toke, snort, or huff his way through graduate school, and he fully expected his daughter to keep to the same straight-and-narrow standard.

Which, apart from a one-night foray into Ecstasy-fueled dancing during my extremely short-lived ska phase, I did. It doesn't hurt that I can't stand the smell of weed. The variety of choice of my high school compatriots was particularly skunky—likely a reflection of quality directly resulting from limited student finances, which made it worse. So, apart from the odd Sidecar—another specialty at the Rusty Nail— Gianna Kostas was, and continues to be, one clean-living human.

Oh, how the mighty have fallen.

My dad's phone lights up again, forcing me to focus. I lean forward and point to his pocket.

"Pops, someone is texting you. And we need to call Taki to come get us, okay?"

My dad ignores this completely and stares down at his wet chinos. "All this comes from crossing the River Styx. But it was worth it, *koritsi*. For now I know the truth. I saw the light. I *know* the light. *Koritsi*—I *am* the light. And so are you."

And he beams his gentle madman's smile at me again.

I give up asking and snatch the phone out of his pocket. He minds this not at all and, instead, leans his head back against the log and begins to hum quietly.

His phone screen has darkened again, and when I ask him for his password, his humming only gets a little louder and a little more recognizably Greek. I think I catch a snippet of a Nana Mouskouri song that I remember from childhood. In desperation, I punch 1234 into the phone, and it opens right up. I don't have the brain power to wonder why his phone is working so far away from any Wi-Fi. Instead, breathing a word of thanks to the Goddess Nana, I open his text message app.

There are seventeen unanswered texts from Taki. I scroll through them quickly. The only one I bother to read all the way through is the last one, which was apparently sent from the village police station. The text is a mixture of Greek and English words, and almost incoherent with panic. It seems he's been trying to organize a search party, but the local police will not agree to participate until twenty-four hours have passed.

I take a deep breath and try to focus my scattered thoughts.

Opening Google Maps, I take a screenshot of our blue location dot hovering somewhere on the southern shoreline of Crete and then start typing.

> Taki, this is Gia. My dad and I are on the beach. We're okay but lost. Somewhere walking distance from our villa—see attached map. Can you help?

I hit reply and then hurriedly add a second message.

> Do NOT bring the police. Will explain all when you get here.

And then I lean back beside my still humming father and watch the stars winking to life, one by one, each piercing the perfect indigo sky.

chapter twenty-one

SATURDAY
Maccu
Gia Kostas, special correspondent to NOSH, in Catania, Sicily

A change of scene from one gorgeous island to another may bring the similarities of the locales to mind, but make no mistake—the cuisines can vary wildly. A case in point is this brilliant Sicilian soup, which plumbs the depths of the Mediterranean for its ingredients but has a flavor so unique . . .

Twelve hours later, and I think I can safely say that everyone—in our little touring party, at least—is no longer stoned. Mind you, my vision is still a little wonky, the periphery inclined to sparkle if I move my head too quickly. Other than that, I seem to be not too physically damaged, at least, by my journey into hell. I'm not sure if it's the early morning or the fact that we are departing his home country or even just a carry-over from yesterday's spaciness, but my dad is strangely quiet.

We are leaving Greece at an ungodly hour today for a sojourn to Italy. It's too early for breakfast, so I hastily wrap the last of Taki's *kalitsounia*—tiny cheese pastries—in a paper napkin for later. When we step outside the guesthouse, Taki and Herman are waiting in a car he has borrowed to drive us to the airport. As he climbs out of the car to help load our bags in the trunk, Taki looks hungover. He is unshaven with red eyes, and even his mustache looks rumpled in the first light of dawn.

Herman, on the other hand, is full of beans and, in the absence of conversation, decides to fill the vehicle with his own voice. He is literally singing an aria as I slide into the back seat of the car. I admit to feeling grateful to be avoiding another ride in the Cretan hillbilly truck, but the price we pay in cockatoo caroling is pretty high at six thirty in the morning. Worse, as I hunt for my seat belt, Herman snaps the napkin-wrapped *kalitsounia* off my lap and lustily gobbles it in a shower of crumbs as we pull away from the curb. I'm still brushing the pastry flakes off my dress when he flutters from his perch on the back of the front seat and alights between me and the window. Nestling right up beside me, he opens his mouth and lets out what sounds like a rolling belch directly into my ear.

This causes Taki to laugh so hard he almost loses control of the car.

"Hermie show how much he like you," Taki insists. "Birds not really burp. Until now, this he do only for me."

"Chairíte," Herman says, and then, *"Kalimera."*

When no one responds, he continues to alternate the two words, unceasingly, several dozen times.

Since everyone else in the car appears to be comatose, I finally whisper, *"Kalimera,"* back at Herman, which makes him bob several times in his spot on the seat behind the driver but also mercifully shuts him up.

Taki and Herman are not accompanying us on this leg of the journey, as we will, apparently, be doing more sailing than driving to get to the next few stops. Besides, Taki has another gig lined up on Crete before he rejoins us back in Athens. After unloading my dad's bag from the back, Taki, his eyes swimming, kisses my father on both cheeks and then does the same to me.

"Is true honor to accompany you and your papa," he whispers to me, the alcohol content of his breath verging on the flammable. "He is great man—strong belief in his work. In searching for truth."

I finally manage to escape his embrace but still feel a pang of regret as I watch him drive off, Herman's beak pressed to the back window. One less person to help me wrangle my dad, perhaps? And one less bird.

Today's journey isn't too arduous, but it does cross a border, thus the early morning visit to the airport. Still, the lineup through security isn't long, and the access to decent airport Wi-Fi is a huge relief after the spotty airwaves of our little villa in Crete.

I have a quick e-mail exchange with Charlotte that makes me happy—her delight at what is really little more than a sketched outline of our upcoming destinations is very sustaining. More thrilling still is her response to my latest submission.

> Before deadline and exactly on word count. And your description of the journey makes my mouth water even more than the food. People are starved for stories about distant shores at the moment. Reader feedback has been fantastic. More of this, please!

On reading this, I can't suppress a sigh of relief. It's got to be a sign. We are leaving Crete, and I'm convinced that all the chaotic and strange experiences of this journey must now be behind us.

These positive thoughts carry me all the way onto the tarmac, where I stop in disbelief.

I should have known something was up when we were ushered away from the main departure hall.

Wordlessly, I grab my dad's arm.

"Yes, darling?" He still looks pretty spacey behind his glasses, but I don't have time to worry about that now.

"What the hell? Can we both even fit inside that plane?"

On the tarmac in front of us stands a tiny Cessna, blue and red, with a propeller on the nose. As we approach, the door swings open, and a set of stairs unfolds from the inside. There is literally a man standing beside the plane pumping gas into it with what looks like the hose you use for a car.

My dad smiles vaguely. "None of the major airlines fly direct, *koritsi*. This will have us there by noon, instead of losing nine hours to a layover." He pats his briefcase. "Our Teresa, she thinks of everything."

When I follow my dad inside, I can see right away that the plane is not only tiny but also decently ancient. The carpet on the floor is worn away in places, and the seats are upholstered in a kind of prehistoric blue Naugahyde that reminds me of movies set in the sixties. There are only five passenger seats, and as I buckle myself into the second row, anxiety flows through me. My dad is still acting uncharacteristically silent, and I don't even have Taki and Herman to look to for distraction. By the time a lone other passenger climbs in behind my dad and me, and the pilot reaches across to hoist up the steps and slam the door closed, my heart is pounding so loud, I'm sure they all can hear it.

I've never been in a plane with an open cockpit before, and the sight of dozens of switches and dials does nothing to calm my nerves. When my dad reaches over to pat my hand from his seat across the aisle, I nearly jump out of my skin.

Worse, I let out a tiny shriek, which is loud enough to make the captain turn around. For the first time, I notice she is a woman. She flashes me a broad smile and, reaching an arm behind the empty seat beside her, beckons me forward.

I look over at my dad, but he's ignoring me, staring blankly out the tiny porthole, so I flip my belt buckle open and walk up the aisle. To be clear, this aisle is made up of the space between the two seats in the row in front of ours, so my walk takes all of three strides. I'm five foot five, but I still have to hunch over, as the ceiling is so low.

The captain grins up at me. Her smile is brilliant white in a very tanned face, and her short dark hair is even curlier than my own.

"Why don't you sit up here?" she asks, patting the seat beside her. "It'll give you a better view, yes?"

"Isn't that—isn't that the copilot's seat?" I cast another quick glance over my shoulder at Ari.

Still staring out the window. I doubt he's even noticed I'm up here, dammit.

She widens her eyes at me. "Not at all. God is my copilot, you know, and he doesn't need a seat."

Her expression of wide-eyed innocence crumbles at my look of horror, and her laugh comes quick and throaty. "I'm kidding you. Really. Sit here with me. It's the best spot for anxious flyers in these little planes. You see more; you feel more in control."

She pats the seat again and then hastily moves her captain's hat, hooking it with her suit jacket on the far side of her seat.

Reluctantly, I sit down, sliding my legs carefully away from the dashboard and under the steering wheel.

That's right. My seat has a steering wheel.

I swallow hard, as beside me, the captain flips a switch causing the propeller on the nose of the plane to spin. As I reach for my seat belt, she stretches a gloved hand over to me.

"Delia Uccello," she says, enclosing my hand in her warm grip.

"Gia Kostas." I can barely get this out, my mouth is so dry.

"Nice to meet you, Gia," she says, and gives a single firm shake before releasing my hand.

In the sleepy, distant past of this morning, I had fully planned to spend this flight toiling over my next piece for Charlotte, but with a steering wheel between my knees, my plans will have to change.

Captain Delia slips on a pair of sunglasses—aviators, of course—and suddenly, she is a no-nonsense professional. A man appears on the tarmac in front of us, waving a pair of orange flashlights, and we lurch backward for a moment before beginning our taxi onto the runway. I clutch the wheel in front of me as the plane shudders, and without missing a beat, Captain Delia reaches across and pats my knee.

"Probably a good idea to keep your hands off the wheel, at least until we get into the air," she yells over the roar of the engine.

I yank my hands backward, horrified, which makes her laugh again.

"There's a handle right there on the door if you need something to hold on to."

I reach out and clutch the worn-looking handle on the door that she indicates, only to have the rubber casing come off in my hand. By this time, we've bumped away from the terminal and onto a runway, the old plane rattling and shaking around us. The propeller on the nose of the plane has vanished into the faintest blur, and my head is forced back as the tiny machine accelerates.

Before I have a chance to give more than a single thought to my own mortality, we are unexpectedly airborne, and everything changes.

My stomach makes the leap back into my body a second or so after the wheels leave the ground, but weirdly enough, it doesn't bother me at all. The ground disappears entirely for a moment as we soar upward, and all I can see is the endless blue of a Grecian sky, dusted only distantly by the faintest wraith of white cloud. For a moment, the edges of the sky take on the unmistakable indigo of twilight. I'm not sure if this is a trick of the windscreen or not, because the effect disappears instantly as we level out over the rippled surface of the Mediterranean Sea.

I am filled with a sense of total exhilaration that I cannot remember ever feeling before. Certainly even my recent experience with mushrooms cannot possibly compare. It's no wonder drug addicts talk about getting high—being literally high in the front seat of this tiny, ancient plane is the most thrilling experience of my life.

I feel a nudge and turn to see Delia grinning at me. "What did I tell you?" she yells. Then she reaches under her seat and pulls out an enormous set of headphones that look even larger than the ones she is wearing.

I slide them over my ears, and the creaks and rattles of the plane magically disappear. Delia points from the cable dangling from my headset to an input on the dash in front of me. As I plug in, her voice appears in my head.

"Does this help?" she asks, and when I nod, she grins again and then turns her attention back to the plane. "There is no mic on your headset," she says, one hand draped casually on her steering wheel. "I can't hear you—sorry. Better than nothing, yes? And saves me from shouting too."

Still grinning, she leans forward to flip a switch on the console. I stare out through the pale blur of the propeller in front of us and drink in the view. From this height, the water looks gently ribbed like blue corduroy—with maybe a bit of lint here and there when the occasional white cap rises up.

The flight passes in what feels like a few minutes, punctuated only infrequently by a remark or two from the patient captain. "To the starboard, there is the island of Capsali," she says shortly after we have leveled out. "And now we fly over the Ionian Sea," she adds somewhat later.

But apart from these few interjections, I am alone with my thoughts. And for the first time on this entire journey, I don't worry.

I can't somehow.

I can't worry about my dad's health or my next article or even about all the wedding planning I'm missing out on. What I can do is marvel at how lucky I am. That I get to see the world from this angle, just once. That I get to share this adventure with my dad. And suddenly, more than anything, I want to tell Raj Malik all about it.

Which is, of course, ridiculous. I should want to tell Anthony. But I can't worry about that either, somehow.

I realize, with a start, that I have tears in my eyes, and hoping the pilot hasn't noticed, I quickly wipe them away.

But a moment later, her gloved hand appears in front of me holding a tissue.

"I'm glad you appreciate what you see," she says quietly in my head.

"Does it make you cry too?" I say back to her, but she just laughs and taps her headphones.

Right. She can't hear me. And I cannot imagine her tearing up over a view she's likely seen hundreds of times, anyway.

I gaze out over the water, tracing the long tail of a tanker ship chugging southward toward Africa. I'm peering down, seeing if I can pick out just what kind of ship it is from the air, when Delia is back in my head.

"Your turn," she says, and by the time I look over at her, she's holding both hands in the air, off the steering column.

Without thinking, I grab my own wheel, and the plane wobbles, dangerously.

"Shit, shit, shit, shit," I hiss between teeth clenched so tight I can feel my jaw locking.

"Relax, Gia," comes Delia's voice in my head. "It's not really a wheel like in your car—more like a joystick, so just keep loose and we'll be fine!"

And once again, she proves to be right. We continue to wobble a little while she points out the dials I should watch to keep the wings steady.

I hear a sudden noise from the back of the plane and look up to see my dad has materialized beside my seat.

"Woo HOO!" he cheers, pointing to my hands on the wheel.

At least, I think that's what he says. I make the mistake of releasing one hand to tap my earphones at him, and the plane yaws off to the right, sending him stumbling into the empty seat behind the captain's.

Delia's laughter rings in my ears as I manage to even things out once more. By dint of sheer determination, I'm able to ignore his antics in the background and keep us in the air for another whole minute or two before she takes pity on me and regains control.

My spiritual lightness never does quite return, but I remember what Raj said about weaving my experiences into my storytelling and decide that steering a plane, even if only for a minute or two, has got to find a place in one of my upcoming submissions to Charlotte.

In the distance, a layer of cloud appears for the first time, coalescing around what must be the island of Sicily. To our right, the land mass of Italy suddenly rises up, the blue of the sea smashing itself into white foam against the shore.

Across the windscreen, a sudden spattering of rain appears, and I feel the engine shift beneath me as the plane begins to descend. The clouds shroud us briefly in a grey fog, disorienting after all the blue sky and water, but then they are above us again. Below us, a breath-taking vista unfolds. From this vantage point, I can't really tell where the island of Sicily ends and the tip of Italy's boot begins. What I can see is the unmistakable silhouette of Mount Etna rising just in from the coast. The ground—or what I can see of it—around the mountain is black as pitch, and the peak is hidden, wreathed in cloud.

The plane's descent is almost as swift as the takeoff, and in moments, we are circling the airport, away from the mountain and south of the city of Catania. As the blinking lights of the runway appear below us, I can see fine lines of mist draping the trees; the whole lush view crowned with the smoke-wreathed peak of Mount Etna in the background.

As we roll to a stop outside the terminal, Delia Uccello reaches across to shake my hand. "Well done, Captain Gia," she says. "It's been a pleasure flying with you."

And in the absence of a flight attendant, it is she who squeezes past me to open the cabin door and drop the steps down to the tarmac. As the three passengers descend, she shakes each of our hands again, wishes us a good journey onward, and then trudges off to chat with the man who is refueling the plane.

Inside the terminal, we have a longer wait than we did on departure to go through security, although the European Union status of both countries means there is no customs line.

My dad, all signs of his earlier exuberance on the plane gone, stands quietly ahead of me in line. After several futile attempts to engage with him about my new prowess as a pilot, I give up and log on to the internet with my phone. I'm worried about the aftereffects of the mushrooms and whether there is some contraindication with the meds he is currently on.

I think about Googling, but instead, I take the easy way out and text Devi. It's the crack of dawn in New York, but she must be on an early shift, because she replies right away.

> To tell you the truth, I've actually read some interesting studies on psilocybin. There's no worry about addiction, and it seems that it does very little long-term damage, at least compared to other drugs. There was one old doc when I was in third year who swore it was not just a good experience but one that changed his life forever— for the better!

Altogether, this is pretty reassuring. But it's not until I slide my phone back into my pocket that I realize that Devi's text repeats, almost word for word, what she told me inside that cave on the coast of Crete.

Except, of course, that she wasn't exactly there at the time.

chapter twenty-two

SICILIAN SATURDAY
Pizza Siciliano
Gia Kostas, special correspondent to NOSH, in Catania, Sicily

As a New Yorker, born and bred, the word pizza *has a very specific meaning to me. However, I am an experienced enough nibbler to know that this word doesn't mean the same thing in Chicago or in Seattle. So finding the vocabulary to express the shock, the delight, the sheer joy of the authentic Sicilian version . . .*

As we walk across the main concourse in the Catania airport, there is no doubt that we have left Greece behind. Unlike the airport in Crete, where the ceiling is made up of huge sheets of glass that allow the dappled blue sky to bounce off the white walls, this Sicilian airport is dark and metallic. But it's just past one p.m. local time, and the food hall is buzzing with loud Italian voices.

I can't stop thinking about Devi's text as I trail along behind my dad toward the exit. I'm torn between feeling calmed by her reassurance that the mushrooms likely will do him no harm and entirely freaked out by the fact that the hell-dweller version of Devi gave me this information already while I was in the depths of my own unfortunate trip into the heart of darkness.

"A moment, darling." My dad suddenly dumps his bags at my feet, and I see with a sinking heart that he is heading into the men's room. Worse, he has the free copy of the Greek paper he was given on the plane tucked under one arm. This means I'll have at least fifteen minutes, and perhaps as long as a half an hour, to kill.

With a sigh, I head out to look around. The airport isn't large, so I find myself an abandoned luggage cart for the bags and go in search of something to eat. I'm just perusing a glass case filled with at least ten varieties of pizza when my phone pings. Worried that it might be Devi, reconsidering her stance on my dad and his mushrooms, I scramble to pull it out of my pocket.

Instead, I discover it's a text from Raj. I stare at his name stupidly for a moment, but then realize with a pang of guilt I must have given him my number sometime during that night of too much lotus-infused wine.

I tap his message.

Gia—it's Raj. Sorry to bother you, but I haven't heard from your dad. We had a FaceTime booked for last night to plan our next meetup, but he didn't call. Is everything okay?

My usual low-grade annoyance with my dad returns, but there's no way I'm going to tell Raj what really happened. *Oh, yeah, sorry, my dad was tripping balls on mushrooms; he must've forgotten to call.*

Not a chance.

Instead, I step forward to the counter and order two slices of pizza to take away. Then I take shots of all the varieties of pizza behind the glass of the food kiosk, even though they look identical to pizza from every street vendor I've ever seen in Manhattan.

Only then do I feel calm enough to flip open my texting app and send Raj a message that all is well, Ari is fine, and will likely contact him once we are settled at the guesthouse in Capo Mulini.

My dad leaps out of the men's room at last, looking refreshed and more like himself again. He accepts the slice of pizza with gratitude and steers me outside toward the taxi rank.

"How far do we have to go, Pops?"

He smiles at me fondly. "Ah, *koritsi*, you remind me of when you were a little girl. 'How much farther, Papa?' you would ask just as soon as you were buckled into your car seat."

I roll my eyes. "I'm just trying to get a sense of the distance, is all. If it's going to be a couple of hours, I'll bring my work into the car with me."

"Is only a few minutes, darling. Put away your work. Enjoy the view!"

And so, even though the last thing I feel like doing is what I'm told, I sit back and take in my first taste of Sicily.

As soon as we are clear of the airport, the taxi motors onto a road that borders the sea. My father, in a rare demonstration that he can actually use technology, pulls out his phone and begins tapping out a text.

Ah. I hope this means Raj is getting an apology, after all.

The cab driver has a local radio station on, which seems to specialize in thrash metal, an odd choice for this jewel of an island basking in the midday sun. Also, it's an old vehicle, with no air-conditioning, so both front windows are wide open. I try to settle in the sweet spot slightly to the right of center in the back seat, where I can stay cool without being entirely buffeted. But as soon as he's done texting, my dad cranks down his own window, so I'm subject to the full force of the airflow from all sides. My hair, which usually retains a natural wave I'm generally quite happy with, has decided to go full out curly on this trip, and at the moment, it's all I can do to keep it on my head.

The drive turns out to be mercifully short, and after a further riotous chorus or two from the radio, the taxi screeches to a halt in a shower of sand near a pier jutting like a crooked, beckoning finger into the ocean. I can't see any sign of a guesthouse. In fact, the pier looks to be part of a marina, with boats small and large bobbing down the length of it. The sun has disappeared behind some low, grey clouds, and here by the water, a light breeze is blowing, bringing with it a musical tinkling from the rigging of the moored vessels. Beyond the pier, the jagged outlines of two rocky islands float what looks like little more than a stone's throw from the shore.

Ari leaps out of the taxi without a glance back and strides purposefully toward the docks. I can see a figure waving from a small motorboat bobbing in the first berth.

My back crackles as I step out of the cab—so unused to all this travel that it clearly needs to complain out loud. I roll my shoulders a few times and retrieve my bag from among an assortment of empty beer cans in the trunk of the taxi.

As I do, my dad comes strolling back, accompanied by a young woman wearing a set of orange coveralls, the longest false eyelashes I have ever seen, and a Sun Devils ball cap.

"Darling, this is . . ." he begins.

"Margarita," interjects the young woman. Her coveralls are unzipped low enough that the black lace of her bra is clearly visible.

She leans forward and knocks her elbow into mine by way of greeting.

"Can't be too frikkin' careful, specially workin' in the tourist industry," she adds. Her accent could not be more American.

"From Tempe, Arizona," she says when I ask. "Left home to see the world for a few years right after high school. I got family here, and I landed in Italy just before the virus struck. Found a job, and I've been here ever since."

My dad reaches into the trunk to retrieve his backpack.

"Margarita has agreed to rent us her motorboat for a couple of hours, darling. I'd like to go over and have a stroll around the islands before the sun goes down. Join me, won't you?"

I glance across at the nearest jagged stack of rock. "That looks more like a mountain climb than a stroll, Pops. I wish you'd mentioned your plans to me earlier."

"Spur of the moment decision, darling. These are the *Isole dei Ciclopi*—the famous islands of the Cyclops. It's literally a tourist haven—the place is covered in walking paths. Come. Let me show you!"

"I'm happy to tour you both around, fer sure," adds Margarita. "It's the most frikkin' amazing place, I swear. The locals say that these islands were the stones thrown at old Odysseus when he angered the Cyclops."

I look over to the islands. Beyond them, just along the horizon, the cloud appears to be breaking up, and there is a line of blue where the sky meets the ocean. I think about it for a solid second or two and then shake my head.

"I'm on deadline, Pops. I thought we were driving straight through to the guesthouse. You go ahead. I'll just find a bar or a coffee shop or something and try to hook up to some Wi-Fi while I wait for you. I need to get another story in to Charlotte by tomorrow, and I haven't even started."

"Well, if you don't want to come, Guido here can take you to your hotel." Margarita bats those long lashes at the taxi driver, once, twice; and clearly smitten, he's already nodding.

My dad rifles through his travel folder.

"We're staying at the *Pensione Castilo*," he says.

"I know that place," says Margarita. I'm beginning to think she runs this entire village single-handedly. "They have a terrace above the water—it's frikkin' *gorgeous.*"

"Excellent idea," says my dad heartily. "Margarita and I will go explore and give you some peace and quiet to get your work done."

I narrow my eyes at him, but he just beams, gives me a quick kiss on the cheek, and hurries off toward the little motorboat.

"I'll keep an eye on him, I promise," says Margarita before jogging off to catch up to my dad.

"But who'll keep an eye on you?" Needless to say, my grumble falls on deaf ears.

"Thees Margarita, she ees such a beautiful woman," says Guido as we walk back to the taxi. "Americano, yes? So beautiful."

"That's what I'm worried about." With a sigh I can't quite suppress, I climb into the front seat.

Guido starts up the taxi, and to the delicate sounds of Radio Catania—backing track courtesy of Slayer—we drive off to find me some Wi-Fi.

While online during the wait for my dad in the airport, I learned that Catania is a city second in size only to Palermo on the island of Sicily, with a population around three hundred thousand. The part of it we're driving through now seems fairly densely packed, especially along the shoreline. Many of the houses are crammed together behind walls of crumbling grey stone and creeping vines. The earth-toned buildings with their terra-cotta roofs blend in with each other, enlivened here and there by a brilliant flash of color, where homeowners have painted their front doors in every shade of the rainbow.

The dock where Margarita moors her motorboat to drive over to the Cyclopean Islands turns out to be located in a place called Aci Trezza. According to Guido, we are just heading a little farther north along the coast to find the guesthouse perched atop Capo Mulini.

As we drive along the coast, the sun breaks through the clouds behind us, lighting up the horizon. The roads in this region are so narrow, oncoming cars have to duck into spaces against the curb to let others by. This means a lot of sudden stops and starts, but amazingly, everyone seems to put courtesy first. It does not hurt, either, that the vehicles are all so tiny.

The view of the ocean dominates everything until we pull onto a small rise above the town, and suddenly there is Mount Etna to the north, much closer than I expect. Clouds still wreathe themselves around the peak, and it looms over the whole region like a gently smoking giant.

Just as suddenly, Guido steers us into a narrow lane, and Etna disappears. Instead we are surrounded by mist-laden trees, everything lush and green in the late afternoon light. The taxi screeches to a halt in a gravel parking space, nestled in behind a tiny villa. The guesthouse is perched on a promontory above the village, with a view that takes in the entirety of the Ionian Sea, spreading out before us like a rolling azure blanket. Along the coast to the south, the three stony peaks of the islands rise out from the water like sentinels.

"This is an amazing view." I take a deep breath of the fresh sea air as I climb out of the car.

But Guido is already revving his engine. He pauses long enough to crank up the radio, then peels out of the lot, waving the handful of cash I gave him out the window in farewell.

While the tiny Italian lady who meets me at the door speaks almost no English, when I point to my dad's name on her register, her eyes light up. I follow her as she bustles up a miniature winding staircase. In spite of the heat, she's dressed entirely in black; including knee-length skirt, high-necked blouse, heavy cardigan, and thick black stockings. The only color she displays is on her feet, which are sporting neon-purple Nikes. I follow those bright sneakers up narrow, steep steps, with each worn riser creaking melodically underfoot. On the second landing, she pauses, puffing a little, at a door with a postcard of the Cyclopean Islands thumbtacked in the center.

"Tuo papa," she says and rests her hand briefly on the door. After catching our breath a moment, we continue our upward climb. At the top of the stairs, she turns a key in a door that has been cut at an angle to accommodate the sharp slope of the ceiling. The postcard on this door is of an ancient castle I'm sure I spied as Guido raced past on our way here. Later, I learn this is the *Castello di Aci*, a fortification that has loomed over this coastline since at least the Middle Ages.

I follow her inside to find a charming, if tiny, little garret room with a round window overlooking the Ionian coast. Far below, I can see both the castle depicted on my postcard and the islands my dad is currently traipsing across, all within the amazing panorama of coastline. The view is incredible, and I could stare at it all day—if I didn't have to work.

Luckily, the little Italian lady, who insists I call her Nonna Rosa, is anxious to feed me. She leads me out onto a terrace that surpasses even Margarita's assessment. The view is indeed frikkin' gorgeous, as is the excellent Wi-Fi. And Nonna Rosa's selection of afternoon snack foods also gets an A+ rating. Teeny little cream puffs sprinkled in dark chocolate nestle on a plate with at least a dozen cannoli, each dusted in powdered sugar.

My heart grows three sizes in that single instant.

The terrace runs around the whole exterior of the guesthouse, and one section of it is shaded by a trellis of thick grape leaves. I settle down to write, happily noshing on cannoli. As soon as I log on to the internet—the password, not too surprisingly, is Etna—a text pops up from Charlotte asking for a few specifics to add to the last article. Hard on the heels of this comes an e-mail from Devi, with an attachment that turns out to be an article on magic mushrooms. I save it to read later and get to work on Charlotte's edits.

Two cups of strong Italian espresso and a slightly embarrassing number of cannoli later, my dad strides onto the terrace, Margarita in tow. I stretch my arms out in an attempt to unkink my back, and Margarita mistakes my intention and dives in for a hug.

So much for caution in the tourism industry.

But whether she's decided we're old friends by virtue of our shared citizenship or just after seeing my dad around all afternoon, it appears I have little to say in the matter.

"Your dad's quite the player, huh?" she whispers when she finally releases me.

"Oh no . . ." I begin, cringing, but she cuts me off with a laugh.

"Ah, it was fine," she says and points to her overalls. "I zipped up a little, and anyway, I think the hiking has worn him out."

I glance over at him, where he is leaning on the stone railing all the way across the terrace, drinking in the view. He does look tired and, as I watch, takes off his sunglasses and rubs his eyes. I realize with a start that his hair, at this distance, at least, looks more white than it does grey.

I turn back to Margarita. "Okay. But I hope he wasn't too pushy."
"Nah." She slaps me on the shoulder. "He's a good guy, and we had a great afternoon. You've got nothing to worry about, I promise you."

As my dad turns toward us, Margarita leaves, pausing to high-five him on the way. She gives me a last wave, scoops a cannoli off the tray that Nonna Rosa is carrying in for my dad, and vanishes, chewing happily.

chapter twenty-three

SATURDAY EVENING
Affogato
Gia Kostas, special correspondent to NOSH, in Catania, Sicily

The truth is that breakfast is not really an important meal in Italy. Most Italians have something small—perhaps a pastry with their coffee—and put so much more of their attention into the later meals of the day. Affogato is the fastest way to combine the rich, dark espresso, which is a required element, with a perfect scoop of . . .

It's a gorgeous evening, the sun spreading a layer of liquid gold across everything—land and sea and more—but the moment Margarita disappears, my dad visibly sags. He assures me he's just worn out and needs a nap, and promises to meet me at eight for dinner. But his skin has taken on a grey tone I don't like at all. Before I know it, he's followed Nonna Rosa off to his room, leaving me with his untouched pot of tea and, more dangerously, a fresh plate of Italian pastry.

Instead of turning back to my work, I feel the familiar worry rise up to take over my mind once more. This place is so beautiful—with its crumbling streets, rocky shores, and ancient castles—but it's not home. And while my dad might be claiming to be merely in need of a nap, I feel the weight of my choice to stay with him settle heavily on my shoulders. He's had all his shots—after the virus swept the world, his whole faculty brought their inoculations up to date. But who knows what he's vulnerable to? His resistance to germs has got to be down after the stroke, regardless of how small he claims it was.

And as for this insane journey? He's not supposed to be here at all. Neither of us is. If his doctor knew he was traipsing around rocky islands, crawling through caves, and—I can't even bear to think of confessing the whole mushroom episode. I brought his medication, yes, and have been on his case enough that I'm sure he's now in the habit of taking it when he should. And I can't think what else I could have done. I mean, he's a grown man. He has to be responsible for his own choices.

Nevertheless, I feel suddenly overwhelmed with guilt. For a person who is here to keep an eye on him, I haven't exactly been great at stopping him from overexerting himself. I haven't even been able to keep him off hallucinogens, for heaven's sake.

I pull out my tablet and start Googling Sicilian physicians. I need someone who speaks English, someone who I can convince or pay or whatever it takes just to have a look at my dad. But my eyes are crossing looking at the list of names, all with addresses which could be anywhere. It's so discouraging.

Before I know it, I have my phone in my hand, texting Devi. Her life is crazy right now, yes, but she's so much better than I am at taking the emotion out and looking at things rationally. I compose a long text, asking for suggestions, even if it means tricking my dad into seeing sense. But the minute I press "Send," I remember. It's Saturday morning there, which means she's on her street beat. Which means her phone is off, for who knows how long.

Dropping the phone to the table, I pop in the last of the cannoli and fret. My stomach is aching, and truthfully, I'm not sure if it's worry about my dad or an Italian pastry overdose.

Probably a bit of both.

The golden light has faded, and the sky has become overcast.

Above the village, thunder rumbles, echoing from the distant slopes of Mount Etna. I shiver and pull a sweater out of my bag. I consider sneaking into my dad's room to steal his phone and find Margarita's number. I have no doubt she'll know who to call.

And then, suddenly, I think of Raj. He's been living here—well, not here, but in the region—for at least a year. I'm fairly certain he's back at the site near Makri in mainland Greece, but he's got to have contacts. Before I can change my mind, I look up his number and text him a note. This one is much shorter than the huge missive I sent to Devi. After everything that's happened, I can't actually bring myself to mention the whole mushroom thing. Just that I'm not convinced I should be managing my father's health issues on my own, and any suggestions from him would be welcome.

There is a flash of lightning from somewhere behind me, followed by an immediate—and deafening—crash of thunder. Abandoning my dishes to the rain, I grab my things and dash under the cover of the awning over the door. And as I do, my phone lights up in my hand.

> Hey, Gia. Glad you are safely in Sicily. Wish I was there to show you and your dad around. The region around Etna is just loaded with fantastic sites. RE your dad: have you considered reaching out to the person who organized his trip? I remember her saying that the company—is it ExLibris?—is on call at all times. She might be able to help you find a local doc. Your dad and I plan to meet up in a couple of days near Rome. Let me know if you need me to come sooner.

Reading this message, my eyes fill with unexpected tears. Setting aside the fact that this guy—even with our slightly embarrassing history—is willing to drop everything to come help my dad, just reading this calm and reasoned advice heartens me.

Outside the door, rain is suddenly sheeting down, a deluge that blocks out the view off the terrace entirely. I tuck my phone in my pocket and pull out my wallet. There, in the back, is the small white card Teresa Cipher had paper-clipped to my dad's itinerary.

I have to step aside as a child, maybe eight or nine years old, dashes past me with a tray and, instantly drenched, collects my remaining dishes to lug back inside. I jam my hand in my pocket and drop the change I find there onto the tray as the child struggles by. This earns me a brilliant smile and reinforces my decision.

I dial the number on the card and, seconds later, connect through to a very reassuring conversation with Teresa Cipher. Speaking to me from London, her first priority is to confirm that no emergency is taking place. Once I tell her that I'm just worried, her voice lightens.

"Every eventuality is included in the ExLibris service package," she assures me, "and we want you to know that your dad is in the best of hands."

This almost makes me tear up again, and when the young child reappears to collect the abandoned teapot, I have to physically restrain myself from reaching out for a hug.

Teresa Cipher goes on to say that she will be back to me before nine the following morning and then wishes me a good night. As I head toward the stairs to my room, an enormous clock near the check-in desk ponderously strikes nine times. Upstairs, my dad's door is slightly ajar, and I peek in to see he is still out like a light, snoring gently. There's a coil notebook on the bed beside him, and his favorite fountain pen dangles from one hand.

I creep in long enough to cap his pen and flip the duvet over him. Then I turn off the light and head up the final flight of stairs to my room. As I cuddle into my own little bed, the gentle breeze whispering in through my window has been cooled by the rain, which has finally stopped. I lie there, staring into the darkness, and think of Raj Malik's kindness and good sense.

And then I think of how he looked that first night, his hands cupping my face, the crease at the curve of his smile that I could not stop kissing. I think of how I watched a single bead of sweat trickle from his hairline below one ear and trace its way down his chest under his open shirt, around one pectoral muscle, and then down across those washboard abs, and . . .

Sitting bolt upright in bed, I blurt, "What the hell, Gia?" so loudly I startle myself.

Embarrassment floods through me. I tell myself it's only gratitude for Raj's help with my dad, but it takes a real force of will to banish the image from my mind's eye and force myself to lie down again.

Of course I'm grateful. Raj gave me the good advice about calling Teresa. He even offered to come and help. Why wouldn't I be grateful for that kind of support?

But here in the deep, slightly humid Sicilian darkness, I can feel heat rise to my face. I know this whole thing, this stupid memory of Raj's perfect, perfect abs—can only be prompted by one thing. I've had almost zero communication with Anthony over the last few days, and anyway, so what? Mental imagery like this only proves I'm normal. Human. A normal, human woman missing her fiancé. No other explanation needed.

I make a mental note to write Anthony a detailed, loving e-mail in the morning, but for some irritating reason, it seems to take a long, long time before I fall into sleep.

chapter twenty-four

SUNDAY
Cannoli
Gia Kostas, special correspondent to NOSH, in Sicily

These sweet, perfect packages made the leap across the Atlantic to America many years ago, but this ideal version, served in its native Sicily, has a certain . . .

I awaken the next morning to the low rumble of what sounds almost like a jet engine. Instead, when I peer out my little round window, I see a majestic yacht slowly motoring toward the rickety little jetty directly below our guesthouse. The incongruity of the elegant ship—complete with helicopter pad—pulling in toward the little wooden dock clears the sleep from my brain. Feeling like it has to contain a celebrity, I race through washing and dressing. By the time I emerge from the twisty staircase into the main lobby, two women are striding across the gravel driveway.

They are both tall, but the first woman is truly striking, wearing a knee-length wrap dress in a nautical Breton stripe and white gloves. The four-inch heels on her elegant pumps impede her progress across the gravel not at all. Behind her, the second woman has dark hair, neatly coiffed in a French knot, a light raincoat open and flapping in the wind, and chic, sensible flats. As they reach the doorway, the first woman removes her sunglasses, and I realize with a jolt of recognition that it is Teresa Cipher.

"Ms. Kostas," she says, extending a gloved hand.

"It's—it's Gia." I can't seem to get out a sentence without stuttering. "What? I—I mean, I certainly didn't expect to see . . ."

Her smile broadens. "Gia, allow me to introduce Dr. Elle Arcetti. Dr. Arcetti is a neurologist and a friend of mine."

The doctor, who is also wearing gloves, shakes my hand firmly. "Lovely to meet you, Gia."

Before I can settle on one of the five or six thousand questions that have just leapt to mind, I hear footsteps on the stairs behind me.

"Ari!" says Teresa Cipher warmly, and indeed my father has arrived.

He clumps up beside us, looking well-rested, if a little thinner than usual. And now that I've taken to noticing things, his hair *is* whiter, even this close up. But his smile is wide, and his eyes take on a look I recognize as he spots the woman in the raincoat.

"Teresa? What are the odds?" says my father, shaking her hand heartily before turning a charming smile on her companion.

Teresa repeats her introductions and then beams around our small group.

"It's such a perfect coincidence," she says in her warm contralto. "Here I was, happily escorting Dr. Arcetti to a reimagining of the dinner scenes from *Under the Tuscan Sun*, and I was struck by our proximity to your itinerary, Ari."

She crinkles her eyes at me for a fraction of a second before continuing smoothly. "And as Elle is a neurologist, she insisted that we stop so she could meet and chat with you both. After all, this has been quite a year for you, Ari, hasn't it?"

If my dad is at all put out by this reference to his condition, he doesn't show it. Instead, he invites the women to share breakfast with us, going so far as to offer his arm to escort the beautiful neurologist out onto the sunny terrace of the guesthouse.

"We'll join you in a minute, Pops," I call out to him. He answers with an airy wave of his free hand.

Teresa Cipher raises an eyebrow at me inquiringly. "I do hope you don't mind me taking things in this direction," she says quietly.

I bulge my eyes back at her and tilt my head toward the front door. The two of us step outside onto the gravel parking surface.

"MIND?" I shout before I can get a grip on my voice.

I manage to tone it down a little, and try again. "*Mind?* I most certainly do *not* mind. I am—I don't know what I am. Delighted? Thrilled? I mean, last night, I called you for help finding a local doctor who might speak English, and you show up the next morning— on a yacht? With a neurologist in tow?"

She laughs at this, but I do hear the note of relief in her voice. "My dear, this is what we do at ExLibris. It's our goal to make the experience a memorable one for all our clients. But we factor in the need to handle emergencies, and I have to say, you sounded quite desperate on the phone last night."

I can't help sighing. "Listen, I think you know by now that my dad is—well, he can be a handful."

Teresa nods. "Everyone has their eccentricities," she says diplomatically.

I lean against the door frame. "Yeah, okay, call it what you like, but it strikes me that my dad may not have been completely up front with you about his health."

Her expression clouds just a little. "Well, yes—we do expect our clients to be forthright, particularly if they have health concerns."

"The problem is that my dad is *such* a Greek male. He'd bleed to death before asking for a Band-Aid. In his defense, I'm pretty sure he had no idea he was ill when he first started planning this whole thing. But you should know that the day I met you, I'd actually flown over to Athens to bring him the medication he was supposed to be taking for his TIA—and that he left behind at the hospital."

All the good humor fades from her face. "Yes, I recall the meeting vividly. And Ari did make a brief reference to some neurological anomalies, which is why I've brought Dr. Arcetti today. However, I admit I assumed these events were well in the past. I had no idea he'd been so recently ill."

"Yep. Sneaky devil didn't want to cancel his trip and wasn't about to tell you in case you canceled it for him."

Teresa Cipher is silent a moment. "And this attack happened when?"

"Two days before he flew here. He was literally in the hospital less than twenty-four hours before signing himself out. I'm sure he didn't tell you because he didn't think ExLibris policies would allow clients to leave under those circumstances."

"Hmm. Well, he likely would have been right. However." She pauses, and her lips twitch at the corners. "I understand how your father is disinclined to adhere to the norm. I'm very glad you called me. You did the right thing."

A wave of relief washes through me. "I mean, he's actually been pretty well, on the whole. It's only when he overdoes it—he seems to crash more easily these days. Yesterday he looked just terrible."

She nods. "Well, in light of all that you've told me, I'm glad we've been able to get here as quickly as we have. Shall we go join them? Let's see if Elle can talk some sense into him."

She sweeps a hand toward the entrance and grins. "I'll be delighted if she is able to offer some good advice, particularly in light of the—naturally, purely coincidental—nature of our visit."

I can't help grinning back. I follow her inside to find that her prediction is, indeed, exactly what happens. Nonna Rosa outdoes herself with an incredible breakfast spread, my dad flirts outrageously with Dr. Elle, and when the neurologist makes a few sensible recommendations, he assures her he has every intention of following each of them to the letter.

Their conversation is so engaged, I'm even able to quietly quiz Teresa Cipher on how the two women really did manage to arrange such a speedy surprise visit. It seems that Teresa, still in London setting up her new office for ExLibris, hopped on an early morning flight to Rome and made good use of the yacht's onboard helicopter to rendezvous with the quite legitimately vacationing Dr. Arcetti—who was indeed sailing along the coast of Tuscany.

Further, Dr. Elle's husband, a hedge-fund manager, is apparently quite happy to stop in Sicily for the day while his wife does her friend Teresa a favor.

"He's found a winery nearby," Dr. Elle confides to me later as I thank her before they leave. "He's a sucker for a Sicilian red."

This reminds me of stories Anthony's told me of how his own father does business. I'm not sure I'll ever get used to the way wealthy people solve problems. All the same, I'm grateful this neurologist happened to be so close by and was willing to talk to my dad.

After a leisurely, almost two-hour breakfast, the women stand up to take their leave.

"Now, Ari," says Dr. Elle, "after our chat, it's pretty clear to me you don't really need another prescription. But you'll remember what I told you, yes?"

My father nods and drains his virgin mimosa. "Site visits spaced out by a day of leisure in between," he says. "I think I can manage that."

"Good." She smiles at him and then nods at me. "Lovely to meet you, Gia."

"And you," I say gratefully, pocketing the business cards both women quietly press on me, just in case.

I turn to Teresa Cipher and reach for her gloved hand. "I haven't thanked you for sorting out my last-minute presence on this trip. There has been an impeccable room waiting for me at every stop."

"I have a wonderful team at ExLibris," she says, returning my squeeze. "As soon as I heard you'd decided to accompany your father, I put one of my best team members in New York City on it immediately. Ramona has recently returned from a round-the-world jaunt of her own that she booked entirely on the fly, so she considers this little journey of yours a piece of cake."

I reach across the table and lift my almost empty coffee cup. "To Ramona! Please let her know how much I appreciate her organizational skills."

Teresa's eyes twinkle. "She's planning her own wedding at the moment too," she says. "So you have something in common."

I smile and nod and try not to think about just how little planning I've actually been doing. I silently vow to spend time on it tonight, as soon as my next story is filed.

We all stand up, and my dad, still not used to a postviral world, attempts to kiss Dr. Elle's hand by way of farewell. She has redonned her gloves but still manages to avoid this ploy by blowing him a kiss instead, insisting it is the new Italian form of goodbye.

This is a woman who dodges like an expert.

My dad smiles and bows gallantly back at both women. And after they leave, true to his word, he retreats to his room only to return with the coil notebook I spied on his bed last night. With Nonna Rosa busy in the kitchen generating delicious aromas, the two of us work companionably in the dappled sunlight of the terrace for the entire afternoon.

In fact, the only down note for the day comes in the form of an e-mail that arrives from Anthony. It's in reply to the love note I've sent him, but his words come across as stilted and odd. Not until I get to the bottom do I realize it's been sent—*again*—via his executive assistant, Melanie Andrews.

Who gets their assistant to e-mail their fiancée, anyway?

chapter twenty-five

MONDAY
Ginger Tea
Gia Kostas, special correspondent to NOSH, on
    the Ionian Sea

Homeric legend has a lot to say about the role of the gods, with Poseidon among the most temperamental—and therefore interesting. Definitely the wrong guy to poke a stick at when you're on a boat, fishing for . . .

I awaken to discover that in spite of his promises to Teresa Cipher, my dad has once again changed his plans and has made a deal with Margarita to speed us on our way. He swears to me that this will mean a shorter journey, as we weren't scheduled to board the boat set up by ExLibris until tonight.

"And by tonight, we will be in Aeolia, ahead of schedule!" he boasts, before adding sneakily, "More time for your papa to relax and take it easy, eh?"

Bastard. I think how hard it must have been on my mother to be married to this man. And it's not like he's letting up. Margarita's at the front door waiting while we bid Nonna Rosa goodbye and settle up our bill. She's ditched her orange coveralls for a tiny jean skirt and cropped t-shirt, and looks every inch the American girl.

Waiting in the parking lot is Guido the cab driver, who is all smiles at this unexpected gig. Or perhaps at Margarita? It's hard to tell.

His cab—a little yellow Fiat, apart from the passenger-side door, which is blue—is sparkling clean this morning. As we step into the parking lot, he leaps out to take my bag and hold the door for me. His gallant behavior is undermined for both of us, however, when my dad arrives with Margarita and ousts me from my spot behind the driver.

"You sit up front, darling. I have a few things to discuss with Margarita about our voyage today. You understand."

This last is a command rather than a question.

Guido doesn't look any happier than I am at this arrangement, and shooting me a disappointed glance, he tucks what looks like a tiny box of chocolates under his seat.

My own bag is on the floor between my feet. I'm extremely full from Nonna Rosa's latest triumph, so I settle in and scroll through the pictures on my phone, deciding which to use for the article I plan to submit on her cooking. There is no question an article will be submitted— Nonna Rosa's skills are unparalleled, and every bite is divine.

Take this morning, for example. I'd planned to just stick to coffee, as I have a history of an unsettled tummy on the water. But when I arrived on the sun-dappled terrace, an entire feast was spread out along the huge old sideboard. It was a brunch for the ages.

In my short time here, I've learned that food seems to be the center of Sicilian life. Everything revolves around slow, leisurely meals shared by families, and to Nonna Rosa? We were clearly family. Laid out along the sideboard were plates containing every Sicilian delicacy I could imagine and several I couldn't. She handed me a cup of coffee, served with sweetened almond milk, to sip while I perused my choices. In addition to what I had come to view as her standards—

the cream-filled croissants called coronetti and the brioche served with a choice of homemade jam and marmalade—there was a platter of what turned out to be goat cheese battered and fried to melty perfection. This was to be scooped up with morsels of a long Italian loaf sliced into bite-sized rings, each piece sprinkled in coarse sea salt. There were fillets of swordfish, grilled to perfection, nestled next to a pasta dish that turned out to have a sauce made with pesto and anchovies. In between these dishes were platters containing tidy piles of fresh sausage, each a different variety and with its own unique spice blend.

So, yeah, it's possible I am feeling a tad uncomfortably full at the moment.

I pull out my tablet. Might as well use the time to write, as it's a couple hours of driving before we make it to wherever it is that we are getting on a boat. Sitting in the front, at least I should get less carsick, and it will distract me from the charm offensive my dad is waging on Margarita in the back.

Before getting ready to leave this morning, I took the time to download my e-mail, planning to go over it while I drank my coffee. But as the choice ended up being to read it or to make time for the last of Nonna Rosa's special brunches, there was really no contest. Now, however, facing a substantial drive through the mountains of northern Sicily, I can take the time to read through them, at least. Replying, of course, will have to wait until later.

But as I bend down to pull my tablet out of my bag, something catches my eye. Guido's driving speed has, not unexpectedly, remained the same, and in fact, may be possibly even faster than yesterday's. We have left the tiny, winding roads of the village and joined an autostrada—a pared-down sort of freeway. The day, by contrast to yesterday, is capped with a clear, beautifully blue sky.

We are hurtling north along a still fairly narrow two-lane high-way as I notice a strange, black cloud up ahead. The cloud is oddly columnar in shape rather than the usual sort of fluffy cumulous mass I associate with a thunderstorm.

In the seat behind me, Margarita is laughing at something my dad says when I hear a low rumble, like distant thunder. I hunch down to peer suspiciously through Guido's window at the ominous cloud. Guido, earphones firmly plugged in his ears and eyes glued to the road, ignores me.

He signals, and we roar past a small white truck with what looks like a handmade mattress strapped to the truck bed. The truck is traveling well below the marked speed, but as we pass, I see that a sheep and two tiny white lambs are in the back. All three appear to be tied in place with rope harnesses. I catch a glimpse of the ewe, stolidly chewing a mouthful of hay, before they are behind us. With the truck out of the way, my view is clearer. The strange thunder-cloud appears to be gathering at the top of Mount Etna.

Because of his earphones, when I reach over to put a hand on Guido's arm, he jumps a little, and the tiny cab swerves.

He pulls one of his earbuds out, and I hear a thin chorus of "Sweet Child o' Mine."

"Sorry—but . . . is that cloud *coming from* Etna?" I point out the window past his nose.

Guido glances out of his side window and nods.

"Yes. Is not cloud, but ash. She's been making noise for many weeks now. Nothing serious, just rumbles. Seems to be worse in mornings, for some reason."

"So, it's a cloud of ash, then?"

"*Si.* If wind is up high, it usually blow out over the water. You see there?" He points up at what looks like a load of white cumulous clouds in the distance. "All ash. It sometimes look white, up high. Not sure why."

I glance nervously over at the black column that I can now plainly see is billowing from the top of the peak, like smoke from a chimney. Craning my neck proves it is indeed floating off to join the distant, larger cloud.

"Is there a way to drive around the mountain to get where we're going? It seems awfully cranky today."

He shakes his head. "We don't get closer than this, no worry. I drive very fast, we be pass her before you know."

Still. I can't seem to tear my eyes away. After a few moments, I begin to feel the black stream might be lessening. Sure enough, as the highway bends to head due north and we are fully past the peak, the smoke is definitely beginning to fade to grey.

In the back seat, my dad and Margarita are discussing the local legends of Odysseus and the Cyclops. I narrow my eyes at him and interrupt.

"You're missing the show." I gesture at the grey column of cloud visible through the back window. "Guido says Etna has been erupting for months."

"Yes, yes," my dad agrees. "I was watching from the window of my bedroom this morning."

He leans back and steeples his fingers together. "It's likely the *Isole dei Ciclopi* were . . ." he begins, when suddenly, from out of the low wreath of smoke surrounding Etna, a perfect white ring appears.

"Look, look!" I shriek, cutting him off.

Guido turns, craning backward to see, and the car swerves crazily again.

"Is smoke ring?" he asks, straightening the wheel without a noticeable change in speed.

"It sure is," says Margarita, looking over her shoulder. "She does that once in a while just to remind us who's in charge."

The white ring drifts upward languidly, holding its shape for almost a full minute before dissipating into grey mist.

"Is it—is it a sign of anything?" I can't take my eyes off the peak of the mountain. "Like, does it mean an eruption is imminent?"

Guido makes a sound very much like a snort. "She rumble a lot, our girl, but hardly ever blow her top. We do our job to keep her happy. The ash, it help the crops, so we grow food and grapes, and we pour out wine in her honor." He shrugs. "Sometimes they have to close airport, and once in a while, lava eats a building, but really? No big deal."

By this time, the peak of the mountain is no longer visible through either the back window or my side mirror. Since my dad has started up again with his storytelling, I turn back to my tablet, and taking a cue from Guido, I plug in my own earphones.

I'm not familiar with any native Sicilian singers, but I flip through my playlists and settle on listening to Ariana Grande the rest of the way, just to keep on Lady Etna's good side.

The rest of the drive is generally adventure-free, apart from a small detour we have to take at a spot where the oncoming lane of highway has buckled and crumbled down the mountainside. There is very little traffic at this point, but Guido is forced to slow down as an oncoming vehicle swerves into our lane to circumvent the problem.

"What the hell?" The edge of the road seems far too close as we go flying by.

Guido gives another of his practiced shrugs. "Is nothing," he says, unplugging one ear again to talk to me. "Quite common through these passes. The volcano, she shake the ground sometimes. And there is not so much money these days, so government slow to fix."

I glance back over my shoulder, and notice the spot where the pavement has crumbled down the cliffside has completely lost its guardrail, which has also fallen into the abyss. I think about Guido having to return this way and can't suppress a shudder. But when I lean closer to ask for more details, Guido has plugged himself back in and is humming tunelessly along with 1980s Axl Rose.

Conversation plainly over, I open up a file to start a new article for NOSH and begin to type. Before I know it, we are careening toward an ever-approaching horizon that is filled with nothing but clear, blue water. Soon Guido is expertly wheeling through what looks like a resort town. We pass a huge marina filled with yachts and high-end motorboats and then take a sharp turn onto a dusty coastal road. A few moments later, we pull up beside a fence topped with barbed wire and a locked gate. This could not be a greater contrast to the marina we just passed. Behind the fence, a few boats bob at a grey pier that is affixed to the shore with only a bit of rope and some old rubber tires.

All the same, I fling open my door and hop out of the car, relieved to breathe the sea air. After a few deep breaths, I turn to see Guido, with his hand on Margarita's arm. She smiles at him, and I see her drop his tiny box of chocolates into the little string bag she is carrying. He leans in for a kiss but is disappointed when she pats his cheek and walks off, pulling a large bunch of keys from her bag.

As my dad hoists himself out of the car, Guido marches past him, looking as stormy as Etna. He reaches into the trunk of his car and comes out not with our bags but with a tiny whisk broom. Starting at the hood of the car, he sweeps away the fine layer of black ash we must have picked up on the drive. He pauses long enough to collect the folded wad of notes from my dad and then returns to his sweeping as we grab our bags and follow Margarita through the gate. She's jingling the keys and whistling as she strides out along the rickety dock.

A young man hops off the larger of the three boats—I notice now, the only one of the three with a real motor—and throws his arms around Margarita. He's topless, skin tanned a golden brown, with matching gold tips in his long chestnut hair.

"This is my cousin Federico," she says, peeling away one of his arms and turning back to us. "He's going to take us to Aeolia on his boat *La Fortuna*."

Federico grins, keeping one arm firmly around Margarita as he shakes our hands. Behind him *La Fortuna* bobs vigorously up and down, bumping the dock with thumps I can feel through my feet.

My dad looks slightly crestfallen at the appearance of Federico. "Oh, I thought I was hiring *your* marine services, my dear," he says to Margarita. "You showed such excellent captaining skills on our tour of the *Isole dei Ciclopi*."

She grins. "This is a better boat for this trip, Ari," she says, and leans across to pat the hull. "Younger and with a bigger—you know—engine." She hops lithely aboard and then turns her smile on her cousin. "I love Federico's big boat," she laughs. "I ride it whenever I get a chance."

Federico roars and then solicitously helps my father onboard before reaching a hand out to me.

Behind us, Guido, having finished sweeping the ash away from his paint job, shoots a final glare at us all and peels out of the parking lot before Federico has even untied his boat.

I'm not sure who looks more disappointed—Guido or my father. I think I have to vote for my dad, who is forced to wear a large and very unbecoming yellow life jacket in contrast to Federico's sleek life belt. And anyway, poor Guido is long gone, back toward the smoke-ring-blowing mountain he calls home.

Uncoiling themselves from each other only long enough to don their own life jackets, Federico and Margarita give us a quick tour of *La Fortuna*. Far from the yachts we passed by only moments ago, this is clearly a fishing vessel, sturdy and low-slung and—a fact which becomes only apparent once we are onboard—reeking of fish. As Federico casts off, we have to wind our way around a tangle of nets and buoys in the main open section near the back. Further forward, there's a small room below the bridge with a long table covered in unwashed dishes and a dozen or more fast-food bags.

"You can sit here," says Federico, waving an arm into the room. Apart from the table, which has five or six stools spaced around it, each bolted to the floor, there is a single love seat, one of its arms attached with duct tape, in a worn, mustard-colored tweed.

Federico and Margarita disappear, and soon we are pulling away from the dock. I stuff all the fast-food containers into a bin, slide the dirty dishes to the other end of the table, and settle in, determined to get some writing done. My dad wanders to the back of the boat and gazes mournfully out as Sicily recedes behind us. Above his head, I can see a single puff of black cloud in a clear, blue sky.

It is *not* shaped like a smoke ring.

About half an hour into what is supposed to be a three-hour journey, the wind picks up. I can attest to this because my iPad spontaneously lifts off the still slightly sticky table and slams down again. There is a flash of color as one of the ship's flags is ripped away by the wind and flung into the wake far behind us. I look around to see my dad has disappeared, and the place where he had been standing is awash in spray. I quickly pack my electronics away in my bag and, holding on with both hands, climb up the steel mesh stairs to the ship's bridge.

There, I find my dad standing, knees bent, firmly planted by one of the windows. At the wheel, Federico's insouciant attitude has disappeared, as he has to navigate waves that quickly grow to three feet high.

Now, three feet doesn't sound like much, but I'm here to tell you, my stomach insists otherwise. I try standing beside my dad, but the erratic up-and-down motion makes me instantly sick. Staggering back down the steps, I aim for a toilet I remember spotting near the back, but before I can so much as open the door, a strong arm scoops me up from behind. Seconds later, I'm retching over the back of the boat while Margarita holds my hair away from my face. "Less to clean up when you do that out here," she says, grinning.

Nonna Rosa's cooking has never been so poorly treated.

When it's clear the tanks are empty, Margarita disappears back up to the bridge. I stand by the side, damp with spray, and try to catch my breath.

Any relief I feel from being sick is short-lived, mostly because the wind doesn't let up, and in spite of Federico's best efforts, *La Fortuna* does not stop bucking. My nausea, even after losing all of Nonna Rosa's brunch, shows no sign of ebbing. I'm so miserable, I curl up, unable to escape the stench of old fish, and try not to cry.

I'm not sure how long this dreadful situation lasts before my dad takes pity on me. He clears off the seedy-looking love seat in the back of the main cabin, finds a blanket, and creates a little nest. After he guides me over, I spend the rest of the journey with my head on his shoulder, eyes squeezed closed and jaw clenched, as he tells the story of Poseidon's feud with Odysseus into my hair.

In the end, our planned three-hour shortcut takes, in fact, a little more than seven. Seven hellish, never-ending hours. I'm not sure what *La Fortuna*—or perhaps Federico—has done to him, but Poseidon takes full measure of his revenge on us today.

The wind dies down as we approach the port town of Lipari on the Aeolian island of the same name, and we stagger off the dock just before ten o'clock at night. I literally have nothing left—no energy, no strength of character, no will to live. And so it happens, when we arrive at our guesthouse, that I find myself in the very odd position of being cared for by my dad.

While he signs us in, I drop onto my bed with all my clothes still on and with the world still rocking. Ten minutes later, my dad appears with a cup of ginger tea that he insists I sip. After the tea, with my stomach settling for the first time since we boarded *La Fortuna*, I feel well enough to clean my teeth and get into my pj's. Sometime later, my dad returns to tuck me into bed, and I fall asleep like a twelve-year-old as he reads aloud a selection of tourist pamphlets from his spot in the easy chair across the room.

chapter twenty-six

TUESDAY
Aeolian Whitefish
Gia Kostas, special correspondent to NOSH, on
    the Tyrrhenian Sea

*Just for a moment, try to remember the best meal you ever had
that was built around a fish. Haddock and chips from newspaper
on a London street corner? Ahi tuna pan-seared to perfection
beside a beach in Maui? Well, here's a recipe to add to your "best
of" file. It begins, of course, with a fish taken fresh from a raging
sea . . .*

I awaken the next morning to a gorgeous, blustery day outside my
window. Clear, blue skies reflect the brilliance of the Tyrrhenian
Sea, and every trace of my seasickness is gone. Lipari is the second-
smallest of the Aeolian island chain, and in the light of day, I am
slapped in the face by the sheer beauty of the place. These islands are
volcanic in origin, though Lipari does not have its own active volcano. Only the aptly named Vulcano and its brother Stromboli still
like to make their beginnings known. From my window across the
water, I can see a gentle wisp of smoke above the top of what I think
is Stromboli.

No smoke rings, though.

My dad must have gone to his own room sometime after I fell

asleep last night. The only hint that he was here at all is the small
stack of tourist pamphlets on the table beside the easy chair.

I wash and brush in record time, determined to get something—
anything—into my very empty stomach. On my way out the door, I
scoop my bag off the chair and knock the top pamphlet onto the
floor. As I stoop to pick it up, one of the headlines catches my eye. I
have to read it twice before the meaning actually sinks in. When it
does, I clutch it so hard it crumples, and then I head downstairs to
find my dad.

He's sitting in a spot by a sunny window in the tiny dining room
of the guesthouse. The house itself is little more than a cottage,
painted a jaunty yellow with white trim around all the windows.
From the size of the breakfast room, the place can't possibly hold
more than four guest rooms or so. My dad is alone, apart from a single
other diner, reading an Italian tabloid covered in what I assume are
lurid headlines: *SCANDALO De Governo!* and *Problemi Fiscale!*

Even with no Italian, I feel headlines like that can't really bode well.

"Good morning, my darling," my father cries, as cheerful as the
headlines are gloomy. He jumps up to give me a kiss on the cheek,
and I see he's wearing a suit jacket and tie.

For the sake of the newspaper-reading guest, I accept the kiss
without a fuss, but I drop the pamphlet literally on top of Ari's soft-
boiled egg as I take my own seat.

As he hastily moves it aside, a young woman arrives to take my
order. Using the translation app on my phone, I ask her to bring me
her own favorite breakfast items on the menu, and she beams and
disappears into the kitchen.

"A very good idea, *koritsi*," my dad says, digging into his egg and
toast. "Getting a sense of what the locals eat should work very well
for your . . ."

"What is *this*?" I snatch up the pamphlet from where he has tucked it behind the saltshaker.

"I don't know, I'm sure," he says, eyeing me warily now. "It is a tourist flyer, I think. Don't you know? You're the one who threw it at me."

I have to bite back my reply when the server reappears with a tiny cup of steaming-hot espresso.

"*Grazie*, Loura," my father says as she sets it carefully in front of my place.

"My pleasure," Loura says, beaming. "*Mi mama*—my mother, she is making 'er special French toast just for you. I will bring when is ready."

She disappears again after refilling my dad's tea, and the old man reading the newspaper at the other table follows her out. I take advantage of the empty room to crush the pamphlet in my fist and shake it at my dad.

"Yes. You're right. It *is* a brochure. It's a brochure for the ferry trip here from Sicily."

He looks at me blankly. "So? We are going north after this, *koritsi*. To Gallura. Not back to Sicily. We don't need a ferry."

I sigh in exasperation. "Pops. I don't want to go back. It took us, like, six hours to get here yesterday in your girlfriend's boat. Or seven."

He looks hurt. "Margarita is not my girlfriend. Merely a wonderful friend who helps us when we need it, yes?"

"If you say so. Anyway, that's not the point. The point is that it took us over six hours. We could have hopped a ferry from . . ." I have to stop ranting to check the now deeply creased pamphlet. "From the marina we passed right by in Milazzo, which would have had us here in an hour and a half. An hour and a half, Pops."

He shakes his head, and after carefully wiping the remains of the egg from his plate with his last bite of toast, pops it in. "Not a chance—not in that weather," he insists. "I'm quite sure the ferries were not even running."

I jab him with my elbow and point out the window, where a ferry is docking into a large berth below us. Beside the ferry, an enormous trimaran bobs at anchor, its lines festooned in colorful flags that snap in the wind.

"It's just as windy right now as it was last night. I bet you anything I would have been less sick on the ferry. And even if I wasn't, we would have been here twice as fast!"

He shrugs. "Darling, how could I know it would get so bad? Anyway, we are here now, and you have a lovely day in front of you. I have one short meeting, and then will join you for a quiet day. We write and rest and recover, yes? Then tomorrow, it's on to Sardinia."

Glancing at his watch, he smiles at me, a drop of vivid yellow egg yolk on the corner of his mustache. "I'm off to meet a colleague, *koritsi*. I will see you back here in a couple of hours, yes?"

Before I can say a word, the server comes in, staggering under the weight of her heavily laden tray. "Ah, Loura," my dad says as she begins to unload the vast array of dishes onto the table in front of me. "Please tell your mama how much I enjoy my breakfast." He kisses his fingertips and then pats her fondly on the shoulder.

"See you later, darling," he says, giving me a jaunty wave.

With the tiniest bit of grim satisfaction, I decide against telling him about the egg on his face. Instead, I turn to see what Loura's mama has come up with.

My dad's meeting must have been super successful, as he doesn't show his face back at the guesthouse until after three. By this time, I've mostly cooled down about the ferry.

Mostly.

The breakfast was enough to feed a family of six, with the added bonus of it being an Aeolian specialty, and was therefore perfect inspiration for my next NOSH entry.

The windy day outside has meant that writing on the back deck of the guesthouse is just not practical, so I sit inside beside a window with a view of the harbor below. Breakfast carries me through the rest of the day, though not without quite a bit of work. When I decline Loura's offer of lunch, her mother emerges from the kitchen looking worried. I put the translation app on my phone to good use explaining that no, I'm not ill, just still full. Even so, every time Loura freshens my coffee, it is accompanied by a variety of tiny, perfect biscotti and small, scrolled butter cookies.

I'm definitely not going to starve in this place.

It's been a good working day all around, actually. By the time my dad arrives back, I've managed to complete one full assignment, including pictures, and sketch out a further two more.

He sits down across from me with a sigh and loosens his tie.

I narrow my eyes at him. "I thought it was supposed to be a quick meeting. You haven't been off wearing yourself out again, have you?"

"No—no. Just a meeting, *koritsi*. It went very well too." He reaches into his briefcase and produces his trusty coil notebook and uncaps the pen that he was given when his emeritus status was confirmed.

"What are you working on?" I ask as he pats his pockets for his reading glasses.

"Oh, just a little project. If it comes together, I'll tell you more about it."

We sit in silence then, both lost in our work for a while. I'm not sure how long later, he tosses his pen down, looks up at me over his glasses, and sighs.

"You work so hard, my girl. And soon—you will be a married woman."

He reaches over to squeeze my hand. "I want to enjoy every minute of this adventure we share together. After the wedding, you will have no more time for your papa."

I roll my eyes at him. "You know that's not true. Nothing will change. We can still go to ball games, right?"

He shrugs. "What if Anthony wants to take you to the ball games? After all, he proposed at a ball game, did he not?"

I wince a little at the memory. "That was just for—" I stop myself and try again. "He was trying to do something that I like, I think. He wanted it to be special."

Devi's voice echoes in my mind. *Yeah—just you and forty thousand of your closest friends.*

My dad waves his hands wide. "As long as he makes you happy, *koritsi*. That is his most important job. He is a lucky man."

"Thanks, Pops," I say, and the two of us settle back down to work in silence. But the warmth of his words carries me all the way through the rest of the day.

The following morning, we board the trimaran I had spotted berthed next to the ferry the day before. The *Celere* sits solidly on the pier below our guesthouse, not even rocking in the waves. The wind, if anything, has risen from the day before, and I clutch a little care package that Loura's mother—who, it turns out, is not only the cook but the owner of our guesthouse—has put together for me. This takes the form of a little mesh bag filled with tea bags and some mysterious-looking candy I've never seen before.

"Eet has ginger," Loura says, translating for her mom. "There's peppermint tea, too, and barley sugar for stomach."

All of which is very welcome.

The *Celere* is huge and sits low and steady in the water as we board, which is almost as reassuring as my care package. It also does not stink of fish, which doesn't hurt either. The sleek lines of this vessel are amazing, and I'm not at all surprised to learn that it is a repurposed ferry designed for quick passage across Mediterranean waters. There are a dozen or so passengers aboard, though it's clear it could hold many more. I don't tell the first mate, who gives me this information, that I thought all trimarans were pleasure craft and instead just nod and take a few notes for my next NOSH article.

The captain, who is a very large, very blond Frenchman, invites all the passengers up to the bridge as we depart. I think about refusing, but clutching my bag of ginger tea, I decide to give it a quick peek. As we leave the harbor, the enormous sails above us billow full to contain the wind, and the boat rockets out into the Tyrrhenian Sea. But almost as soon as we turn away from Lipari, while the wind still blows, the waves settle down to a gentle surge. Above the wake of the boat, the volcanic peaks of the island chain recede into the distance.

It's not until we have been aboard a day that I learn this was the boat Teresa Cipher had originally booked us on for the trip to Lipari. Not only does the *Celere* offer a smoother ride than Federico's motorboat; it apparently made the crossing from Sicily in under an hour.

When I confront my dad about this, he surprises me. Instead of making excuses, he is repentant and promises me to use only ExLibris-approved transportation for the rest of the journey.

This feels like good news. And it doesn't hurt that this boat is so fast and comfortable. With the wind at our back, the *Celere* doesn't have to fight the waves, instead skimming along the water's surface in a way that feels almost like flying. The biggest added bonus for me is that every trace of my seasickness has vanished.

Apparently there is state-of-the-art satellite Wi-Fi onboard, so I plant myself for the day in one of the large and elegantly appointed lounges, far away from the sea spray, and work on my next column. The Sicilian feast prepared single-handedly by Nonna Rosa has left me struggling a little to find the words to do it justice. For inspiration, I open one of Charlotte's recent e-mails that actually includes circulation numbers. Whatever I have been doing so far seems to be working, and it appears this is making my editor happy.

> People are starved for travel stories. This adventure you're on is
> really catching fire.

I read the words *catching fire* over a few hundred times, until I have to stop because my face is starting to hurt from my giant smile. It somehow makes things even better that I get to shine a light on a few of the places my dad loves so much.

When an announcement goes over the public address system that we'll be docking at Gallura in less than an hour, I head upstairs to look for my dad. I find him standing near the front of the enclosed deck, staring through the dark at the lights of the island that are just winking on in the distance.

I give him a peek at Charlotte's e-mail on my phone, and he reaches an arm around to hug me.

"I'm so proud of you, Gianna," he says, his voice barely carrying over the low thrum of the ship's engines. "You have made something of yourself, and all on your own."

"Maybe." I tuck my phone away. "I mean, I'm only contracted for the one series, so it's not like it's a regular gig. But it's a start, I hope."

"So it is," he says, squeezing me again. "Better than *my* start. Did you know I ran away from school when I was sixteen?"

I stare at him in surprise, but he nods. "Yes, I did. Crewed on a boat that ended up right here." He taps the glass of the window.

"Here? You mean *here* in Sardinia? I thought you came to America straight from Athens."

He shakes his head, staring out into the darkness. "From Ithaca, actually. With quite a few detours along the way. I fell in love with a beautiful girl," he adds, and I'm shocked to see his eyes fill with tears.

"What? Who was she?" I'm suddenly rabid with curiosity about his youth—a time in his life he's never really even mentioned to me. I pepper him with questions, but he waves them away.

"Ah, it was a long time ago. I was here for three months, and the girl—well, her parents wanted her to be with a local boy."

I grin at him. "Weren't interested in a Greek boyfriend for her, huh?"

He shakes his head firmly. "They did *not* approve. In fact, they sent her away to school." His voice drops even lower. "We never saw each other again."

He wipes his eyes, and I can't find any words to comfort him, so I try distracting him by asking about something he mentioned earlier.

"Just a minute—did you say Ithaca? I thought you were born in Athens?"

He clears his throat, and his voice resumes its normal timbre. "I went to school in Athens, but my family came from Ithaca. I was five or six before my papa moved us to the city. The economy was terrible, and he didn't have the money to hang on to his olive groves—and so we moved. But I never liked it—I never fit in. So I ran away."

He reaches down for his briefcase. Outside, the lights grow ever closer, and some of the details of the port come into view. It's hard to make things out in the dark, but Santa Teresa di Gallura looks to be a small village tucked neatly into a sheltered cove.

240 · kc dyer

My dad straightens, and I see he's holding the ExLibris itinerary. He turns to the last page.

"You see? Our final destination is Ithaca—for that very reason. Odysseus began there, and so did I," he says.

I shake my head, my mind roiling with all the new information about this man I thought I knew.

"I haven't really thought about it before now," he adds, "but visiting my first home might be even more important to me than this project." He tucks the itinerary away, and we go to collect our bags.

As we are walking down the gangplank, I vaguely recall a reference Raj Malik made to Ithaca way back at the very first site, outside Mitra. I'm suddenly awash in shame that Raj—a total stranger to me until so recently—might know more about my dad than I do.

chapter twenty-seven

WEDNESDAY
Malloreddus
Gia Kostas, special correspondent to NOSH, in Sardinia

These tiny Sardinian swirls offer almost a French twist on the lightest, most delectable riff on gnocchi you've ever tasted. When served in combination with the local spices, including . . .

Considering Sardinia is the second-largest island in the Mediterranean Sea and has been inhabited since basically the dawn of time, it is remarkably unspoiled. We are staying near the little town of San Teodoro on the west coast, not far from the spot we came ashore. All I know about this stop is that my dad has plans to visit the gravesite of some giants, which are apparently pivotal to his research project. We can't seem to get away from giants on this journey, somehow.

I sleep late and wake to discover something I hadn't noticed before crashing hard last night—my tiny room has its own balcony. After throwing open a pair of enormous wooden shutters—painted a vivid turquoise—I step out onto the little stone terrace. It's encased in an elaborate wrought iron railing, rusted and wound through with fragrant bougainvillea. The combination of the vivid purple flowers and the brilliant blue shutters is so eye-catching, it wakes me up immediately.

My view is not down to the sea but of verdant hillsides and dense, lush undergrowth. Many of the bushes are flowering, and the vista is breathtaking. This part of the island is all rolling hills, most dotted with grazing herds of sheep. There's no wind today, and the sound of songbirds is very peaceful after so much time on the water lately.

Behind me, there's a quiet knock, and thinking it must be my dad, I step back into the room to open my door. Instead, a young woman is standing outside carrying a tray.

"Caffè?" she says and, when she sees my expression, steps inside. She strides through the room and sets the tray on the tiny ceramic-topped table out on the deck. The tray holds a small steaming pot that smells so fragrantly of espresso that my mouth actually waters, a wee pitcher of foamed milk, and two almond biscotti.

I beam at her. "Thank you so much. *Grazie, grazie!*"

"Prego," she replies and disappears, closing the door behind her, leaving me to enjoy a leisurely breakfast on my sunny deck. There doesn't appear to be Wi-Fi in my room, but I know I saw a password posted above the check-in desk downstairs, so I decide to just take in the view for a few minutes before I head down to connect online.

Below me, I can see a trail—too narrow to be a road—snaking down the hill toward the small village in the distance. Seconds later, a cyclist pedals by, pumping hard to make it up the hill. A pair of young girls run past in the other direction, heading down to the village, followed by a woman pushing a stroller. I stare idly at the passersby, enjoying sitting on a chair that isn't rocking with the motion of the sea; perfectly content with being a land-based creature again.

I'm just finishing the last luscious crumbs of my biscotti when I notice a familiar straw hat pass by on the path below. I jump up and lean over the rail to call out to my dad, but he carries on down into the village, oblivious. By the time I've gathered up my things and made it downstairs, he's long gone, which suits me just fine. I've got a piece ready to send to Charlotte, but my main goal for the day is to check in with Anthony. If I plan things right, I can call for a quick FaceTime before he goes to bed.

Unfortunately, it turns out the woman behind the desk (name tag: Estella) speaks exactly zero English, and I—needing a Wi-Fi code—have no translation app with which to ask for it. When I finally think to point at the triangular logo above her desk, her expression clears.

"*No weefee—mi desolato,*" she says. "*É rotto.*"

Which means, I think, that I'm out of luck.

She reaches to collect a business card from the rack beside the desk and slides it across to me. "*Due minuti,*" she says, holding up two fingers. She comes out from behind the desk and walks to the front door. "*San Teodoro,*" she says, pointing at the path and repeating, "*Due minuti.*"

"*Grazie.*" I'm grateful I can at least manage to thank her without a translation app.

After a quick trip back upstairs to collect my big hat, I set out down the hill.

The village of San Teodoro is small, little more than a few streets fanning out from the hills down to meet the sea. This has got to be good news, in that it should be easy to find Estella's recommendation, called the *Caffè Sardini*, according to the card. Remarkably, in spite of the tiny size of the village, I spy at least three other coffee bars on my way down the main road. But as I stop to enter the first of these, I discover that it is set up with a counter only and no seating area. The counter is crowded, and while the place smells fantastic, lingering is clearly not encouraged. Both the other places turn out to be exactly the same.

As I step back outside and look again for the *Caffè Sardini* sign, I see my dad's unmistakable straw hat bobbing along the street toward what looks like a market square. I'm just about to call out when I lose sight of him again. Hurrying along, I enter the village square, which at the moment is the site of a bustling marketplace. There are mostly women here, both selling items in the stalls and carrying shopping baskets. A few small children skip about, and I nearly trip over a chicken that struts past me, not at all concerned about getting in my way.

I'm just about to give up when I spot the logo for the *Caffè Sardini* hand-painted on a wooden sign. And there, directing a woman to a seat at one of the tables outside, is my dad. The woman is carrying six or seven large baskets. She has her back to me, and as I approach, Ari appears to be doing all the talking. I catch sight of that charming smile, and I can feel my temper start to rise.

All I want to do with this day is talk to my fiancé. The man I have abandoned to ensure my father is safe. My father, who claims to be on a research trip to find some mythical holy grail—his Odyssean Ark of the Covenant or whatever it is that he needs to imprint his name in history. But we are into the second week of this wild goose chase with no sign of any arks or grails in sight.

What there has been, however, is a large collection of attractive women. And each and every one of them has been subject to the patented Ari Kostas charm offensive. Dr. Elle in Sicily, with her good advice that he has ignored. His pursuit of Margarita and her bra-bearing coveralls meant that we took a time-wasting, stomach-churning boat trip. Even Teresa Cipher, although she's admittedly turned out to be more of a colleague, is an undeniably gorgeous woman. And now, here in this tiny village in Sardinia, yet another woman is in his sights.

All the warmth and good feelings that this trip with my dad has fostered in my heart evaporate in an instant. It is exactly as my mother always said—he is a philanderer. Always has been, always will be. This is how he's wrecked two marriages and countless other relationships with women. *Good* women.

This has got to stop. Right now.

Blood fully boiling, I stomp through the gated entrance to the *Caffè Sardini* in time to see them ordering drinks. The woman is wearing a light cotton dress, and her hair is tied back with a matching scarf. She's in the process of setting down all her baskets, and for the first time, I get a good look at her face. She is undeniably attractive, but most certainly middle-aged, and this stops me in my tracks. As the oldest of the potential conquests on this trip, Dr. Elle was in her early thirties at most, and this woman is definitely older than that. Which should take her off my dad's nothing-if-not-predictable radar. All the same, she's got to be twenty years younger than my dad and is certainly closer to my age than to his. Still, after everything else, it's just too much.

As I begin to weave my way through the tables, my dad jumps up and walks inside. Filled with equal parts fury and determination, I hurry over to the table where the woman is seated. She's not wearing sunglasses and shades her eyes to look up at me.

"Do you speak English?"

She looks a little startled. "Yes. A leetle. Can I—can I help you with something?"

I shoot a quick glance into the café. It's quite dark inside, but I can just make out my dad standing beside the cash register and reaching for his wallet.

"Listen, I think you should leave. My dad . . ." I shoot a thumb over my shoulder into the café. "He's a notorious womanizer."

"Womanize . . . ?" she repeats dazedly. "I not . . ."

Inside, my dad is counting out bills onto the counter.

"Look." I don't have time to gather my thoughts but continue anyway, a little desperately. "My name is Gia Kostas, and that's my dad, Ari. I have literally been chasing him around the Mediterranean for the past two weeks, watching him hit on women. If you're smart, you'll get away while you can."

"Did you say Ari? Ari Kostas?" the woman asks. "The history professor from the television?"

I roll my eyes. "Yes, yes, that's him. That show was over years ago. I can't believe he's still getting mileage out of it."

The woman, her face suddenly pale, stands up and, without a word, steps around the back of the table, hurriedly scooping up all her baskets. In seconds, she disappears into the crowded marketplace.

At that moment, my dad arrives carrying a tiny espresso cup in each hand.

"Gia!" he says delightedly. "I can't believe you found me. I'm just about to . . ."

His voice trails off as he notices the empty table for the first time.

"She's gone." Seizing one of the cups from his hand, I drain it.

The coffee is searing hot, and tears of pain spring to my eyes, but I'm so furious I pretend I haven't just scalded my esophagus all the way down.

My dad looks aghast. "Darling—did you burn yourself?" He sets down his coffee cup and offers me a paper napkin to wipe my watering eyes.

"I'm fine." This is a lie. "She's gone, Pops."

He looks off into the bustling marketplace.

"Gone?" he asks, sitting down. "To the ladies' room?"

"No. She's *gone*, gone. I sent her away. I've had it, Pops. I've had it with you and all the women. It's been one after another this whole time. I'm so mad at myself that I bought into all your shit. All your plans for your legacy—your noble ideals. What happened to retracing Odysseus's journey? What happened to putting a crown onto your life's work? You're seventy-two years old, for heaven's sake. Give it a rest!"

And to my total mortification, I burst into tears.

I turn and flee into the coffee shop. Inside, after tripping over a chair, I stumble blindly into the restroom and slam the door.

I lean on the sink and have just turned the water on to splash my face when the stall door opens behind me. A very old man teeters out, leaning on a cane with one hand and still doing up his fly with the other. He looks at me, his mouth forming an O of surprise.

"*Scusi! Scusi, signorina!*" he cries and bolts out the door at a remarkable speed for someone using a cane.

I hastily turn off the tap and, grabbing a handful of paper towels, sidle back into the coffee shop.

The barista behind the counter raises her eyebrows at me but says nothing. By this time, my throat is burning so badly I'm not sure I could have spoken even if I did have the right Italian vocabulary to apologize.

There is a water-filled pitcher at the end of the bar, so I stop and pour myself a glass. Condensation beads the outside of the pitcher, and the water is filled with slices of lemon. The first sip helps cool my burning mouth at least, so after draining the glass, I refill it and carry it outside.

My dad hasn't moved except to pull his sunglasses down over his eyes. He stares glumly into the crowded marketplace as I sit down.

Before I can say anything, he takes one of my hands.

"I'm sorry you feel this way about your papa," he says quietly. "I know I deserve every word of your anger. But tell me—is your mouth okay? Did you burn your tongue?"

I nod and lift the glass. "I'm okay. I got some water."

The noise and bustle of the market rises up as silence falls between us again. When he releases my hand, I pull my tablet out onto the table, but I don't log on. I feel gut-punched in a way that has nothing to do with the espresso.

After a while, my dad drains his cup. "I know I deserve every word of what you say to me, Gianna," he repeats quietly. "But this time? Is not what you think."

He sighs. "I told you before of my first love, my Penelope. What you don't know is that I first met her here, many years ago—in this very market. She was selling olive oil—her mama's olive oil. When I got up the courage to speak to her, I teased her that her oil is no good because it's not Greek."

He smiles a little. "So, this morning, when I came down to this market, I have many old memories. Suddenly, I see a woman. The woman you spoke to."

I open my mouth, but he raises a hand before I can say anything.

"I know what you think, but you're wrong," he says firmly. "I just see her—she catches my eye, and I think—no! She looks so much like my Pene! And then I think—this place is so small. Maybe she knows her?"

"Pops, I *saw* you following her. You can't *do* that. It's so creepy."

"Gia. My darling girl. I only have good intentions. I only wanted to ask her a question."

"For goodness' sake, Pops. This is the twenty-first century— you've got to know you can't just stalk some random woman in a marketplace. It's not enough to have good intentions. It doesn't *matter* what your intentions are."

"I know, I know," he says apologetically. "I wasn't really thinking."

"Oh, man." I drop my face into my hands. "It's a miracle you haven't been thrown in jail somewhere."

"You're right," he says. "But I promise you, I only asked her to coffee. Nothing creepy." He leaps up. "I'll go find her again. Apologize."

I grab his arm and pull him back down into his seat. "You'll do no such thing!"

He stares at me a little wild-eyed and then suddenly laughs. "Okay, okay—I see. More stalking, right?"

Face? Meet palm.

He sighs at my expression and leans back in his seat. "You're right. What's past is past. Someone told me years ago that Pene moved away. Life has carried on. She is long gone, and we are both old, if she is even still alive. It's just—that woman looked so familiar . . ."

His voice trails away at the look on my face.

"Fine. You're right. I'll leave it. You'll stay here to work today? Do you want another coffee before I head off to the site?"

"Do you think they do iced coffee?" I twist around to stare at the chalkboard menu on the wall.

A shadow falls across the table, and my dad makes a tiny choking sound as I turn around.

The woman is back. This time, she's no longer carrying the armful of baskets and instead holds a roll of paper and what looks like a small black-and-white snapshot. Her face is still pale, and when she speaks, her mouth sounds dry.

"I—may sit with you a moment?" she asks quietly.

My dad shoots me a triumphant look as he pulls out a chair. When I glare back at him, he drops the grin.

"I want to apologize for my forwardness earlier," he says to the woman awkwardly. "I haven't been here for so long, and when I saw your face, it brought back many memories. I hope I didn't . . ."

Before he can finish his sentence, the woman slides the photograph across the table at him. He lifts it up and then scrambles for his reading glasses, dropping his sunglasses in the process. I scoop them up from the ground and set them on the table before leaning across to look at the photograph.

Then I have to remove my own sunglasses to look at it again.

It's old, the blacks mostly faded out to grey, but there is no question that it's a picture of my father as a teenager. He looks like a baby—face still round, no mustache, or at least, when I look closer, maybe only the start of a mustache. Regardless, it's a very young Aristotle Kostas, and he's holding the hand of a young woman. Someone who could be this woman's younger sister.

The color completely drains out of my dad's face.

"My Pene . . . ?" he whispers, looking up at her. "This is my Penelope."

The woman nods. "Yes," she says, her voice sounding stronger. "But this is also my mother."

chapter twenty-eight

 STILL WEDNESDAY
Culurgiones
Gia Kostas, special correspondent to NOSH, on the island of
Sardinia

*These brilliant little pockets are a splendid surprise, fashioned out
of durum wheat to form dumplings stuffed to the brim with ricotta,
with the startling addition of local mint, plucked fresh from . . .*

It might be only eleven o'clock in the morning, but it takes a full
bottle of red wine for Aristotle's color to return. He's so busy asking
questions, the woman, who gives her name as Talia, can barely
keep up.

At this point, even I have kissed any thought of productivity on
this day goodbye and had a glass of red myself. The wine does a hell
of a better job at soothing my burned throat than the water did.

Just saying.

It's not until Ari has fired every possible question about the health
(generally pretty good, with a bit of arthritis in her knees), well-being
(same, without the arthritis), and whereabouts (not here, which is all
that matters at the moment) of Talia's mother that she finds time to
take a deep breath. She drains her own glass and, with a sideways
glance at me, slides the document over to my dad.

His brow furrows as he unfurls the page and stares at it uncom-
prehendingly.

Even reading upside down, I can tell immediately what it is, though not what it says.

I can see right away it's a government document.

A birth certificate for a baby, *Talia Angelina Natale*. The name of the mother is listed: *Penelope Assunta Consolata Natale*. The name of the father is blank.

My dad looks confused, and after a moment, Talia reaches across and places her finger under the date of birth.

He looks up at her then, and his face is a revelation. He's still got his sunglasses off, so I watch his expression morph from puzzlement to stunned shock and finally to clarity. And this is how we both learn that yes—I have a half sister.

My dad manages to slide the page over to me before losing it completely, dropping his head onto his arms on the table and sobbing. Over his head, I meet Talia's eyes and see in them the same stunned shock that I am feeling.

Maybe not quite the same. But it's shock, no doubt. The two of us sit in silence as our father cries his eyes out.

Inside the café, I see the barista just shaking her head. I'm quite sure she's had her fill of crying Kostases for the day. And of course, no one—*no one* cries from the heart like a Greek male. I feel so stunned myself, I don't know what to think. I mean, his earlier pretty vague belief that this woman, this *stranger* he spotted on the street and whose face reminded him of his young love—it turns out to be justified.

Talia is her mother's daughter, and his own too.

I don't know if it was my earlier outburst or the fact that I've just been so angry with him all morning, but in this moment, at least, I don't feel even a little bit tempted to join in the tears.

The truth is, I really don't know what to think. I mean, I grew up knowing I had two half brothers, but I only got to see them a few times on family holidays, and *trust me* when I say it was always awkward.

But a sister? A sister who lives half a world away from me? A sister I had no idea until this moment existed.

I risk looking over at Talia while my dad is still in full flow. She's sitting beside him, one hand on his arm and the other on his shoulder, just watching him. Not saying a word. He's been mopping his face with paper napkins from the table, but after a few minutes, she pulls a handkerchief from somewhere and wordlessly places it in one of his hands.

Her eyes have not left his face since she passed him the certificate. I realize that she herself never thought this moment would arrive. A life-changing moment on a day when she had only set out expecting to sell her baskets in the town marketplace.

The handkerchief seems to help in the end, and after mopping his face several times and blowing his nose in a way I would never tolerate under any other circumstances, my dad seems to get a grip on himself.

"I'm sorry," he says and reaches to take Talia's hand. She looks a little startled at this but doesn't pull away. With his other hand, he reaches for mine. "I am so sorry—to both of you. Not for crying—but for all the mistakes I have made that led to this moment."

He shakes his head, and his eyes well up again. "So many, many mistakes."

I hastily pull my hand away and, using the handle of a knife, poke the damp handkerchief back toward his hand.

"Do I need to take you back to the guesthouse?" I glance over at Talia. "Should we talk in private?"

He shakes his head. "No, no, I'll hold it together, *koritsi*, I promise."

He doesn't, of course.

But what the hell? We've come this far already, and I desperately want to hear Talia's story too.

Focusing on her hands, which she folds in front of her, Talia takes a big, shaky breath.

"I don't know many of details, because my mother, she—she very sad and also angry whenever I ask. A bit better now, but when I was *adolescente*—a teenager—she almost never want to talk about—about you," she says, shooting a quick look at Ari. "I think she was around fifteen when you met, yes?"

My dad nods and pats the table. "We met here—right here in this market," he says. "It's the reason I came down this morning. To revisit old memories. But I never dreamed . . ."

He smothers a half hiccup, half sob in his sodden handkerchief.

I reach across and pat Talia's clasped hands, and she looks at me, startled.

"Just carry on," I whisper. "He's going to keep doing this. Greek men."

"Greek men," she says at the same moment, and the accidental chorus of our voices is so entirely unplanned, we both have to laugh.

She angles her chair then so she can see my face along with my dad's—*our* dad's—and my heart suddenly feels tight in my chest. "Go on."

I'm more interested in distracting myself than rushing her. But my dad clears his throat.

"I was sixteen, and Pene was eleven months younger," he says. "I was crewing on a ship, but fishing? It's not so important here as back in Greece, so after I meet your mama, I quit the ship and take a job at an inn. The building I work was just up the hill, over there."

He points across to where the hills rise up from the other side of the village. "I wash the dishes and sweep the rooms and change the sheets. And I meet your mama whenever we can."

Talia nods. "Yes. She told me you work on fishing boat—she say you left and never come back."

My dad shakes his head suddenly. "No, no, no. I never did that. We were in love. One evening, I went to see her after work, to the little shed behind the house where the jars of olive oil were stored. I got to the door, and Pene was not there. Her mother arrived instead with her broom. She beat me like I was a carpet. She was crazy with fury."

He mimes a madwoman swinging her broom extremely convincingly.

"I pleaded to see Pene, but her mother said she was gone. Gone to a new school, far away."

Talia nods at this. "My nonna," she whispers. "She love me so much, but she will never say name of my father. She spit, give sign of evil eye."

I think about my Dutch *oma*—who cycles everywhere, wears sensible shoes, and feeds me stroopwafel and milky tea—and feel a moment of strange relief.

"She did go to convent school, I know that," Talia adds. "Over in Porto Torres, I think. The nuns help when I was born. They want to give me to another family, but my mother refuse."

My dad wipes his eyes. "I went back to the inn—I boarded there too, you understand, and the innkeeper threw me out. He had heard from Pene's father, he said. And if I knew what was good for me, I would leave town."

"So you left?" asks Talia.

My dad shakes his head. "No—not then. I slept in the olive grove, and then when I got caught, I moved my blanket to the cork forest.

I stayed for weeks—maybe a month—searching for the school." He pauses and sighs deeply.

"I never knew—never even guessed that Pene was going to have a baby. I mean—I was so young. She was my first love. In those days . . ."

He sighs again. "But, you know, I had to eat. I tried to make it home to Greece but found a job on Malta and worked there a long time. Later, I got a job on another ship, this one to England. I sent many letters to Pene to tell her that I loved her, but I heard nothing back."

He pauses to wipe his eyes. "In London, I worked in restaurants and cafés, and I got lucky. I was accepted back into school, and I worked very hard on a scholarship. The only one I could get was in Classics, and it reminded me of all the stories I heard growing up in Greece. When I got an invitation to study in America, I sent one last letter. Still no reply. My heart broke to pieces in my chest, but what could I do? I took a big ship to New York, and there I became me— who I am now. But I never forgot my Pene."

Talia's eyes widen. "She wrote you too," she says softly. "At least, she say she did. But she never spoke to me of your letters. I wonder . . ." She's quiet a moment.

"When I was small—before school—my mother fight with her family. One night, she pack up all our things, and we move away—to Roma. That was where I grew up and went to school. I only came back here when my grandparents die. They leave me the farm. Not much land left—they had sold the orchards, but I have the old house. My mother would not come with me. She is retired now and has her own place near Santa Maria di Leuca."

Talia glances at me. "On the heel of Italian boot," she clarifies and then turns back to Ari.

"When I was growing up, she would tell me of my father living in America. I even saw you once on the television when I was eight— or maybe nine. I beg Mama to call you, but she say no. Again and again, I ask her why she not reach out. 'I call him when I need him and he did not come,' she would say. 'I don't need him anymore.'"

Even I cry, then.

We end up sitting at our little café table for most of that day, sharing stories. Laughing a lot. Crying a bit too. Periodically, food arrives, and we all eat some of it, but not much. I don't take a single picture or make a single note. As the light of day begins to fade, Talia stands up.

"I'm sorry—I have to go now," she says quietly. "Perhaps we can have a chance to meet again before you leave?"

We exchange numbers, and then she is gone.

My dad goes in to pay the bill, and I thank the staff for their patience over this long, strange day. As we walk up the hill to our guesthouse, dusk falls, and the stars begin to wink into the sky above our heads. My dad, rather than looking exhausted, has a bit of a feverish glow in his eyes that I don't like the look of at all. But the wine has made him drowsy, and I manage to convince him to get some rest.

After he goes up to his room, I head back down to the front desk, where the Wi-Fi has been miraculously repaired. On a whim, I send a text to the number Talia gave me earlier.

A strange and wonderful day.

Seconds later, my phone pings.

Is strange you my sister. But also wonderful.

258 · kc dyer

And then, after a moment . . . she adds something more.

My mother tell me very terrible stories about my father.

I laugh a little and type back:

My mother too. And some of them were true. But not all.

There is no reply.

But much later that night, as I brush my teeth, my phone lights up one last time.

No, I read in the darkness. Not all.

chapter twenty-nine

THURSDAY
La Mungetas
Gia Kostas, special correspondent to NOSH, on the island of
   Sardinia

*These wonderful arthropods, their twisty secrets hidden within,
range in size from the miniature* minudda ciuta *all the way up to
the giant* ciogas, *and elevate the experience of eating snails to a
gourmand's delight . . .*

The sun is streaming through my window as I awaken, and I take
a minute to be grateful that my dad decided to embark on this
crazy trip at the perfect time of year. The weather has been mostly
splendid, and all this sunshine is waking something up inside my
skin that I didn't even know was there.

And not only that—I have a sister!

Even cuddled under the warm duvet, this gives me a little shiver
of joy.

I remember asking my mom for a sister when I was really small—
maybe the Christmas I was seven? I added her to my list for Santa,
along with a selection of Beanie Babies. My mom looked at the list
and laughed, which made me sad. It wasn't a joke. I wanted someone
to share everything with. Older half brothers, who lived far away and
I never got to see, didn't fit the bill.

260 · kc dyer

Before I went to sleep last night, I lay in bed and typed the whole story, beginning to end, in an e-mail to Anthony. I tried calling him first, of course, but once again, his phone went straight to voice mail. I reach across to the end table—which in this room is a little wrought iron patio table painted white—and unplug my phone from its charger.

My heart sinks. Nothing from Anthony. I almost dial straight through to him when I remember to check the time—after two a.m. in New York.

Dropping the phone on the bed, my mind wanders back to Talia Natale. Talia Kostas, by rights, not that I hold with the whole old-fashioned patronymic system. And in any case, her last name has no bearing on the fact that she is my sister. Her face floats in my mind's eye as she was yesterday—beautiful olive-colored skin, rich chestnut hair. She has a tiny streak of grey emerging from one of her temples, which she had neatly tucked behind one ear. I can totally see my dad in the lines at the corner of her eyes, emphasized by her tan. I realize, with a shock, that she must be two or three years older than my own mother. Under normal circumstances, that would feel pretty icky.

But then—nobody knew. And by nobody, I mean my dad.

And if he had known, what are the chances that I would even be here?

I make an executive decision. The joy stays.

Checking my phone, I see there's still nothing from Anthony. Yeah, yeah, it's the middle of the night in New York, and I shouldn't expect anything, but still . . .

The birdsong from outside the window—combined with a too-full bladder—gets me out of bed at last. When I emerge from the shower, I find a text from Talia, offering to meet up later today. She's got a work commitment until five. I agree immediately and then go down to find my dad to tell him I will come to see the giants' archeological site with him today, after all.

A ri has hired a car to take us to the site, which is across the other side of Sardinia from where we are staying. The drive is not too long, and the vistas are incredibly beautiful, but I have to say—I kind of miss Taki. And I *really* miss Herman. His salient, single-word observations have enlivened my NOSH pieces more than I would like to admit.

The Giants' Graves at Arzachena are incredible. The island of Sardinia has been inhabited since time immemorial, and the ancient civilizations here put many other world sites to shame. Before the Romans truly made their presence known from across the water, this island was in the clutches of the Nuragic culture, which takes its name from a very specific form of structure built by the ancient Sardinians. These structures—known as nuraghes—are kind of a cross between a monument and a fortress, and can be found all across the island. Upward of seven thousand of these amazing stone towers have been identified in all, though probably at one time, there were many more. The best part is that no one can really agree on what these buildings were used for—military strongholds, residences, meeting places, religious sites—or perhaps any and all of these things. What *is* known is that they formed an integral part of a culture that was so ruthlessly swept away by the Romans that only mystery remains. Today, we don't even know what these people called themselves.

But the *Tomba dei Giganti* are a different form of mystery—and monument—altogether. Whether it was a grave, or even a funerary site at all, is in total dispute. The site is small, not far from a busy roadway, and pretty much surrounded by vineyards and olive groves.

The boulders that form the gravestones look like giant chipped and crooked teeth lined up around the site of the possible tomb. All the same, it strikes me as more of a tourist attraction than an actual archeological site. There are, in fact, a handful of tourists walking around, but the only language I hear spoken is Italian.

My dad, though, is in his element. For the first time, he's using his phone to snap photos, and he's got his trusty coil notebook in hand, taking notes. I even see him jotting down measurements.

After a quick look around, I fall into a bit of a "if you've seen one site, you've seen 'em all" kind of mood, so I find a spot in the shade and secretly try to tether my phone to the mobile of one of the tour guides. When my phone pings, I'm not sure if I'm more delighted by my skill at stealing Wi-Fi or the distraction of a new text.

In spite of the fact that it is now well into Anthony's working day in New York City, the text is not from him. It's an invitation from Talia for my dad and I to join her for dinner at seven. Do we need directions? When I check with my dad, he looks stricken, and I fear a return of the Kostas flood, but somehow he manages to keep it together.

"Please tell her I will remember the way to that house forever," he says, one hand over his heart. "Tell her I could never forget."

I type a quick reply.

We'll be there. No directions needed.

A few hours later, we arrive on the stroke of seven, freshly showered and with appetites primed by our day in the open air. This turns out to be a good thing, as Talia? Can cook.

The meal she serves us makes me forget I have ever eaten before. It is nothing short of magnificent.

Her table, a behemoth that takes up most of the large farm kitchen, puts even Nonna Rosa's selection to shame. She has set up a smaller table on the shady veranda behind the kitchen and hops up periodically to bring new dishes out for us to try. There is sausage and salad and pasta and seafood—and seafood pasta!—and fresh bread with home-churned butter, plus a spicy frittata made with eggs from her own chickens in the coop out back, and rich fruity wine to wash everything down.

We have nearly demolished a tray of *ciusòni*, which are small, perfectly cylindrical dumplings, when it occurs to me that I have not yet documented a single meal in Sardinia. When I broach the subject to Talia, she agrees enthusiastically and plunges into the process of food journalism with great glee. As each new course arrives, she pauses to arrange it beautifully on her table, even running to get a couple of lamps to improve the lighting for the photographs before we can take a single bite.

This focus on the food turns out to be a good thing. Our plan is to leave tomorrow, and Talia helping me with my job takes some of the attention away from the fact that my dad is going to have to say goodbye. And even as the evening is drawing to its natural close, as we drink coffee and eat the tiny *aranzada* that melt away as my mouth closes on them, Talia is one step ahead.

She pulls out pen and paper and carefully copies down Ari's entire itinerary from his ExLibris file.

"I have already made arrangements," she says, smiling. "You are here for one more week, yes? I think that is enough time for you to meet up with my mother. Do you think you might want to do that?"

And for the first time in my life, I see Aristotle Kostas at a total loss for words.

His face reddens as Talia speaks, and he clasps her hands—pen and all—into his own and silently nods before throwing an arm around each of us and—not a real surprise—bursting into tears.

Both of us caught up in this awkward group hug, Talia catches my eye over Ari's shoulder and, closing her eyes, gives her head a tiny shake. The idea of watching our father face the music with Pene after all these years is clearly as interesting to her as it is to me. The end of the journey is going to be more eventful than any of us ever expected.

My dad manages to get a grip on himself after not too long, and we walk away from Talia's house full of love and hope for the future and possibly a few too many of the round, sweet *sospiri*.

On our last morning in Sardinia, I wake to a weird sort of pseudo-apologetic e-mail from Anthony.

My dearest, sweet Gia,

I'm writing you this note in bed after an eighteen hour day that's left me completely done in. You might say I'm exhausted but exhilarated—the IPO went off without a hitch! I tell you, the complexities of bringing this company into a public offering felt like nothing when I was invited to ring the bell at the stock exchange this morning. You should be so proud of me. What a rush!

But listen, babe—I've got a big surprise in store for you. You thought that wedding dress was the best thing that ever happened—after meeting me of course, ha ha—but this is going to blow that out of the water. Talk to you soon as I can get a minute to call. Really sucks how badly the time zones clash with you, bolting off on your little unplanned adventure. Get ready to have your mind blown!

Love ya, babe.
Anthony xoxo

I bring the phone into the bathroom with me and read the e-mail a second time while I brush my teeth.

He makes no mention at all of my news of meeting Talia, nor of any of the many voice mails I've left, excited about the success of my series with NOSH. I'm not sure if I should be upset that he's showing exactly zero interest in what's going on with me or relieved that he's not completely freaked out by my sudden—and unique—change of family circumstances.

He must feel a *little* bad at not taking my calls, however, because of the promised surprise. If there's one thing Anthony is good at, it's surprises. The wedding dress thing was a little misstep, sure, but to be fair, I haven't really had a chance to share my thoughts on the subject. As a swimmer since I was a child, I've always secretly dreamed of being married in a mermaid dress—one that celebrates my curves, not hides them.

I spit out the last of my toothpaste, my finger hovering over the "Reply" button. Should I send Anthony a note to remind him just exactly what I've been doing all this time? I settle on sending him a reply expressing excitement about his surprise, along with a selection of the pictures from Talia's amazing meal last night that I plan to feature in my next installment for NOSH.

And then, as I jam the rest of my clothes in a bag, I begin to feel annoyed with myself for justifying to Anthony what I'm doing here. I'm here to support my dad and to further my career. Also? The groom never has a say in the selection of a wedding gown. And in any case, the silhouette of the dress should be nobody's business but my own. No self-respecting food writer should have to camouflage her assets.

Should she?

My heart lifts as I follow my dad back onto our old friend the *Celere*, which is waiting for us—and a few other passengers—in the

266 · kc dyer

port of Olbia. This is going to be a much shorter sea journey than the last two. Today we will arrive at San Felice Circeo, a tiny spot on the coast just south of Rome. My dad waves his coil notebook at me and starts in on a long explanation of the importance of yet another cave associated with his research. As I lean on the railing of the boat and look across the water to the distant mainland of Italy, I can't help tuning him out. The next week is going to hold the reunion with Pene, a couple of more stops in Italy, and then on to Athens before we head home. But before all that, we'll be in San Felice Circeo, and I remember that Raj will be there.

For some reason I'm not willing to examine too closely, I can't wait to see him again.

chapter thirty

FRIDAY
Spaghetti a Napoli
Gia Kostas, special correspondent to NOSH, in Naples, Italy

This most commonplace of American dishes is taken back to its roots here in the brilliant Mediterranean city of Naples, where the garlic is fresh and the pasta is without . . .

The trip across the gently rolling waters of the Tyrrhenian Sea is as short as a ferry ride, and it's not even ten o'clock when the boat docks in Naples. This is the first major city I've been to since Athens, and the noise and activity of the docks remind me a little of home. Container ships, huge cranes, the bustle of stevedores loading, unloading, and yelling. Everybody yelling.

Strangely, I find I haven't missed that part at all.

Through the glass to the waiting room, I spot Raj and wave eagerly when we come through. In return, his greeting is very reserved.

He reaches out to shake our hands. "So nice to see you again, Dr. Kostas, and you, Ms. Kostas."

Ms. Kostas? I feel a sudden, irrational surge of disappointment. He's still perfectly polite, of course, but the warm friendliness of the last time we were together is noticeably absent.

"I've arranged a car to take us to the site, sir," he says before turning to me. "Happy to drop you off wherever you'd like, first, of course. Perhaps the guesthouse?"

"That sounds ideal," says my dad heartily and, hooking an arm through Raj's, launches into his plans for the day.

I trail along behind, expertly third-wheeling it, as usual.

As we step out onto the street, Raj raises a hand, and a car pulls up to the curb, the trunk springing open.

"No motorbike today?"

Raj swings open the back door, and my dad hoists his bag into the trunk. "Change of plan now that you're here. I can double, no problem," he says, laughing. "But the last time I've ridden three on a bike was in Delhi, visiting my cousins when I was fifteen."

I slide into the car beside my dad, and Raj hops into the front passenger seat. While he gives an address to the driver and then turns around in his seat to chat with my dad, I sit quietly, thinking.

Of course plans have had to change since I'm here. I might be here keeping an eye on my dad, but my very presence is making more work for everyone, including Raj. No wonder he's acting so reserved.

And regardless of his motivation, I feel annoyed with myself. I mean—one nice dinner does not a friendship make. And what do I need to be friends with this guy for, anyway? I *have* friends. And I *am* engaged, after all.

At this thought, my hand goes to my neck, and I make a decision. While my dad machine-guns questions about San Felice and Raj does his best to answer them, I carefully undo the clasp to my necklace, take my ring off the chain, and slide it back onto my finger.

Twenty minutes later, after pulling up to the guesthouse, I head in alone.

"I'll check us in and get some work done," I insist, and the two of them, eager to go explore the next site, drive off without looking back.

Which suits me just fine.

The place we are staying is on the seaside, north of Naples and south of Rome. The coast here is craggy and rocky and absolutely beautiful. The white wind-weathered cliffs have a similar look to the shoreline of Crete, where we got lost in the caves.

And in our own minds, at least for a while.

After checking in, I walk out to the communal terrace, which happens to be on the roof of the guesthouse. Directly below me, the water is emerald green and very shallow at the moment. Even from way up here on the rooftop, I can see purple and red sea stars filling the rocky tide pools far below.

To my left and just up the coast a bit, a broad stream tumbles down from the rocky highlands into the sea. Where it meets the shore, it runs beside a public campsite, its entrance dotted with snack bars and sea sport equipment rental shacks.

According to the ExLibris itinerary, this is the last stop of any length on this crazy trip, and I stare down thoughtfully at the little rental shacks. I decide that if I get my next article for NOSH ready to go by this evening, I might take the morning off for a little ocean exploring. Why should Ari and Raj have all the fun?

Inspired by the thought of a swim in those crystal clear waters, I get down to work on my next piece right away. This rooftop terrace is empty of other humanity and dotted with the ubiquitous cast-iron tables, each topped with a furled white umbrella. I choose a likely spot, crank the umbrella skyward, and settle down to work.

I'm now getting almost daily updates from Charlotte, giving me an idea of the numbers my stories are generating. After a fairly slow start, the readership has soared, with the pieces on Sicily and Crete apparently being the special favorites.

As I log on to the Wi-Fi, I decide I'm going to blow those earlier likes and numbers out of the water with this next story. Between the careful step-by-step instructions Talia walked me through—and we photographed—and the incredible dishes she shared with me, I feel like the Sardinia piece is going to be the jewel in the crown of this series.

Before I can get down to work, though, my inbox updates with a staccato series of pings. The first several are notes from Charlotte, and I star those to read—and gloat over—later. There's also a short message from Devi, telling me that she aced her specialist training over the weekend and can now go back to her normal—but still crazy—schedule.

Hard on the heels of Devi's e-mail is a note purportedly from Anthony, but with Melanie's DNA all over it. I mean, his last note to me was so lovey—all "kisses" and "babes"—so I know that she must have written this one. It's terse and merely says that he's read my e-mail and will be replying as soon as he is able.

I feel a bit ambivalent about this. Does this mean Melanie is reading my private correspondence to my fiancé? I don't need anyone else knowing about the whole thing with Talia—at least until I'm ready. I haven't even told Devi about it yet.

I lean back in my seat—wicker, luckily, not cast iron, and with a very comfy seat cushion—and have a moment of gratitude that Devi is in my life. We've been friends since we shared that double desk back in third grade, but these days, we hardly get to see each other. My internship at NOSH meant that I've no longer been keeping the more relaxed schedule I had when I was in school, and of course, Devi is up to her eyeballs at the hospital. Lately, it seems that our interactions are mostly electronic, and that makes me a little sad.

I decide that I need to make some girlfriend time happen as soon as I get back to New York. And then I settle down to pick out the photos that do Talia's incredible meal the most justice.

Three hours later, the sun has just dropped below the umbrella enough that I am considering finding a spot inside so I can better read my tablet screen, when I hear footfalls pounding up the stone steps behind me.

Turning, I see Raj Malik pelting up the stairs.

He spots me and clutches at his chest, panting. "Christ—that was more stairs than I expected."

I spring to my feet. "What's wrong?"

"Nothing," he gasps and then tries again. "At least not—*not* actually nothing. It's just that I'm not sure it's medical. I mean, he's just acting a wee bit strange."

I've already tossed everything into my bag. "Where is he?"

"Downstairs. I got him into his room, and I'm almost positive he'll be all right, but . . ."

"Let's go." My mind reeling with possibilities, I follow him back down the stairs.

chapter thirty-one

STILL FRIDAY
Mushrooms Redux
Gia Kostas, special correspondent to NOSH, near
    Naples, Italy

*The wide and varied use to which Neapolitans put mushrooms
speaks to the truly remarkable creativity in a cuisine that dates
back millennia . . .*

My dad's room is across the hall from mine on the first floor of the guesthouse. Raj, who reaches the door before I do, steps back to let me in first. The room turns out to be a little larger than mine, with its own en suite bathroom. As I hurry inside, he's sitting in a lovely old chair beside the open window, gazing out over the water. The dark wooden shutters, each with a tiny brass keyhole, run from the floor almost all the way to the twelve-foot ceilings. At the moment, they've been unlatched and thrown open to a view of the Mediterranean. There is no balcony, but outside the window, an elaborate wrought iron screen has been affixed across the opening to act as a safety barrier.

My dad looks fine, but when he turns to smile at me, his pupils are huge, making his eyes look like creepy black marbles.

My heart sinks like a stone.

"Darling!" he says. "My beautiful girl. My second beautiful girl—conceived in love, wrapped in love." He turns to Raj. "Thank you for bringing her to me, my friend. My dearest supporter."

He waves a hand to encompass the room. "Can you see it—can you see the room is wrapped in shades of love? Blue and turquoise and . . ." His voice trails off and his eyes close gently.

Wincing, I turn to Raj. "Thanks very much for bringing him back. I think I know what the problem is."

My dad, still smiling, turns his gaze to the sea outside the window.

Raj tilts his head, indicating the door to the bathroom. Reluctantly, I follow him inside.

"I'm just worried this is a cognitive . . ."

I sigh and raise a hand to cut him off. "It's not. It's . . ."

My mind races to find an alternative to the truth—and fails. Raj looks so worried. His hair is sticking up, and he's all sweaty from his race back to the guesthouse, so in the end, I just turn and march back into the room. I kneel down beside my dad, and he's still smiling out the window at the universe.

"Pops—look at me," I say, patting his hand. "What did you eat for lunch?"

Nothing. His smile doesn't falter.

"Dr. Kostas," Raj says, and I can hear how hard he's working to keep the panic out of his voice. "Can you hear us? Gia is here."

"Gia?" my dad says suddenly. "My Gianna—is the future." He points to the sky outside the window, which, now that the sun has set, is turning an ethereal pink and gold. "But there—you see her? There is Magdalena—my grandmother. Magda! Magda!"

Before I can react, he is on his feet, reaching out the window. Raj grabs hastily at his sleeve, but the top of the wrought iron rail is high enough to ensure there's no danger of a fall. Luckily, he doesn't fight us and returns compliantly to his chair almost immediately.

"Pops," I say again. "What did you eat for lunch?"

"The future meets the past," my dad says, beaming. "Magda—

this is my Gia." He gestures to me and then out the window. "Gia, this is Magdalena. And of course, you both know Consolata."

Raj looks from the open window to my father and then back at me. He raises his hands, palms up.

Do you want me to go find a doctor? he mouths. Out loud he says, "We had those prosciutto sandwiches for lunch, remember, Ari? And what about the olives? Weren't they delicious?"

My dad just beams his gentle smile into the ether, communing with ghosts.

I sigh and force myself to meet Raj's eyes. "I think he's eaten mushrooms. We—we had a little problem with this already, back in Crete."

My dad clutches at Raj's sleeve. "It's great stuff, dude," he says and then dissolves into helpless laughter.

"Mushrooms?" Raj says, slowly. "As in . . ."

"Psilocybin. Magic mushrooms."

And then, before I can stop myself, I tell him the whole story. Even though I try to keep it short, this is no easy task, as my dad keeps interrupting us with tales of crossing the River Styx and introductions to various ancestors, visible—of course—only to him.

"That's—quite a story," says Raj, his voice low. "Was this inside the caves? It's a miracle you found your way out."

I nod. "I thought he'd finished all of them in Crete." As soon as it comes out of my mouth, this sounds like I'm making an excuse. "I mean, I didn't even ask him at the time. I thought they all went into the omelet that morning."

"Consolata knows," Ari hisses suddenly. He holds one hand to the side of his mouth, like someone trying to sell you something out of the trunk of a car. "She's shown me the way."

"The way to . . . ?" Raj asks, politely.

I roll my eyes. "Don't try to talk to him. He's not going to make any sense at all until this stuff wears off."

"The way to the answer, of course," replies my father, the stoner. "The route. The path. The artifact. The answer." He waves his hands in Raj's face, sketching out an elaborate pattern that means absolutely nothing to either of us.

"This is pure nonsense, Pops, and you know it."

I've clearly reached the point of peak humiliation when I'm forced to castigate my stoned father. He's not hearing a word I say anyway and, ignoring me completely, launches back into a conversation with whoever is speaking to him out of the now purpling sky.

I rub my eyes and turn back to Raj, but I'm too embarrassed to meet his gaze. "I can take it from here. He should be back to normal by the morning."

Raj clears his throat. "Are you—ah—sure there are no medical implications?"

I shake my head. "Apparently not. I mean, beyond him trying to throw himself out that window to talk to—to Consolata, whoever *she* is."

"She is Magdalena's great-grandmother," my dad says from his chair. His eyes are, once again, tightly closed. "She has come to show me the way."

Walking across the room, I swing the door open for Raj, hoping he'll take the hint and leave. "We'll see you in the morning."

Instead, he squats down by my dad's chair, dropping his hands onto the old man's knees. "It's been a long day, Ari," he says quietly. "Perhaps we can chat about things over breakfast in the morning?"

My dad pats one of Raj's hands. "A fine idea. By then, I should have the exact location for you. And we can find the answer together, yes?"

"For crying out loud, Pops!" My patience is entirely gone, but Raj just stands up and smiles at him.

"Good. See you in the morning, then," he says. By the time he's made the three strides over to the door, my dad's head has fallen back into the wing of the chair, and he is snoring gently.

"I am *so* sorry," I find myself whispering, but Raj shakes his head.

"You didn't know. Anyway, it's my fault. I watched him cleaning out the contents of a little plastic bag just as we walked into the cave. I thought it was granola or something, but when he didn't offer me any, I didn't ask."

"Oh, thank god he didn't." I stare at him wide-eyed, horrified at the very thought.

Raj shrugs. "It doesn't look like it's done *you* any long-term damage," he says and, for the first time, gives me a real smile. He turns to leave.

"Listen." I reach out to touch his arm. "I'm sorry I didn't tell you about the mushrooms before. I was just so embarrassed. After the situation with Paulo and the wine at your site that time—I mean, this is not the norm, is all I'm saying."

"I know that," Raj says, quietly. "I've worked with your dad for over a year, remember."

I follow him out into the corridor. "Okay. It's just—the mushrooms really were just an accident, at least the first time. I don't want you to think he's some old hippie, tripping out and wasting your time."

Raj laughs then. "It's okay. I don't think that at all."

A wave of relief washes over me. "Good. And thank you very much for looking after him so well."

"Don't give it another thought. Perhaps I'll see you tomorrow?"

"Yeah. See you then."

I watch him walk down the hallway toward the stairs and then close the door. I spend the next hour searching my dad's things like a hound dog on the scent of an escaped convict. I start with the room, looking through every drawer and under the mattress like an FBI pro.

At some point about halfway into my search, my dad rises and goes into the bathroom. I redouble my efforts, but after searching every bag and the dividers in his briefcase twice, all I find is a single plastic baggie, tattered now, and jammed into the pocket of his jacket.

Emerging from the bathroom smelling like toothpaste, my dad wanders over to his bed and collapses into it. He is completely oblivious to me going through all his stuff.

"G'night, *koritsi*," he mumbles into his pillow. "Don't forget to kiss your great-grandmother, eh?"

This reminds me to close—and lock—the enormous shutters and pocket the tiny brass key.

Jamming the tattered baggie into my pocket, I head for my own room.

I never want to see another mushroom again as long as I live.

chapter thirty-two

SATURDAY
Amargoso Amaretti
Gia Kostas, special correspondent to NOSH, near
San Felice Circeo, Italy

These sweet nothings are the most delectable macaroons you'll ever taste. They cross the boundary from bitter almond to sweet and back again in a way that makes the palate sing. Begin with . . .

I wake up to a text from Devi in reply to one I'd fired off to her after getting my dad to bed the night before. After hearing the whole story, she is clearly just as amused as Raj had been and insists that there is likely no contraindication from the hallucinogen in the mushrooms to my dad's blood thinners.

> Did you read that article I sent you? If anything, he
> probably had a better trip.

I can hear the chortle in her words, which does nothing for my mood.

My dad is waiting for me, looking fresh as a daisy, at a table on the patio. Beside the table, the server has driven over a cart bearing a complete coffee service, still steaming, and a selection of biscotti.

"You look very well this morning, Ari," I say, pouring myself coffee from the carafe. I sit across from him, my back to the splendid view of the Mediterranean.

He looks hurt. "Ari? What is this Ari? You are my baby, don't forget. The last of my children to call me Papa."

I snort and reach across for a biscotti to dunk in my coffee. "You're not acting much like a papa these days. Taking unregulated hallucinogens. Scaring your colleagues—*and* me."

The biscotti melts away into the coffee, and I have to retrieve it with a spoon. It is absolutely delicious and even improves the flavor of the coffee. Tilting the remaining biscotti on the saucer, I manage to snap a shot or two before my dad scoops it up to eat.

"Darling," he says, dunking thoughtfully. "You know that before everything, I am a scientist. Science rules my every decision. Yes, I made a mistake in Crete. It was an honest one, I promise you."

I sigh and sip my coffee. "I believe you."

"I should hope so. I abhor drug use, you know that. It's never crossed my mind to ingest any hallucinogenic substance, let alone psilocybin—well, ever. And I certainly would never have given it to you, my baby girl, knowingly."

This makes me laugh. "Oh, I'm sure of that. All those lectures when I was in high school. You even made me watch *Reefer Madness*—remember that?"

He laughs too, then. "Guilty as charged. But look at the result!"

He stretches an arm out toward me proudly.

"Thanks a lot. You make it sound like I'm a prize heifer brought to the market. Just so you know, most kids rebel against that kind of hard line. It just wasn't my thing, is all." I drain my coffee. "And anyway, what happened to *you*, Mister High and Mighty?"

"That's Dr. High and Mighty, thank you very much," he says, grinning.

"Well?"

He's quiet a minute, finishing his coffee. "I did some research."

"What kind of research?"

"Online. And I e-mailed Dr. Elle."

At this moment, the server arrives, replacing the carafe and bringing a fresh basket of biscotti. The Italian tradition of breakfast being the least important meal of the day is definitely upheld here, but the biscotti *are* divine.

When the server leaves, I pounce on my dad's remark.

"Dr. Elle? You mean Teresa Cipher's friend? Just to be clear, she brought that doctor in strictly to check on your health because I was worried about you. Until you decided to—you know—hit on her."

He shoots me a haughty look. "You mistake me, my girl. I love women, yes, of course I do. I love them because they are strong and beautiful but, above all, because they are smart. Take your mother, for example. She is a terribly clever woman."

"That's true, though I'm not sure I've ever heard *you* say it before."

He shrugs. "She is too clever to stay with me."

"Also true. But quit changing the subject. Are you telling me you've been in touch with Dr. Elle since that day on Crete?"

He nods. "She sent me some information. A few articles and a piece from *The Lancet*."

Pulling his phone from his pocket, he flicks through the screen for a moment and then holds it out to me.

"Since when have you been doing e-mail on your phone?"

He chuckles. "Your papa might be an old dog, but . . ."

"Okay, okay, I get it."

I glance down at his screen and then scroll to the top and take a closer look. It's the very same paper Devi sent to me. Speechless, I hand his phone back.

"This research raises some very interesting theories on brain function and the role of the human conscious." He shrugs. "So, I want to raise my consciousness. Who cares? My brain's not very trustworthy these days. Who knows when it's going to give out on me for good?"

"Don't talk like that."

He reaches across to pat the back of my hand. "This journey— every stop I make is for a reason, *koritsi*. All these years, I've felt like something is missing. Somehow, somewhere, there is proof—hard proof—that so far, everyone has missed. Again and again in my work, I find references to a piece that depicts Odysseus's story that is contemporaneous to his journey."

"A piece? Like a piece of writing?"

He lifts his shoulders. "It could be a depiction of the journey on an amphora or other vessel. It may be the words themselves pressed into the side of an everyday object. But somewhere, those early verses of Homer's exist as written proof. Proof that the journey—or at least the story of the journey—took place in the third century, or perhaps even earlier."

I shoot him a skeptical glance.

"*That's* your holy grail? Somebody's old stew pot etched with a story told by an ancient blind poet who may or may not have even existed?"

His smile is sad. "For the past year, my girl, I plan to come here. All my hopes are pinned on finding the key—the final puzzle piece to cement my research. And you know what I got so far?"

"No . . ."

"Nothing, that's what. A big, fat zero. And time is running out, if not for me, for this journey. So yesterday, I visited the cave, and I am sure—so sure—that the evidence will be there. I looked through all morning with Raj, but we find nothing. So I think—I maybe am looking at things the wrong way. I might need some new insight. And then I remember that I have a few—just a few—of those special mushrooms left."

He sets his coffee cup into the saucer with a clatter. "And what can I say? I was right. So I send what I learned to Raj this morning, and he tells me he can go once more through his site near Circe's cave." He sighs. "Perhaps we shall find nothing. But once I complete this journey, in my heart, I will know that I have given the theory my all. If I can't cement my place in history beside Homer, at least I will have tried my best."

"So, is the site here the last of the digs, then? What about—don't you plan to visit Malta on the way back to Greece?"

His eyes twinkle. "Ah, yes, at first, but no longer. Last night, I sent a message to Teresa, and she agreed to a little change of plan."

Change of plan. Those words have never bothered me before, but after this trip, I hope I never hear them again.

"And that means?"

He shrugs. "I spent the unhappiest days of my life in Malta. After I lost Pene, I crewed on a ship back to Greece, but it was a disaster. One night, when the ship stopped in Malta, I was robbed and beaten up and thrown in jail for fighting. By the time I got out, my ship had sailed. I lost all will to do anything after losing Pene, and so I ended up staying there seven years. It's where I met Helena and where Tomas was born."

"Tomas? My brother Tomas? Doesn't he live in London?"

He nods. "Helena and I took a chance to make things better, and we moved to England, but—well, long story. It didn't work out."

He falls silent.

"So, we're not going to Malta, after all?"

His face brightens. "No. Instead, we take the train from Napoli across to Taranto, and we pick up the boat to Ithaca there. It's quicker, and we can stop on the way in Santa Maria."

"Okay, I finally get it. Santa Maria di Leuca. Where Pene lives."

"Where Pene lives." His smile lights up his face. "I have so much to tell her."

"Pops, I love to see you so happy. It's—it's amazing. I can see how much meeting up with Pene means to you. But you've got to remember what we talked about. She may not even want to see you again."

"No, no, you are right. I remember what you said, and I have turned a new leaf. This decision must be completely hers. I cannot plan her life for her, I know that. But just to see her again will be enough. It means everything."

"I can tell."

"And for you—we complete our circle of the Mediterranean, and you can finish your assignment, yes?"

"Okay—yes, that still works for me." I pause a moment, then smile at him. "Thanks for thinking of that, Pops. It means a lot. I finished my latest piece last night. I just need to submit it this morning, and I might actually be able to take a day off to explore Capri."

"Good, good." He claps his hands and then rubs them together. "It's a beautiful place, you'll see. You can lie on the beach or even climb the Via Krupp while I visit with this new colleague. And the day after that, we take the train from Naples, eh?"

The thought of a day on the beach is too good to miss. It's a matter of seconds to log in and send the piece off to Charlotte, and ten minutes after that, we're striding down toward the docks and the water taxi that will buzz us over to what the tourist brochures all call "the magical Isle of Capri."

In retrospect, I'm guessing that reads better than "Capri—site of one disaster after another."

It just doesn't have the same ring to it.

chapter thirty-three

STILL SATURDAY MORNING
Parmigiana Melanzane
Gia Kostas, special correspondent to NOSH, in Naples, Italy

Mythology has it that nothing is more powerful than the siren's call to the sea, but in this case alone, it might be worth holding out. When this Neapolitan wonder is served without shrimp or scampi, this dish makes a delicious option for vegetarians. The secret is a delicate pairing of eggplant with a version of local mozzarella called fiordelatte, *combined with . . .*

R aj Malik is waiting for us by the water taxi when we arrive, as it is to his friend that my dad is to be introduced today. Apparently Raj also needs to collect a piece of equipment from the guy to use on the excavation of his site at San Felice. My dad, while technically sobered up, is still completely unrepentant about his mushroom-fueled adventure of the day before. He spends the trip across the water explaining to Raj how the vision that was carried to him in the form of one or another of his great-grandmothers might prove his theory after all.

Raj's demeanor, at least when he speaks with me, has reverted back to frustratingly formal once again. I find myself feeling unaccountably annoyed with him about this. I mean, considering all that we have been through on this wild goose chase of my dad's, you'd think he could just loosen up a little. This morphs, of course, into feeling angry at myself for even caring. We agreed to forget anything that happened between us. Why should it matter how this colleague of my dad's acts?

But somehow, it does.

Making things worse is the complete radio silence from Anthony. I decide to spend the day ignoring my frustration with all of them—my doping dad, my unresponsive fiancé, and even the carefully polite Raj—since they all are leaving me extremely cranky at the moment.

Capri is a brilliant, multicolored jewel floating in the balmy Gulf of Naples, a very short distance off the Amalfi coast. We disembark from our water taxi on the tourist dock of the Marina Grande, and the town of Capri climbs up the mountainside above us with a splash of every color you can imagine. From this angle, the houses look like brilliant building blocks set against the cliffside, one atop the next. The blues and reds and yellows pop against the rocky cliffs and sparkle in the morning sunshine.

We agree to meet back on the pier at four, and still internally fuming at both of them, I stomp off toward the tourist office. I'm quite sure neither one even notices as they hurry away to meet their colleague without even a backward glance. Considering this is my first real day off on the entire journey, I resolve on the spot to forget about all the men in my life and enjoy Capri to the full. Collecting a small paper map from the quiet tourist office, I set off in search of the Via Krupp.

All the signs are in both English and Italian, which makes finding my way a piece of cake. I pay two euros to step inside a very clean and efficient funicular, which scoots me up the side of the mountain. It's a vehicle that feels like a bizarre cross between an elevator and a subway car. Just over four minutes later, I step out into the city's main piazza, and from there, I follow my map all the way across to the Augustus Gardens.

The Via Krupp is a cobbled walking path, zigzagging its way down the cliffside in a series of tight switchbacks. Ostensibly it was built for Herr Krupp, a scientist, to make his way between his shipboard laboratory and his cliffside home. However, the whispered story is that the road made it easier for Krupp to scoot down to a hidden grotto at the base of the cliffs, where he indulged in extracurricular orgies and other debauchery.

The views of the island and across the water are astonishing, and below me, the path winds its way down in a series of tightly cobbled switchbacks all the way to the beach. While I have no inclination to find out if the orgy thing is still happening, my plan to take the jagged path down to the beach is thwarted, however, when I discover access to the Via Krupp is blocked. The sign, in both Italian and English, notes that the path is closed due to recent rock falls.

Pausing to catch my breath, I lean against the wall and look out over the island, trying to decide which beach will be nicest to plant myself for the rest of the day. Suddenly, I hear a yell followed by a distant splash. Just up the coastline, I spot a group of small brown dots moving around on a promontory jutting out from the cliff face. As I watch, one of the dots leaps off the cliff and lands with a splash in the waters far below. A second jumper follows the first, and then two who may or may not be holding hands join in.

I have less than zero interest in hurling myself off a cliff, beautiful setting or no, but the water below the jumpers appears to be a little cove, and I can see several paddle boarders and even a kayak floating on the azure sea. Aside from a gentle ripple, the water looks as clear and calm as a swimming pool.

Since none of this experience even resembles a normal sort of vacation, I have, of course, had zero time for shopping. The only bathing suit I have with me is my training suit from my time on the university team. Swimming was my go-to exercise in university, and it meant I got a workout three times a week, no matter what the weather. My training fell off considerably during the internship at NOSH, but I still managed at least two trips to the pool most weeks.

So, while my navy blue NYU training suit is technically for swimming, the only other people I see wearing one-piece suits are all grannies. In the changing room, I lock my phone and the rest of my things—except for my big hat—away and tell myself that it doesn't matter. I don't know a soul here. No one is going to point and laugh. And I'm not going to let my lack of a cute bathing suit spoil my day.

Twenty minutes later, I'm wearing a neon yellow life belt—much more fetching than a full life jacket, to my mind—and getting the feel for paddling my jaunty orange kayak. This place has it all, from scooters to surfboards, but a kayak seems like the best choice, somehow. The shortest rental time is two hours, which seems excessive, but the idea of taking a gentle tour along this part of the coastline appeals to me tremendously, so I choke down the expense and settle in to enjoy the chance to paddle on this gently rolling, very salty sea.

I've never paddled an open kayak before, and the experience is exhilarating. As soon as I'm outside the confines of the marina, I lose myself shooting across the waves, which are admittedly a little choppier outside the rope boundaries. I'm essentially just sitting in a series of deep dents atop the kayak, with nothing more complicated than a little rope attachment to assist in raising or lowering the rudder. Pausing to get my bearings, I spot the jagged trail of the Via Krupp farther along the coastline, just past a rugged outcropping of rocks on the shore.

The waves begin to rise up a little as I approach the rocky finger poking out into the water, and I can see white foam shooting up where the water is crashing against the rocks. Beyond the outcropping rests the tranquil, sandy cove I spotted earlier.

As I paddle closer, I get a clearer view of the jumpers on the cliff face high above, and I suddenly realize that the cliff walls are essentially awash in a wide selection of gorgeous men. I mean, I've heard Capri is supposed to be a destination for the beautiful people, but this is ridiculous. I've never seen so many tanned six packs in my life. These guys wear swim suits in a rainbow of jewel tones and patterns, ranging from speedos to board shorts. Their water-slicked hair is every shade from fairest blond to black, and I even spot a single redhead with hair well past his shoulders. It's impossible not to stare.

Someone somewhere must have a boom box, because music is echoing weirdly off the cliff walls, which, by the time it makes it down to me, takes the form of an ethereal, unearthly sound. There must be dozens of jumpers lining the cliffs, yelling joyfully before they leap skyward and then plunging into the crystalline waters below.

This wide selection of beautiful boys catcall across the cliff face to egg each other on, and a few of them even appear to be dancing. Strangely, I don't see a single woman. High above, a jumper launches off the cliff in a giant, curving arc, executing a perfect somersault before landing feetfirst with almost no splash.

I suddenly realize, with a start, that in the time I've been staring, mesmerized by the movements of these ideal, male bodies, my kayak has been slowly drawn toward the rocky outcropping near the cove. And the stretch outside the rocks is filled with some suddenly substantial waves.

So substantial, in fact, that when I hear a shout behind me, I turn my head to see an extremely buff surfer dude careening right toward me.

"Woooo HOOOO!" he screams, and all I get is a glimpse of tanned abs and curly dark hair before he does some kind of swivel of the hips, and his board zigs off behind another wave.

I aim myself at the quiet cove again and paddle with all my might, but it's no use. My kayak has taken on a mind of its own and is shooting through the waves toward the rocks. Two more surfers appear, moving fast. There is a sort of roaring whoosh, and the closest one careens sharply past me and disappears over the waves. The other surfer, whom I notice is sporting earphones, must make a wrong move, because his board is suddenly flying skyward with no sign of him on it.

As this second guy disappears, I hear music again, less distorted now. I have a momentary flash of recognition as Taylor Swift tells me to "Shake It Off" before she is drowned out by the sound of the waves crashing against the rocks. The wind picks up suddenly and swirls my hat off into the water.

I manage to scoop it up with my paddle and jam it underneath my seat for safekeeping.

Lack of any sort of recent swim practice means my arms feel like they are about to fall off, but as soon as I take a rest, the nose of my kayak rises alarmingly. Worse, no matter how hard I paddle, the waves somehow pull me inexorably away from the cove and toward the rocks. I briefly consider bracing my paddle against the frame of the boat to push myself clear of the rocks when the choice is taken away from me. The next wave hurls the nose of my kayak even higher, and I'm suddenly watching it shoot into the air without me as I sink beneath the choppy waves of the brilliant blue Tyrrhenian Sea.

chapter thirty-four

SATURDAY AFTERNOON
Calamari a la Capri
Gia Kostas, special correspondent to NOSH, on the Isle of
Capri

The sheer bounty of the sea is one that all cultures and races around the Mediterranean never take for granted, and even fishermen who have plied these waters for decades know the importance of granting each sea creature its due . . .

D rowning is never a question.

I mean, I'm wearing a life belt, after all. And people—people who are good swimmers—who wear life belts don't drown.

Do they?

The music, of course, is cut off the instant the water sweeps over my head. A different sort of noise altogether takes its place. A low, deep thrum, but not at all like the bass line of a pop song. It's the call of the ocean, somehow deeper than sound, pulsing in my ears. The rushing and roar of the waves is gone too, and above me, momentarily, the outline of my little kayak is dark against the transparent crystal of the water.

Luckily, the life belt in question is very buoyant, and I pop up to the surface almost immediately. As I do, I inhale a big, panicked gasp of air, which, that close to the top of a wave, is just about half water.

Coughing, spluttering, and panic-flailing, I bob in the waves, retching the salty water out of breathing passages not designed to accommodate it.

I say "bob," but really, after that first sort of rocketing trip to the surface, I'm almost immediately slapped under again, and this time, when I frantically kick upward, my right knee hits something so hard the shock reverberates through me. The pain is not quite instant, but when it comes, it's so intense my entire leg goes momentarily numb.

This is a problem, as you might imagine, when attempting to swim.

My mind flashes back to my dad telling me the story of how Odysseus so angered Poseidon that the god made it his business to attempt to drown the adventurer. But what have I done to infuriate the god of the seas?

Whatever it is, he must be pretty angry. This time, when my life belt pops me and my nonfunctional leg to the surface, I gasp again for air, only to find the tide is still sweeping me in a collision course for the rocky point. And yet, just past this spot, past where the waves are foaming and slapping against the rocks, just out of reach, the water looks calm and blue—and yes, even inviting.

But over here in this vortex, I'm being churned like a single sock in a washing machine.

The feeling comes back—with a vengeance—to my knee, and I have just enough undrenched brain cells left to know that these submerged rocks are going to kill me before the water does. The next time, it could be my head instead of my knee.

As if the sea is listening, at that moment something smacks me on the back of the head. I flail—because, let's face it, all I'm capable of at the moment is flailing—and hook my elbow on something.

It's my paddle.

This is less good luck than it was good planning, as I only now remember how the rental company had tethered me to it with a wrist strap before I set out. I make the mistake of clutching it like a life ring, and the paddle instantly shoots back down under the surface, which is exactly where I do not want to be at the moment. As I drag it back up toward me by the tether, I realize the paddle blades float, though not enough to hold me up. Still, it does help a bit. After tucking it under both my arms I find I can kick my legs and keep my face above the waves fairly easily.

There is no sign, any longer, of the kayak itself, but I don't have time to worry about that now. I put my head down, concentrate on not inhaling more water, and kick. This time, I smack my ankle bone into one of the submerged rocks, which shoots pain and panic through me in equal measure.

I need to get out of here.

Suddenly, my ears clear out enough to hear the cliff divers' music, again pounding from the boom box on the shore. This is both good and bad news. The tide has sucked me back near land, but this part of the shore really, really wants to smash my bones.

"Concentrate, Gia." I don't, of course, realize I'm speaking out loud until my mouth fills with water. *Smooth move, idiot,* I think, this time keeping my mouth closed. Then, more as an effort not to kick another rock, I lift my legs and stop fighting for a minute.

Flipping the paddle under my neck, I attempt to float on my back. Floating is the wrong word for what I'm doing, but I'm not drowning, at least, at the moment. My arms are useless since I have to clutch on to the paddle to keep it from drifting away, but I aim myself on an angle away from the rocks and try tiny flutter kicks.

And, miracle of miracles, it works. Kick by kick, inch by inch, I edge my way out of the clutches of whatever undertow has held me in its grip. I feel so relieved to be actually moving under my own power again, I just stare at the blue, blue sky and keep kicking.

By the time I dare to dangle my feet beneath me into the water, I'm more than a hundred feet away from the rocks. I take a quick look down, and there is no sign of anything—anything—below me, which is freaky in its own way. Flipping the paddle under my arms again, I frantically tread water for a minute to get my bearings and look back toward Capri. The quiet cove has vanished, faded back into the general silhouette of the island. The crash of the surf is gone, but so is the surreal, echoey music.

This isn't a problem. I'm a good swimmer. Now that the threat of the rocks is gone, I just need to redirect myself toward one of the open, sandy beaches. I take a deep, steadying breath and pretend the paddle is just a kick board, and I'm in the pool.

When I stop to check again, I can't say that I've made any noticeable progress. In fact, looking around, I see I'm now farther out than the last of the surfers. To give myself a little rest from kicking, I turn over and try floating on my back for a minute with the paddle tucked underneath my head. Staring across at the island, I realize the docks of the Marina Grande have faded from view, and in spite of all my work, everything looks even farther away. It comes to me that I am slowly and inexorably being swept out to sea.

Strangely enough, all sense of my earlier panic has left me, but I'm also incredibly worn out by this unaccustomed spate of physical activity. When most of what I've been doing lately involves moving my fingers across a keyboard, a day with a big walk, a paddle, and now a life-or-death swim is a somewhat startling contrast. So, for the moment, I float and stare at the sky and try to look for positives.

The first thing I realize is that all the morning's animosities seem to have been washed away by these salty, blue depths. Compared to being lost at sea, Anthony's lack of communication no longer bothers me at all, and I can't even dredge up a shred of annoyance at my dad. Also? It occurs to me that if I ever do manage to get myself ashore again, I'd like to thank Raj properly. He's helped me every step of the way on this crazy journey with my dad, and I've never really acknowledged it. No wonder he always acts so stiff. I hate being unappreciated myself, and I'll bet he does too.

I'm not sure when the sound of the motor begins to register within these internal musings. When it finally does, I pop upright as much as the life belt will allow and try to spy-hop myself high enough to see which way it's coming from. Apart from a sense that I've drifted a long time—possibly days—I have zero idea as to where I am. The thought of being spotted by any kind of watercraft would be just about ideal at this moment.

The opportunity for rescue by motorboat morphs so rapidly into the likelihood of death by motorboat, it's shocking. One minute, I'm trying to bob above the waves to look for rescue, and the next, I'm back to fast-kicking to save my life as a fishing boat roars by. It's so close I get pushed aside by the bow wave, and then suddenly I'm caught in a tight little eddy behind the boat's wake that spins me like a cork.

The next minute or so goes by in such a blur, it's difficult to describe. A wash of water, a scrape of rope, and a horrifying sense that someone or something is watching me—from below. There is a sudden mechanical noise—a sort of repetitive clanking whir. My foot gets tangled in something for just long enough to jerk my head below water. There is a brief sense that I'm stuck, and when I frantically slide my hands down to free my foot, I feel something thick and soft squeeze my ankle briefly before slipping away. Then my face bobs back out of the water again, and when I gasp for sweet, sweet oxygen, instead I inhale the overpowering reek of gasoline. This is immediately followed by the sound of shouting voices and a big jerk, and I'm suddenly airborne. The next moment I'm hauled bodily aboard a boat, paddle and all.

My life belt catches on a metal cleat on the side of the boat, and the arms that have been dragging me aboard suddenly release. This is not really a problem, as I tumble inward, landing on a sort of spongy surface, equal parts soft and rough. The skin of my arms feels like it has been excessively loofahed, but I'm so happy to be out of the water, all I can do is just lie back and cough. My head feels incredibly heavy, and I'm not sure I could sit up if I wanted to.

Which I don't, not really.

A babble of voices makes me open my eyes. *"Ce l'abiamo fatta! Lei è una sirena! Si! Si una sirena!"*

Three swarthy young men dressed in shorts, colorful Hawaiian shirts in various states of disrepair, and each wearing bloodstained leather gloves are kneeling around me. It's like a scene from an operating theater in a surreal movie, their heads forming a perfect circle around my line of vision.

One of them is holding something that looks like a giant yellow shepherd's crook, and they are all smiling broadly.

I turn my head and see that the spongy bed I'm lying on is actually a bulging fishing net. And inside the net, looking back at me, is the same enormous eye I felt resting on me earlier, deep under the water.

And just like that, I'm back on my feet.

"What the hell?" I manage to shuffle my way backward onto a narrow walkway surrounding the open deck at the back of the boat.

"Americano!" the young men say delightedly to each other, but I'm no longer looking at them.

Whatever is in the net absolutely fills the deck of this boat, which has to be fifteen feet long. Its rubbery body is mostly grey, with a kind of pinkish tinge at the margins. The only other thing I can see in the net is a small, silvery fish, which flaps feebly a few times and then lies still.

One of the fishermen, sporting a substantial *Magnum P.I.*–style mustache, kneels down and lays a reverent hand on the monster in the net. "Is squeed," he says and then mimes something which kind of reminds me of the way one would munch a cob of corn. "*Calamari gigantesco.* We catch heem. Then we catch you!"

They all laugh again, and the one with the yellow crook taps it on the deck like a soldier banging his spear.

The squid does not join in and neither do I. Instead, I fold my arms across my stomach and shiver. The squid just stares upward with one baleful, pale blue eye peering through the mesh of the fishing net. The tip of one of its tentacles has slipped out through the net, displaying two neat rows of suckers.

I am awash in relief at being out of the sea, but my primary bodily urge at the moment is to throw up. Something in my expression must translate itself to the fishermen, because the one with the mustache barks orders at the others, who dash off immediately. He leans into the cabin of the boat and pulls out a ratty, oil-stained towel. Flapping the towel skyward with the air of a conjurer performing a trick, he wraps it around my shoulders, wrinkling his nose.

"*Spiacente*—sorry, sorry. Is no much nice. Santo get something— mmm—*meglio.*"

The towel is stiff and threadbare, but it's such a relief to have something to wrap around me that I try smiling, though I'm sure it comes out more as a grimace.

"Thank you," I manage, at last. "*Grazie.*"

This use of his own language clearly delights him almost as much as my nationality. Pulling off one of his gloves, he holds out a hand. "*Mi chiamo* Mattia Forzani," he says, patting his other hand to his chest.

"Gianna Kostas," I say and shake his hand.

His face falls. "Ooo, so cold," he says, and after squeezing my hand once, he yells something else, this time to the man who disappeared down the stairs.

"*E miei fratelli Santo,*" he adds, pointing first to the man inside the cabin, "*e Giuseppe.*"

Santo has a ponytail, and Giuseppe looks like he hasn't shaved for a few days but has neither ponytail nor mustache. Apart from the variation in hairiness, their smiles are so identical there's no question they are all brothers.

Giuseppe's head reappears at the top of the stairs. He is carrying a silver thermos in one hand and a striped blanket in the other.

"Sit, sit," says Mattia, pulling forward a plastic chair that may have once been white. "*Lei ha freddo,*" he says to Giuseppe, twirling his finger. "*Fretta, fretta.*"

Giuseppe pours steaming dark liquid—immediately identifiable as coffee—into the lid of the thermos and holds it out to me.

"*Uno momento!*" commands Mattia, and reaches down between Santo's feet inside the cabin. Pulling out a metal flask, he pours a shot of something into my cup.

"*Salut,*" he says and clinks the flask against my cup before draining it into his mouth.

"*Salut,*" I whisper and swallow the whole thing in one gulp.

As the wave of warmth washes through me, Mattia takes the blanket from his brother's arm and, after removing the oil-stained towel, tenderly wraps it around my shoulders. "We go dock, *sì?*"

As if on cue, the engine revs up again, and the boat lurches forward. Santo has taken the wheel inside the cabin, and there's nothing for me to do but sit here and watch Capri come thankfully, speedily closer.

From my spot on this fairly rickety chair, I can see the boat is pretty much an exact replica of *La Fortuna*, the boat that carried us on our disastrous crossing of the Aeolian Sea. The resemblance between the two carries right down to the smell, which, to be fair, should only be expected of a fishing boat. In any case, I am not complaining because, unlike the *La Fortuna*, this boat has me stepping back onto land in a matter of minutes.

By the time Mattia and his brothers pull their boat up to a mooring spot on the dock, I feel completely back to myself again. I'm not sure what was in Mattia's flask, but all the circulation has returned to my fingers and toes, and I'm no longer shivering at all.

I turn down the Forzani brothers' kind offer to escort me to the lifeguard station, but they refuse to take back their blanket. So with the striped blanket still draped over my shoulders and the paddle in hand, I wave goodbye as their boat—which I now see is called *Athena*—putts away from the dock. After which I turn and head off down toward the rental place, trying desperately to come up with a good explanation for how I find myself missing exactly one kayak.

chapter thirty-five

STILL SATURDAY
Ravioli Caprese
Gia Kostas, special correspondent to NOSH, on the Italian
Isle of Capri

With a basic dough unique to this jewel of an island, made of only
a special flour and hot water, this ravioli combines the best of the
flavors this locale has to offer. Start with the creamiest ricotta . . .

Since my phone, my bag, and all my dry clothes are locked up in the public changing room by the rental place on the Marina Grande, I really have no choice but to go and explain to them what happened. Maybe if I throw myself on their mercy, they won't charge me the full replacement fee. I can't be the only person to have been tossed from a kayak, after all.

Still, the thought of having to pay a huge fee makes my heart sink. It means almost all the money earned for my series of articles will go to cover this one mistake. Why couldn't I have been content to just sit on a beach? I tuck the blanket under one arm, take a tighter grip on my paddle, and hurry away from the dock.

Pausing to wait for a break in the traffic, I hear a clock tower chime from somewhere on the cliffs high above me. I count the chimes absently while crossing the street and then stop stock-still as the last chime fades away. Twelve chimes. Twelve chimes.

"That's impossible," I mumble to myself, and then nearly jump out of my skin when a car, impatient to turn the corner, honks at me.

I scramble across to the sidewalk as quickly as I can—considering I'm a barefoot New Yorker with feet that have never seen pavement—and make a beeline toward a gelato vendor parked on the corner with his cart.

"*Ciccolato, dulce le leche, gelaaaaaatoooooooo,*" he bellows. "*Caramello*, matcha tea!"

"Excuse me," I say as he turns his best salesman's smile on me. "*Scusi*—do you have the correct time?"

"Ees good time for gelato," he says, beaming at his own cleverness.

"No, thank you." Still, even after all that's happened this morning, I am unable to stop myself checking out the contents of his freezer case. The selection looks wide-ranging and very tempting.

"At least—maybe later. My money is locked away."

At his look of puzzlement, I mime turning a key, and point toward the kayak rental place, as if that might make things clearer.

It doesn't.

"No money." I point to my own bare wrist and then to his wristwatch. "I just need to know the time."

"No money, no gelato," he says. No more salesman smile either, apparently.

I step around the cart and clutch pleadingly at his arm. "Please—I just need the time. I'll come back for the gelato when I get my money."

He swats me away like a fly. "No money, no gelato," he repeats firmly. "*Andarsene!*"

"Fine." Turning away so quickly that my fish-scented blanket flares out behind me like a striped cape, I stomp off.

But not before reading the time on his watch.

Point Gianna.

I hurry along the waterfront with new purpose. As unbelievable as it seems, the chiming clock was correct. It is now just a few minutes after twelve noon. Which means my entire adventure—from strapping on my life belt, which I suddenly realize I'm still wearing, to being drawn in and nearly crushed on the rocks by the call of the six-packs, then swept out to sea, sucked down in a whirlpool, and finally plucked from a watery grave by a trio of Italian fishermen—took just over an hour.

I'm not even expected to return the kayak until one p.m.

Which gives me a thought. Maybe I won't have to pay the replacement cost, after all.

Bypassing the rental kiosk entirely, I follow a sandy path past the end of the docks and work my way around the rocky headland. The path weaves through some low, scrubby bushes, but I use the paddle to push aside the worst of the thorny branches. After only a few minutes, the path takes a sharp turn, and—

I'm at the cove.

What are the chances my kayak has made its way back here? After all, I fell off while almost inside this cove. My efforts to escape the nautical version of jumping out of the frying pan—getting crushed on the rocks—meant, of course, that I ended up inside the fire—in this case, getting sucked out to sea. Okay, so the whole frying pan–fire thing is maybe a bad metaphor. My point is, I might be able to pull one good thing out of this day if I can actually recover the kayak.

Both the wind and tide have shifted in the last hour, and the surface of the water is no longer glassy smooth. Instead, small steady waves, some up to a foot high, are coursing in orderly lines and

AN ACCIDENTAL ODYSSEY · 303

breaking on the shore. Gazing upward, I see all the cliff jumpers are gone. Or perhaps they've just swapped venues—the waters past the rocky promontory are now filled with dozens of surfers, riding the waves.

Shading my eyes, I scan the coastline inside the cove.

And sure enough, at the far end of the now rapidly disappearing beach, I spot a splash of orange bobbing in the waves near the rocks.

The tide is coming in fast, and I've had enough swimming in the Mediterranean to last a lifetime, but I figure if I scoot along the edge of the rocks, I should be able to wade in, nab the kayak, and return it with no one the wiser.

I drop the smelly striped blanket and the paddle on the shore, hopefully far enough back to be out of the reach of the incoming tide. But just as I sidle sideways along the somewhat slippery edge of the rocks, I hear a shout.

Looking up, I see one of the surf gods is hailing me. Unlike the rest of the crew that are out in the choppy waters beyond the cove, he's not standing on his board. Instead, he's lying on his stomach, paddling his way in to shore.

At this distance and staring right into the sun, I can't make out much. Dusky skin, a bit sunburned on the shoulders. Dark hair, a mass of wet curls swept back from his face. It's not until he hops off the board and into the water that I realize it's Raj.

Holy crap—those abs can compete with any of the surfer gods, I think wildly, before remembering that I am still wearing the stupid life belt over my university training suit.

I feel like a toddler in water wings.

Raj comes slogging up through the water, his surfboard tucked under one arm. "I thought it was you," he says, smiling.

It's a real smile too, with teeth and everything. Not the polite, upward curl of the lips he generally reserves for his conversations with me lately.

I can't help smiling back. "I didn't know you were a surfer."

"I'm not," he says quickly.

I gaze pointedly at his surfboard, and he laughs. "Okay, well I'm very new at it. And not exactly brilliant, as you can tell from the lame way I've just paddled in here."

I cross my arms in front of the life belt. "I thought you were going with my dad to meet some guy?"

He hauls his board out of the water with a grunt and props it up awkwardly in the sand.

"Right. Did that first thing this morning. Introduced your father to the mad monk himself, picked up the camera I'd loaned him, and . . ."

His voice trails away for a moment, and then he adds suddenly, "He's an odd duck, Brother Wilde, but he and your dad got along famously. They didn't need me hanging about."

With his free hand, he points to the top of the cliff. "The museum is right up there, so afterward . . ."

"I thought it was a monastery," I ask. "Isn't Brother Wilde a monk?"

"Yeah, well, it used to be a monastery but it's mostly a museum now and a school. As for . . ."

"Whoops," I say and lunge for his board, which is beginning to tilt dangerously. He grabs it with both hands and, after a moment's struggle, leans it back against his shoulder. "Hopeless," he grumbles, grimacing.

"So, are you heading back to return that now?"

He nods but doesn't seem in any hurry to leave. I risk a quick glance over my shoulder in time to see one end of my kayak bash up against the rocks.

"I s'pose so. It's not due in until two, but I think maybe I should take a lesson before trying again." He gestures at my life belt. "What about you? Where's your board?"

I puff up for a single moment that he would even consider me in the same category as a surfer girl, and then, as my kayak bashes a second time against the rocks, this time with an audible crunch, I sigh.

"I don't surf. I've been out kayaking, but I sort of—ah—got thrown off. And if I don't go rescue it right now, there won't be much of it left to return."

"Christ—is that it out there?" he says, following my gaze to where the hapless craft is bashing itself to death on the rocks.

"Yep. So, if you'll excuse me . . ."

"Let me help," Raj says, hoisting his board. "I can paddle out and tow it in."

"Not a chance. The undercurrent is terrible right there by the rocks, which is why I got sucked in. You don't want your board to get wrecked too."

"Fine," he says, replacing his board on the sand firmly. "But I'm not letting you scramble over those rocks by yourself. You'll get all scraped up."

He glances down at my legs and then does a double take. "Whoa—what happened there?"

I look down to see a large purple bruise blooming on my knee. "It's where I bashed myself," I begin, but then he drops to the sand, and I see he's actually peering at my ankle.

It's ringed in a neat double row of bright pink sucker marks.

"Holy mackerel," I whisper, shocked at the sight. "He really did grab me."

Raj turns a confused face up to look at me. "Who grabbed you?"

"It's a—long story." To avoid further explanations, I begin scaling the sandy side of the rocky promontory.

From here, I can see the remains of what must have once been a pier. Most of the wood has rotted away, but in places, an old, slippery plank or bit of cement piling emerges from its rocky foundation.

Without a word, Raj climbs up beside me, and we begin to gingerly clamber our way along the outcropping. Down here, the rocks are wet, slippery, and covered with sharp barnacles, but somehow we slither our way down to the water's edge.

There is a dull sort of thudding sound as the water smacks the poor kayak repeatedly against the rocky outcropping, just beyond reach.

"You wait here," he says, edging his way closer. "I can lower myself down and pass it up to you."

"Be careful," I yelp, but it's too late, and he slides off the rocks and into the water. Instead of disappearing under the waves, though, he's somehow only waist-deep.

"Ledge," he gasps and then, "Got it."

Clutching a blackened shard of rotting wood, he's managed to reach out with one long arm and snag the bit of rope on the prow of the kayak. Fighting the pull of the surf, he yanks the boat closer, but as he does, the wood under his hand gives way, and with the next wave, he loses his footing.

The rotten old piece of dock has essentially crumbled away under his grip, but as his arm flails, I spot the rusting bolt that once held the wood in place. Slithering down the rock to where Raj is still fighting the kayak, I hook my elbow around the old bolt, grab his hand as it flails by, and pull.

Seconds later, we're both lying atop the rocks beside the battered remains of my little orange kayak. One of the fiberglass panels on the front is completely caved in, but the rest of the boat looks relatively unscathed.

I can't say the same for the two of us.

Raj's chest sports a diagonal scrape from one shoulder to his navel—the result of slipping against the barnacle-covered rock. I've only scraped one arm, but in combination with my bruised knee and sucker-scarred ankle, I feel like I've been through a war.

An enormous wave slaps the rocks and soaks us, driving us to our feet. We carefully retrace our route back to the beach, each of us holding one end of the kayak and trying not to slip. Stepping onto the warm sand of the cove feels like a victory, and as we drop the kayak onto the beach above the tide line, Raj reaches in and pulls a wet sodden mass out from under the seat. When he holds it up, I see that through some miracle, my hat has survived. Raj shakes it out, hands it to me, and then gives me a triumphant high-five.

Then we both collapse onto the beach, gasping and laughing like idiots.

"I can't believe we got it! Thank you so much. I could never have done that without you."

He sits up enough to give a sort of half bow, and for the first time, I notice that he's not in a bathing suit. I mean, he's shirtless, which accounts for why I mistook him for one of the surfer boys, but he's also wearing khaki shorts.

And a pink scrunchie around one wrist.

"It's my locker key," he says, by way of explanation. And maybe because I am completely exhausted, I start to laugh.

Once I start laughing, I find I can't stop, and then Raj is laughing too.

It takes us quite a while to recover.

He tells me that after leaving my dad at the monastery, he'd been walking along the rocky cliff top and saw the divers jumping off.

"I considered it for about a minute and then I decided to try surf-

308 · kc dyer

ing instead. I mean—it's not a big center for surfing here in Capri. I think the water is usually too calm. So I thought, why not?"

Hard to argue, considering I had followed a similar line of thinking myself, and told him so.

But he didn't have trunks, and so he decided to just go in his shorts.

"And here I am," he says. He sits up, wincing as he does so. The barnacle scrape is at least an inch wide and runs up almost his entire torso. It's fire-engine red.

"Ugh, that looks really sore." Guilt surges inside me. "I'm so sorry."

"Don't be!" He prods his stomach gently. "It looks worse than it is, I think. The skin is really just scraped, not torn. I'll slap some antiseptic on it when we get back, and I'll be good as new."

We lapse into silence. With the music gone, there's only the sound of the wind and the waves at the moment.

"Listen." I swallow hard, trying not to sound as awkward as I feel. "While I was out there earlier, I remembered that I haven't thanked you."

He shrugs. "Nothing to thank me for—you did half the work. *And* you stopped me from falling off that ledge."

"No, I'm not talking about the kayak. I mean, yes, thank you for helping me get it back. But what I need to thank you for is all your support of my dad. This—nothing like this has ever happened to me before. With him taking off on this trip and everything. Anyway—I know neither of us could have made it this far without your help."

He looks at me without speaking for a long moment.

"Listen," he says at last. "About that . . ."

And right at that moment, a tiny crab sidles out of one of the patch pockets of his khaki shorts and scuttles across his knee. We both shriek, just a little, and this starts me laughing all over again.

"You think that's funny?" he says and reaches across to pull a piece of kelp out of my hair. "Having a crab in your shorts is macho," he adds, grinning. "But having kelp in your hair just makes you a mermaid." And as we both burst out laughing again, a shadow falls across our legs.

An immaculately suited shadow.

chapter thirty-six

 SHOCKINGLY, STILL SATURDAY AFTERNOON
L'impepata di Cozze
Gia Kostas, special correspondent to NOSH, on the Italian
Isle of Capri

*This dish, an ancient tradition attributed to the fishermen of this
island, takes mussels found on the treacherous rocks along the
coast and pairs them with the finest fresh spices and a splash of . . .*

I squint up through the sunshine to see the face of Anthony Hearst.
My Anthony. My beloved. My fiancé. But instead of smiling or
sweeping me into his arms, he just stares down at me, looking furious.

"What the hell's going on here?" he asks. "Who is *this* guy?"

After a day filled with so many crazy emotions, all I've got left at
the moment is puzzlement.

"Anthony?" I manage. "What are you doing here?"

I'm suddenly convinced that I might be dead—or at the very
least, hallucinating. Anthony looks all stiff and pale in his dress shirt.
Extraordinarily pale.

Raj has jumped to his feet and offers me a hand to help me up,
but I manage it on my own.

"What are you . . . ?" I begin again and then stop. "Anthony, this
is Dr. Raj Malik, my dad's colleague. Raj, this is Anthony Hearst, my
fiancé."

Neither man extends a hand. There is a long moment of silence, which Raj finally breaks.

"Right," he says, his voice strangely formal. "I'll just go collect my board, then."

I stare at his back as he strides across the sand and then turn toward Anthony.

"What the hell was *that* about? And why didn't you tell me you were coming?"

He narrows his eyes at me and adjusts so he's standing where he can't see Raj at all.

"This is the surprise," he says flatly. "I told you to expect a surprise. Ta-da."

He's making the pretense of a smile now, at least with his lips, but it never gets to his eyes. In fact, it looks more like a grimace, and he drops it almost immediately.

Stepping closer, he lowers his voice. "I've come all this way to bring you home, and I find you cavorting with some asshole on the beach?"

I take a step away and look up into his face, incredulous. "*What* are you talking about? This is my dad's colleague! Why on earth would you call him an asshole?"

"In any case," says Raj, who has reappeared with his surfboard under one arm and a towel around his neck. "We most certainly were not *cavorting*. In fact, we were merely . . ."

And right at that moment, for the first time in the history of our relationship, I see my fiancé take a swing at another man.

I believe a pause is required here, just to clarify a few things.

First of all, I have never—ever—even *seen* a fistfight. I have an aversion to violence so intense that if a fight arises in a movie I'm watching, I fast-forward through it. Tarantino is clearly not my jam.

And in spite of my natural inclination toward buff, muscled men—as evidenced by how I nearly met my end earlier today from too much staring at cute boys—this has zero to do with what they actually *do* with those muscles. Fighting men are scary to me, not appealing.

Even so, the two men in front of me might be the least likely combatants ever. I mean—Suit Man versus the Archeologist? It's like nerd on nerd.

And worse—So. Much. Worse.—is the fact that a crowd is beginning to gather.

From where? My theory is they came from the cliff diver / surfer crowd, but where they were before this moment is anyone's guess.

Right now, though, they are forming a rough, cheering semicircle with their backs to the cliffs. Someone's playing music again, but Taylor Swift has been supplanted by a cover version of "Pumped Up Kicks" sung in what I think must be Italian.

I force my way back through the crowd of onlookers pushing past me to get closer to the two men, now shuffling around each other on the sand.

Anthony's fist is absolutely aimed at Raj's face, but he misses wildly, mostly because the sleeve of his suit jacket doesn't offer a lot of mobility. He is dressed, after all, like he just stepped out of the first-class compartment of a plane.

Which he likely did.

I'm sure Raj's look of shock echoes my own, and after easily dodging the blow, he simply stands there, staring from Anthony to me and back.

"*What* are you thinking?" I hurry across the sand toward Anthony, but my way is blocked by a curvaceous brunette. She's wearing a bikini designed to look like it is made of lettuce leaves, along with a fetchingly coordinated green manicure.

"Ay-yi-yi," she says, hooking her arm through mine.

"Scusi!" I try pulling my arm free, but she's having none of it. "Look, I need to stop this."

"No, no, no," she says, tightening her grip. "Let the boys 'ave dere fun, eh?"

"This isn't *fun!*" I try again—unsuccessfully—to pull away.

She just laughs and nods her head at a nearby blond girl, who takes possession of my other arm. The blonde is wearing a bathing suit that is little more than a collection of strings guaranteed to give her interesting tan lines, but like her friend in the lettuce bikini, she's got biceps of steel.

Meanwhile, in the center of this cheering group of enablers, Raj and Anthony are still circling each other warily. It's hard to know which of them looks more ridiculous; Anthony in his dress shirt and tie—he has somehow managed to doff his suit jacket—or Raj, who is clad only in khaki shorts, with his barnacle war wound and the neon pink scrunchie still encircling his wrist.

"Christ," he blurts. "What the hell, Hearst?"

For some unknown reason, this seems to further incense Anthony, who practically leaps forward to take another swing. This time, his highly polished handmade shoes—extremely impractical for Capri beach wear—slide out from under him. He falls flat on his back in the sand.

A roar rises up from the crowd.

Inexplicable as this whole thing is, seeing Anthony lying there seems the appropriate result of such farcical behavior. What's happening here is completely bewildering, and it's leaving me with a feeling I'm not quite ready to examine just yet.

Instead, I'm still staring openmouthed when Raj reaches a hand down to help Anthony up. Instead of accepting it, Anthony grabs the towel around Raj's neck with both hands and yanks him down onto the sand.

Raj's look of shock turns to something else, and his face reddens.

"I knew I recognized that girlish flailing," says Anthony. "You couldn't fight then either, as I recall."

"What?" I try again to wrestle myself loose from the lady surfers. "What does that even mean?"

Raj doesn't reply. I suddenly realize that Anthony is actually choking him with the towel, but before I can do anything about it— throw myself between them? Make a plea to their sanity?—the two of them are rolling over and over in the sand.

"*La lotta,*" choruses the crowd. "*La LOTta!*"

I give up struggling with my captors and just watch, heart in my mouth. Apart from the moment with the towel, neither one of them has managed to strike any kind of a blow. Anthony has somehow lost his grip on the towel and is jamming his hand under Raj's chin in some kind of awkward attempt to pin him down.

Raj looks shocked at this tactic and, struggling to get away, manages to roll on top of Anthony in spite of the fact his head is still being forced backward. From this position, he's able to jerk Anthony to his feet.

"I don't know why you're doing this, you wanker," Raj hisses. "You're the one who broke her heart."

In response, Anthony grabs wildly at Raj, and his fingers close on a handful of his hair. He pulls it so hard, Raj roars with pain.

Still holding Raj by the hair, Anthony sneers at him. "Oh, for god's sake. It was nothing. We were kids," he spits. "I think the *real* problem here is that you're making some pathetic attempt to get your own back with *my* fiancée. Which is ludicrous."

With a sudden, violent shake of his head, Raj manages to jerk his hair out of Anthony's grasp, but Anthony takes another wild swing and, this time, connects with Raj's eye. Raj reels, staggering backward, and the crowd explodes.

"And anyway, as I recall," says Anthony with a smirk. "The better man won. And it looks like I win again."

Raj doesn't really recover, as he's still holding a hand to his eye, but he kicks recklessly out at Anthony. The kick misses by a mile, but sand flies up and sprays into Anthony's face. He pauses for an instant to wipe his eyes just as Raj swings out wildly and smacks him in the nose. The fountain of blood so startles them both—and me—they jump apart.

And the fight is over.

The crowd gives a satisfied cheer, and while a couple of the buff surfer dudes pause to pat the combatants on the back, everyone else just sort of melts away.

This includes my girl-power team, who each attach themselves to the arm of a different muscular male. They walk away, all chattering happily.

Stomping over, I retrieve Anthony's jacket from where it lies crumpled in the sand and then whisper at him furiously. "What the hell happened between you two? How do you even know each other?"

Anthony snatches up a corner of my smelly striped blanket and holds it to his nose.

"I might ask the same of you," he says huffily, and this is so not the right answer, I turn my back on him and stride over to Raj.

He's blinking hard and touching the skin below his left eye, which is already starting to swell.

"Are you okay?" I ask quickly.

"I'm fine," he says, his voice sounding pretty formal for a guy with a burgeoning black eye. "I don't think his nose can be broken. I only hit him with the palm of my hand."

"I'm sure he's all right. But—what was that even about? Why didn't you tell me that you knew him?"

"You should go see to him," Raj replies shortly. "He might need some ice for his nose. And I have to take back my gear, so I can return your boat for you."

"Thank you." But I'm not even sure he hears me as he tosses his towel over one shoulder and stalks off.

chapter thirty-seven

 STILL SATURDAY AFTERNOON, NOW WITH BLOODSTAINS
Insalata di Arance
Gia Kostas, special correspondent to NOSH, on the
Isle of Capri

*Sometimes, after a day filled with the heat of a Mediterranean sun,
a salad is the perfect solution to cool things down. This beauty
begins with the finest . . .*

By the time I get back to Anthony, he's made his way onto the path toward the Marina Grande. Someone—no idea who—has given him a handkerchief, and he's dropped the striped blanket at the edge of the beach.

I gather up the smelly blanket—now with added bloodstains!—and fold it under my arm. The string of sucker-shaped bruises around my ankle will fade, but this blanket is hard proof of my insane day, and I'm not ready to let go of it yet. Scooping up the paddle with my other hand, I hurry after him.

As soon as he steps off the sandy beach, Anthony turns around to wait for me. I have to admit, he's got kind of a rakish look at the moment. His blond hair is ruffled and sticking up on one side. He's managed to wipe most of the blood off his face, but there is a spray down the front of his no-longer pristine dress shirt. He's carrying his suit jacket over one arm, his sleeves are rolled up, and his tie is hanging loose and off-center.

I feel a brief moment of tenderness toward him mixed in with a whole lot of confusion.

"Well," he says, as I come hurrying up. "That was not exactly the welcome I was expecting."

Without a word, he grabs my face and kisses me, hard. He tastes of blood and Tic Tacs, with maybe a little hint of stale coffee.

Pulling away almost immediately, I feel a surge of complicated emotions. I stare up into his face, not even knowing where to start, when he wraps his arms around me again, drawing me close.

Or, you know, as close as you can get when one of us is wearing a thick, yellow foam life belt.

"Dammit, Gia," he says, cupping my butt with one hand. "Perhaps I should battle for your honor more often."

This remark serves to shoot a dose of reality into a very weird day, but it doesn't provide much clarity. I step back and glare up at him.

"My *what*? Look, Anthony, I have no idea what just happened, but if you were under the misguided impression you were battling for my honor, you are completely off base."

I fold my arms across my chest. "Now, how about we start at the beginning here, and maybe you can tell me why you took a swing at my dad's colleague?"

Anthony takes a deep breath and stares off into the distance for a long moment. At last, he sighs and looks down at me with his usual genuine, charming smile. "Never mind all that," he says. "But you're right—we need to start again."

Turning his back to me, he pulls on his jacket, smooths out his hair, and straightens his tie before spinning around and holding out his arms.

"Surprise! I'm here to spend the weekend in Italy with you! I've brought presents and a bunch of wedding stuff, and I'm ready to have a good time. Are you happy to see me?"

I manage to force a smile. He still looks nothing like his usual self, but he's right. This *is* better.

"Of course I am," I say and reach out to take his hand. "But what about . . . ?"

He holds up a hand. "Only good things for the moment." He links his arm through mine and marches me down the path toward the Marina Grande. "We need to find you some shoes."

I turn back to see how Raj is managing with my battered kayak, but I can't see any sign of him at all.

I'd like to say this new start makes everything better between us, but it just doesn't. Anthony waits outside the public changing rooms while I gather my things. Inside, I try to collect my roiling thoughts. Something has changed, something I knew even before Anthony threw that inexplicable punch at Raj. But I'm not ready to look at it quite yet.

Instead, I throw my sundress on over my suit, drop the life belt into a return bin, and hurry back out to meet him. My mind is still reeling, but when I emerge, he's tapping on his phone.

"I've been on to George Martini," he says, pocketing the phone as I come out. "You remember George?"

When I shake my head, he shrugs. "Finance guy in my fraternity. Anyway, he's got a place in Naples and has given us the use of it for the weekend. Gorgeous spot, at least according to the pictures he's sent me."

"That's nice," I say cautiously, steering him toward the gelato cart that's still parked on the corner near the rental place. Even with all that's happened, I'm so hungry I can hardly think straight, and the gelato cart is the closest food purveyor I can see at the moment. "We've got a hotel in Naples too, but I'm sure my dad can do without me, so we can have a chance to talk, at least."

We pause to look at the selection, and I see that with the arrival of my new wallet-bearing companion, the cart man is back to wearing his big salesman smile. Anthony selects a delicate lemon sorbet in a cup, but I go full cone, with a scoop of chocolate and a scoop of dulce de leche.

It is, hands down, the best gelato I've ever tasted. It's so good, I can completely ignore Anthony's raised eyebrow at my selection. "That's going to melt before you can eat it all," he says drily.

I grab a huge handful of paper napkins and set out to prove him wrong.

And really, in the end, the gelato turns out to be the only reason things stay civil as long as they do. I'm so busy devouring the icy deliciousness that Anthony is able to go on for a full two minutes about someone named Minetta before I think to stop him.

I pause to wipe my mouth with yet another paper napkin. "Sorry—I'm not clear on the whole Minetta thing. I thought your assistant's name was Melanie."

He dabs at the corner of his mouth with his—lone—paper napkin and then sighs, impatiently. "Minette is not *my* assistant. She's for your father. This is why I am here. I've hired her away from George to help out your dad when you're gone."

He tosses his cup and napkin into a bin as we walk by. "You haven't been listening, Gia. She's the best part of my surprise. She's going to step in to look after him—make sure he takes his medicine, gets enough sleep, whatever. And after we have two mind-blowing days in Naples, you'll come home with me."

I pause before the last bite of my cone as this finally sinks in. "You—want me to come home with you? Like, back to New York? Now?"

He sighs, grabs one of the remaining paper napkins, and wipes something off my chin.

"Not *right* now," he says patiently, as though explaining something to a child. "After that gorgeous round ass of yours and I have a naughty weekend in Naples. This is the *surprise*, Gia. I've looked after whatever your father needs by hiring a very capable woman. Her name is Minette. You won't need to worry about a thing, and we can head home Sunday night. My mother has a meeting scheduled with her event planner for Monday afternoon, and she wants you there to finalize some of the details. We're three months out, babe— this stuff should be set in stone already."

He grins at the expression on my face. "Look, I know it's a lot, but this is what you do when you love someone. And listen"—he leans in and puts his mouth beside my ear—"Minette is a total fox—the complete package, if you know what I mean. She's one hundred percent your dad's type, and when I say she'll do whatever he needs, I mean it. That girl? Is a *force*. He's not going to miss you at *all*, honey."

I don't even know where to begin unpacking all of this. Anthony bragging that he's procured a hot babe to answer my dad's every whim makes my mind want to turn off immediately. Instead, I start with something I can at least wrap some vocabulary around.

"Anthony," I say, slowly. "I don't want to leave right now. I have two more articles to write for NOSH, which I am contracted for. It's work—an actual job. And my numbers have been really great—the readership is incredible. I might be able to jockey this into a full-time position when I get home."

He snorts. "Why would you even try to be a journalist when the job market is so terrible these days? You *have* a full-time job when you get home. Just wait until you see the list my mother has ready for you. Not much sleep in your future, at least until July, is what I'm saying."

"Until the wedding, you mean?" I ask. I can scarcely believe what I'm hearing.

He shrugs. "We can decide what you want to do after that. But, babe—it's so gorgeous here. What do you say we change our honeymoon plans for Capri? I had no idea the place was so beautiful, and I'm sure George can find us fantastic accommodations."

I wipe my fingers carefully on the remaining napkins and then toss them in the bin.

"My dad does not need an assistant. He needs *me*. For work stuff, he's got Raj. But this trip has been different than we both expected. I found out I have a sister, Anthony. And my dad needs my moral support when . . ."

But that's as far as I get.

He turns back to me, his eyebrows drawing together. "Gia. I'm here to take you home. I mean—look at this from my point of view. I've gone to a lot of trouble to arrange all this, do you understand? Like—reaching out to George, sorting out the place—even organizing a capable—a VERY capable—assistant for your dad. And then I get here, and what happens? I go to all this trouble to surprise you, and not only do I find out your father's got some kind of a lackey already here, but you're messing around with him on the beach?"

I can feel my own temper start to burn. "Messing around? We were NOT messing around. He was helping me rescue my kayak, for crying out loud."

"That's not what it looked like to me," he snaps. "You told me that your dad couldn't do without you. But instead, when I show up, I find you fraternizing with some piece of shit on a beach? It's not exactly like you're looking after your ailing father, is it?"

I put my hand on his arm. "Just a minute. I *have* been looking after . . ."

He seizes my hand by the wrist and holds it up between us. "How can you," he spits, "a woman wearing the fifty-*thousand* dollar ring I bought for her, betray me like this?"

"*Betray* you?" His anger, the fact that he would throw the cost of the ring at me, and the vastness of the sum itself combine to stun me into silence. I'm not sure if he takes this as a sign of my guilt, but without a word, he turns and strides off toward the water taxi dock.

Not knowing what else to do, I follow him.

I stand beside him silently, my mind reeling, as he goes up to the ticket counter, buys two tickets, and then steps into the shade of a palm tree. There's a breeze blowing across the water, but it's mid-afternoon, and the heat is intense. His face flushed, he removes his jacket, takes his tie off, and folds it neatly into his pocket.

"We only have ten minutes before the next water taxi," he says, his voice sounding calmer. "We can go back to George's place, and you can meet Minette. We'll all feel better after we have a drink— George keeps an excellent bar."

I narrow my eyes and look out over the bright blue water. The wind has picked up, and while it's not terribly wavy, each peak is topped in white foam. I focus on keeping my tone even.

"I'm not going back to George's place, wherever that is. I'm supposed to meet my dad here at four. I would never leave without telling him."

"You can send him an e-mail, surely," Anthony says. "Or call his hotel and leave a message."

He uses the cuff of one sleeve to wipe a trickle of sweat away from his forehead.

"Anthony. You gave me no hint that you were coming—not even a note from your executive assistant, even though she's been handling all my e-mails. You can't expect me to drop everything with no notice."

His face darkens again. "I *said* it was a surprise! I was trying to do something spontaneous, for god's sake."

"Okay—okay. I see that now. I see your intentions were good. But you need to know that you completely misread that whole thing with Raj on the beach—he works with my dad, full stop. Nothing—*nothing*—has happened between me and Raj . . ."

My voice trails off as I realize that this is not—strictly—true.

My mind spins. Could Anthony have somehow found out about what happened at the nightclub in Athens? Is that what this was all about?

I look up to see Anthony sneering at me. "Really? Because the first thing I saw, Gia, was the two of you half naked on the beach with your heads together. Him brushing the hair out of your eyes?"

"It was kelp . . ."

"I *saw* you," he barks, and then when several people turn to look, he stops and takes a deep breath. After a minute, his voice is calmer, but his words emerge through gritted teeth.

"Whatever happened, I've made it clear, I'm prepared to forgive you. I should never have let it go this long—I should have come and collected you right away. Things happen in places like this, I know. I blame myself. If I hadn't had the IPO to deal with, I would have done something about it earlier."

My even tone deserts me. "Like what? Like you making my choices for me? That's not my idea of how a relationship works, Anthony."

The crowd of people filing off the water taxi are all staring at us now, but I don't care. "You can't pretend to be worried and to care about me when you really just want to make all the decisions."

His eyes narrow. "That's not true and it's unfair. I've been missing you, Gia, and thought you were feeling the same way. I thought you wanted to be with me. I guess I was mistaken."

He hands me the second water taxi ticket.

"I'm going to change my flight to leave tonight. If you want to come with me, you know where to find me."

Still holding the little red ticket in my hand, I watch as he jumps on the water taxi just before it pulls away.

chapter thirty-eight

FINALLY SATURDAY EVENING
Pezzogna
Gia Kostas, special correspondent to NOSH, on the Italian
Isle of Capri

If you consider salad only as a starter, there is no better follow-up than this dish, local both in ingredients and preparation to the island of Capri. Begin with fresh-caught red sea bream . . .

It's a good parting line, I have to admit, but it isn't at all true. As the water taxi shoots off toward the mainland, I realize I actually have no idea where to find Anthony at the airport—not what airline he's flying on, nor his flight time. And after everything that's happened, do I really want to find him, anyway?

My mind is churning as I make my way slowly off the dock, and I'm so lost in my thoughts that I don't see Raj coming until I practically bump into him. Unlike me, he has clearly taken the time to shower, and as he walks up, he smells of shampoo and sea air. However, the shower has done nothing to wash away the dark ring forming under his left eye, and I see his hand go to it unconsciously.

His expression lightens when he sees me.

"Gia, I was certain you would have gone. Are you—okay?"

I take a deep breath. "I'm not really sure at the moment, to tell you the truth."

"Mm." He shifts the bag he is carrying to his shoulder.

"Is that the equipment you needed?" I switch to the safer ground of work talk.

"From Brother Wilde," he says. "It's a camera that can give me a better look at the site near Circe's cave. Your dad seems pretty convinced we'll find something there."

"What do you think?"

He shrugs. "I think this has been an amazing journey. Even if his theory doesn't pan out, I've learned so much from working with him."

I give a bitter laugh. "So you *do* think it's a wild goose chase."

"Hey—that's the *opposite* of what I just said."

Since my sunglasses are somewhere at the bottom of Naples Bay, I have to shade my eyes against the sun to see his face. I suddenly decide to take the plunge.

"How do you know Anthony? It's obvious you have some kind of history."

Raj's face closes down. "He didn't tell you?" And then, as if to himself, "Well, of course he didn't."

"No. He didn't tell me. But neither did you. I meant to e-mail him after you mentioned knowing an Anthony Hearst at dinner that night, but then—the mushrooms happened."

He shakes his head, not meeting my eyes. "It was nothing. Years ago. You must know he attended Oxford for a while?"

I have to stop to think about this. "I guess he mentioned he was in England for a semester as an undergrad. Is that where you met?"

Raj nods. "Right. We had a few classes in common. I hardly knew him at all."

"I think I remember him telling stories about wild parties in all the pubs and how tough the exams were."

"I don't know anything about the pubs," he says, shrugging. "We didn't exactly frequent the same places. We shared a tutor, and he was quite terrible to a girl we both knew. There wasn't much more to it. We just—didn't get on."

"There's got to be more than . . ."

"Darling! Here you are, right on time!"

As my dad strides onto the dock looking sunburned and cheerful, Raj turns away. My dad claps him on the back by way of greeting. And then, after dropping a kiss on my cheek, he turns and waves to a figure standing across the street from the marina dock.

Squinting against the setting sun, I see a man wearing a brown robe, his long white hair blowing in the wind. He waves back at my dad enthusiastically.

I look over at Raj. "Is that your monk?"

Raj lifts one shoulder. "Brother Wilde is more of an eccentric academic, I'd say. He's considered one of the preeminent Homerian scholars."

"An absolute inspiration," my dad says heartily. "We spent a very informative afternoon going through his herb garden."

I glance back to see the man hurrying off in the direction of the funicular. He's tiny—little more than five feet tall—and when he turns, the setting sun reflects off a bald spot on the top of his head.

"Takes his cosplay seriously, then?"

But before either of them can answer, my father catches sight of Raj's eye. "My dear boy—what happened? Did your surfboard do you wrong?"

"Something like that," Raj says and pulls a pair of sunglasses from his pocket. "But I'm fine. Nothing to worry about. Shall we go?"

He turns and leads the way toward the water taxi.

My father, following behind, pauses to fish around in his wallet

chapter thirty-nine

LONGEST SATURDAY, EVER
Soppa Tal-Armla
Gia Kostas, special correspondent to NOSH, in Naples, Italy

This incredible soup can be eaten as a starter or, served with a crusty loaf of Maltese peasant bread, can be a hearty meal in itself. The secret is found in the fresh cheeselets and beaten . . .

After trying unsuccessfully to find a cab, I actually end up taking a city bus to the airport. Our guesthouse is right downtown, and a friendly Neapolitan tourist guide wearing a red vest points me to the bus station as both the quickest and the cheapest option. It's a direct route and has Wi-Fi, so it gives me time to google the flights to New York. It also helps me avoid thinking about what I'm going to say when I get there, if I do manage to find him at all.

It turns out there is only one terminal building, and two direct flights departing to New York City this evening, which should simplify things a little, anyway. All the same, the bus stops outside the terminal, way before I feel ready. My nerves jangle as I walk inside.

The entrance to Naples International Airport is more cosmopolitan than any other I can remember, and glass cases containing art installations pepper the concourse. The overriding theme of the moment appears to be Italian fashion with a focus on shoes. I walk past displays featuring Fendi, Bruno Magli, and Ferragamo, among others.

Teresa Cipher would love it in here.

At literally the first bar I look into on the concourse, Anthony is sitting at a booth talking on his phone. Behind him, an ice sculpture of an enormous stiletto-heeled shoe glistens in the soft light of the bar. It looks like it's resting on a bed of diamonds, but these are actually ice cubes, enclosed in a mammoth fountain. It might be the most over-the-top ice sculpture I've ever seen.

Anthony's expression lights up like a beacon when he sees me, and he almost spills his drink trying to end his call and jump up to greet me at the same time.

And there it is.

I know as soon as I see his face that it's over. The fact that I've just said goodbye to Raj—probably forever—and didn't have the courage to tell him how he makes me feel is like a fist, twisting and crushing my heart in my chest. But I can't deal with any of that now. Now, I have to face Anthony, and I'm not going to take the coward's way out again.

I need to tell him the truth. And I need to find a way, if I can, to not hurt him. I at least owe him that much.

When he bends in to kiss me, I turn my face, so that his lips only brush my cheek.

He immediately raises a hand to the server. I want to keep my head clear, but he looks so disappointed when I ask for mineral water that I agree to a glass of wine.

While we wait, I point at his phone, not knowing where else to start. "Did I interrupt a business call?"

"Um-hmm," he says, sipping his Manhattan. "But it's okay. The news is all good."

He reaches across to take my hand. "Thank you for coming, Gia. I don't know what I would have told my mom if I'd shown up without you." He slides a paper ticket across the table to me. "Bet you didn't fly first class coming over here. You're not going to believe the difference. Champagne on takeoff, baby!"

"Anthony—I'm not—that is, I haven't decided to fly home with you."

I pause to take a sip of wine, furious at myself for copping out already. Taking a big gulp, I try again.

"Things have changed while I've been here. Between us, but also with me and my dad. The stroke was bad news, and he's had a few setbacks since. The chance for me to be with him . . ."

Anthony's phone tings, and he glances at it before turning the screen off.

"Anyway, it's really important that I see this through. Also, I've promised Charlotte a piece from Ithaca, which is our last stop. I'll be home in just a few days, Anthony—a week at most. And then—you know—we can talk things through properly."

"How is this not properly? We're talking, aren't we?"

"Well, yes, but—I mean, your flight's in just over an hour, so . . ."

He laughs smugly. "Babe, we are all checked in. We can stroll onto that big bird thirty minutes late if we feel like it, and nobody will say a word."

He reaches an arm out to hug me.

I pull away and stare at his face. He's just not getting it, but before I can say anything, his phone tings again. He smiles at the message and clicks off the screen an instant later.

"Was that a text?" I ask. "That looked like a text."

"It was work," he says shortly. And then when I stare pointedly at him, he pats my hand and laughs. "Okay, okay—so my assistant has talked me into texting, but only for important shit, right? It's an 'old dog, new tricks' thing, I guess."

I narrow my eyes. "You sound like my dad. The difference is that he *is* an old dog, but you're not."

He waves a hand dismissively. "Anyway. I'm just getting the hang of it. To tell you the truth, I hate the unpredictability of texting. I much prefer e-mail, where I can keep a record of everything said and schedule time to deal with it every day."

"This is what I don't understand." I lean back in my seat to get a clearer look at his face. "You've always been Mr. Predictable."

"I prefer to think of it as Mr. Dependable, myself," he counters, smirking.

"Okay, fine. But what is Mr. Dependable doing hopping on a plane to come get me—on a whim? Taking a swing at my dad's colleague for only talking to me? It's—it's just weird."

He shrugs. "I was worried about you being over here on the other side of the world, and—well, it just so happens I'm in a position to do something about it. So I did."

"You're dodging the question, Anthony. Does it have something to do with Raj Malik? How do you know him?"

"I don't," he says stiffly. "Not anymore. The time I spent in England, he was in a couple of my classes, I think. Had a lot of ridiculous ideas, as I recall. A bit of a socialist." He spreads his hands. "That's it."

"He said something about a girl. Was there a problem over a girl?"

The corner of his lip curls. "Oh, you don't need to worry about her. That lasted maybe a month. I'd forgotten all about her until I saw you with him. And speaking of dodged questions"—he arches an eyebrow at me—"how about *you* explain what you were doing with Rupinder, anyway?"

"That's not his name. His name is Raj—Rajnish Malik. Dr. Malik, actually."

Anthony snorts and drains his Manhattan. "Rupinder, Rajinder—whatever. So he managed that PhD after all, did he? He wanted to hang out with us, as I recall. He was good at rowing, but not much else. Anyway, he had his own friends."

I remember Raj saying, *"We didn't exactly frequent the same places."*

"Okay, so what about the girl, then? What was her name?"

He lifts one shoulder dismissively. "No idea. But she was gorgeous. I do remember that. Sachi, maybe? Suki?"

"What happened?"

He shrugs again. "Like I said. I can barely remember, it was so long ago. I was overseas with three other guys from my fraternity, and I was, like, twenty-one. At that age, all you really want to do is party, right?"

"Okay, but what happened to her?"

"To who?"

"Dammit, Anthony. The girl—Sachi."

He glances away. "Not a clue. She moved to New York for a while and got a part in a Broadway show. I think she might have been one of the Cats? Anyway, I only saw her once or twice after that. I had a lot of shit going on, right?"

Right. I lean back in my seat. So something definitely happened with this girl, whose name he can't remember but who clearly followed him to New York.

"In any case, babe," he says, interrupting my musings, "it's all water under the bridge. I don't want to know about your previous conquests either, right? Like I said—all is forgiven. We just need to get you home."

He picks up the tickets and tucks them into his passport. "We should probably head to the gate," he says. "I just need to take a piss. Keep an eye on this stuff, okay?"

He sets the passport containing the tickets on top of his phone and slides out of the booth.

Feeling desperate, I stare after him. He hasn't heard a word I've said, and I guess I'm the same, because nothing he's said has changed my mind either. My dad needs me. I need to—I *want* to—finish my series for NOSH. And the truth is, I suddenly know what I *don't* want.

I don't want to be with Anthony anymore. I most certainly, absolutely, do not want to marry him.

I consider bolting while he's in the restroom, but I can't bring myself to leave his passport unattended on the table. Instead, I slide the ring off my finger. I think briefly about just what I could do with fifty grand and then set it down beside his passport.

Suddenly, his phone begins to buzz so violently it dances across the polished surface of the table in front of me. In an effort to save the phone from falling, I clutch at it. I manage to grab the phone but miss the passport, which drops to the floor under the table. On the screen is a one-line message I can't help reading before the phone goes dark. Bracketed in two eggplant emojis, it reads:

Tony. Missing you, babe. We have lots to catch up on
when you get back . . .

This is followed by a second message, which only contains the winking emoji with its tongue out.

It's from someone called "Mel."

When Anthony returns, I'm standing beside the table. As he walks up, I thrust both hands out at him. With one hand I return the ring, and with the other, the phone. I've lost the desire to consider his feelings, somehow.

When he glances down to read the message, he doesn't even blush. Instead, his expression grows annoyed.

"It's a joke," he says. "Certainly not anything to return a ring over."

I feel strangely calm. "I'm not returning the ring over that text. I'm returning it because I don't want to marry you. I'm not sure why I ever did. And I'm not going back to New York with you."

"She's talking about work plans, Gia. Obviously, it's written in jest," he splutters. "There's even a zany smiley face, for god's sake." He sets the ring on the table and crouches down to retrieve his passport.

"I don't know. It seems more inappropriate than funny to me. Especially from a coworker."

He takes a deep breath and then stomps over to pay his bill at the bar.

"Hey," he says to the bartender and holds up his phone. "If you see this thing—this winking symbol thing—what does that mean to you?"

The bartender—who, like his brethren everywhere, is wiping a glass—shrugs. "That was funny?" he mutters.

Anthony turns on me triumphantly. "See?"

"You didn't show him the first part." I stride over to the bar. "He doesn't have the whole context. And besides—he's a guy. Of course he's going to read it differently!"

Anthony stops suddenly. "You need to be able to take a joke, Gia. Lighten up a bit. I mean, what's wrong with you that you can't even see when another *woman* is teasing?"

I—I don't even know what to say to this. So instead, I go back to the table and pick up my things.

"Goodbye, Anthony."

He narrows his eyes. "Where do you think you're going?"

"I think it's obvious. I'm leaving." And then, to be perfectly clear, I add, "Back to the guesthouse to finish the trip with my dad."

I point at the ring, still sitting on the table.

He bulges his eyes at me. "You don't leave a ring like that sitting on a table. It's worth . . ."

"I know, I know. Fifty thousand dollars. And you know what? You're right."

I reach down and scoop the ring into my hand. "Why did you ask me to marry you if you were going to sleep with someone else?"

He narrows his eyes at me and shrugs. "Gia, I didn't plan to sleep with her. But then you were gone so long, and there she was."

"Oh, so it was my fault for leaving? To help my dad?"

He puts on his patient face. "Babe, it didn't mean anything."

I take a deep breath and try again. "Just be honest with me for once. Why did you pick me?"

His eyes narrow. "Okay, you want the truth? My dad wouldn't turn over control of Hearst Publishing unless I was"—he pauses to make air quotes—"'settled down.' And besides, I like that nice round ass of yours."

He grins, and in spite of his words, I get a brief glimpse of the man I once fell for.

Too brief—and too late.

"And when I found out you came from nothing, I decided that way, I could meet my dad's stupid requirements and still piss him off."

This hits me like a blow to the gut. "From—nothing? What does that mean, 'came from nothing'?"

He waves his passport dismissively. "You know—whatever. Your parents were divorced. You grew up in poverty. You had nothing." He laughs derisively. "Except that cute little ass, of course."

He leans back and looks me up and down, and adds, "Maybe not so little anymore, huh?"

Under any other circumstances, I'd shoot down a remark like this with the scorn it deserves. But instead, I'm stuck on "came from nothing."

I'm quiet a minute as I think about all that's happened with my dad. The importance he's given to showing me where he came from. I think about his grandmother—my great-grandmother—Magdalena and *her* grandmother Consolata. Okay, so they were the product of a drug-induced hallucination, but they were once part of him. And now that I've been here, they'll always be a part of me too.

Anthony drains his Manhattan and sets the glass on the bar. "Come on, babe, you need to show a little sense. Let's get on the plane. And if you don't want to wear the ring, at least put it in a safe place."

He reaches out a hand, but I step backward.

"Good suggestion," I say and do the most sensible thing I can think of under the circumstances. I toss the ring over my shoulder. It lands dead center, sinking instantly into the sparkling ice cubes surrounding the sculpture.

And then I turn and walk out.

Watching a grown man leap knee-deep into an ice-filled fountain while wearing a bespoke suit is not the most satisfying moment I've ever had in my life, but it comes a close second.

chapter forty

SUNDAY, BUT ONLY JUST
Delizia al Limone
Gia Kostas, special correspondent to NOSH, in Naples, Italy

When it's late at night, and a certain something is essential to sweeten your dreams, this incredible zing of citrus might be just what the doctor ordered. Begin with the zest of . . .

By virtue of it being after midnight, I manage to make it back into my room in the guesthouse without running into my dad. I take a cab straight back, late-night public transit being no place to angry-cry with any hope of peace—at least in New York, which I assume also applies in Naples.

I'm not willing to risk it, anyway.

I try holding my breath while waiting my turn in the airport taxi rank, but this only results in an unexpected and possibly even more embarrassing case of the hiccups.

The cab driver takes one look at me in the rearview mirror as I climb into the back and tosses a tattered pack of tissues on the seat beside me before roaring out into the still-busy streets of Naples. Perhaps as a show of compassion, he turns his radio up loud. The rest of the ride takes place with me alternately weeping and hiccuping in the back seat, while the voices of Andrea Bocelli and Ed Sheeran soar from the front.

By the time I make it to the entrance of the guesthouse, I've managed to get a grip on the worst of the weeping. The very sleepy man in charge hands over my key, looks briefly startled as I hiccup my response, and then points me to the stairs. It's nearly twelve thirty as I close the door to my room.

Inside, I uncap the complimentary bottle of water on the bedside table and take a swig. When that doesn't really help, I flop onto the bed, hang my head off the side, and take another drink upside down. Only when I'm sure the hiccups have stopped for good, I FaceTime my best friend.

"Holy shit," Devi says as the screen lights up. "What's happened?"

Annoyingly, as the story pours out of me, she's nodding and, whenever I pause for breath, making interjections like, "Yep, saw that coming," and "No surprise there."

This conversation is not going at all the way I planned.

"Devi, I called you for support. You're supposed to be on my side, here."

"Darling girl, I *am* on your side." She laughs derisively, and then she must catch a glimpse of my face. "Oh, honey! Don't look like that. Not now. There is no doubt left to give this man the benefit of. He's tried to control you from the moment he met you. He's dressed it up in flowers and dinners out and . . ."

"And a giant diamond ring." I'm not about to tell Devi what Anthony said he paid for it—not yet, at least.

"And a fucking giant diamond ring, presented to you *way* too soon in your relationship in such an over-the-top setting that you couldn't say no." She shakes her head. "And I have to admit, he's really good. At the start, I thought I'd just have to wait out the love haze, and then you'd see the light. But he preempted me and asked you to marry him when you'd only really been together a couple of months."

"Three," I whisper. "Three months."

"Okay, three months," she says. "But right now, you're in Greece, girl. Ain't no better cure for a broken heart than one of those beautiful Greek boys."

"I'm actually in Italy," I counter. "But I take your point."

"Greek, Italian—I don't care. Just get out there and hit that hard. Then take a selfie with his beautiful face and e-mail it to Anthony while you're still mad."

"I don't know," I say, unable to suppress a sigh. "I still feel more sad than angry."

Her voice softens. "Listen, Gia, you've done the right thing. You've kicked him to the curb. Let him rot there with the rest of the trash. And promise me you'll at least try to have fun while you're still away, okay? When are you coming home?"

"I—I'm not sure. Not more than a week, I think. We've got a couple more stops, and I've got two more pieces due for NOSH, but . . ."

"Oh my god, Gia—I forgot to tell you. NOSH is amazing!" Devi drops the phone to rustle some papers, so I get a quick look at the ceiling. "Did you know they were the featured magazine inside the *New York Times* on Saturday? And guess whose story was on the cover?"

Her face suddenly reappears, this time smiling broadly.

"No—that is, I knew the piece did really well, but—did they use my photos too?"

"I guess so—I only checked the byline, not the photo credits. But there was an amazing shot of this perfect cannoli on the cover. Was that yours?"

For the first time in what feels like forever, I feel a stab of pride. My story—my photos—in the *New York Times*? Okay, in NOSH,

AN ACCIDENTAL ODYSSEY · 343

but still technically inside the actual, physical Old Grey Lady of a newspaper.

"Yeah, that was mine."

"Well, GO you! And do *not* feel bad about dumping Anthony's ass. He doesn't deserve you."

We agree that I am better out of the relationship than in, and then, in a moment of weakness, I tell her about the fistfight.

Her eyes light up.

"What? Are you saying he took a swing at your dad's colleague without any provocation? Like—straight out of the blue?"

I take a shaky breath. "He says he thought he saw something between me and Raj, but he totally, totally misread the situation."

"Hold on, back it up a minute here, sister. What was there to misread? Misread like, you're not even in the same room with the guy? Or like, Anthony caught you guys being meaninglessly flirty with each other and misread that?"

"Neither. Raj helped me rescue my kayak after I got thrown off and . . ."

"What? What? Okay, Gia, this changes everything. Who is this Raj guy? I thought he was some old dude who works with your dad?"

A vision of Raj—wet hair swept back, his already-mocha torso tanned even darker by the Mediterranean sun, sitting beside me on the sand and laughing—leaps, unbidden, into my mind.

"No, he's not an old dude," I say carefully. "But he is my dad's colleague, and really? He's been nothing but super polite and almost standoffish . . ."

And suddenly I realize why.

"Dev, I've got to go. I have to look someone up online, and I can't do that while I'm on FaceTime with you."

"No!" she shouts and then, glancing over her shoulder, repeats more quietly, "No. I still have too many questions. And you totally *can* look something up—it just sometimes makes the camera go off. Anyway, I'm sitting at my computer. What do you need?"

And so, together we look up the name of the girl Raj told me about. There's a little detour while we search for "Sasha," but as soon as I remember her name was Sachi, we find her almost instantly.

Sachi Gee.

"She's an actress," Devi says, but by this time, I've found her too. She lives in London, and she's gorgeous. Like, Chrissy Teigen gorgeous. Since she's currently starring in a play in the West End, Devi opens IMDB and learns she got her start on Broadway. I google the play, hit images, and find a picture from opening night.

She wore a skintight sheath dress that fit her body like molten gold.

Her date was Anthony. My Anthony. Or rather, my Anthony no longer.

"Who *is* she?" cries Devi's voice from my phone's speaker. I click out of Google, and her face replaces Sachi's.

"She's—the reason for the fistfight, I think." This gives me pause. "It really did have nothing to do with me—or with that night in Athens—after all."

Devi looks entirely baffled. "What the actual fu . . ." she begins, and then behind her, I see a door open.

The image disappears so fast, it takes me a moment to realize she's pulled the covers over her phone. This effectively muffles the voices, but I hear her saying, "Right away, Auntie. Just let me finish this chart."

There is the sound of a door closing, and then suddenly Devi's face pops back into view.

"Look," she whispers, "you're going to have to give me the short version. I'm at my aunt and uncle's house, so I can use their desktop to upload some giant files from work, and as soon as I'm done here, they want me to go drink chai and talk about why I'm not married yet."

"Have you finished the files?"

"Yes. It only took two minutes. I'm stalling, of course. Now talk. Who is this gorgeous woman?"

"Raj and Anthony went to school together for a semester at Oxford about five years ago, and my guess is, they both liked her."

"Your guess? She's so gorgeous, *I* like her, and I don't even lean that way, as a rule!" She's quiet a minute and then laughs out loud. "Maybe I'll tell my auntie *that's* why I'm not married yet. That'll give her something to talk about over chai!"

She peers into the screen. "Anyway, why does it matter? It was five years ago at least, and her Wiki page says she's married now. Five years ago, you went to prom with Henry Tuttle, for god's sake. Who knows where *he* is now? Who even cares?"

"That was seven years ago, but I know you're right. It's just . . ."

"What? What?" Devi jams the phone so close I can see right up her nose. "There's something missing in this picture. Who cares if stupid asshole Anthony fights with someone over an old girlfriend? I always told you he was the jealous type. Did the other guy—what's his name?—did he win, at least?"

"Raj. I guess so. Anthony got a bloody nose, so they sort of just stopped."

"Yay! Go other guy!" Her eyes narrow. "So, tell me again who this Raj is?"

"He's a colleague of my dad. He's—uh—remember that night I got drunk and . . ."

Devi shrieks and drops the phone. "Holy shit, Gia—he's not the hot Prince Charming?"

Behind her the door opens, and the image suddenly vanishes again as a muffled voice speaks out.

"Are you all right, Devi dear? I thought I heard a scream!"

"I'm fine, Auntie. It was just—a—a difficult photograph. Accident victim, you know."

"Oh, darling, I'm so sorry you have to deal with that. But just part of the job, eh? We have a fresh pot of chai waiting for you in the front room, as soon as you are done."

"I'm coming, Auntie. Two minutes. And you'd—you'd better close the door. I'll be quicker if I'm not distracted."

"Fine, fine. Mrs. Gupta has brought along some of those biscuits you like, darling. See you in two minutes!"

The door finally closes, and Devi's bulging eyes reappear. "Okay, she will literally be back here in one minute fifty-nine seconds, so you need to spill, and fast. Are you telling me that the guy you nailed that first night in the toilet—the Prince Charming who found your shoe—is RAJ? And he works with your dad?"

"It was a janitor's closet, not a toilet."

"Listen. To. Me," she whispers hoarsely. "Do NOT let that get away."

"Too late," I say as lightly as I can manage. "He's gone."

This shuts her up. "I'm sorry, Gia," she says, at last. "But don't forget what a rock-star journalist you are. That's going to be the best thing that comes out of this whole crazy adventure, right?"

"Right. Thank you for being here for me, Dev."

"I love you," she says simply. "Where else would I be?"

Sure enough, the door behind her opens again.

"Love you too."

And with that, she is gone.

S o. I'd like to say I take my best friend's advice and run off to have my way with assorted Italian stallions. But since there's only one stallion I'm actually interested in and there's nothing remotely Italian about him—and worse, he's not only *not* interested in me back but has actually left the building—I am seriously out of luck.

Of course I am. Even if I wasn't his colleague's daughter, as far as he knows, I cheated on my fiancé. Which, plainly, he has a bad history with, in light of Sachi. So, even if he actually does believe me, I'm still the unreliable party in this scenario.

I get it. I do.

And so, for once in my life, I take the only sensible option open to me and go to bed.

chapter forty-one

SUNDAY FOR REAL
Tiramisu
Gia Kostas, special correspondent to NOSH, on
    an Italian train

*You may have tasted this dish at the finest of Italian restaurants
Stateside, and if you have, you will know that nothing cures a
broken heart like the true delicacy and flavor . . .*

I sleep through until my dad knocks on my door just after seven, telling me we have ten minutes before we need to go catch our train.

After one look in the mirror, I throw myself in the shower. I'm not going to be able to do anything about the dark circles under my eyes, but I can at least rid my face of all the mascara streaks from crying.

I lay the phone on the counter beside the sink while drying my hair. I'm so tired, I can hardly think, and the shower hasn't helped as much as I hoped. The only thing I can say for myself is that when my dad shows up at the door, I'm dressed and have at least managed to get some eyeliner on.

We don't have time for anything—coffee or conversation—but manage to make the train just before it pulls out of the station. I follow my dad, who has the good sense to march us down to the café car and secure us a table. We are drinking steaming espresso and eating cannoli and croissants before Naples stops flashing past outside the train windows.

I'm on my third coffee before my dad leans forward.

"It's my fault," he says so quietly, I almost can't hear him over the sound of the engine. "I told Anthony where we were going to be. I thought he was just checking in—I had no idea he was going to show up in Capri."

Sighing, I push away my cup. "It's okay. You didn't know. *I* didn't know things would go so wrong." I look over at my dad's face. His nose is sunburned, but he looks somehow pale all the same. He's probably just as tired as I am, and his worry over me doesn't help.

"I thought you liked Anthony." I finish the last bite of my cannoli. The old, pre-odyssey Gia would never have eaten a pastry this rich for breakfast. But if Italy has done one thing for me, it's shown me that it's never too early for dark chocolate and cream. Especially combined with morning coffee.

He shrugs. "I like him well enough. I just think you can do better."

This makes me laugh. "Better than the heir to a publishing empire?"

He laughs too, and drains his coffee. "Okay, you may not be able to find someone richer. But I want you to be happy. Happy is more important."

I sigh, not—truthfully—feeling very happy at all.

"Well, whatever the result, I've broken it off with him. We're done."

My dad wipes croissant flakes off his fingers, then reaches across to squeeze my hand.

"That you are happy is all I want. Even if you find no one, as long as you are happy, I am happy."

"Wait a minute—are you saying that *you*—my Greek father, who has spent a good chunk of my adult life trying to marry me off—are *you* saying that you think I'm not going to find anyone?"

He laughs and signals for the bill. "You need to find the one who is right for you, my sweet *koritsi*. When you find him? You will know."

This advice would be more heartwarming if I didn't know my dad's romantic history.

Just saying.

O nce we clear the city limits of Naples, our train picks up speed until it's flying along. The scenic beauty of what I think must translate roughly to the instep of the Italian boot whizzes by so fast, it's a blur outside the windows. After breakfast, we find our assigned seats, which are just comfortable enough that I conk right out for the rest of the journey. A couple of hours later, I awaken as the train slows down outside an Italian town called Taranto and disembark, blinking into a brilliant, crystal clear afternoon.

We alight at the Taranto Galese train station and take a taxi down to the waterfront, where we'll pick up the boat Teresa Cipher has arranged for us. Our taxi takes us along the shores of the Mare Piccolo—the Little Sea—which is separated from the Mediterranean by a tiny arm of land. On this land stands the Castel Sant'Angelo, a huge fortification built on the ruins of older castles by the then king of Naples, Ferdinand of Aragon, in 1496. The stone of the castle walls is brilliantly white against the cerulean blue of the sea, but this glimpse is all I'm going to get of it, as our trimaran is waiting.

It is the *Celere* once again, and I could not be more delighted. The Wi-Fi connection onboard means I'll be able to submit my stories to NOSH on time without worry, and since my job is the only thing really going right in my life at the moment, I am happy to put all my attention there, at least for now.

As we climb aboard, my phone pings, which surprises me for a moment, before I realize it's just reconnected itself to the onboard Wi-Fi.

The ping is a text from, of all people, Raj Malik. My heart lifts at just seeing his name, but the contents are obscure enough that I have trouble following at first.

> Bad signal, so only time for a quick note. Tell your dad I've found something. Can't believe it, but he might have been right all along. Not a vessel: a tablet. Will need carbon dating to confirm, but will try to catch you with the piece I've found before you leave the country to be sure. Stay tuned!

When I show it to my dad, all the color drains out of his face for a moment, and then he insists I read it out loud to him. When I finish, he grabs the bag out of my hand, tosses it carelessly to the floor, and dances me wildly around the deck, much to the amusement of the crew.

After a final twirl, he drops me into a deck chair and runs over to shake the captain's hand. "This boat—she is taking me to find my destiny," he crows joyfully and then rashly runs down to the galley to order a round of champagne for the crew for after dinner.

I take a quick look to make sure my iPad has survived this rough treatment, which thankfully, it has. However, moments later, my hat is not so lucky. There is a huge gust of wind as we round the corner of the point at San Vito, and my hat sails off so high in the sky I lose sight of it long before it hits the water.

I stare out to sea while the boat skirts the point of land, and then watch as both the wind and the waves settle back into their usual placidness. Losing the hat doesn't matter so much now—we have only a couple of days before we have to fly back to New York, and anyway, if I want to, I can buy another one at our next stop in Gallipoli. But somehow, after all we've been through together on this trip, I feel deeply sorry to see it go.

Once we pull out into the sea, I head back to my favorite spot in the lounge and settle in for a good writing session. I need to sort through all the pictures I have taken of the various meals so far on the trip and decide what recipe to feature for my penultimate article. Outside the large, rectangular window, the coastline of Italy streams by, an unending vista of long, deserted beaches. The land is very flat here, and the sky is overcast, which should make it easier to concentrate on my work.

But before I get a single word down, my dad slides into the seat across the table from me. He's got his phone in hand, and he gives me what I can only describe as a shy smile.

"I have something to confess, *Gianitsa*," he says, eyes twinkling. He slides his phone across to me, which is open to an e-mail. I read through the e-mail and then read it again before looking up at him.

"So, you pitched this book to publishers before you had even finished it?"

He actually giggles. "I know. Naughty of me, isn't it?"

"I don't know about 'naughty,' Pops, and—correct me if I'm wrong here—but you still haven't got the hard evidence to prove your theory. How long have you been up to this?"

"A few weeks, maybe." He shrugs. "In any case, young Raj has

AN ACCIDENTAL ODYSSEY · 353

found something at Circe's cave. You read the text he sent—this is really happening!"

"Okay, I admit it sounds promising for sure, but you haven't seen an artifact with your own eyes yet, right? And there's also the minor detail that you pinpointed the location when you were high on mushrooms."

He narrows his eyes. "I've never known you to be such a doubter, Gianna. In any case, I have finished it now. I made a printout of the first draft of the book in Naples. You can read it for yourself whenever you like."

"I'm not doubting you, Pops. I'm just trying to think critically. With scientific principles."

He smiles gnomically. "As do I. But, mushrooms aside, you can't discount the value of serendipity throughout history to scientific discovery."

I look back at the letter on his phone. "Okay, fine. But—am I reading this correctly? You've got a publisher interested in the manuscript?"

He laughs delightedly. "Apparently so. Over the last few weeks, I've been pitching my idea to all the big publishing houses in New York . . ."

"Have you promised them proof that your long-shot theories are true?"

"Yes," he says vehemently. "And now it seems I was right. Raj would not make this trip for nothing."

"But you didn't know he'd found the urn or whatever it is until today. These letters go back weeks."

"Details." He waves a hand dismissively. "I knew I was onto something all along. I believed it was true, and now I'm going to have the proof. This book is going to shake academia to its foundations.

Look!" He taps the screen of his phone. "Even your fiancé's publishing company is in the mix."

"Ex-fiancé," I counter gloomily.

He scrolls a bit more and then shows me another letter. "Take a look at them apples!"

I read through the letter with the Hearst Books logo and then look back at him. "When did this come through, Pops?"

"It just came in. But I don't have to go with Hearst Books if you'd rather I didn't, *koritsi*. The point is, there is definite interest in my theory. It's creating a storm in the publishing world! This makes our whole trip worthwhile, my girl. Can you see that?"

I don't know what I see, and that's the problem. I mean—I understand too little about publishing to know if a financial executive has any influence on the choice of books they print. Is it far-fetched to think that Anthony is somehow finding another way to make me beholden to him again? Regardless, there is no way I want to say anything about this to my dad. I have never seen him look so joyful and excited. After all we have been through, I am *not* the one who is going to bring him down.

That evening, the *Celere* pulls in to the harbor at Gallipoli. It is an astonishing sight, as one section of the city stretches along an isthmus into the sea. It is also, I soon discover, in no way related to the more famous Gallipoli, site of horrendous losses for the Allies in the first world war. That spot is located far to the east, past even mainland Greece, along the shore of Turkey.

Tomorrow, we are slated to arrive in Santa Maria di Leuca, and this pushes even his impending publication to the back of my dad's mind. I get a text from Talia just as the boat is pulling in to its berth for the evening, telling me that she and Pene are expecting us the following afternoon.

When I read this to my dad, his face reddens so much I make him sit down.

"What if she won't see me?" he whispers, mopping his suddenly sweaty brow. "What if she still hates me?"

"She's invited us, Pops." I sit down beside him. "She knows we're coming. Talia says she's looking forward to seeing you again. It's all going to be okay."

But I can tell he is hardly hearing me. Between Raj's find and his impending meeting with Pene, he is too excited to go ashore for dinner. I'm not about to miss my dinner, so I go without him. This is an excellent decision, as I bring back what ends up probably being the best takeout I've had on this entire journey. We sit on the deck as the swallows dive above us through the twilight and nibble on paper-thin slices of sopressa served with creamy polenta. This Italian salami is flawlessly complemented with local olives and fresh, chewy bread dipped into a perfectly spiced hummus. After dinner, as the stars come out, we drink sweet red wine, and my dad gently clinks his glass against my own.

"You know," he says, "of all the mistakes I've made in my life, the biggest was leaving Pene."

"Are you sure, Pops? I mean—there's been some decently big mistakes in there. And I'm pretty sure I'm one of them."

I can see his teeth gleam in the dark. "If you are, then you are the best mistake I ever made."

He's quiet a minute, then drains his glass. "When we're done here, *koritsi*, I want you to know—whether this damn book gets picked up or not, I'm coming back here. I want to return to Ithaca, not just to visit but for good this time. And I'm going to make things right with Pene and Talia."

He gets to his feet, a little unsteady with the wine, and pats my shoulder. "An early night, I think. I want to be rested when we arrive. I want her to see the best of me."

We both chuckle a little at this, but I don't follow him downstairs.

Instead, I say a little prayer of gratitude to Teresa Cipher and her crew at ExLibris for booking us onto this Wi-Fi enabled vessel. And then, as the boat glides out silently into the still waters of the Mediterranean, I file my second-to-last article and take myself to bed.

The ship is already docked in Santa Maria di Leuca when I awaken, so I get myself washed and dressed, and then head up to the deck to have breakfast. Surprisingly, my dad's not there, so I sit down and begin without him. The coffee, as with every cup I've tasted in Italy, is absolutely perfect—hot and rich and without a trace of bitterness. I've just guiltily ordered a fresh pot so my dad will be able to have some, when the first mate comes racing up the steps from below, his face ashen.

When I follow him downstairs to the berth, my dad looks like he is sound asleep. One of his hands rests on the printout of the manuscript that he threatened to make me read. And in the other hand, he holds the picture Talia gave him. Sixteen-year-old ne'er-do-well Ari Kostas, with his arm around the shoulders of his first—and only—true love.

chapter forty-two

MONDAY
Can't imagine a single dish I want to write about
Gia Kostas, missing my dad already

The sky has clouded over in the last few minutes—nothing serious, no real rain-bearing clouds, but a sort of gentle, grey mist is in the air. The first mate left almost immediately after we found my dad to make contact with—someone. He told me who, but I just can't remember at the moment.

I'm sitting on the deck, feeling numb and blank and empty. There are so many people I should contact—Talia and her mom are expecting us today, and I'm fairly certain Raj said he was coming to meet us. And what about Teresa and her team at ExLibris? There must be a million other things, but I don't have a clue where to even begin.

In the end, I dial Anthony. It's the middle of the night in New York, and he's not even been back there for long, but I feel like he should know my dad is gone. I scroll through my phone to find the number for his landline at home since I know he generally leaves his cell phone downstairs at night. The phone rings five times before it's picked up.

"Hello?" says a breathy voice that in no way belongs to Anthony. My own voice dies in my throat.

"Hello?" the woman says again. Somewhere in the distance, I can hear water running and then Anthony calling out.

"Was that the phone, Mel? Just leave it, okay?"

The woman giggles. "I hear a landline ring, Tony, and I can't help myself. I mean, I do it all day at work, right? It's just a habit."

Anthony's voice, closer now, repeats, "Melanie, don't pick up the phone."

"Hello?" she says again. "Hello?" And then, after a pause, "See what I mean, babes? It doesn't matter. There's no one even there."

As I touch the screen to end the call, all I can think is *Tony? Really?* No one—including me—has ever been allowed to call him Tony. I slump back onto my deck chair and stare blankly at the phone screen when it suddenly rings in my hand.

"Gia! You made it! You are NOT going to believe this. I can't wait to show you."

"Raj," I say quietly, but I'm not sure he even hears.

"It's definitely a tablet, a huge fragment, the biggest I've ever seen. The text is clear as a bell, and I'm almost positive it's third century. Which, if it's true, is *incredible*, because the Homeric scribes didn't even start writing until the eighth century. And listen! Late last night, we also unearthed a ewer, and—I can't even believe it—an urn. Your dad was right, dammit!"

"Raj," I try again, but he's talking so fast now I can't even follow him and he's so breathless I think he must be running. "I need to tell you . . ."

His voice is still on the line, but suddenly, he appears, flying into the far end of the marina. He waves his phone madly at me as he dashes up the dock, lugging a heavy canvas bag under one arm. He bypasses the small gangplank of the *Celere* completely and vaults over the side of the boat. Pausing only to drop the bag into my chair, he wraps me in a huge hug, swings me around—and kisses me.

There is a sudden taste of salt and sea air and toothpaste, and then it's over.

The events of this morning have left me so shocked, I can't do anything but stare up at him. In the moment of awkward silence that follows, his face flushes a deep red.

"I'm *so* sorry," he blurts. "That was only a—a *friend* kiss, I promise you. In—ah—*celebration*."

His hands are still on my shoulders, and he gives me a gentle squeeze. "I'm just so excited for your dad."

His eyes search my face—I think maybe looking to see if I'm offended?—and he finally, slowly releases me and steps back.

"Was it a terrible crossing?" he asks slowly. "You look so tired . . ."

I open my mouth to reply and instead just burst into tears.

"Gia—Gia, I'm so sorry," he says. "I know I overstepped, but it was just in the heat of . . ."

"It's not the kiss, you idiot." I manage to pull it together for a minute. "It's my dad."

And, to give him credit, he stops talking then. By this time, I'm crying so hard I've lost the ability to speak myself, so he takes my hand and leads me over to one of the benches that line this open part of the boat. We sit together, not quite touching, and soon enough, I find I can talk again.

He only gets up long enough to pass me the napkin I was using at breakfast, and I clutch at it gratefully.

"Tell me what you need," he says, at last, when my sobs finally quiet to that shuddering state where even breathing doesn't come easily.

"I don't know. I don't know what I need, Raj. I don't even know where to start. How am I going to get him home?"

"I don't know either," he says, looking worried. "But we can find out. This must have happened before—they must have systems in place. Have you talked to the captain yet?"

I'm just shaking my head, when the first mate climbs back aboard, followed by several people who immediately disappear down below.

"Is doctor," the first mate says quietly. "And harbormaster, to talk to the captain. After they see to your papa, they come up and give you more information, okay?"

"Okay."

The first mate is joined by the captain, who offers me his condolences before they both follow the others down to my dad's cabin.

After they leave, Raj points to my phone. "Do you need to reach out to your family in America? What about calling Anthony?"

This sends a surge of emotion through me that I can't quite identify before I realize it is anger. I wipe my eyes hard and shake my head.

"Anthony and I are history. I need to handle this on my own."

Something changes in his face, and he's quiet again. After a long moment, he asks, "Okay. What do *you* want?"

I stand up and walk over to the rail, looking out across the water. "I want what my dad wanted. To make things right with Pene and Talia, and to go back to Ithaca. But now—now he'll never have the chance."

My eyes fill up again, but I fight the tears back. Anger surges in my chest; fury at all the stupid, selfish choices I have made.

"I can't believe we didn't talk about this—I'm such an idiot. I should have made him talk this through with me. But instead, I was too busy dealing with NOSH and with Anthony and with everything else except the possibility that my dad could die."

Raj walks over to stand beside me. "We're mortal," he says quietly. "We all know that, right from the moment each baby is born. But if we think about dying all the time, nothing would ever get done. So getting caught up in the regular adventures of daily life just means we're human."

He laughs a little, then. "And this latest adventure? It's been enough to take anyone's mind off all our human realities."

"That's true." I think back to all that's happened over the last—can it only have been a couple of weeks?—and then I laugh too. Just a little.

But somehow, it feels better than being mad at myself.

"What do *you* want?" Raj asks again.

I take a big, shaky breath. "Well, he did say he wanted to go to Ithaca. I know that for sure."

He smiles. "Then it's settled," he says. "We're going to finish this journey for him."

And that is what we do.

B y the time Talia arrives, we have everything settled on the boat. It turns out that transporting someone who has died to a different country, even a different EU country, is a lot more complicated than if the person dies at sea. Our plan all along had been a brief stop here in Santa Maria di Leuca, en route to Ithaca, so the captain agrees to keep to this itinerary. Talia's brought her car, however, so we take an hour to go meet up with her mother.

Penelope Natale is, of course, Ari's age but, like her daughter, looks much younger. Far from awkward, we end up sharing a lot of laughs over lunch, admittedly mostly at my dad's expense. Pene admits to always secretly holding a torch for Ari and to following his career from afar. But seeing how his marriages failed reinforced all the terrible things her parents had said about him, and over the years, she became convinced that her decision to never contact him had been the right one.

"When Talia call me the day you met, I sure he was—you know—no good," she tells me. "It took Talia hours to make me believe he truly honest."

"Hours," echoes Talia, widening her eyes dramatically.

I reach across and touch one of the old lady's hands. "He made so many mistakes, it's true. But he loved you."

I clasp both her hands in mine. "And he wanted more than anything to tell you so."

After spending the afternoon sorting out funeral plans with Talia and Pene, Raj and I board the boat just as dusk is falling. The sun sinks into the water as we pull out onto the Mediterranean for the last leg of our journey.

Raj, who has stayed beside me all day, mostly not saying a word, leans on to the railing. The wind is just enough to ruffle our hair, and I think of my hat, floating off somewhere out on this vast sea, and for some reason, it makes me laugh.

Which then, I have to explain so as not to sound like a crazy person.

Luckily, Raj laughs too. "Maybe it will have its own adventures," he says. "The odyssey of Gianna's hat—volume two."

"Why volume two?"

He grins. "Think of all the adventures you had together. Those were certainly enough to fill out volume one."

The slimmest white trace of a fingernail moon appears just above the horizon in front of us, barely visible in the twilight. I take a deep breath.

"I need to thank you."

"No, you don't," he says. "This is just . . ."

But before he can finish, I reach up and kiss him.

He kisses me back. And we kiss underneath that tiny little trace of a moon for a long, long time.

I take another deep breath when we finally break apart. "That was *not* a friend kiss," I clarify, and his smile gleams down at me through the gathering dusk.

"I was going to say that this is just what good friends do," he says, reaching for me again. "However, I am perfectly willing to take it back."

But after a much shorter time, he breaks off the kiss and actually physically steps away from me.

"Maybe we should stop," he mutters. "This is just too much, all at once. Losing your dad right at the end of the journey like this. What if you go home after all of this and make things up with Anthony?"

The very thought makes my stomach clench, but for the first time today, Raj looks truly worried.

I reach out my hand and shiver a little. "You asked me earlier what I want," I say, staring up at him fiercely. "Did you mean it? Does it *really* matter?"

He takes my outstretched hand in both of his warmer ones. "Of course it does. You can always talk to me," he begins, but I cut him off again. Talking is *not* what I have in mind.

Kissing him, I slide my cold hands up under his shirt, making him jump, just a little, before he folds me into his arms.

There are times, you know—even for a writer—when actions speak louder than words.

chapter forty-three

TUESDAY
Ithaki Rovani
Gia Kostas, special correspondent to NOSH, in
    Ithaca, Greece

*Possibly the sweetest offering of this epic journey, we present this
concoction of honey, oil, and rice that combines together to make
an appropriate end to any meal, let alone this series. The secret,
as always, is in the spices . . .*

And so, three weeks after I left New York City to chase him down,
I begin the process of burying my father on the other side of the
world. It takes me a day and a half to sort out the funeral. I have
never organized a funeral before, and I think maybe it shows. I
mean, it's complicated. My dad is technically Greek Orthodox, but
he hasn't been inside a church in my lifetime. I wouldn't call him an
atheist, but monotheism has never been his thing either. I try to explain this to the priest who Pene has found to take the service, but
even with Talia's excellent translating skills, I'm not exactly sure how
it's going to come together. I suspect Zeus isn't going to get a mention.

Raj had to leave that first night, but he promised to help from
afar, and he has. I gave him my dad's phone, and he's reached out and
notified everyone on it, from my dad's university colleagues to my
half brothers and their families.

I did make the call—FaceTime, actually—to my own mom, who shocked both of us, I think, by offering to fly over. In the end, she agreed that attending the small memorial his department at the university plans to hold in the summer might do just as well.

"But are you sure you're okay, honey?" she says, her face suddenly looming closer on my phone screen. "Do you have everything you need there?"

"I think so." I glance down at my list. "It's likely going to be pretty quiet. And I'll be heading home the day after tomorrow."

"We'll get together for lunch soon, okay?" she offers. "With mimosas or something? Raise a glass to the old reprobate." I agree this is a fine idea, and we say goodbye.

The morning of the funeral, before I start to get ready, I submit my final column to NOSH. The featured dish is a local sweet called rovani—made from rice, honey, olive oil, and spices—which I tasted for the first time with dinner the night before. It's sticky enough to pull the fillings out of your mouth and sugary enough to cause a dozen more, but it seems fitting to end this journey with the sweetest possible finale.

I append a quick note to Charlotte telling her about my dad and send it off, awash in mixed feelings. It's my first real commission as a writer, and in spite of everything, I'm so proud of myself for seeing it through to completion. The few notes I've had from Charlotte have all been positive, and—according to Devi, at least—there's been a pretty good reception.

I pull on the new dress I've bought for the funeral. It's got cute little shoulder ties and is in a pink floral I can wear with my teal cardigan. Shoulder ties are not exactly de rigueur for funeral-wear, but I know my dad would roll over in the grave he's not quite in yet if I wore black. I've only managed one sleeve of the cardigan when an e-mail pings through.

Gianna!

I'm so sorry to hear about the loss of your father. I know how important a figure he has been in your life, and his presence is felt in every part of the story you've woven through this series. I know he will be dearly missed.

My plan was to save this offer for once you were home and rested, but considering your circumstances, I expect this may be a bit of a hard day for you. Let me lighten it to this extent: we at NOSH would like to extend you the offer of a full-time writing position. We're in the market for a roving foodie columnist, and we believe the series you've just completed shows you are more than up to the task.

Think about it, and once you're home and have caught up on your sleep, we can talk details.

Sending all my best to you as you celebrate the life of your colorful father,
Charlotte

PS: It might amuse you to note we have been fielding requests to loan you out as a "culinary expert" from some outfit I've never heard of before. It's called ExLibris—apparently they recreate literary journeys? Sounds pretty sketchy to me. Keep a wary eye out!
—C

And with this cheering news, I finish putting on a funeral dress best suited for a person with a colorful father and head out to say goodbye to my dad.

I f Ari had died at home in New York City, I expect there would have been hundreds of people at his funeral, all in one way or another beneficiaries of the lifelong Aristotle Kostas charm offensive. By this standard, the ritual that takes place at the tiny chapel in Ithaca is a quiet affair, but the attendees? Are anything but.

The tiny white chapel stands near the harbor mouth to the town of Ithaca. It is walking distance from the little guesthouse where we are staying, and so I walk over, with Talia holding one of my hands and Pene the other. The chapel is painted in the classic Greek colors of white and blue, with a slate roof and a teeny bell tower. The bell is ringing as we approach, and the blue front door, which faces the sea, is flung wide open.

Inside, the chapel has room for perhaps thirty people, and as I walk up the stone steps, it is overflowing with familiar faces. Taki is there, crying already and blowing his nose into a large, red handkerchief. Herman is with him too, perched atop the reading lamp on the pulpit. And at the front of the chapel stands Raj. He looks impossibly handsome, wearing what I'm pretty sure is the same suit he wore the night I met him in Athens, though I suspect it's been laundered since. He smiles and indicates the front row of seats, and the three of us slide past him and sit down.

At the front of the church on the altar is the picture of my dad taken with both my half brothers on the occasion of Tomas's university graduation. I was about nine when it was taken, I think, and it's the only picture I have of the three of us with my dad. The other photo is the tiny snapshot of Ari and Pene as teenagers. I have to take a deep breath when I see these two images, and suddenly, I feel Raj's hand in my own.

Talia has done her job well, because the service—which, apart from a few words of welcome at the beginning, is entirely conducted in Greek—takes no longer than fifteen minutes. During each of the three hymns, Herman sways on his perch, raising his crest and occasionally rubbing a cheek against one of the framed photos. There is a slight disruption in the middle, when Brother Wilde, trailing a cloud that smells distinctly like a mix of patchouli oil and weed, pushes through from one of the rear pews and offers a prayer in Italian. Other than that, things go pretty much as expected.

After the final hymn, mostly chanted as a solo by the attending priest, there is a stirring at the back, and six enormous men stride forward. At the head of the group is Paulo, his face serious.

I shoot a wide-eyed glance at Raj, and he grins a little sheepishly.

"Paulo offered to carry it by himself, but then I remembered your encounter with the basketball team in Crete. I checked if any of them live nearby. Only five did, but they all wanted to come, so . . ."

The coffin looks ridiculously small in the hands of these giants as they all pause to nod their heads at me on their way out the door. I can't imagine how even two of them could fold themselves into the Mini Cooper that day, but the sight of them here makes me smile at the memory.

And, strangely enough, I don't stop smiling for the rest of the afternoon. Afterward, we follow a collection of almost completely spherical ladies, all dressed in black, to a nearby hall, where a table groans under the weight of the Ithacan equivalent of finger foods. While the men seem to gather in one corner and the ladies in another, one by one, the amazing and wonderful people I've met on this crazy journey come up to say hello or to offer a memory of my dad.

Margarita swings up first, accompanied not by Federico of the fishing boat but by Guido the cabbie. She looks lovely in a black dress covered in tiny white polka dots and fitted to flatter her cleavage in a way her orange coveralls could only dream of. Guido has his hair slicked back with enough oil to thoroughly lube his cab and is wearing a black dress shirt, done up right to the neck, and tight jeans. Not once do I spot him letting go of Margarita's hand.

Most of the basketball players are clustered near the food, and among them, I spot Sikka. Today she is wearing the black sparkly miniskirt, but this time topped with a comparatively modest t-shirt, emblazoned with a Def Leppard logo. Her Ivo sits beside her, his face like thunder, as she chats amiably with one of the players. When she catches my eye, she points silently at Raj and slowly and deliberately performs an unmistakably obscene gesture with her fingers before then pointing at me. Luckily, Raj misses this little display, but the basketball player she's standing with grins widely and shuffles a little closer, effectively blocking my view.

I worry a little about Ivo, I have to admit.

In a corner near the savory dishes, I spot Paulo holding forth with two or three of the other basketball players. He's wearing exactly the same clothes I remember from the day by the cave near Mitra, right down to the eye patch. As I watch, he mimes taking a shot at a basket and then spreads his arms wide.

"And who could beat that shot?" he cries.

"NOBODY!" chorus the men around him, and they all roar with laughter.

"It might have been a mistake to call Paulo," Raj whispers. "I— think he brought some of his wine."

I grin. "I wouldn't mind trying some of that . . ." I begin, when there is a stir across the room.

The basketball team uncluster themselves to allow an elegantly clad woman through the door. In her heels, she is as tall as any of them, and she is wearing what I find out later is a Hervé Léger wrap dress in deep red. It would a hundred percent meet with my dad's approval, knowing his fondness for scarlet on a woman.

Teresa Cipher removes her sunglasses and scans the room before striding toward me.

"Gianna, my dear, I am so sorry," she says, reaching out to squeeze my hand. "I would have been here sooner, but I was at a wedding and couldn't get away until now."

She turns to Raj. "Thank you so much for tracking me down, dear boy. I would have been devastated to miss being here."

He beams back at her. "I remembered you said you were working in London, so I thought it might be worth at least sending you an e-mail."

"I'm so glad you are able to be here, Ms. Cipher." I release her gloved hand. "Is the wedding nearby?"

She smiles. "Close enough. It's a pair of my staff members being married, if you can believe it, in the Eiffel Tower. The service was held in a tiny, private room at the top. I've left my partner there guarding the champagne."

"All the way to Paris? Will you be able to make it back in time?"

She pats my hand. "Darling, jet helicopters were invented for this very situation." Leaning forward, she places her head beside my ear. There is a sudden faint scent of white roses and bergamot.

"This isn't the time or place, my dear, but I just want you to know I've put in a word at that lovely magazine you work for. I have a little commission in mind that I think might suit you."

"That—that would be amazing." I can't help wondering what Charlotte will make of this blond goddess.

Teresa gives my hand a final squeeze. "I'll be in touch, darling."

Then she turns to Raj and offers him her hand. "Lovely to see you again, Dr. Malik."

"And you, Ms. Cipher," he says, but as he shakes her hand, I see his eyes widen.

"I was terribly fond of Gianna's father," she says quietly. "And I do hope your intentions with his daughter are—noble. I would so hate to see her hurt in any way."

"Absolutely," Raj gasps, as she releases him at last. He shoots me a sideways glance and flexes his hand a few times.

"Marvelous," she says, her eyes twinkling. "Until we meet again."

And with that, she sweeps out of the tiny hall and is gone.

Before we leave the reception, Raj shows me an urn he has found, a near replica of the piece in Circe's cave that was discovered buried next to the stone tablet. "For the ashes," he says. "If you want it, that is."

We leave it with the priest, and Talia promises to pick it up when it's ready.

"I'll keep it until you're set to come back," she says. "We'll find the best place for him together, yes?"

I think I'm going to like having a sister.

That night, still wearing my sundress, and with Raj still in his suit, we walk barefoot along the clean, white sands of the beach near the guesthouse. The sea is crowned with a thin golden line, and the stars are just beginning to wink into the sky one by one. There isn't another soul to be seen in any direction.

"I can see why your dad loved it here so much," he says quietly. "It's so incredibly beautiful."

I sigh a little. "I don't want to talk about my dad. It'll make me cry again."

"It's okay if you cry," he says, "if you still need to. It's good for you."

"I think I'm done for now. But let's talk about something else."

We're both quiet a moment.

"So," he says at last, "you're really through with Anthony, then?"

"Ugh, yes. And I don't want to talk about him either."

Raj shoots me a sideways glance. "I once heard your dad say you needed to be with Anthony. That he was good for you."

I shake my head firmly. "He didn't know the real Anthony. And anyway, what he actually said was that it didn't matter who I was with, he just wanted me to be happy."

"Good," says Raj. "I just want to make sure you're not carrying a torch for him."

I laugh. "No torches. Unless I can have one to burn him at the stake, maybe?"

He slings his arm over my shoulder and pulls me close. "That won't be necessary. Enough blood has already been spilled."

I pretend to not notice that he preens a little as he says this.

Instead, I laugh. "Okay, well, speaking of torches—why don't you tell me about the girl in London. About Sachi?"

He shoots me a startled look. "Seriously? Listen, you don't need to worry about all of that. It was a long time ago."

"I know. And I'm not worried about it. But I'm interested. What happened after she went off to New York with Anthony?"

He jams his hand—his other hand, the one not around my

shoulders—into his pocket. "She came home after about four months," he says quietly. "Turns out he'd had a girlfriend in New York he neglected to mention."

I, of course, have never met this girl, but I fume on her behalf. "So he broke her heart?"

Raj laughs wryly. "Yeah. She broke mine and then he broke hers. I'll never know, of course, but I get the feeling he only wanted her to get her away from me. After that, I wonder if the thrill was gone."

"Why didn't you get back together?"

He sighs. "Ah, it was a long time ago. When she came back, things just weren't the same. Anyway, last I heard, she's happily married with twins. *And* I think she's doing a play at one of the theaters in the West End."

"So no torches being held for her, then?"

He shakes his head firmly. "Nary a one." And then, for the first time since before the funeral, he pulls me close and smiles down at me. "Besides, my parents were relieved. They thought it meant they'd have a shot at choosing for me since I'd done so poorly the first time."

I look up at him, startled. "Like—like an arranged marriage?"

He laughs. "My family are two generations away from India, Gia. My own parents married purely for love. But they are desi parents, right? They're more than willing to find me a suitable girlfriend."

"Which is . . . why you are here and not living in London?"

He laughs again. "You see right through me."

"Exactly." I pull away from him into the darkness.

He releases my hand and then takes a few hurried steps back as something flares out between us.

"What was that?" he says. I can't see his face any longer, but his voice sounds a little startled.

"It's my blanket from the Forzani brothers. You know—the guys who saved me from the giant squid?"

"You kept it?" he says, sounding incredulous. "As I recall, at the time it smelled pretty ripe."

I laugh and sit myself down. "It was also covered in Anthony's blood, thanks to you. I was kind of hoping the bloodstains would stick around, but there's no denying the skill of Italian laundry ladies. Clean as a whistle now."

I pat the blanket beside me and undo the top button of my teal cardigan.

It's so dark, I sense rather than see him sit down beside me. His arm brushes mine, and the feel of his skin on my own sends a shiver through me that has nothing to do with the temperature.

"I'm glad you kept it," he says, tracing a finger down my neck.

"Of course I kept it." I try not to squeak as his finger travels across my collarbone. "That was, I think, the single strangest day of my life. I might have lost my big hat on this trip, but I plan to keep this blanket forever."

"It seems pretty useful right now," he says, and I feel his fingers tracing my wrist under the cuff of my cardigan. I start to yank my arm out of the sleeve, but he stops me.

"Uh, can you leave it on?"

"Seriously?"

"Yeah. That's the one you were wearing in the club that night, correct? I have some very—uh—*happy* memories of the hot girl in the blue cardigan."

"Literally hot. That place was steaming."

"I remember," he whispers, his breath warm on my skin.

And the shoulder ties on my sundress turn out to have been the correct choice, after all.

Somehow we're lying down, and then he's running his finger back up and around the outer rim of my ear, which makes me laugh.

He laughs too, low in his throat, and then we stop laughing for a while and concentrate on other, far more important matters that suddenly arise.

Sometime much, much later, Raj's phone lights up where it's landed between us on the blanket.

"How are you getting a signal?" I murmur, still drowsy.

"SIM card," he whispers and then kisses my shoulder as he reaches for the phone.

Seconds later, he gives a little squawk and sits up suddenly. In the light from the screen, I can see the paler skin below his tan line that arcs just beneath his hip bone. I trace my finger along it lightly, which makes him shiver. He drops the phone and rolls back down to kiss me again.

After a minute, I pause for breath. "What did it say?"

I catch a glimpse of his grin in the moonlight. "You need to quit distracting me," he says and then hands me the phone.

Squinting a little at the brightness, I read the screen. "A biopic? For Netflix?"

"That's what they're saying. Someone told me you can get anything on Netflix these days, so with your dad's blessing, I pitched them a re-creation of this trip. Apparently the discovery of the clay tablet—right where your dad predicted it would be—sealed the deal."

I think about reminding him that that particular location was pinpointed by my father's long-dead ancestors and then decide to let sleeping Greeks lie.

Instead, I settle on, "That's amazing!"

He laughs incredulously. "Looks like I have an appointment next week at their New York office. Hmm—if only I knew someone willing to show me around the city . . ."

I laugh and throw my arms around his neck to kiss him. Which is when we both realize my dress is still muddled in an untidy pile on the sand.

Half an hour or so later, I manage to get my dress back on for real, bows fully retied and everything. After we shake all the sand out of the striped blanket, we meander back along the beach, aiming ourselves at the single twinkling light that marks the entrance to the guesthouse.

I pause for a minute to gaze up at the stars shining down on the land of my father. A land that feels more like my own after all that's happened. And now that he's here forever.

Raj's hand is warm in mine as we start up the sandy path to the guesthouse. This might be the last night of my accidental odyssey, but I know I'll be back soon.

First, though? I've got a New York foodie tour to organize.

ACKNOWLEDGMENTS

I write these words of thanks after what has been a tough and terrible year for our small planet; a time that is not yet done, I'm sure. While writing is a solitary occupation under the best of circumstances, the distance that we have been forced to keep between us means that writing *An Accidental Odyssey* has not been business as usual. Technology has been a lifeline for me this year—my only connection with most of my friends, family, and colleagues.

I am so lucky to belong to a close and warm collection of writers and artists, friends from whom I drew support regardless of the distance that separates us. Much love to my friends Kathy Chung and Pamela Patchet for their unwavering support, and to Lee Födi, Marcie Nestman, James McCann, Laura Bradbury, Mahtab Narsimhan, Tyner Gillies, and my whole SiWC family for always being there.

For their generosity in sharing information, experiences, and nuances of language, I'd like to thank Christiane Kypreos, Marina Atunes, and from the Litforum, Karen Henry, Maria Pecora, Elle Druskin, and Kelly Claytor.

My endless appreciation goes out to the amazing team at Berkley: Cindy Hwang, Angela Kim, Will Tyler, Stacy Edwards, Jessica Mangicaro, Brittanie Black, and to Vi-An Nguyen for her gorgeous, funny covers.

My deepest gratitude goes out to my brilliant, patient, and kind agents—Laura Bradford and Taryn Fagerness—for helping my peripatetic stories find readers all over the world; especially heroic considering the epic projects they each accomplished this year. Thanks also to my new assistant, Christine Sandquist, for helping organize my scattered mind, and to Mary Robinette Kowal for introducing us.

I had last read *The Odyssey* back in the dark history of time when I was in high school. Thus, when I decided to write this story, it was a complete joy to discover Emily Wilson's 2018 translation. If you are in the mood for a little Homerian fancy, I cannot praise this edition highly enough, from her lyrical style to her renunciation of the trite conventions and careless misogyny that litter the earlier translations. I can also highly recommend the audio version, brilliantly presented by the talented Claire Danes. Having this resource near to hand made my cheeky, gender-swapping romp through Odysseus's travels—along wine-dark seas—all the more fun to write.

As always, much love goes out to Peter and Alicia, with deep appreciation for their tolerance of the eccentric writer in the family. Love, too, to Meaghan and Jürgen, with both thanks for the archeological tips and apologies for any details I got wrong. Thanks also to my sister, Lisa Dempster, for editorial advice always offered kindly, and from a safe distance. I should note that Taki's Herman owes his very existence to my friend Norma Rodger's boy Barney, and also to Topaz, whose huge personality shines out through Herman's eyes.

These stories of travel and adventure were first born with Emma's search for her one true love—a character from a book, of course—in *Finding Fraser*, so I need also thank the two writers—and friends—who have most inspired my writing before Emma and since: Jack Whyte and Diana Gabaldon. In this year where so many have lost so much, we had to say goodbye to our Jack, and I miss him terribly. Jack was a man who loved a good story, and he loved to laugh, so really his inspiration lives on—I've done my best to try to create both here in these pages.

As always, for all the help and support from brilliant writers and industry folks along the way, every mistake you find herein is mine alone.

Finally, thank *you*, dear reader, for sharing these journeys with me.

Now—where shall we go next?

An Accidental Odyssey

kc dyer

QUESTIONS FOR DISCUSSION

1. As the story opens in *An Accidental Odyssey*, Gianna Kostas leaves New York with the idea of chasing her dad down and then quickly returning home. Have you ever traveled to any Mediterranean countries? Which of Gia's destinations would you most like to visit?

2. What are the questions Gia wrestles with when it comes to weighing her options between planning her wedding, finding a job she loves, and dealing with her exasperating father? Would you have made the same choices she did?

3. Gia's internship as a food writer for NOSH has been her dream job. Have you ever wanted to write for a living? If not, what is your dream job?

4. When Anthony calls Gia after their big fight, he denies that he broke things off with her and then says he is sorry if she mistook his intentions. How is this problematic? What other hints do you see of an imbalance in Gia and Anthony's relationship?

5. In this story, Gia enjoys writing about food, and she becomes very good at it. How does her love of food and culinary writing help shape

her sense of self as her journey progresses? Did any of her suggested recipes strike your fancy?

6. Gia's friendship with Devi is so long-standing and rock-solid, they are almost like sisters. Do you think Devi did a good job of communicating her conflicting feelings about Anthony? What would you do if your dearest friend had a relationship with someone of whom you disapproved?

7. In spite of their fiery initial attraction, why do you think Raj tries to keep his relationship with Gia professional? Have you ever found yourself in an awkward situation with a work colleague? Should there be hard-and-fast rules for work relationships? And if you were in Raj's shoes—or in Gia's—what would you have done differently?

8. *An Accidental Odyssey* is a story about love in just a few of its many forms—love of friends and family, romantic love, but also a passion for discovery and even for work. As a journalist, a classical historian, and an archeologist, Gia, Ari, and Raj each love the job they do. How do the professions of each character define the choices they make when it comes to both work and family? Do you agree with these choices?

9. While paddling off the coast of Capri, Gia is mesmerized by the sights and sounds of a collection of buff surfer dudes, and nearly crashes her sea kayak into some treacherous rocks. Aside from these gender-swapped sirens, did you recognize any other echoes of Homer's *Odyssey* in Gia's adventures as she chases her father around the Mediterranean?

10. How does Anthony's surprise arrival in Italy epitomize his vision of himself as the ideal hero for Gia? What signs do you see throughout the story that this relationship is not as perfect as it looks from the outside?

11. After all their ups and downs, why do you think Gia was so driven to complete Ari's quest? What were the unexpected outcomes of Gia's accidental odyssey? If you had a chance to take a journey like this one—would you?

Photo by Martin Chung

kc dyer loves travel and has literally flown around the world in search of fantastic stories. When not on the road, she resides in the wilds of British Columbia, where she walks her dogs in the woods and writes books. kc is the author of *Eighty Days to Elsewhere*, the madcap story of a young woman so desperate to save her family's bookstore that she undertakes a race around the world, but ends up falling for her competition. Her most recent novel in the ExLibris series is *An Accidental Odyssey*. kc is also the author of *Finding Fraser*, an international bestseller in romantic comedy. You can read more about kc and her books online at kcdyer.com.

Ready to find
your next great read?

Let us help.

Visit prh.com/nextread

Penguin
Random
House